ANNE RICE & CHRISTOPHER RICE

RAMSES
THE DAMNED
THE PASSION OF CLEOPATRA

Anne Rice is the author of thirty-six books, including The Vampire Chronicles and The Lives of the Mayfair Witches. She lives in Southern California.

annerice.com

Christopher Rice published four *New York Times* best-selling novels before the age of thirty and has twice been nominated for the Bram Stoker Award. He is the cohost of the YouTube channel The Dinner Party Show with Christopher Rice & Eric Shaw Quinn (www.tdps.tv).

christopherricebooks.com

Prince Lestat and the Realms of Atlantis
Prince Lestat
The Wolves of Midwinter
Interview with the Vampire: Claudia's Story
The Wolf Gift
Of Love and Evil
Angel Time
Called Out of Darkness
Christ the Lord: The Road to Cana
Christ the Lord: Out of Egypt
Blood Canticle
Blackwood Farm
Blood and Gold
Merrick
Vittorio, the Vampire
The Vampire Armand
Pandora
Violin
Servant of the Bones
Memnoch the Devil
Taltos
Lasher
The Tale of the Body Thief
The Witching Hour
The Mummy
The Queen of the Damned
The Vampire Lestat
Cry to Heaven
The Feast of All Saints
Interview with the Vampire

UNDER THE NAME ANNE RAMPLING

Exit to Eden
Belinda

UNDER THE NAME A. N. ROQUELAURE

The Claiming of Sleeping Beauty
Beauty's Punishment
Beauty's Release

ALSO BY CHRISTOPHER RICE

A Density of Souls
The Snow Garden
Light Before Day
Blind Fall
The Moonlit Earth
The Heavens Rise
The Vines
The Flame: A Desire Exchange Novella
The Surrender Gate: A Desire Exchange Novel
Kiss the Flame: A Desire Exchange Novella
Dance of Desire

RAMSES THE DAMNED

THE PASSION OF CLEOPATRA

RAMSES
THE DAMNED

THE PASSION OF CLEOPATRA

Anne Rice &
Christopher Rice

ANCHOR BOOKS
A Division of Penguin Random House LLC
New York

AN ANCHOR BOOKS ORIGINAL, NOVEMBER 2017

Library of Congress Cataloging-in-Publication Data
Names: Rice, Anne, 1941– author. | Rice, Christopher, 1978– author.
Title: Ramses the damned : the passion of Cleopatra /
Anne Rice & Christopher Rice.
Description: First edition. | New York : Anchor Books, 2017.
Identifiers: LCCN 2016057153
Subjects: LCSH: Mummies—Fiction. | Ramses II, King of
Egypt—Fiction. | Cleopatra, Queen of Egypt, –30 B.C.—Fiction. |
Immortality—Fiction. | GSAFD: Occult fiction.
Classification: LCC PS3568.I265 R36 2018 | DDC 813/.54—dc23
LC record available at https://lccn.loc.gov/2016057153

Anchor Books Trade Paperback ISBN: 978-1-101-97032-4
eBook ISBN: 978-1-101-97048-5

Book design by Steven Walker

Printed in the United States of America
10 9 8 7 6 5 4 3 2 1

Anne and Christopher
both dedicate this novel to their coauthor,
and to the People of the Page

Contents

RAMSES THE DAMNED

THE PASSION OF CLEOPATRA

Proem

It was a tale told by the newspapers in 1914—of a spectacular find by a British Egyptologist in an isolated tomb outside of Cairo—a royal mummy of Egypt's greatest monarch and, beside his painted sarcophagus, a vast collection of ancient poisons and a journal in Latin, written in the time of Cleopatra, comprising some thirteen scrolls.

Call me Ramses the Damned. For that is the name I have given myself. But I was once Ramses the Great of Upper and Lower Egypt, slayer of the Hittites, father of many sons and daughters, who ruled Egypt for sixty-four years. My monuments are still standing; the stele recount my victories, though a thousand years have passed since I was pulled, a mortal child, from the womb.

   Ah, fatal moment now buried by time, when from a Hittite priestess I took the cursed elixir. Her warnings I would not heed. Immortality I craved. And so I drank the potion in the brimming cup . . .

   . . . How can I bear this burden any longer? How can I endure the loneliness anymore? Yet I cannot die . . .

So wrote a being who claimed to have lived a thousand years, slumbering in darkness when the great kings and queens of his realm had no need of him, ever ready to be resurrected at their command to offer wisdom and counsel—until the death of Cleopatra and of Egypt itself drove him to an eternal rest.

What was the world to make of this bizarre tale, or the fact that Lawrence Stratford, discoverer of the mystery, died in the tomb itself at the moment of his greatest triumph?

Julie Stratford, daughter of the great Egyptologist and sole heiress to the Stratford Shipping fortune, brought the controversial mummy to London, along with the mysterious scrolls and poisons, to honor her father's discovery with a private exhibition in her home in Mayfair. Within days Julie's cousin, Henry, made frantic claims that the mummy had risen from its sarcophagus and tried to murder him, and talk of a mummy's curse astonished Londoners. Before rumors could die down, Julie appeared in public with a mysterious blue-eyed Egyptian named Reginald Ramsey, who then journeyed with Julie back to Cairo in the company of beloved friends Elliott, the Earl of Rutherford, and his young son, Alex Savarell, and the aggrieved Henry.

More shocking events unfolded.

An unidentified corpse stolen from the Cairo Museum, grisly murders amongst the European shopkeepers of the city, and Ramsey himself sought by the Cairo police, and the disappearance of Henry. Finally, a fiery explosion left baffled witnesses and a frantic Alex Savarell grieving for a nameless woman who had fled the Cairo Opera House in terror, driving her motorcar into the path of an oncoming train.

Out of chaos and mystery, Julie Stratford emerged as the devoted fiancée of the enigmatic Reginald Ramsey, traveling Europe with her beloved, while in England the Savarell family sought to understand the exile of the Earl of Rutherford and the grief of young Alex for the woman he had so tragically lost to the flames in the Egyptian desert. Gossip dies down; newspapers move on.

As our story opens, the country estate of the Earl of Rutherford will soon be the location of the engagement party for Reginald Ramsey and Julie Stratford, as others far and wide hear echoes of the story of the immortal Ramses the Damned and his fabled elixir, though the mummified body itself, brought to London with such fanfare, has long since vanished.

How can I bear this burden any longer? How can I endure the loneliness anymore? Yet I can not die. Her poisons can not harm me. They keep my elixir safe so that I may dream of still other Queens, both fair and wise, to share the centuries with me.

—RAMSES THE DAMNED

3600 B.C.: Jericho

"We are being followed, my queen."

She had not been a queen for centuries, but her two loyal servants still referred to her as such. Both men flanked her now as they approached the great stone city of Jericho on foot.

They were the only members of her royal guard who had refused to take part in an insurrection against her. Now, thousands of years after freeing her from the tomb in which she'd been placed by her traitorous prime minister, these former warriors for a lost kingdom remained her constant companions and protectors.

It was their companionship that mattered most. She knew a loneliness which she could never fully describe to another being, a loneliness she had long accepted but she feared might one day destroy her.

There was very little else from which she needed to be protected. She was immortal, and so were they.

"Continue to walk," she commanded quietly. "Do not pause."

Her men obeyed. They were close enough to the city to smell the spices coming from the market just beyond the stone walls.

She towered over most people, but her servants were both taller than she by almost half. To her right walked Enamon, with his proud but bent nose, broken in an ancient battle between tribes who had long since died out. Aktamu was on her left, his round, boyish face out of place atop his lean, muscular body. They hailed from no specific lands; immortality had made the world their home. But today they dressed as traders from Kush, in skirts of leopard skin that shifted over their long legs, with broad golden sashes stretched over their bare, muscular chests. Her swaddling of blue robes allowed her slender arms to move free. The walking stick she used was a show for mortals. She did not tire or require rest as they did.

The road before and behind was clear of wagons in this moment, and so it was no surprise the three of them had drawn notice from someone outside the city gates, and yet to hear Enamon tell it, this attention was sustained, and suspiciously so.

When Bektaten looked back over one shoulder, she saw the spy.

His skin was a few shades lighter than her own, the same color as those who inhabited the city ahead. He stood a good distance up the barren hillside off to their left, wrapped in robes and latticed by the frail shade from an olive tree. He made no attempt to conceal himself. His stance and position were a warning, a threat of some sort. And his eyes, they were as blue as those of the men with whom she'd traveled for centuries.

They were as blue as her own.

They were eyes changed by the elixir she had discovered thousands of years before. A discovery that had caused her kingdom's fall.

Is it he? Is it Saqnos?

The memories of her prime minister's betrayal would never fade, no matter how long she walked the earth. The raid he'd staged upon her quarters with members of her own guard. His demands that she hand over the formula she had discovered quite by accident, the one that had allowed a flock of birds to fly above the palace in endless circles without ever tiring.

Saqnos, handsome, thoughtful Saqnos. She had never seen

anything like the transformation that had overtaken him all those centuries ago. And it had only worsened when he saw her eyes, once brown, had turned startlingly blue.

That there was a substance on this earth that could abolish death, and that she had consumed it without consulting him, these facts had driven him mad with a thirst for power.

If he had simply asked for it, if he had not betrayed her, would she have handed it over without question?

There was no telling now.

With the spears of her own men raised against her, she had refused.

Despite the great strength afforded by her transformation, the royal guard numbered enough men to overpower her. They dragged her to the rock tomb Saqnos had already prepared. And during this humiliation, the architect of her fall raided her quarters and even her private work chamber for every vial of the elixir he could find. Immediately he distributed them to his soldiers. But he did not find the precious formula itself, for she had taken care to scatter the ingredients among her other tonics and powders.

It was then that his plan went to ruin.

Upon discovering that they had been granted eternal life, upon realizing that they had been made impervious to most fatal wounds, these once-loyal soldiers laid down their arms and abandoned their new leader. What need did they have for a ruler? What need did they have for the shelter of a kingdom when they could explore the world endlessly without fear of cold, starvation, or the serpent's bite?

Saqnos . . .

But the man who watched them now was not him.

"Once we are inside the city walls, prepare the ring," she said quietly.

"Yes, my queen." Enamon caressed the leather pouch at his side with a long-fingered hand.

They made frequent visits to this place. They were assumed

to be traders from the land of Kush, and they never disabused anyone of this notion. Their bags always bulged with blossoms and spices, many of which she'd plucked from peaks so high and dangerous, so battered by powerful winds and drenching rains, no mortal could reach them. The other visitors to the market did not know this.

These journeys to Jericho filled her with joy, for they interrupted her long wanderings. The vast, forbidding landscapes her immortality allowed her to visit spoke their own languages; there was a certain music to the whisper of winds through the leaves of jungles where no humans dwelled, a harmony to the contrasting winds that swept high mountain peaks. But the languages spoken in Jericho, and the tales of loves, deaths, and newly born cities, they were a music without which she could not endure. And after days of collecting these stories, of listening to mortals tell their tales, she would then return to her camps and record them in her leather-bound papyrus journals, clumsy books she had made herself and kept throughout her centuries of existence, books she had vowed to keep for all time.

Bektaten would not allow her love for this place to be spoiled by the sudden appearance of strange immortals, immortals she had not made.

Immortals like the one who was following them now from just outside the toss of a stone. Or the one who stood poised next to the city gates, regarding them with a fearless and penetrating gaze.

We are being hunted, Bektaten thought. *Someone has heard tell of tall black-skinned people with blue eyes visiting Jericho, and they know what we are and they have come here to lie in wait for us.*

As they passed through the gates and into the tunnel just beyond, Enamon used the cover of shadow to follow her instructions. He held one open hand out to his side, indicating she should fall behind them by several steps. She complied.

Enamon swung his leather satchel around to the front of his

body, then removed a bronze ring Bektaten had fashioned with her own hand. He passed it to Aktamu, who quickly unscrewed the small jewel, revealing the tiny chamber and pin underneath. Enamon then removed a small fabric pouch.

Bektaten watched them closely.

The next few steps could be very dangerous for all three of them, but as long as the contents of the pouch did not pierce their skin, all would be well.

Unless she was soon given cause to use the ring.

Once the ring had been filled, its jewel fastened back in its place, Enamon handed it to her, and she slid it gently up one long, dark finger.

They continued to walk as if no transfer of a great, secret power had just taken place.

And then she saw him.

He stood in the shadows of the rectangular towers behind him, the bright glare of sun at his back. His swaddling of robes matched those of the two spies he'd sent to watch her approach.

Saqnos.

The man who had condemned her to immortal life trapped beneath the earth. The man who, in his desperate desire to re-create the elixir, had harvested every plant in Shaktanu, penetrated jungles she had forbidden her subjects to enter. The plague he had unleashed had brought down a civilization that once stretched across the seas.

So much had been lost to the man who now stood before her, she was rendered speechless by his presence. And yet she felt no rage.

What had she expected to feel upon seeing him again after all this time?

They had been lovers once. And now, despite herself, she felt an unwanted kinship with him. *Ah, the loneliness, the unspeakable loneliness, how it presses on the heart.*

There were so few like them. So few who had witnessed the

fall of the first great civilization since Atlantis. So few who had known the vast desert when it had been dotted with trees and shimmering pools and animals and the scattered palaces and temples of Shaktanu. That was before the plague. Before the great heat of the sun had scorched the earth she once ruled, driving the survivors towards the Nile, where they would eventually form the empires they now called Egypt and Kush.

A great hunger, a great desire for companionship, arose within her, even at the sight of a man who had been willing to condemn her to eternal darkness.

It would not have been quite such a fate. For what she'd realized as soon as the stone slab had been placed over the tomb was that, without the light of the sun, she had begun to slowly weaken. Soon after, she had fallen into a gentle sleep that became a stupor until Enamon and Aktamu freed her, exposing her body to the sunlight once again.

But Saqnos could not have known these things at the time. The elixir was too new to them both. Saqnos had been perfectly willing to let her wither away to dust.

And yet still, she could not help but see him now not as a lover, or a prime minister, but as a brother in immortal life. Yes, that was it. He was her kindred in immortal life.

Saqnos fell to his knees before her, took her hand gently in his, and kissed it.

Would a mortal woman have recoiled?

"My queen," Enamon said softly.

She lifted her free hand to one side. *Stay where you are*, the gesture said.

"You are surprised that I live?" Bektaten finally asked. "How can you possibly feel this when you have hunted me to this place?"

"*Hunted.* This is not the right word."

"Then provide me with the right word, Saqnos."

He still held the hand he'd just kissed. A gentle tug was all that was needed to bring him to his feet.

"Walk with me, my queen. Walk with me so—"

"Did I not cease being your queen when you placed me in the earth?"

If only she could be convinced by the woeful expression, the bowed head, the seizure of remorse that seemed to grip his powerful body. But she was not convinced. And she saw his true motive: to separate her from her men. And from his men as well. This latter fact intrigued her.

"There is much I must repair," Saqnos whispered.

"Indeed, the theft of my creation."

"Your creation?" he asked. Anger in his eyes now, the remorse quickly gone. "You were in search of medicine, not the secret to eternal life. Do you no longer give the gods credit for the accident of its discovery?"

"Which gods? There have been so many. The fall of our kingdom, Saqnos. How do you plan to repair this?"

"You cannot lay blame for the plague at my feet."

"I cannot? You entered jungles from which no creature returned. We knew there was sickness within. And yet you slashed them to ruin."

"Because you would not give me the formula."

"Because you demanded it at the tip of a spear."

It was impossible to read his expression now.

"Please, Bektaten. Walk with me."

And so he had granted her request to stop calling her his queen. Did that earn him some small measure of obedience? Perhaps so.

"A few paces. Nothing more."

He reached for her hand, the same one that wore the ring, and she withdrew it. And so they walked side by side, without touching, towards the clamor of the market. But she dared not leave the shadows. Not when his motives remained so unclear.

"If you blame me for Shaktanu's fall, would you give me the chance to rebuild it?" he asked.

"There is no rebuilding Shaktanu."

"I do not speak of resurrecting temples out of what is now desert sand."

"Temples out of desert sand? This is how you refer to what you destroyed? Our empire crossed seas in ways unknown to the people of this age. We charted the stars with maps now lost to dust. Lands that remain unknown to the people of this city were our colonies and our outposts and full of our loyal subjects. And all of this you now dismiss as *temples in desert sand*?"

"Do not chain me to the past when I offer you a better future," he whispered.

"I am listening, Saqnos. Speak to me of this better future."

"The people of the lands around us claim control of what was once Egypt. But I have walked its length. There is great chaos there, and wars between its people. There is an opportunity for us, Bektaten. An opportunity among their confusion to remake what we have lost."

"There is no remaking what we have lost."

"Then something new. Something greater."

"To what end, Saqnos?"

"To bring order."

"*Order?* This is a concept that possesses you even now? You have eternal life and you speak of something *greater*? This is madness. The same madness that turned you against me. To see it unchanged after centuries . . . I have no words for it. No words for you."

"This city, this Jericho, is but a pile of sand compared to what we once had. A great empire, an empire ruled by immortals, people of our vast knowledge and experience, it could bring about a new age."

"And so it is not order you seek but control."

"You were a queen. You know there cannot be one without the other."

"How can you be so unchanged, Saqnos?"

"I do not seek to change!" he said.

"I see. And so your remorse over what you did to me, it was a display, as I suspected."

He did not bow his head now. He did not look away. Anger burned in his blue eyes. The anger of one confronted by an unwanted truth.

"Leave me out of your dreams of a new kingdom. I shall never be your queen again."

"Bektaten—"

"Do not grovel, Saqnos. It demeans you. If you wish to create an immortal army to claim Egypt as your own, you have everything you need. Don't seek to enlist me so that you can be free of your regrets. You betrayed me. This is history now. It is our history and it shall never change."

"I do not," he said, seizing her wrist in his powerful grip. "I do *not* have everything I need." Rage now, rage that flared his nostrils and exposed the whites of his eyes. "The formula . . . it is corrupted. These men, they will not last. Not as long as we have. They are *fracti.* At most I have given them two hundred years of life. Then they will decay and I will be forced to make others. I need the pure elixir. I need it as *you* made it."

And so this is why he had sought to separate her not just from her men, but from his own, so that they would not hear this secret. So that they would not know that somewhere on this earth was an elixir more powerful and potent than the one Saqnos had given them.

"And so, after thousands of years, you seek exactly what you sought in the final hours of our kingdom," she answered. "You seek what I shall never give."

He withdrew from her suddenly and let out a high, piercing cry.

They came from both ends of the tunnel, men just like the two who had followed them into the city. Six in all, daggers drawn. In an instant, Enamon and Aktamu were surrounded. Saqnos had fallen back entirely, leaving his men to do his bidding.

They were focused on wresting the leather satchel from Enamon's body. But two grabbed Bektaten's arms from behind to restrain her. She had already unscrewed the jewel on her ring, revealing the tiny bronze pin within. It didn't take much movement. She simply drove the knuckles on her confined hand upwards towards the forearm of the man attempting to hold her in place.

The ring pricked his skin and he let out an anguished cry. If the strangle lily worked as it always did, the man would not have much time for screams.

He stumbled away from her. Extended one accusing finger in her direction, and then the finger turned to ash. His wide, terrified eyes blackened in the same moment his jaw withered into dust. All around them, the fighting came to a halt. Suddenly, the man she'd poisoned was nothing more than a pile of robes laced with ash.

The remaining men, these fracti, as Saqnos had called them, fled in desperate terror.

And when she turned to face Saqnos, it appeared as if he too wanted to flee.

There was something of this earth that could end him in an instant. This knowledge had paralyzed him. He was breathless and wide eyed.

Carefully, Bektaten picked up the ring's jewel from where she had discarded it and screwed it back into place.

"You shall dwell in the shadows of kingdoms and never again in their royal palaces," she said quietly. "Should you refuse this command, should you ever seek to raise an army of immortals, I will find you, Saqnos, and I will end you. Let this be the last command you ever hear from your queen."

It seemed for a moment that her former prime minister would not be able to tear himself away from the sight of his mercenary's emptied, ash-strewn robes lying in a puddle on the dirt. Then a fear unlike any he had known for centuries seized him. He raced past her towards the city gates.

Once he was gone, Bektaten felt a hand come to rest on her shoulder, and then another. They were on either side of her once again, Enamon and Aktamu, wordlessly alerting her to their constant presence and their enduring commitment to accompany and protect her for all time.

"Collect the ashes and the robes," she said. "And then we go to the market. This is a good city full of good people. And we have successfully expelled its invaders."

"Yes, my queen," Enamon whispered.

Part 1

I

1914: Outside Cairo

The young doctor had never met a woman as enchanting as the one who lay beneath him now. Her desire was insatiable. Her hunger for him seemed a hunger for life itself.

When he'd first been called to her room days before, they'd assured him her death was imminent. *Burned from head to toe*, the nurses had cried. Her body had been pried from underneath the crates at the very bottom of a freight car. No telling who she was or how far she had been carried by the train. Or how on earth she was still alive.

But when he'd pulled back the mosquito netting, he had found her sitting up in bed, so beautiful it had been almost painful to look at her. Her unmarred features exquisitely proportioned. Her rippling hair, parted in the middle, making a great pyramid of darkness on either side of her head. Words like *fate* and *destiny* crossed his mind. Still, he was instantly ashamed of how the sight of her nipples beneath the bedsheet had aroused him.

"What a handsome man you are," she'd whispered. Was she a fallen angel? How else to explain the miraculous physical recovery? How else to explain her complete absence of pain or disorientation? But then there was her accent. Perfect, polished British. And when he'd asked her if she had any friends, anyone he should contact, she had said the strangest thing: *I have friends, yes. And appointments to keep. And accounts to settle.*

But she made no further mention of these friends in the hours after he spirited her away from that little outpost on the edge of the Sudan. Hours in which he'd thrown himself into her arms, ridden the serpentlike undulations of her unblemished, golden-skinned body.

First, she insisted they go to Egypt. When he asked her if these friends she'd mentioned could be found in the land of the pharaohs, she said simply, *I have had a great many friends in Egypt, Doctor. A great many.* And her smile had disarmed him once again.

In Egypt, she claimed, she would reveal more of her mystery.

In Egypt, she would give him some sense of how it was she could go without sleep, consume great quantities of food at all hours without gaining a pound. How she could make love with a consuming passion that never tired her in the slightest. And perhaps she would offer too some explanation for the dazzling blueness of her eyes, so rare in a woman of her Mediterranean complexion.

But would she share with him the most important detail of all? Would she tell him her name?

"Theodore," he whispered to her now.

"Yes," she answered. "Your name is Dr. Theodore Dreycliff. A fine British doctor."

Even after the time they'd spent together, she said these words as if they were vaguely unfamiliar. As if they contained facts of which she needed to be constantly reminded.

"Not so fine in the eyes of my colleagues, I'm sure," he said. "A fine doctor doesn't abandon his hospital without explanation. Doesn't just run off with a beautiful patient at a moment's notice."

She didn't greet this remark with the indulgent giggle he would have expected from one of those wretchedly boring women back in London his parents had wished him to marry. She merely gazed at him in silence. Perhaps she truly didn't understand, or perhaps she sensed there was more to his story he hadn't shared as well.

He had no fine reputation, that was for sure. He'd done good work at that little outpost in the Sudan, but it was a terrible, youthful mistake that had banished him there years before. Fresh out of medical school and desperate to appear competent to his elder colleagues, he hadn't asked the questions he should have during his first weeks of practice. As a result he'd nearly crippled a patient by prescribing her an obscenely inappropriate amount of medication.

Inappropriate was hardly the word his colleagues had used for it, however. *Reckless. Criminal.* Their practice had been spared ruin only by God's good grace. They'd railed against him for placing his vanity over the needs of a patient. And they had only agreed not to report him provided he did one of two things: left the practice of medicine altogether or left London.

What a grim satisfaction he'd taken from their wretched hypocrisy. They cared little whether or not he harmed a patient in some far corner of the world, so long as the repercussions didn't travel the breadth of the empire back to their doorstep.

Vanity indeed, he'd thought.

That's how he'd wound up practicing medicine in what his old college chums would sneeringly call *darkest Africa*. He'd arrived a different man, brash and arrogant, but also coddled and spoiled. Africa had changed him, shown him the weaknesses and limits of the British Empire, shown him miraculous experiences for which the Christian church of his youth had no explanation or even language.

Like her. Indeed, it was easier to think of her as an experience than a person.

The word *person* was far too ordinary to describe the magical impossibility that was her very being.

And yet, even as they lay twined in each other's naked limbs, her expression radiant with bliss, his thoughts were still occupied by the second and perhaps unsurvivable scandal he'd surely set into motion with his sudden absence from the hospital.

A modest amount of money had been enough to save his hide the first time, covering his travel to the Sudan and his living expenses in the months after his arrival. Now he wasn't sure what the exact cost to his professional reputation would be. Or if he could afford it. There was no going back to his family. Once he tallied up the expenses from this journey, there was precious little for him left to even live on. Two hired motorcars, one for the tents and supplies, one for the two of them, and a driver for each. Enough food and water for days. Or not, if his beautiful companion's appetite didn't flag at some point. And dynamite. Several menacing sticks of dynamite.

But she had promised him, promised them all, that whatever they found at the end of this desert journey would be enough to pay off all of their debts, now and forever.

In the ensuing quiet, the tent flaps shuddered in the desert wind. He could make out the distant laughter of the drivers. He'd told them to keep a respectful distance from the tent. So far they had obeyed.

"Teddy," she whispered.

Her fingers grazed his cheek.

He was so surprised by this sudden touch he jumped.

"Soon I shall tell you my name," she whispered.

*   *   *

He felt like a foolish boy for plugging his ears with both fingers. But he'd never been this close to an explosion before. He had no idea what to expect.

His beautiful companion showed no fear as she watched the men disappear in between the ridges up ahead, strings of dynamite in their hands.

Before them lay an island of eroding sandstone spires. They formed a loose cage around a high mound of golden sand. Teddy knew precious little about Egypt's archaeological digs aside from the webbing of tents they threw across the landscape. There were no signs of any such excavations here.

They were a two days' drive from Cairo. In the middle of nowhere, it seemed. And yet she had directed them here with utter confidence simply by watching the stars. And now, as the men scurried across the sand, lit fuses abandoned in their wake, her body coiled with an almost sexual tension.

He drove his fingers deeper into his ears.

The men, still running, clapped their hands over their own.

The blast sent a shimmering shock wave through the sand at their feet. A plume of smoke rose high into the air. She actually clapped, his female companion. Clapped her hands together and smiled as if dynamite contained a magic as powerful as the kind he sensed coming from her.

Once the smoke cleared, he could see one side of the mound blown away. A stone doorway had been punched through by the explosion, its shattered remains left behind like rotting teeth.

The ground here had not been disturbed for ages, and she'd known the exact location of this buried temple.

The Egyptian men fell back.

Were they right to be afraid?

There'd been all that talk in the papers recently. A magnate of some powerful British shipping company had discovered a mummy's tomb, filled with inscriptions proclaiming it the final resting place of RAMSES THE DAMNED. Also within, Roman furniture and a statue purported to be of Cleopatra, the last queen of Egypt.

The whole affair was utter lunacy, the journalists had cried. Ramses II had ruled a thousand years before Cleopatra's reign. And his body lay in the Cairo Museum. Everyone knew that!

But when the man who discovered the tomb suddenly fell dead within its once-buried walls, talk of ancient curses overtook academic quarrels. The mummy's body had been shipped off to London, the last he read, at the request of the late archeologist's daughter. Stratford, that was their name, he remembered now.

Where had she put it? he'd wondered. In her drawing room? How ghoulish! Clearly she had not feared any mummy's curse.

Perhaps it wasn't a curse the men all around him feared now, but the woman who had brought them to this place.

His lantern barely pierced the darkness within. She walked far enough ahead to remain just inside the halo. But she was eager to strike out into the black, he could tell. This tomb, even in deep shadow, was utterly familiar to her.

When the light from his lantern fell across the glittering treasures up ahead, he gasped. She halted and waited for him to catch up, waited until the glow filled the space with the strength of a dozen candles.

Nerves alight, he spun in place, looking for a sarcophagus or some other sign of a desiccated mummy slumbering within this dark place. But all he saw were piles of coins. An ancient vault of untold treasures. And his beautiful companion walked among them leisurely, sweeping the dust and sand from atop the glittering piles with one gentle passing hand. There were statues of varying sizes as well, lined against stone walls without elegance. They had been brought here in haste, it seemed, and for their protection.

"How did you know this was all here?" he asked.

"Because I ordered my soldiers to bring it here," she answered.

His laughter was sharp, disbelieving. Then he saw the face of the statue closest to him. His breath left him along with any sense of an orderly, rational world.

"You have been very kind to me, Teddy," the woman said. "May I expect more kindness from you in return for some of these riches?"

He tried to answer. He could only make a dry, rasping sound that reminded him of the one time he'd almost choked on a piece of steak.

Her breath was at his ear now, her slender arms curving around him from behind. Her moist lips grazed his neck. Living, breathing, alive. The statue staring down at him through the lantern's flickering light bore her exact likeness, as did every statue stashed inside of this crypt. The same perfectly proportioned face; the same raven-colored hair and rich olive-toned skin. Only the color of the eyes was different. On the statues the eyes were dark, not blue, but they were of the same generous size and seemed full of life and calculation even beneath layers of dust.

"A modern man would look upon this crypt and accuse me of simply looting my own kingdom in its final hours. Of having no faith in my own lover. No faith that the Battle of Actium would halt Octavian's advance."

Octavian. Actium. A woman who did not sleep and could not die. The woman before him and behind him. Alive, alive, alive . . .

"This isn't . . . ," the doctor tried. "Impossible. This is . . . impossible."

"No one knew more than I that an empire's greatest protection was in its wealth, not its army. It was riches that bought us peace with Rome for years. Riches and grain. So it would make sense to these historians, wouldn't it? That in my kingdom's final hours, in my final hours as queen, I did little more than grab for treasure.

"But they are wrong, you see. Very wrong. Once it was clear Octavian could not be stopped, once I'd chosen to give my life to the serpent's bite, I couldn't bear the thought of my likeness being destroyed by their soldiers. Let them write my history as the harlot queen, but before Isis, I would not surrender my countenance to the dismemberment of Roman hordes."

It wasn't just the statues, he realized. It was the coins, it was the treasures. She appeared on all of these coins. And they'd all been hidden here in this vault for more than two thousand years.

"Ask me again, dear Teddy," she whispered. "Ask me my name."

"What is your name?" he whispered.

She turned him gently, cupped his chin in delicate hands that possessed a supernatural degree of strength. But her kiss was gentle, lingering, and she delivered it while gazing into his eyes.

"Cleopatra," she answered. "Cleopatra is my name. And I

wish for you to show me all the joys of this new world, so that I may share those joys with you. Would you like this, Teddy?"

"Yes," he whispered. "Yes, Cleopatra."

*   *   *

It was a remarkable tale she told. A tale of immortals and awakenings and terrible, tragic accidents.

She spoke of her death as a great lake of blackness from which she had been suddenly pulled.

Before its discovery, her corpse had been preserved by the mud of the Nile delta. For decades afterwards, it lay in the Cairo Museum inside a glass case, branded with the drab label UNKNOWN WOMAN, PTOLEMAIC PERIOD. Thereafter, countless historians and tourists had pressed their faces to the glass without realizing they were gazing upon the same likeness that had entranced Caesar and Marc Antony.

And then, two months prior, she had been recognized in death, recognized by a man from her ancient past who walked again.

Ramses! And so they were true, those wild tales in the papers about the recently discovered tomb whose mummified occupant had left scrolls claiming he was, in fact, Ramses II, one of Egypt's greatest pharaohs. The Roman furniture inside, the impossible tale of an immortal counselor who had served and advised many of Egypt's great rulers for thousands of years. All of it, so resoundingly dismissed by academics and historians, was absolutely true, and the woman before him was living, resurrected proof of it.

Ramses II. He walked even now, she claimed. In London, perhaps. Or maybe some other place, Cleopatra did not know. What she knew was this: He had been awakened by the sun after his tomb had been discovered and the body shipped back to London. Then, upon recognizing her in the Cairo Museum, he had awakened her with the same elixir that had given him immortal life, an elixir he had stolen from a mad Hittite priestess during his reign as Egypt's pharaoh.

Their reunion was a reversal of their first meeting two thousand years before, when the old priests in Alexandria had told her tales of a wise immortal counselor who had been raised from eternal sleep by her own great-grandfather. She had laughed at them, these priests, and demanded to be taken to the crypt of this so-called immortal. Upon seeing the withered mummy within, she had ordered the shutters in his tomb opened so that the place would flood with sunlight. Her disdain for old myths had turned to awe as this bath of celestial light brought skin and hair and handsome features back to the lifeless form on the slab.

The tales had been true! And the man she awakened, Ramses the Great himself, had served as her chief advisor and lover for years afterwards.

And then came his betrayal.

He had approved of her affair with Caesar, advised her to pursue it, even. But in Marc Antony he had glimpsed the seeds of his queen's undoing. And so, when she came to him on the eve of the Battle of Actium, demanding the elixir, not for herself, but for her lover, so that he could create an immortal army to stop Octavian's advance, Ramses had refused. And she, in despair, had eventually given herself over to the serpent's bite.

And now?

The Ramses of this new century had fallen in with a group of London aristocrats, friends and relatives of the man, Lawrence Stratford, who had discovered his tomb and died shortly thereafter. Together, this group had traveled to Egypt. For what precise reason, she did not know. She knew only that when Ramses came across her body in the museum he had been overtaken by grief and had performed an act he'd never once performed before.

He had poured his precious elixir across the remains of her corpse. Then, apparently, he had fled, abandoning her to the madness and confusion that had beset her in those first few days. A madness she spoke of in the most general of terms.

Teddy did not press.

But it was clear, terribly clear, that Ramses had fled in horror from what he'd done, that she had been left in the care of one of the members of his traveling party, a British earl, Elliott Savarell. This man had a son, Alex, but when she came to the part of the story in which he played a role, she became distant and distracted again. She said this name twice ... Alex ... Alex Savarell. As if its very mention overwhelmed her. As if the sound of it placed weight upon her tongue.

Was it anger or guilt or heartbreak she felt when she remembered this man, this viscount from London? There was something there, for sure. Something between her and this Alex that was enough to distract her even now.

And there were other gaps in the story, other moments when her pauses became long silences that suggested either a failure of memory or riots of emotion to which she refused to surrender. And Teddy could sense from these silences that in those first days of madness, of not knowing what she truly was, she had taken life.

And so be it.

She was not a creature governed by natural laws. How dare he impose upon her the laws of man?

"And the accident?" he asked finally. "The one in which you were so terribly burned?"

It was the first thing he'd said in an hour. The winds had finally died down, and the excited chatter of the men nearby was no longer being blown away from their tent. Of course they were excited. She had promised to give them a percentage of the treasures to which she had led them all that day.

"An accident, yes," she said. "It was a terrible accident."

And she would not say more.

And so it had ended badly. Terribly, perhaps. Two tragic ends with this immortal Ramses, and she did not want to speak of either one. But in those first few hours after her miraculous healing, she had alluded to revenge. And now, he realized that whatever she asked of him, he would give himself over to it.

"You wish to see these people again?" he asked, knowing as he spoke that there was a very real possibility she wished to do these people harm.

For a while, she gazed at him. He wanted to believe she was assessing him, judging whether or not he was a worthy companion now that she had revealed her truth. But he knew that was unlikely, and it pained him. It pained him to believe she was gazing through him and into her own history.

"In time," she whispered. "In time."

"And so what do you wish to do now?"

"I wish to be alive, Teddy." Her smile gave him as much pleasure as the feel of her fingernails along his spine. "I wish to be alive with you."

No other words had ever brought him such joy.

2

Venice

Ramses felt he was living in a dream. Never had he beheld a city more magnificent. He gazed out the window now, across the Grand Canal at the endless row of palaces facing him, and looked to the brilliant afternoon blue sky above, and then down once more at the dark green water. Sleek black gondolas streaked past, crowded with brightly costumed Europeans or Americans gazing with awe and enthusiasm on the same wonders that held him captive and silent. So many luxuriant hats, laden with plumes and flowers. And on the banks the flower markets with their radiant blooms. Ah, Italy. Ah, paradise. He smiled, marveling that he could not learn modern languages fast enough to unpack their treasure load of words to describe this loveliness. There were dazzling names for the faded red and dark green of these old buildings, for their decorative arches and balconies, names for the periods of history and the styles which had given birth to them.

Ah, this great earth, this splendid earth, and this time of all times that it could nurture such dense metropolises where commoner and noble alike could enjoy such beauty so effortlessly. He wanted to see more, he wanted to see the whole world, and yet never to leave here.

The afternoon heat was being swept away by the breeze off the Adriatic. The city had risen from its siesta. Time for him to go out as well.

He closed the green shutters and moved back into the splendid bedroom, which was in itself magical to him, a treasure. Kings and queens had lodged in this gaily painted chamber, or so he had been told.

"Appropriate for you, my darling," Julie had said to him. "And the cost means nothing." His Julie gave him her all with perfect trust.

Stratford Shipping, the great corporation she'd inherited from her father, was back on track under the watchful eye of her remorseful uncle, and gold, she assured Ramses, would always be plentiful. But no amount of gold in Ramses' time could have purchased this level of luxury.

Floors of patterned wood as hard and lustrous as stone, inlaid bed and dressing tables trimmed in shining brass, and mirrors, ah, the enormous mirrors. Everywhere he looked he saw himself smiling faintly in these vast dark mirrors as if his duplicate lived and breathed on the other side of the glass.

This was a glorious age, no doubt of it, and the culmination of many glorious ages during which he'd slept in his tomb in Egypt, lost to time, lost to consciousness, and not even dreaming that such wonders might await him.

Ramses the Damned, who had closed his eyes rather than witness the utter fall of Egypt. Ramses the Damned, who had known that once he was buried away from the sun, he would grow powerless, and then slumber, slumber unendingly—until brought into the sunlight by unwary mortals of a future age.

He might have pondered all this in quiet here forever, what he had missed, and what enchanted him now everywhere that he turned.

But Elliott Savarell—the Earl of Rutherford—and his beloved Julie were waiting for him, and this city waited for him, waited for him again to travel its lovely watery alleyways to the Piazza San Marco, where he must again enter the church that had almost brought him to his knees when he'd first seen it. All over this land, he'd seen churches filled with statues and paintings of unimaginable perfection, but no hallowed sanctuary had subdued him as had San Marco.

Quickly, he finished his toilet, adjusting the black tie at his neck, and putting on the gold cuff links that Julie had given him. He ran the pearl-handled brush through his thick brown hair. And applied the smallest amount of cologne to his smooth-shaven face. In the mirror he saw a modern man, a European man of dark tan skin and radiant blue eyes, and nothing of the ruler he had been to thousands in a time that could not have imagined this one.

"Ramses," he whispered aloud. "Never, never go to that passive and hopeless sleep again. Never. No matter what this world offers you or does to you. Remember this moment and this bed-chamber in Venice, and vow you will have the courage for whatever is to come."

With a springing step, he made his way down the broad marble staircase and through the busy hotel lobby to the docks.

Within seconds the liveried attendant had a gondola at his disposal.

"Piazza San Marco," he said to the brightly costumed gondolier as he handed him several coins. "And if you will get me there quickly—"

He sat back, gazing up at the buildings once more, trying to remember the name for the arches he most admired. Were they Moorish? Were they Gothic? And what was the name for the finely turned little posts on the balconies? Balusters. So many words ran through his mind, with their infinite connotations— *decadent, baroque, grandeur, rococo, monumental, enduring, tragic.*

Ideas, concepts, stories, stories without end of the rise and fall of kingdoms and empires, of far-off lands beyond wide seas, and mountainous terrain and realms of ice and snow—all crowded in upon him wondrously.

Such a world needed a wealth of words to define it, all right. And enthralled as he was, his mind drifted back, back to his own pleasure barge on the Nile so long ago, with his precious naked maidens pulling the oars, and the breeze that hovered over the broad river where the simple folk gathered on either shore to bow to their passing pharaoh. How slow the pace without ticking and chiming clocks, and how eternal seemed the golden sand and the patches of dark river silt with their carefully tended green fields. Palm trees swaying against a perfect sky, and the limits of all that could be known so very certain. It seemed the dream now, this bygone time, and not these great substantial palaces towering over him.

"No, never retreat into sleep again," he whispered aloud to himself.

Soon enough the long black boat reached the dock and he was entering the huge crowded square in search of the restaurant where he was to meet his beloved and their dearest friend. Tourists thronged the shadowy portals of the great church of San Marco. He would have liked to slip inside alone now and see once more all that glittering gold and those splendid mosaics.

But he was late as it was. The church would have to wait for now, for tomorrow or the day after.

Perhaps they did not care, his beloved friends. Perhaps they too were swept up in the beauty and gaiety of this most splendid of cities.

He saw them before they caught sight of him, and he stopped amid the loitering tourists merely to look at them—Julie and Elliott at the outside table beneath the red awning, Julie dressed smartly as a man in her white linen suit with a brilliant blue silk tie, her hair swept back and up into a man's straw hat with a black band above the brim, her blue eyes vibrant as she spoke passionately, earnestly, to the youthful-appearing Earl of Rutherford, who lounged in his woven chair, ankles crossed, nodding to Julie as he gazed past her.

How the elixir had transformed both of them—these mortals, the only living beings to whom he'd ever given the divine fluid.

How it had cured their subtle fears, and dissolved their many inhibitions.

They could not see it for themselves, really, not as he could see it, because he had known them both so well before giving them the magic brew. And he marveled now, watching them, that he had done this thing, this bold thing of sharing the elixir, when in all those centuries before he had offered it to no one. No one, that is, except his dark love, Cleopatra, who in life had refused it, and who in death had had no choice; Cleopatra whose rejection had broken his soul.

A dark shiver passed through him. His Cleopatra. He wanted to forget forever that only two months ago, he'd come upon her unmarked corpse in the Cairo Museum, and in a moment of utter madness, he had poured the precious elixir over the body to bring it back to life.

Ah, the shame of it. The horror. And he had done this, not some bumbling mortal, but he, Ramses the Great, had committed this unforgivable act, only to see that miserable resurrected Cleopatra—that muddled and mad and impulsive creature—lost to him again forever when her motorcar collided with a train roaring across the desert.

Could he ever atone for that blunder? Could he ever forgive himself for pouring out the precious fluid over that half-rotted corpse that had been his greatest love, and regenerating a murderous monster with broken memories and a monster's heart? With all his soul he wanted to forget it.

He stood there pondering as tourists made their way past him. That sin would be on his soul forever, even though he had been born to believe he could never be guilty of sin and that his smallest impulses spoke for the gods of Egypt. Well, there was another blunder, another terrible crime, yes, Ramses had to admit that as well.

There was an earlier act of unforgivable rashness, an act committed thousands of years before. It had been in an enemy country, and committed against a mad and mocking priestess from whom he had claimed a treasure that was his by right of conquest—the elixir, and the secret of its ingredients, that had transformed him into this immortal man that he was now.

The thoughtless slaying of that priestess before her impotent altar had been a hideous mistake indeed. It had always haunted him. It haunted him even here in this dreamlike realm where the soft electric lights were going on in the windows, where the candles were being set out on the dining tables, where streetlamps were being lit all around him in the radiant azure twilight.

It haunted him because it had been stupid to slay the one human link he had to the origin of this strange liquid that gave him millennia to ponder its origins.

No matter. The sin of having resurrected and destroyed Cleopatra was enough to darken this sublime evening for him, and the sight of his splendid companions.

And he thanked the gods, whoever they were, and wherever they were, that he was no longer alone in the power given him by the elixir, that Julie and Elliott shared this with him now.

Julie saw him. In a passing glance, she saw him, and he saw the smile on her lips. The raised terrace before the restaurant was now a sea of twinkling candles.

He moved towards her quickly, and bent to kiss her upraised face lightly, respectfully, as European men do it, and then turned to shake the firm hand of Elliott Savarell.

Elliott had risen, and now pulled back the chair to his right so that Ramses might take his place facing the piazza, between himself and Julie.

"And at last," said Elliott. "Are we not all famished?"

"Bring on the feast," said Ramses. "I'm sorry for keeping you waiting. I needed time alone, time to be quiet, time to think about all this," he said, smiling as he looked out at the crowds. "All I want to do now is travel, see more, know more, learn more."

"I so understand you," said Elliott. "That's an obsession we share, my king," he said. "You've given me the world and I want to travel the world, but I have a pressing task that won't wait."

"But what is that, Elliott?" Ramses asked.

"No use discussing it," said Elliott. "Allow me to say I'm off to Monte Carlo, and other gambling resorts. I've found as the result of the elixir I have a knack for cards I never exhibited in the past. And I have to use it for obvious reasons."

"Elliott, all you have to do is ask—" Julie said.

"No, my dear. No. We've been through that, and that I cannot do."

Ramses understood the man's pride. He'd understood it from the time of their first meeting. This was a nobleman without a nobleman's usual means, a man of privilege and breeding without the resources to support the houses he owned, or the style of life he was pressured to provide for those closest to him. Elliott knew the world; Elliott knew books, history, literature; and Elliott knew the silent shame of being in debt, and on the brink of ruin always. Now Elliott had within his veins the elixir of eternal life, and he was still not free of the bonds of the heart.

"Well, maybe I have a solution for you, Earl of Rutherford," said Ramses. "Yes, go to Monte Carlo, and gamble with your newfound gifts," he said. "But this will give you something for the future." He felt his inner pocket. All these European clothes were so thick, so padded, so filled with secret pockets. Yes, it was there, the piece of paper on which he'd drawn the map. He gave it now to the earl. "Can you make this out?" he asked.

Elliott took the piece of hotel stationery in his hands and studied it intently before answering. Ramses could see the curiosity in Julie's bright blue eyes, but he waited.

"Of course, I know this, this is the Gold Coast of Africa, you've used all the modern names," said Elliott. "I've never been there . . ."

"Buy the land there, exactly where I have marked," said Ramses. "No one is looking for gold there. But you will find it there if you look, and you will find the remains of ancient mines which were once the property of the pharaoh of Egypt."

"But why do you give this to me?"

"Take it," said Ramses. "I have other resources just as rich. I've asked questions, many questions, of the bankers we've met here and everywhere, of the agents who handle Julie's affairs. These resources of mine have been forgotten by the world. I can draw on them when I need them. This is only one gold mine, and it is my gift to you, and I command you to take it."

Elliott smiled, affectionately but with faint disapproval. Ramses saw the tragedy in his eyes, the humiliation. *And he will live forever,* Ramses thought, *and someday centuries from now, he will not even recall the agony of this moment. But we are in this moment, and this agony is real.*

"I'm serious," said Ramses. "You took the elixir from me, Earl of Rutherford. Now take this. I demand it."

Elliott reflected for a long moment, the lights playing in his blue eyes, eyes almost the same shade as those of Julie, as those most surely of Ramses. Blue eyes of a certain shade that were the infallible evidence of the elixir. Then Elliott folded the map and slipped it into his pocket.

"Go to Monte Carlo," said Ramses again. "Be wise with your winnings, and clever. And you'll soon have the means to explore that mine."

Elliott nodded. "Very well, Your Majesty," he said with a faint ironic tone. "This is very gracious of you." Elliott smiled, but there was defeat behind the smile.

Ramses shrugged. "Talk to your bankers about the land now. A delay in developing the land will be in your favor. But you should purchase it as soon as possible." He glanced at Julie. "As for my precious one, I have other maps, as I said."

Julie was gazing at him with unreserved admiration.

It was now full dark. And the magical realm of the Piazza San Marco had been further transformed as the sky above vanished in the mist, and strains of string quartets rose from the restaurant terraces around them. Perhaps the great golden church would close its doors. Ah, well, he would see it tomorrow. He would go during the quiet afternoon hours while the Italians slept.

Waiters were buzzing about, wine was being poured, and a raging hunger suddenly rose in Ramses as he caught the aromas of other meals being laid out around them. This hunger was never really appeased, nor the thirst that rose with it for wine or beer that would never make him drunk. *Bring on the food,* he thought excitedly. Intoxication was a thing of the past, but he wanted that flash of warmth from the wine that lasted just a few minutes after each drink.

Julie was speaking in rapid Italian to the waiter. But someone had touched her arm. It was one of those many English people who knew her from London.

She rose, acknowledging the well-dressed man who stood before her, and gave a quick kiss to the woman—a London merchant family.

"But your eyes, Julie!" said the woman. "Your eyes are blue. Julie, your eyes!"

Ramses glanced at Elliott. It was always the same, and now with the same conviction, Julie told the tale of the mysterious fever in Egypt that had changed her eyes from brown to blue. Utterly preposterous. Elliott was hiding his smile. But the couple was moving on, mollified as much as amazed. They had not recognized the Earl of Rutherford, and Julie had made no introductions.

"Spared again," said Elliott with a sigh. "But why do they believe it?"

"What?" asked Julie, settling in her chair once again. She picked up her glass. "That a fever caused my eyes to change color? I'll tell you why they believe it. They have to believe it."

Ramses laughed. He knew precisely what she meant.

"The eyes of human beings simply don't change color," said

Julie. "So they welcome the explanation, and they accept it, and then they go back to the ordinary world in which such things simply don't happen." She sipped the wine. "Lovely," she whispered. She disguised her thirst, and only in small sips consumed the entire glass.

Over her shoulder appeared a waiter's hand to fill the glass again.

"Makes perfect sense," said Elliott. "Yet still it surprises me. It's even been in the papers in London, you know. STRATFORD HEIRESS SUFFERS FEVER IN ALEXANDRIA, CHANGING THE COLOR OF HER EYES TO BLUE. Something like that. Alex sent me the clipping."

"What is it, Ramses?" asked Julie.

He realized he'd fallen to staring at her. He didn't reply at first. He looked at Elliott.

In the dim light of the candles, they looked impossibly beautiful to him, his immortal companions.

"You are gods to me," he whispered. He picked up the wine, and drank it slowly in one draught, and didn't wait for the waiter to refill his glass. He savored the rich taste of the Chianti, and then he smiled. "You can't imagine what it is like," he said. "After all those centuries alone, alone with this power, alone on this journey, and now you are with me, both of you. And I've asked myself why, why was it so easy for me to give you the elixir when for centuries I'd suffered this loneliness, this isolation. It's because you are like gods to me, you two, you paragons of this time."

"You are the god to us," said Elliott, "and I think you know it."

Ramses nodded. "But you can never know how you seem— how learned, independent, strong."

"I think I understand," said Elliott.

"And you can never know what it means to me to have you as companions." Ramses fell silent. He drank the second glass of wine and sat back approving as the waiter set down the first course of the meal, a pungent soup of seafood and vegetables simmering in a red broth. Food, how he hungered for it, always, and how they hungered for it now, too, both of them, but they were too young yet in the elixir to be weary of the hunger.

Julie clasped her hands and bowed her head. She murmured a silent prayer to gods Ramses didn't know.

"And to whom are you praying, my dear?" asked Elliott. He was drinking the soup with ungentlemanly haste. "Do tell me."

"Does it matter, Elliott?" Julie asked. "I pray to the god who listens, the god who knows, the god who may want a prayer from me. Perhaps the god who created the elixir. I don't know. Don't you ever pray anymore, Elliott?"

Elliott glanced at Ramses. Then back at Julie. He had already finished the soup, and Ramses was just beginning. A shadow of sadness passed over Elliott.

"I don't think I do, my dear," said Elliott. "When I drank the elixir I didn't think of God. If I had, perhaps I wouldn't have drunk it."

"Why?" asked Ramses in astonishment.

In that long-ago Hittite grotto, when Ramses had reached for the goblet of the elixir, he'd been convinced that he as pharaoh always did the will of the gods. And if this liquid, this sacred liquid, was the property of a Hittite god, well, then it had been Ramses' right to steal it.

"I would have thought more of Edith, and of my son," Elliott said. "As it is, I'm forever separated from them. And I'm not sure that is the will of the domestic gods worshipped by us British."

"Stuff and nonsense, Elliott," said Julie. "Your only thought now is to take care of both of them."

"That's true," said Ramses. "And you have ahead of you your adventures in Monte Carlo. Someday I want to see Monte Carlo. I want to see everything."

"Yes. As a matter of fact, I'll be taking a car out this very night," said Elliott. "I think my winnings here in Venice have begun to attract notice."

"You're not in any danger?" asked Julie.

"Oh, no, nothing of that sort," Elliott replied. "Just a major streak of luck among gentlemen, but I don't mean to push it. And I must say, I will miss you. Both of you. I will miss you terribly."

"But surely you're coming to London, aren't you?" Julie asked. "I mean for the engagement party. You know I've promised Alex that he and Edith can host this party? They're doing this for us. They so want to make us happy."

"Engagement party," Ramses muttered. "Such strange customs. But if Julie wants this, I will go along with it."

"Yes, I've heard from them both on that. I'm honored that you are allowing this. I wish I could be there. But I don't think I'll be seeing you that soon. However, I do want to thank you for your kindness to Alex, Julie."

Ramses could see complete sincerity in Elliott when he said these words, with none of the usual bite. What was the word for it? *Sarcasm*? *Cynicism*? He couldn't remember. He knew only the Earl of Rutherford loved Julie, and he loved his son, Alex, and it was a sadness to Elliott that Julie and Alex would never be married now, but the Earl of Rutherford accepted all this perfectly.

The young Alex Savarell had really quite gotten over Julie. He was in fact mourning for the mysterious woman he'd known in Cairo, the nameless and tragic woman he'd loved, the woman who might have killed him as easily as she had killed others—the Cleopatra awakened so fiendishly from the sleep of death by the elixir.

The familiar flush of shame passed over Ramses again as he contemplated this. *All my life, however long, wherever that I go, that sin . . .*

But the night was too beautiful, the roast fowl set before him too savory, the air too moist and sweet, to think of those things. He wasn't sad himself that they would be returning to England for this party. He wanted to see England all over again, see the green and forested parts of England, see the fabled lakes of England, all of England that he had not seen before.

A small orchestra nearby had begun to play, one of those dreamy waltzes that Ramses so loved, but there was no floor here for dancing, and only a few violins fed the swelling sound, yet it was still delightful.

Ah, yes, remember this moment, always, with the music playing and your darling smiling at you, and this new friend Elliott at your elbow, and no matter what the future holds, do not ever yield to the darkness again, do not ever yield to sleep, to escape. This world is simply too wondrous for that.

An hour later they said their farewells to Elliott in the bustling lobby of the hotel before going up to their rooms.

Julie peeled off the constricting male clothes and stepped out of them, a pink blossom escaping from a sheath of white. She fell into his arms.

"My queen, my immortal queen," he said. The tears stood in his eyes. He allowed her to remove his jacket and throw it aside, to unbutton the stiff and cumbersome shirt.

Naked together, they embraced in the enormous bed, amid linen that smelled of sunshine and rain, as the singing of a passing gondolier drifted through the windows.

And she will never die as all the others died, Ramses thought, kissing her hair, her breasts, the tender flesh inside her shapely arms, her smooth legs. Never die as they all have, all those other mortals with whom he'd ever struggled in darkened chambers. "My Julie," he whispered.

As he entered her, he saw her face flush and grow moist, the blood beating in her cheeks, her lips slack and her lids half closed. Such trusting surrender, when she was now as powerful as he. He lifted her tight against him as he came.

Thank you, thank you, god of the elixir. Thank you for this blessed spouse who will live as long as I live.

*   *   *

Early morning. He never really slept. Yes, he dozed now and then, rested, but he never really slept, yet Julie slept, nestled among the pillows, pink as the roses in the nearby vase, her shining hair on the pillow. He was looking out the window again, at the dark shimmering canal below, and then up at the black sky with its inscrutable stars. Once, as pharaoh, he had thought he would journey there on his death, one of the immortals, and now he knew the truth about those stars, the modern truth of the vast reaches of space and the truth of this tiny, insignificant planet.

He thought of Cleopatra, or the monster that he had raised from the dead. He saw that blaze as the car hit the train and the gasoline in it had exploded.

Forgive me, whoever, whatever, you were! I didn't know. I simply didn't know.

He padded silently across the polished floor, back to the bower of down coverlets and pillows in which he'd left his Julie. "This one lives," he whispered. "She lives and she loves me, and there is a bond forged between us that will give me the strength to forgive myself everything else."

He kissed her lips. She stirred. She stared up at him. He couldn't stop kissing her, her neck, her shoulders, her warm breasts. His fingers found her nipples and pressed them hard as he kissed her open mouth. He could feel the warmth between her legs against him. *Forever. Forever with her, the future brilliant and magnificent as this very moment. Discovery and wonder, and love without end.*

3

Alexandria

She liked this Teddy, this Dr. Theodore Dreycliff.

She liked the way he made love to her, his ministrations hungry and solicitous.

She liked that he treated her as a queen.

She liked that his pale skin turned pink under her slaps.

She had made him rich beyond his wildest imagining and still he clung to her, still he showed devotion.

But it had been a mistake, asking him to bring her to Alexandria.

There was little he could do to fix it now. They stood together on the seawall, staring out at the Mediterranean. Meditating on a sea crowded with ugly steel ships was easier than exploring a city so terribly changed from what she remembered. From what she wanted to remember of it.

To see Cairo overtaken by the mad growl of motorcars had not rent her heart in this same way.

During her time as queen, she had been no stranger to the length of the Nile. And yet even then the Upper Nile had been shrouded in the feel of the ancient; its inhabitants spoke a language most of her advisors could not. She had made it a point to learn this language, but that did not mean those regions had felt like home to her. Alexandria had been her home, and so to see it robbed of its great lighthouse and library, webbed with dark alleyways where there had once been glittering, vine-dappled streets, all of this was more than she could bear.

She found herself clutching Teddy's hand as if it were the only rail on a steep, open staircase.

"Darling," he finally whispered, "you're in pain. What can I do? Tell me and I shall do it."

She kissed him gently, cupped his face in her hands. There was nothing he could do. Not in this moment. But everything he had done up until then had been a triumph, and so she refused to make him feel anything other than great confidence in his abilities.

In Cairo, he had found the collectors, brought them to the tomb she'd unearthed, and arranged for the quick sale of everything inside.

He had returned without them so that he could ensure she concealed herself in the nearby hills before they arrived. Should their potential buyers see her likeness so near to the statues carved in her image, he had insisted, she would be exposed to the world.

But she had harbored suspicions over this request. Dark suspicions.

Had he cut some secret deal with these men? Would she be forced to snap his neck with one twist of her powerful hand? And so she had not hidden in the hills as he'd requested, but closer, behind one of the cars, where she could hear their rapid English. And it had all transpired much as Teddy had predicted. With astonishment and handshakes and warnings from these private collectors that the academic community would be in an uproar as soon as word of this place and the speedy sale of its contents reached the press. But what could they do? Men had to make a living, these men said several times.

A curious phrase, she thought. To make a living.

There was no room for gods nor queens in this phrase. In this belief that each man, each human, each person, was making a life rather than living one. The more she learned about this modern era, the more she thought it a time of bumbling rulers who took poor care of their subjects, or too many rulers for any one to rule effectively.

Teddy was exuberant when the men left. The rest would be taken care of back in Cairo, he'd informed her. Deals signed, funds transferred. Their customers had retained the Egyptians they'd hired to stay on as guards.

Their account, he added with a gleam in his eye.

He had not betrayed her. He had not stolen from her. And so she had not been forced to kill again in this, her second immortal life.

"What's next, my love?" he'd asked. "What can I do for you now, my Bella Regina Cleopatra?"

A stab of pain when he called her this. She had been called this before, by a man who had showed her Teddy's same level of devotion, but with twice the charm.

Must not think of him, she told herself. *Must not think of the young and innocent and noble Alex Savarell. Or his father, Elliott, the Earl of Rutherford. Or that pale, mewling little kitten, Julie Stratford. If I am to be free of death itself, let me be free of Ramses and his wretched twentieth-century lot.*

And so perhaps this tumult of feeling had caused her to answer too quickly, caused her to say words she now regretted.

"Please, Teddy. I wish to see Alexandria."

And here she was, standing amidst a gray and dusty relic of her empire that bore no resemblance to the city from which she once ruled.

There was something else that afflicted her, something which she had not shared with her new companion, but which seemed to have intensified since their arrival here.

Her returning memories were partial, broken.

Some were vivid, but others were retreating behind a veil, becoming more indistinct with each passing day. And who knew what she could not remember at all and might never remember? She felt cheated.

The sight of the sea, slate gray in the setting sun, brought back vivid recollections of her opulent galley's oars dipping into these same waters. On that long-ago journey, to Rome and to Caesar, it had taken an eternity for Alexandria to retreat across the horizon, the lighthouse the last piece of her home to vanish into a void between dark water and night sky.

She could remember the fear around that journey, the desperate uncertainty about how she would be received by Caesar, by Rome itself. She could remember the city's drab ugliness upon her arrival, its narrow, filthy streets, the whole place a veritable sewer compared to gleaming, sun-bleached Alexandria. That such world-changing might was originating from such a rank, brutish place had filled her with a sense of dread and injustice. These memories flashed through her, pulses of pure emotion with the power to transport her back to her time as queen.

But she could not remember Caesar's face.

Many of her memories from that time were like this. Mosaics glimpsed through water pierced by shafts of near-blinding sunlight. Bright things, beckoning things, but still cloudy and unresolved. The events of her past, their chronology, were clear to her now, but the senses and smells and tastes of it all seemed remote still. And how much of her supposed clarity was the result of having read so many history books on the train ride there?

Yes, she could remember the way Caesar suckled her neck, the way he gripped the sides of her face during his moments of focused and powerful release, and she could also vaguely recall a masculine smell that mingled with the sharp metallic odor of his armor and knew with a strange kind of certainty that this was his smell, Caesar's smell. She could also recall the stark difference between his lovemaking and that of Marc Antony, who claimed her body with boisterous and vocal ferocity.

But many of these things were facts. They came to her as knowledge, not richly detailed recollections of lived experiences.

Not yet, at least. Maybe it would take time. Or maybe with each successive resurrection, more of her old lives would be lost. This thought horrified her.

To be cut off from every memory of her time as queen if she suffered another conflagration like the one in Cairo? Unthinkable.

And how infuriating that she could remember her every encounter with Ramses in excruciating detail.

Was it because he'd been there at the moment of her resurrection? His had been the first face she'd seen as the elixir drew her forth out of withered flesh and dried bone. Perhaps the sight of him, standing over the display case as she shattered it with her skeletal, outthrust arms, had awakened all her memories of him just as it had awakened her body. Like the imprinting between a newborn animal and its mother.

The thought sickened her. Ramses was no mother, no father. No true parent to anyone.

For Caesar and Marc Antony to be retreating behind some great watery veil, while Ramses, the man who had been her ultimate undoing, danced vividly throughout her mind; this was simply intolerable.

Such confusion still. It didn't compare in the slightest to those first few awful days after her awakening in Cairo, when her body had been full of gaping wounds, her mind a riot of memories which would vanish and reappear only to vanish again.

There was greater stability now, in her body, and in her soul. But her mind was not entirely healed. She wanted her memories.

On the train to Alexandria, she'd devoured the history books Teddy bought for her. And it hadn't surprised her in the slightest how the Romans had told her story. A powerful whore, whose only true power lay in between her legs. As if lust alone would have been enough to subdue a man like Caesar, a man who could have helped himself to any queen he wanted, and often did.

Would this be a curse of immortality? she wondered. To witness the degree to which victorious nations simplified and cheapened the narratives of their rivals?

It infuriated her that she was in no position to put her version of events to paper, given the uneven and unreliable return of certain memories over others.

When reading her own history became too much for her to bear, Teddy had sought to gently lecture her on the world they were traveling through. Of those inventions she had yet to encounter, of conflicts between nations whose names she had never heard spoken before.

Every now and then he offered her some piece of knowledge of which she was already in possession, and in those moments, she would place a hand gently on his thigh and inform him that even in Alexandria all those years ago, men of science had begun to speculate that indeed the earth itself was round.

Still, the extent of the known world now shocked her. It seemed impossibly large. Far too large for a single city, London, to serve as its center.

But this is exactly how Teddy described the city of his birth. The center of a vast and chaotic world that stretched between two frozen poles. It seemed akin to securing a giant tent in desert winds with only one reed. Surely, the dance of empires which had at times ensured long periods of stability during her reign could not tame such an expansive world.

And now there was talk of a great conflict brewing on the continent of Europe, which she understood was the name given to much of what had once been ruled by Rome.

But these thoughts could only occupy her mind for a short moment. For in this new, gray, growling Alexandria, the past and present fought for control of her mind. Which one would win? She was not sure.

"It was a mistake to bring you here, my love," Teddy finally said. "A terrible mistake."

"It was nothing of the kind," she answered. "I asked you to do so and you complied. Where is the mistake in this?"

He took her in his arms so they could avoid getting trampled by a regiment of pale-skinned soldiers in uniforms more drab than any Romans had worn in her day. Were they Romans? Or were they British, like the people Ramses moved among now? And what explained their presence here? Here in her Alexandria.

No, not mine. Not mine anymore. Not mine for two thousand years.

They would leave here at once, the two of them. She could easily flee this grief, this regret, simply with another train ride. The fear of death had been removed. And she had Teddy. Boyishly handsome Teddy who hung on her every word. Who . . .

. . . he was fading right before her eyes. Teddy's smile became a look of concern as he saw the expression on her face. She tried to speak, but his very image wavered before her, and then, instead of his face, she saw another's. A woman's face. A woman she did not recognize. And there was darkness crowding in on all edges of this woman like an expanding frame of starless night sky.

The woman was pale skinned with tumbles of golden hair, and her expression showed the same bafflement Cleopatra now felt. As if they were mirroring each other. What was the woman wearing? Some sort of lacy robe. A sleeping garment of some kind.

She reached for this woman, and amazingly, this woman appeared to reach for her.

And then she was gone.

And the traffic was blaring all around her, and Teddy had gripped the hand with which she had reached out to her vision.

Nausea, dizziness; two things she had not felt since her resurrection. They seized her now with fierce power. She stumbled into the nearest wall. For some reason, her body preferred the support of cold concrete to Teddy's arms.

A vision. A vision that had taken her outside of herself. How else could she explain it? But could she explain this to Teddy? Would he understand? Worse, would his devotion to her flag when her mystery and magic took on a dark tint?

Who had this strange blonde woman been? Where had she been?

It was no memory from her past, she was utterly sure of this.

And why had this woman regarded her with the same curiosity?

"Something is not right," she whispered. "Something is . . ."

"I'm here, Cleopatra. I'm here. Anything you need, just ask it of me. Please."

Damn you, Ramses. Just as I seek to be free of you . . .

"Cleopatra," Teddy whispered.

"There is nothing you can do, dear Teddy. There is only one who could possibly help and he is . . ."

"Ramses," Teddy finished for her.

She turned to him, accepting the comfort of his embrace again.

"What did you see?" he asked. "It seemed as if you were look-ing through me."

"A vision. A woman I didn't recognize. She was in some other place."

"It was a dream."

"I am wide awake. I do not sleep. I have no need for it."

"That's just it, don't you see? You don't sleep, but your body is still human and your mind is still human and so your mind must process things in the same way. Mortals do it through dreams. And so you must do it through a kind of dreaming while you're awake. That's all, my darling. That's all it is. Truly."

Oh, how she wanted to believe this pronouncement. And how touching the earnestness with which he delivered it. He was, after all, a man of medicine and science, despite the scandal in his past.

"Dearest Teddy, I fear the treatment of a being such as myself lies far outside your area of expertise."

"Indeed," he answered. "And so there's only one who might have the answers to what ails you. Ramses the Great."

"Ramses the Damned," she whispered.

When he pulled away from her suddenly, she was afraid she had lost him. But he was rifling in his jacket pocket. He found it quickly, the folded-up piece of paper he'd been searching for.

"I went back to the Shepheard's Hotel in Cairo. I know you said you didn't want to see them again. But Ramses and his friends, I thought perhaps they might be looking for you, and if there was a search under way, you should be aware of it. There was no sign of them except for this. A cable that had been sitting at the front desk for only a few days."

"A cable?" she asked, baffled, taking the paper from his hands.

"Yes. They're transmissions. Words. They come over the wires and are written down. Do you need me to read it to you? This was for Elliott Savarell, the man who took care of you. This friend of Ramses. It was his son who sent it. He obviously thought his father was still in residence at the hotel, but the front desk said he had not been there for some time."

But she had read it herself already.

```
FATHER ARE YOU WELL STOP BETROTHAL PARTY
FOR JULIE AND RAMSEY EIGHTEEN APRIL OUR
ESTATE YORKSHIRE STOP MOTHER THRILLED
PLEASE COME OR WRITE YOUR SON ALEX
```

Alex Savarell was the author of this message. The beautiful, adoring man with whom she'd shared a single, unforgettable night in Cairo. A man who had promised her everything, even though he hadn't been truly aware of what she was, of how she'd come to live again.

There was so much to absorb in this simple, terse message. And yet, that was the word that seemed to drift towards her off the paper again and again, as powerful as the strange vision she'd suffered only moments before.

Alex . . .

"That's him, isn't it? Mr. Ramsey? That's his alias. He's to be married, to this Julie Stratford. That's the daughter of the man who discovered his tomb, isn't it?"

"Yes," she answered.

"You wish to go to him?" Teddy asked.

She forced herself to look into his eyes, to banish all thoughts of other men she'd lain with, and women she had almost killed.

"I do not. I do not wish to go to him. I wish to find answers that only he will possess. And so, I have no other choice."

"We, my darling," he said, taking her hand. "*We* have no other choice, my Bella Regina Cleopatra."

*   *   *

It was she! The woman in the picture. And her companion was a handsome young man, probably British, just like the men who were supposedly searching for this woman.

The man had followed them there from the train station, and now he was sure. It was a fine sketch, done by an expensive artist, so there was no mistaking the resemblance. It had been delivered to him weeks before by his cousin, who claimed a friend of his from Cairo was searching for this woman. His cousin knew little else, except his friend, a Samir Ibrahim, had been the compatriot of a famous British archeologist who had recently died, and the man's relatives were desperate to find this woman for some reason.

Ever since then, he had visited the train stations whenever there was an arrival from Cairo. Searched for the woman's face in the crowd.

And today, just as he'd grown weary of this pursuit, he had spotted her emerging from the morning train on the arm of her handsome companion, and he had followed them throughout their wanderings.

He had been ordered to follow her long enough to establish a detailed report and nothing more. She was dangerous, this woman, or so these British thought.

He had seen enough.

He fell back into the crowd, then hurried in the direction of the nearest telegraph office.

4

Chicago

Sibyl Parker was desperate to record the contents of the dream that had just awakened her. She pulled her diary from the nightstand drawer without turning on the lamp.

In the pale sliver of light coming through the cracked bedroom door, she wrote feverishly.

> *Again, I saw the woman, a beautiful woman with skin darker than my own and raven hair and blue eyes. She stood with the sea behind her in a city I did not recognize. She gazed back at me. She even reached for me at the very moment I seemed to reach for her. And then the dream ended. In this dream, there was no violence like the others. A blessing, it seems. Could my plague of nightmares be coming to an end?*

Scribbling just these few sentences exhausted her.

The first peaceful dream since the nightmares had begun. She should savor this relief, she knew. But as soon as she blinked, images from her other nightmares filled the deep shadows around her canopied bed.

The first one had been the most awful. The one in which she'd stared up at a handsome Middle Eastern man who seemed terrified by the sight of her. His fear baffled her until she saw the hands with which she reached for him were withered almost to the bones. She'd heard splintering wood and breaking glass, and then, in the moment before she woke, she realized she'd been crawling out of some sort of display case.

Then, a week later, she'd dreamed of closing her hands around a Middle Eastern woman's throat, of watching the life drain from her eyes. And if those two had not been disturbing enough, she'd then suffered another nightmare. In this one, two giant trains bore down on her out of night darkness, coming from opposite directions, the lights from their locomotives like the eyes of angry gods. Then she'd found herself sailing into the sky on a bed of flame, and had awakened with a scream that had drawn everyone in the house.

Impossible to forget, these nightmares. But a part of her did not want to forget. She was sure these dreams were elements of some sort of experience for which she did not yet have a name or a true understanding, and so documenting them in their entirety was absolutely essential.

After several minutes, Sibyl's shallow gasps turned into deep, sustaining breaths, and her bedroom seemed to be her own again.

Had she cried out in her sleep?

Probably not. If so, Lucy would have come. Or one of the housemaids. Or perhaps one of her brothers, Ethan or Gregory, whichever one had not yet drunk himself into a stupor.

Powerful winds off Lake Michigan battered the immense house. A few of the shutters had come loose, and now they were tapping out a rhythm against the stone walls that sounded like the loping gait of an injured giant.

Parker House was one of the first mansions built on this former patch of swampland north of Chicago's commercial district, and her parents had left it to her, and her only, to ensure that its maintenance would not become prey to the vices of her younger brothers. They'd done much the same with the family business, installing Gregory and Ethan in vanity positions which gave them the illusion of power and control while those more qualified kept them from making a mess of things.

All her life she had been a woman of distinct and powerful dreams. But up until recently, they had been long, languorous experiences, fueled by the books she'd consumed voraciously ever since she was a little girl. Dreams of romance and adventure and faraway lands. Recording them in her journals the following morning had been a delight. And many of those older journals still provided inspiration for her *little stories*, as her brothers sneeringly referred to them, despite the fact that those *little stories* now provided the most substantial sum of income their family had left.

For as long as she could remember she had dreamed of Egypt. She'd lost count of how many times she had ridden Cleopatra's pleasure barge on a cushion of blossoms. The gleaming streets of Alexandria were as real to her as Michigan Avenue, and as a young girl she would often shed tears over the cold reality that the latter was not the former.

Too much Plutarch, her mother had scoffed.

But she'd read far more than Plutarch. She had devoured everything she could find on Egypt's last queen, from slender little volumes for children to the largest collections of archaeological photographs she could find in the library. And every artifact, every illustration of gleaming Alexandria and its lost library and museum, inspired dreams and fantasies in her that were as vivid as they were fevered. In these obsessions and fantasies, only her father had seen the first stirrings of talent.

"You will learn as you get older, my dear girl, that not everyone reads as you do. Not everyone has the same encounter with language. There is a heightened sensitivity in you, to be sure, but you can embrace it. It's far more than just a nervous condition, these tears you shed when you read of Cleopatra and Marc Antony's fall. You are a rare and beautiful thing, Sibyl. For most people, words are just symbols for sounds, made on paper. For you, they can create all new worlds in your mind."

And her dreams were a reflection of this, her father had insisted, and so he encouraged her to write them all down, so that a journal of dreams became her first real writings. Now the author of some thirty popular romances set in ancient Egypt, she knew more perhaps than her parents ever had about how people respond to language. Hers might not be the haute literature of the age, but she moved her loyal readers, outselling H. Rider Haggard and Conan Doyle and a legion of other popular American writers.

The role played by her dreams, however, was her secret. And of late her dreams were full of fear and torment. It was as if some dark and once-buried part of her had been unearthed by a great upset she couldn't identify.

Could grief for her parents be the cause? But it had been three years now since the terrible boating accident that had drowned them both.

Were her brothers and their drunken antics to blame? If so, why were so many of them strange dreams of a faraway place, viewed through a stranger's eyes, a stranger capable of murder? And if her brothers were the cause of these nightmares, why didn't they appear in any of them?

If the sudden commotion in the foyer was any indication, her brothers were about to make an appearance downstairs.

"Sibyl!" Ethan's voice boomed up the grand staircase. "Gin! Gin for everyone!"

My dearest mother and father, she prayed. *I pray that your spirits return on the wind and knock your terrible, ungrateful drunk of a son flat on his face!*

"Sibyl! Wake up. We've got company!" Gregory was joining in now. "'Less you've got a suitor up there with you, in which case give him our condolences!"

There was a riot of laughter at this remark, some of it female.

It was past three in the morning, the servants were asleep in the attic, and she was being summoned like a housemaid. And to serve whom? What company could one reasonably expect at three in the morning?

She swung her feet to the chilly hardwood floor and gathered the waistband of her robe about herself.

When she reached the top of the grand staircase, her brothers and their female companions stared up at her from the foyer far below as if Parker House were a hotel and the four of them were being rudely ignored by the bellman.

Ethan was the taller of the two. He had been a handsome devil before strong drink had convinced him to treat his shaggy mane of black hair as an afterthought, and given him a blotchy complexion and a bulbous red nose. Gregory was half his older brother's height, with a pear-shaped body and a bushy ginger mustache he maintained solely because it made him look older and therefore more accomplished in business than he truly was.

Their dates for the evening were both clad in spare but flowing dresses that managed to drape and reveal their long legs at the same time. This particular style of fashion had just started to take hold in young women who frequented jazz clubs, and Sibyl didn't care for it, which is why she always managed to forget its brusque name. Something to do with a bird, she thought.

Both women only glanced at her before returning their attention to the surroundings: the giant grandfather clock in the front hallway, the grand staircase beneath a stained-glass dome worthy of a statehouse.

"It is past three in the morning," she said quietly. "Am I really expected to entertain?"

"How many rooms this place got?" one of the women asked.

"Plenty, honey," Ethan answered. "Parker House's got plenty of rooms and we're gonna show you all of 'em. Where's Lucy?"

"I'm right here, madam," Lucy stammered. Ah, poor dear Lucy. Still struggling into her robe, Sibyl's beloved maid emerged from the stairs to the servant's attic. She was blinking at the chandelier's sudden glare.

"You may conduct a tour in the morning," Sibyl offered as she descended the stairs with Lucy behind her. "Or perhaps when you return at some later date. For now, Lucy and I both need our sleep."

Both of her brothers paled at the thought of spending more than a few lustful hours with their current companions.

"Gin, Lucy," Gregory bellowed. "Gin for everyone!"

"You may go back to bed, Lucy," Sibyl said.

"Fix us a drink, Lucy," Gregory cried.

"Go to bed, Lucy. This instant. I insist."

Lucy turned on her heel and proceeded up the stairs from which she'd come.

"Hey, what's this?" one of the women said. She picked up a parcel wrapped in brown paper off the console table and shook it as if it were a baby's rattle. "One of you fine gents get me a gift? You boys! We just met!"

"Oh, no, that's for Sis here," Ethan answered. "See, Sis is what you might call a collector. She enjoys dusty old things from all over the world 'cause they remind her of her love life."

Ethan snatched the package from his date's hand and shook it next to one ear.

"Ethan, put it down," Sibyl said. She stood at the foot of the stairs. "Please!"

"Doesn't sound like a piece from a pharaoh's scepter," Ethan said.

"Might be more bones," Gregory chimed in. "Remember the time the old man sent her some bones and she spent hours studying them at her desk like some mad scientist? Should have put her in a madhouse right then!"

"Put it down, Ethan!"

But Ethan only raised his arms high above his head so the package was just out of Sibyl's reach. The women cackled as if it were the funniest thing they'd ever seen.

Most of the items she'd purchased from her antiquities dealer in New York were far too delicate to stand up to this kind of abuse. And the mere thought of her ghoulish brother breaking some valuable artifact just so he could impress his date was more than she could bear.

Here she was, at thirty, an internationally known author, and her wastrel brother was treating her as if she were a child putting on airs.

"Sibyl loves little stories, you see," he cried. He hopped back just far enough to keep her baited. "Always making up stories in that precious little head of hers. Wants to be somebody else, probably."

Sybil drove one foot down atop her brother's. The sudden jolt of pain caused him to release the package. She caught it in both hands instantly.

When she spoke again, it was as if her voice came from some other, more distant place.

"You would do well to remember that my *little stories* provide a substantial source of income which helps finance your little racing tours about town in the middle of the night! And while I'm sure you've dazzled these fine ladies with tales of your skillful management of Parker's Dry Goods Emporium, should you continue to disrupt my sleep and Lucy's, I would be more than happy to explain to them how the actual management of the company takes place at the hands of those whose skills extend beyond the ability to refill a flask without drawing the notice of their colleagues!"

Oh, what she would have given for a portrait painting of the expression on her brothers' faces in that moment. It looked as if her tirade had chased every drop of liquor from their veins.

Inside, she was as stunned by her outburst as they were, but she was determined to hide that reaction, lest it should portray her as a creature less fearsome than the one who had just startled them all into silence.

She was used to words flowing unbidden and vigorously from her pen, but not from her own lips.

"Show's over, ladies," Gregory said. He steered his date

towards the front door by her right shoulder. Ethan did the same to his.

Just before the door closed behind the two women, she heard one of them say, "Well, that one thinks she's some kinda empress."

If only, she thought ruefully. *If only.*

When she reached the top of the grand staircase, she looked back over her shoulder and found both of her brothers staring up at her like frightened dogs.

"It was just a parcel," Gregory whined.

She responded by closing her bedroom door.

* * *

Just as she suspected, the package was from her antiquities dealer in New York, E. Lynn Wilson. She tore it open with her bare hands. God forbid she go downstairs for a letter opener and risk running into her brothers again.

The statue was intact, thank God. And in pristine condition. The goddess Isis seated atop a tiny platform, her wings outstretched on either side of her; her right leg pressed flat against the platform from knee to foot and her left leg bent, so that she could turn her gaze to the expanse of her left wing.

Dear Miss Parker,

I must apologize for the length of time it took to locate the statue you described to me some time ago. But I am proud to say I have finally managed to find one that should fit the bill. While it is a reproduction, it has been faithfully re-created from descriptions of and illustrations from the Ptolemaic period and such, so that I am confident it will make an excellent addition to your collection. Because you have been such a wonderful customer and because I remain a loyal and steadfast admirer of your highly entertaining novels, I have chosen to send it forthwith without the expectation of a deposit.

As you can see from the illustration I have also included,

it is highly likely that the prow of the oared galley on which
Cleopatra traveled from Alexandria to Rome may very well have
been carved with a rendering of the goddess Isis quite similar
to the statue included here. And as I'm sure you're aware given
your overall interest in the subject, most statues and portraits
which claim to be of Egypt's last queen are in fact closer to being
common representations of the goddess she worshipped, such as
the one you see here.

I hope it is as you described to me some time ago. If it is
not, please don't hesitate to keep it as a simple token of my
appreciation for your business and your wonderful books. If it is,
I have enclosed an invoice for the full amount which you may pay
at your earliest convenience.

Yours,
E. Lynn Wilson

P.S. Because I know we share the same passion for all things
Egypt, I've included some news clippings sent to me by a friend
in Cairo about an intriguing affair that made the papers there,
which I am presumptuous enough to assume might form a fine
basis for one of your thrilling tales in the future!

He'd folded over several pieces of newsprint and taped them
to the inside of the box.

Her first instinct was to toss them in the trash.

Even though he seemed like a nice man, the last thing she
wanted was some sort of specious claim brought against her by
either the subject of the article or Wilson himself, should something she wrote in the future bear even the slightest resemblance
to whatever lurid tale the article told.

But curiosity got the best of her.

She unfolded the pages within.

Her breath left her in a long startled hiss and she found herself
sinking to the foot of the bed as she read.

The headline screamed MYSTERIOUS EGYPTIAN CLEARED IN CONNECTION WITH MUMMY THEFT AND GRISLY MUSEUM MURDER.

Beneath it was an ink drawing of the handsome man she had seen in her nightmare.

He stood beside a camel, the camel driver off to his left. The pretty woman in the drawing with him—she was either American or English, Sibyl couldn't tell—was not identified, but the print just below read "Valley of the Kings." Proud, handsome, and gentlemanly in his trousers and white silk coat, the man showed none of the terror he'd given off in her dream as she'd reached for him with a skeleton's hands.

But it was him; she was sure of it. His remarkable eyes and sculpted chin. His regal bearing.

It felt as if a great weight were sitting on her chest. Her hands shook.

She forced herself to read.

Someone had stolen a mummy from the Cairo Museum and murdered a museum maid in the process. The mummy in question had been the perfectly preserved remains of a woman from the Ptolemaic period who had spent centuries entombed in the mud of the Nile delta before she was discovered and transported to the museum. For a time, the police had suspected Mr. Ramsey, a "mysterious Egyptian" who had been on holiday in Egypt with members of the Stratford Shipping family. Now that he had been cleared of suspicion, Ramsey had been permitted to return to London with his traveling companions.

And that was that and everyone was supposed to be satisfied.

But the amateur detective in her could sense the holes in the story. She'd seen what families of influence and wealth could do. The fingerprints of one were all over these articles.

If Mr. Ramsey had been cleared, then who now was the primary suspect? And what of the whereabouts of this mysterious stolen mummy from the Ptolemaic period?

She was distracting herself with this little game of detective, distracting herself from a new sensation that filled her limbs. A tingling that suggested shortness of breath. But also another feeling that was harder to explain.

Excitement. A thundering, almost incomprehensible sense of excitement.

Her nightmares had become so vivid and wretched this past month, the fear that she was losing her mind had become as steady and persistent as her heartbeat. But now, the suggestion of a more miraculous explanation had quite literally arrived on her doorstep, an explanation that spared her sanity, an explanation that suggested there was as much true magic and wonder in the world as she had tried to write into it with her little stories.

The man in my dream exists, she thought. *We are connected somehow. And if I follow that connection as far as it goes, perhaps my nightmares will come to an end!*

Quickly she removed several sheets of her best stationery from the desk drawer and began to write. The letter was to her London publisher.

"I have reconsidered your many invitations and now agree with you that it is an excellent idea for me to visit London, and accept any invitations you might recommend for speaking engagements or appearances. . . ."

As soon as the sun rose, she'd call her New York agent.

*   *   *

At breakfast Sibyl dropped two aspirin tablets in front of both her brothers, neither of whom looked up from his half-eaten swirls of scrambled eggs, neither of whom seemed to care in the slightest that it was almost noon on a Monday and he'd made no attempt to get started on the week's business.

"I'm leaving," she said.

It took Gregory several seconds to pick up his aspirin. He swallowed them with a sip of water small enough so as not to upset his tortured stomach.

Ethan stopped massaging his temples, opened one bloodshot eye, and did his best to look at her with it.

"Another stroll through the Lincoln Park Conservatory?" he grumbled. "So you can pretend like you're an ancient lady in one of those gloomy novels you love?"

"Further than the park, actually."

Gregory looked up from his plate and saw that she was dressed in her traveling costume. A tailored jacket checkered in squares of white and blue, the outward-facing flaps of the collar lined in blue satin. The band on her otherwise plain hat was also a matching shade of blue. She'd never been one to wear her corsets like something out of an illustration by Charles Dana Gibson, but Lucy's nervous hands that morning had left her with a particularly tight fit. And that made sense, she thought. It made her feel as streamlined as the prow of the ship she planned to soon board.

"How much further?" Ethan whined. "You've got writing to do."

"Yes, and I'm not sure if you've heard, but it's only possible to write in the city of Chicago now. President Wilson just signed it into law."

"Well, I'm not sure what the president would have to say about your sharp tongue," Gregory grumbled.

"Who knows?" Sibyl responded. "Perhaps he's a fan of my books."

"Ha! No one in the corridors of power is reading *your* trifles, miss," Gregory responded.

"Where are you going, Sibyl?" Ethan demanded.

"London."

"*London!*" they both cried at once, their mutual outrage having pierced the veil of their hangovers.

Her brothers began to bellow and cry about responsibilities that weren't actually hers, which neither was capable of attending to on his own. She had expected just this sort of response. But she always knew that Ethan and Gregory were just lazy enough that if she presented her imminent journey as a fait accompli, they might not protest it with all they had.

"For how long?" Gregory finally asked when he saw she remained unmoved by all their previous allegations and complaints.

"For as long as it takes," she answered.

"For as long as *what* takes? Why must you be cryptic as well? There's talk of war, you know. They've already had one in the Balkans and at the rate they're all going Germany and Austria will make some sort of trouble soon."

"Serves them right," Ethan grumbled. "Jamming all those countries onto that tiny continent like horses in a barn. What'd they think would happen?"

"And you can't go off traveling alone, all by yourself, I won't permit it!" said Gregory. "No, I say no. Besides, you've been to Europe five times with Mama. You've seen everything in Europe."

"It's time I went off on my own," said Sibyl. "What have I been waiting for, after all?" But the dream came back to her, and the article in the paper, the face of that man.

"By the time I've returned, Ethan," she said, "I'm sure you will have assumed an important role in world affairs, and you can share that great insight with our president."

"We need you here," said Gregory. "The staff needs you."

"What you mean is you'll have to manage them on your own," she replied.

She was almost to the front door when Ethan called after her, "Fitting you'd make your escape just before the week started!"

"It's *Monday*, gentlemen," she called back. "The week started hours ago!"

She slammed the front door behind her just as she heard the tinkle of overturned glassware and chair legs scraping the dining room's hardwood floor.

Old Philip was waiting for her in the driveway and so was Lucy. All the bags had been loaded into the Rolls-Royce, and now Lucy and Old Philip were both smiling at her, as if they were proud of the speed with which she'd managed to escape from the house that morning.

This was new, this authoritative voice she had discovered within herself, this assertiveness as well. When she unleashed it fully, this sense of power made her feel twice her size. In the past, she would have snuck out without saying anything to her brothers at all, and then, on the ride to the train station, she would have worried ceaselessly about their reactions to her sudden absence, and whether or not she was shirking the promise she'd made to her late parents to care for her brothers even amidst their terrible self-indulgences.

But now, she felt like a different Sibyl Parker altogether, one capable of crossing the globe on her own and flattening anyone who dared step in her way.

5

Paris

Samir Ibrahim dashed across the Place de la Concorde towards the most famous restaurant in the world. In one hand he clutched the telegram that had terrified him to the bone.

He had to find Julie and Ramses at once.

As politely as he could, he pushed his way through Maxim's front bar, past the men in their tuxedos and the women in their flowing, lustrous gowns. All the while, the hypnotic strands of the "Morning Papers" waltz guided him through the din of boisterous conversation and into the restaurant's main dining room.

He spotted them immediately.

The floor was full of other impeccably dressed couples performing the Viennese waltz, but he was sure most of the attention in the room was on Julie Stratford and her handsome Egyptian dancing partner.

For the briefest of moments, Samir forgot his dark mission as he watched the only child of his dear, departed friend Lawrence, the man with whom he had traveled the world, unearthing tombs and relics, spin across the crowded dance floor in the confident grip of a former pharaoh. There had been a time, just after they'd traveled to Egypt in the wake of her father's death, when it had seemed as if Julie's grief for her father might overtake her. But now it was clear her spirit had been beautifully restored.

Indeed, she danced with such confidence and beauty, tears came to Samir's eyes.

Her male attire reflected impeccable taste. Black tails, her pile of curls crowned with a top hat, the delicate hands with which she held her dancing partner sheathed in white gloves.

And then there was the dancing partner himself, her new fiancé. The man whose tomb her father had discovered in the hills outside of Cairo. This man had rescued her from an attempted murder at the hands of her own cousin. For he was not just a man, but an immortal who had once ruled Egypt for over sixty years, before faking his own death so that the secret of his immortality would remain hidden from his subjects, and from history itself.

Ramses the Great. Proud, handsome Ramses. Ramses the pharaoh of ancient Egypt who had shattered Samir's sense of the limits of this world in which he lived, and transformed his view of it forever.

It was an astonishing thing, Samir thought, to know the man's true, ancient identity amidst the bustle and swirl of this opulent place with its colorful murals and liveried waiters and great clouds of cigarette smoke in which the scents of dozens of perfumes mingled and became an aroma that seemed otherworldly. It was an astonishing thing to worship this man, accepting the rectitude of Ramses' immortality, accepting the superiority of Ramses' mind, accepting the power and seductive charm of this true monarch to whom Samir had pledged immediate and unquestioning loyalty.

Samir knew this was a moment he must relish and savor.

Oh, Lawrence, Samir thought. *You would be so happy to see your daughter now. So happy to see that she is not just safe and protected, but electrified by immortality. More alive than she has ever been. And oh, if only you might have shared these revelations with me, that Ramses the Great lives, walks the earth, the very same king who once rode his chariot at the head of an army of chariots into battle against the Hittites. Oh, if only you could have heard the words of this man as he reflects on those long-ago centuries, answers the most complex questions about them so effortlessly. . . .*

His thoughts returned to the dancing figures before him, to the present moment.

Why did it fall upon him to shatter their happiness?

But he could wait. Another few minutes at least.

And so, along with the crowd, he watched them dance. He marveled at the immortal strength that allowed them to swirl and turn without pausing for breath, even as the dancers around them seemed to tire. The same strength that allowed each of them to dance without once looking away from the adoring gaze of the other.

Did any of their onlookers notice that their eyes were an almost identical shade of blue? Perhaps. Or perhaps they were too distracted by the spectacle of the dance itself.

Ramses saw him the minute the dance concluded. So did Julie. They moved towards him through the crowded tables, offering smiles to diners still applauding their performance.

They were not surprised to see him. He had planned to meet them in Paris, but he had not planned to bring with him such frightening news.

"Samir, my friend," Ramses said, clapping him on the back, "you shall join us at our table at once. We have made new friends here and we shall be happy for you to join them."

"I'm afraid not, sire," Samir answered.

Mustn't go into details in this crowded place. He handed Ramses the telegram.

"I'm afraid she's been found," Samir said.

Ramses read. Julie stiffened next to him.

"In Alexandria," Ramses said, his mood darkening.

"Yes."

He handed the cable to Julie, whose expression had become an icy mask. *No surprise there,* Samir thought. Before becoming an immortal, Julie had almost died at Cleopatra's hands.

"I see," Julie said softly, with a faint smile. "Well, perhaps we should look at it this way: now we know we too are capable of surviving great fire." Her face went white and she swallowed, her lips trembling.

Ramses curved an arm around his fiancée's waist and steered her towards the bar.

"Come," Ramses said. "Let's all return to the hotel at once and discuss the implications of this."

*   *   *

This lavish suite at the Ritz, with its soaring, draperied windows looking out onto the Place Vendôme, had been their home for a week now—their last stop on the Continent before the return to London. Ramses loved it, as surely as he'd loved all of the grand hotels in which they'd lodged, dined, made love.

The staff had been faithful in delivering great heaping platters of pastry and quiche at all hours, along with buckets of champagne, just as they had requested.

Ramses, seated at the dining table, read the cable again, as if the brief message might reveal some hidden clue upon subsequent examination.

> WOMAN YOU SEEK IN ALEXANDRIA STOP MALE
> COMPANION SHE CALLS TEDDY UNKNOWN STOP
> BOTH ARRIVED FROM CAIRO ON MORNING TRAIN
> STOP ADVISE IF YOU WANT FURTHER ACTION

He would do better to question Samir than to focus on these terse strings of words. He wanted more champagne. It was Samir who lifted the bottle from the bucket of ice and filled the crystal glass for him. Samir then sat back puffing on his small dark cheroot. Julie too enjoyed one of these little "smokes." And indeed the smoke to Ramses was like perfume. Long centuries ago, tobacco had been very rare in his kingdom, coming from unnamed lands far across the sea. Just one of the many luxuries he'd known as a king.

But again, it crossed Ramses' mind that no pharaoh of his time had ever enjoyed the vast luxury known to a world of business-men and commercial travelers in this day. And even the common people had their vintage wines and tobacco. He drank the cham-pagne in one long draught.

How he hated this dark intelligence from Alexandria.

This was their last week in this great capital before they had to attend the betrothal party hosted by young gentle Alex Savarell, the very man Julie had once seemed fated to marry. Ramses wasn't dreading it, precisely, merely waiting eagerly for it to be over. He understood the goodwill behind the gesture, and the impor-tance of the family to his beloved companion.

But he longed to travel again as soon as it was over, to see the Lake District of England, and the castles of the north, and the fabled lochs and glens of Scotland.

Now this startling news cast its dark shadow over all their plans, here in Paris, and tomorrow and tomorrow.

Julie rose and opened one of the windows so the smoke from her cigarette could escape. The drapes fluttered in the cool night air.

She was no longer a delicate thing. She had not been for some time. Long gone was the trembling young woman who had seen him rise from his sarcophagus in her very house in London, just in time to prevent her murderous cousin Henry from poisoning her in her own drawing room with a cup of tea—the same incor-rigible man who had poisoned her father in Egypt, all in a bum-bling attempt to raid the family's company to pay off his gambling debts. But Henry Stratford was gone now, and so too was the version of Julie he had almost killed. She'd been outspoken but naïve, under pressure to marry a man she had not loved, and on the verge of being exposed to the true evils men can do in the name of avarice.

Yes, quite completely gone now, that Julie for this ever-resilient bride of his heart, to whom he did not need to pledge his undying loyalty with rings and ceremony.

On the ship carrying her back to London from their Egyptian adventure, that Julie had attempted to end her life, only to land in his powerful arms before the dark sea could claim her, accepting the elixir from him hours later with trembling hands.

She radiated an effortless confidence and poise, this Julie, who had begun to see the world around her from an entirely new perspective. And all the world had been theirs to explore only moments ago.

Ramses looked at Samir. How he treasured this mortal friend and confidant, an Egyptian of this age, dark of eye and face, with a deep understanding of Ramses and his ways that these lighter people of the north, even his beloved Julie, could not quite so easily discover. Someday, someday, perhaps, the time would come to confer the elixir once again, to this man, but there was time to ponder this, and Samir would never ask for this gift, never assume for a moment that Ramses, his lord and master, should be approached for such a thing, or so taken for granted.

"What do we know of this man she travels with?" Ramses asked. "Aside from his first name."

"Not much of which we are sure. But I have suspicions."

"Do share them, Samir."

"As I wrote you some time ago, one of the trains that struck her car that night continued on. Much of its cargo was bound for an outpost in the Sudan. After some investigation, my men came across a report there of a body that had been discovered in one of its boxcars."

"From where did this report come?"

"A local journalist."

"And the local hospital?" Ramses asked. "Did you contact them?"

"No one would speak of it. The nurses who had been on staff that night had since departed."

"This was only two months ago," Julie said.

"This man she travels with," Ramses said, "you believe him to be someone from the hospital? Her doctor, perhaps?"

"Perhaps, sire."

"And the others who departed?"

"More murder," Julie whispered.

"Maybe, Julie," Samir answered. "Or maybe not. One of my men in Cairo just contacted me about a rather large sale of artifacts. A private sale. The archaeological community is outraged, of course. Whoever made the sale has taken steps to conceal their true identity. But the rumor is they claimed the tomb in question was a secret storehouse of treasures kept by Cleopatra herself. That many of the coins and statues inside bear her likeness. There's been some coverage of it in the Egyptian papers. I had them send the articles to my office at the British Museum by post."

"She sent vast stores of treasures south when it was clear Egypt would fall to Rome," Ramses said. "I remember this."

A simple response, but it had sent him stumbling down a corridor of memories.

How he had wanted to believe her a monster, the creature he had raised. A terrible aberration raised from death by his own arrogance. But on the night of her terrible accident, in the moments before she'd fled the opera house in shame, stealing off in a motorcar she couldn't control, careening right into the path of two speeding trains, she had been far from a bumbling, voiceless ghoul. She had been full of focus and control and a desire for revenge. Moments before, she had confronted Julie in the ladies' powder room. Menaced her, threatened her life. Delighted in Julie's fear.

During her rampage through Cairo, Samir and Julie had both done their very best to convince him that she was a soulless creature. Not Cleopatra, but some terrible, monstrous shell. But when they had finally faced each other at the opera, there had been no denying it, the sight of the old spirit in her eyes.

And now? She lived still. Truly indestructible, it seemed.

But what did she want? Why had she traveled to Alexandria on the arm of this young man? Was it to say goodbye to her old city, the same reason he had traveled the length of Egypt himself only months before?

Everything about her was a mystery to him. He'd been a vital man in his prime when he drank the elixir; she'd been a corpse when he poured it over her. He'd never been subjected to fire of the kind she had apparently survived. And so he could not guess as to her state of mind now, any more than before, or her motives, to say nothing of what might lie ahead for her body, her will. And indeed she had a will, a will as fierce as his own. He had seen this for himself as she'd fought to go on living.

He rose to his feet and walked about the large suite, gesturing for Samir to remain seated. He knew that Julie was watching him.

He was remembering, gathering for himself, all he had ever learned of the elixir.

In the thousands of years since he'd first stolen it from the cackling old Hittite priestess, he had tested the elixir's strength and limitations, learned its blunt simplicity. When he was still king of Egypt, he had sought to create an immortal bounty. But the crops he grew with it couldn't be digested. They had to be uprooted and sunk to the bottom of the sea. For they had killed droves of his own people in pain as soon as they were consumed.

As the years advanced, he learned the extent to which the rays of the sun could awaken and sustain him. The extent to which he could wall himself off from the sun's life-giving power, inducing a sleep that was close to death, a sleep in which his body dried and withered. Natural light, from the sun or reflected across the night sky, sustained him. Only once he was sealed off from it altogether for a period of several days did the deep sleep return.

This was what he had done two thousand years before, when his refusal to give Cleopatra the elixir on behalf of Marc Antony had resulted in her suicide and Egypt's fall to Rome.

An agony to think of these things now, as it always would be.

To remember her pursuit of him after they'd discovered Marc Antony's corpse, dead by his own hand. The way she'd called for him, begging him to bring Marc Antony back from the dead. Insisting that he could do it with his precious, secret elixir.

He had slapped her! A terrible thing, but he had slapped her at the mere suggestion that he use the elixir in this way. And to think that two thousand years later, he'd used the elixir for just such an end, not on Marc Antony's remains, but on her remains.

Now that his actions in Cairo had resulted in a menace from which they might never be free, would her love for him turn to bitterness and anger?

Julie sensed the torment in him, and stood beside him, laying a hand gently on his shoulder.

"And so you believe Cleopatra is behind the sale and she used proceeds from it to buy the silence of anyone at the hospital who might remember her?" Julie asked.

"As well as anyone who might remember how quickly she healed," interjected Samir. "But who knows if such things are even necessary? Who would believe tales of her strange resurrection?"

"And do we have reason to believe she has killed again?" Julie asked.

"Not quite, no," Samir said. "But we know she is very much alive. That she has traveled the length of Egypt. And that she is not alone."

"There is something else we know," Ramses said.

"Yes, darling?" Julie responded.

"We know that if she does decide to kill again, there is very little we can do to stop her."

When he saw darkness overtake the expressions of his companions, he regretted the words. But they were the truth. An unavoidable truth that had to be addressed.

Once he found the courage to meet Julie's stare, he saw that it was not fear in her eyes, but sympathy and concern. For him. This astonished him.

"I will not have you lost to regret over this, Ramses."

Quietly, Samir said, "I shall leave you now. They lost sight of her in Alexandria, but it's possible they might be able to find her again. I can arrange to have them watch the ships from Port Said when they reach England, if you wish. Let me know what you would have and I shall make it so, my king."

"No, Samir," Julie said, "you mustn't go so quickly. You must be exhausted. Stay here with us. Rest. Have something to eat. Let me arrange rooms for you."

"No, but thank you," said Samir. "I am staying with an old acquaintance of mine from the British Museum. In the morning, I'll return to London and make sure your house remains secure."

"Secure?" Julie asked. "Well, of course it's secure."

"Indeed. But it will comfort me to be sure. Just as it comforted me to see you at Maxim's tonight, so beautiful and full of life."

He rose and received Julie's two hands and her loving kiss on his cheek.

"Good night, dear Julie. Good night, Mr. Ramsey." Samir offered a coy smile when using his alias. "I would say, *Sleep well*, but alas . . ." And then he was out the door.

*   *   *

Once Samir was gone, Julie turned her gaze on him. It was the first time in weeks she'd seemed so disturbed. Ramses hated the sight. Hated that their dreamlike journey across countries and continents had been brought to such an abrupt end.

Or had it? For she seemed more troubled by his mood than the knowledge that Cleopatra lived and breathed.

"Do you believe we should fear her, Ramses?"

"She threatened to snap your neck like a reed. Those were her exact words."

"Well, she can't now. And besides, she said this only moments after she failed to do it. She was alone with me then for a good length of time, if you remember, and all she made were threats."

"Yes, but you were interrupted, were you not? Do you truly believe she had a change of heart?"

"It's impossible to say for sure."

"Then I will say this," said Ramses. "It was shame that drove her from the opera house. Shame and rage at me for allowing Marc Antony to be defeated all those years ago. She was overcome. It's why she lost control and drove onto those train tracks. She had never wanted the elixir, you see. I offered it to her when she was queen, and she refused it. Only when her lover, her compatriot, was poised for defeat did she ask for it, and even then, she wanted it for him and him alone. For some mad dream of an immortal army."

"And you were right not to give it to her, Ramses. Think of how the world might have been terribly changed as a result. Sometimes death is the only thing that can free us from a despot. Should that divine hand be removed from those in power . . . Well, I fairly shudder at the thought."

"I don't know," he said. His voice had fallen to a whisper. "True, she was a queen, but she would have outlived her despotism. I was a king and I outlived mine; I withdrew from the chambers of power. I don't know. I'll never know. I know she lives now and she kills without hesitation or regret. And I am responsible for this—who she is now, in these times. And I fear she is far more dangerous now than she might ever have been in those ancient days."

Julie did not respond. He looked at her. She had taken a seat again at the table, and was gazing up at him with such sadness.

"I don't love her, my dear," he said. "This is not longing for her that you hear. This is remorse for what I did in awakening her."

He drew close and dropped to one knee in front of Julie. He saw patience in her eyes and the deepest affection.

"You are my love and my only love," he said. "Ours is a true partnership of mind, body, and spirit, of two immortals. But now her shadow falls across our path again, this creature that I have admitted to our paradise."

Julie urged him to his feet, and turned to face him as he sat across the table from her. "It's two months since her terrible accident," said Julie. "If she seeks revenge still, she is most certainly taking her time."

"One more reason why I'm coming to believe she wants no contact with us at all."

"Is there anything you want to say to me?" asked Julie. "Ramses, don't fear schoolgirl jealousy on my part for this creature. Whatever she is, I'm equal to her now in strength and in invulnerability."

"I know," he said.

"And I believe, as I did in the past, that she is not the real Cleopatra."

"Julie, who else can she be?"

"Ramses, she cannot have Cleopatra's soul in her. She simply cannot. And I believe we all possess souls. Now, where those souls go when we die, I don't know, but surely they do not rest inside our corpses in the earth or in a museum for centuries."

He reached out and caressed her face. How radiant and quick she was, how fearless, and bold.

Souls. What did any of us know of souls?

There were so many things moving through his mind, so many ancient prayers, so many chants. He saw the faces of ancient priests. He felt in one dark flash the burden of duty that had been his for so many long years as king, in which he'd participated in rituals at dawn and at dusk and at noon. He had gone down into the new tomb being prepared for him during his reign and asked that the endless inscriptions on the walls be read aloud to him.

His soul was to travel through the heavens after his earthly death. But where was it now? Inside of him, of course.

It was too much. He knew that creature was Cleopatra! Julie might speak of the impossibility of it, call it a revenant, a monster, and speak of Christian realms to which souls flew on invisible wings. But he knew that thing he had raised in the Cairo Museum was Cleopatra.

"Come," Julie said. "Let us walk. We are in one of the most beautiful cities in the world and we have no need for sleep. If we are soon to return to London, let us walk these streets without fear of pickpockets, accidents, or Cleopatra herself."

With a delighted laugh, he allowed her to pull him to his feet with a strength she had not possessed months before.

6

Julie had feared rivers once.

As a young girl she had refused to venture near any rail above the Thames, convinced she might slip and fall through and be swallowed up by the black water.

She felt no such fear now as she and Ramses walked along the Seine towards the great looming shadow of Notre Dame.

She could swim the length of this river without tiring if she chose. Together they could follow it all the way out to sea and take up residence on some isolated island where terrible storms and shorelines composed entirely of jagged cliffs would make it impossible for mortals to intrude. There they would find a seclusion that would allow them to study their every passing thought as one would jewels.

For a delirious instant, she thought perhaps she and Ramses should do just that, right now. But she knew that they had no choice but to return to London, and the sooner now the better.

It was a warm spring evening and they had shed their coats, and she her top hat, so that her hair hung loose in a tangle of curls against the back of her white dress shirt. Passersby must have thought her an elegant street musician with a penchant for men's fashions. Warmth and severe cold, as well as the intrusive social prejudices of others: these things would never trouble her again, thanks to the elixir. Also among its gifts, heightened senses which allowed her to detect whether or not there was actual substance in distant shadows and to commit large volumes of text to memory in several minutes' time. When she was blessed with these things, it was nearly impossible not to shirk off tiresome, everyday obligations.

"You are troubled?" Ramses asked, taking her hand in his.

"No, not troubled. Merely thoughtful."

"Share these thoughts with me."

There was some of the king in this command, but also the counselor. For he had played the latter role for thousands of years and reigned as pharaoh for only sixty.

"I was thinking on what might cause someone in our position to eventually prefer seclusion," she answered.

"Interesting. Without a companion, the thought seems unbearable to me. For me, seclusion meant only sleep. It was preferable only when the demands of those who had called me into service became too much to bear."

"And so you don't dream now of our taking up residence on some distant island where mortals cannot dwell?"

"Is this what you dream of, Julie?"

"I'm not quite sure. The possibility seems utterly tempting. But as one of a thousand. Or a million. All of which we have time enough now to sample."

Ramses smiled and drew her close to him as they walked. "It is such a different thing to enjoy this gift with you, Julie. Such a different thing to enjoy it with anyone. But most especially you."

"It must be. You refer to it now as a gift. Before it was a curse and you, Ramses the Damned. But I can't imagine you referring to yourself in this way now. This pleases me, Ramses. It pleases me greatly."

"Yes, I see now that it was not immortality that was a curse, but the role I gave to myself. That of counselor. I regret it not for a moment. But it became unbearable. And I can no longer blame my past torment solely on Cleopatra's fall."

"Or Egypt's fall," Julie whispered.

"Yes. There was a hunger in me for a new life. But I couldn't envision it. So I gave myself over to the sands of time itself. Your father's discovery of me, my awakening. These are pieces of a grand destiny, and you, Julie, the most wonderful part of it."

Impossible not to fold into his arms at this, to delight in the feel of his hot breath against the back of her neck as he embraced her. The hour was late, but before the elixir, such a public display of affection would have seemed beyond the pale. Even in Paris.

"We need not return to London, Julie. Not if it isn't what you wish."

"Oh, but it is. It isn't simply for Alex, Ramses. I want this party, this betrothal, for myself and for you. I need it. I can't quite sever all ties. And I need to walk into the offices of Stratford Shipping and make certain all is well for myself. And besides . . . what if this creature can find Alex? What if she has enough knowledge to track him to London?"

"She can easily find him and find us," said Ramses. "Such are the times. Newspapers, telegraphs, photographs."

Julie was beginning to realize they might have to remain in England simply to protect Alex Savarell. But she didn't want to commit to this as yet. Only time would reveal whether the revenant Cleopatra was interested in any of them. And then there was Elliott. Elliott was now quite capable of defending his son from any assault by the monster. How she hated to disturb Elliott now, to distract him from the things Elliott felt he had to do.

She steered Ramses to a bench along the river, a comfortable iron bench on which they could sit and watch those strolling past.

"Should we cable Elliott?" she asked. "Let him know about Cleopatra?"

"Not yet," said Ramses. "We'll leave for London tomorrow if you wish. I would rather Elliott completed his plans. His family is depending on him. I love these people because you love them; and I am bound to them because you're bound to them. If it does turn out that Cleopatra comes to London to search for young Savarell, well, then we can send for Elliott."

This moved her deeply. She wasn't sure it was wise to say so. What a complex and loving being Ramses was. And Julie realized it would have broken her heart had he not loved Elliott.

Elliott Savarell had been her father's closest friend. She even suspected the two men of having been lovers in their youth. In fact she was sure of it.

She remembered a strange summer afternoon when she was a girl. She'd been with her father visiting Elliott's country estate, and she'd gone off roaming with Alex only to drift back early and alone, a bit bored, and tired, and come upon her father and Elliott alone in the library.

She had caught them unawares only for a moment.

But it was a strange moment. They'd been before the window with their backs to the door. Elliott had had his arm around Lawrence, and he'd been talking to him in an intimate whisper.

It was something about the way the two men stood so very close, about the manner in which her father leaned close to Elliott, the way their lips almost touched, that had startled her and impressed her.

She must have made some small sound then. The men had broken off to greet her. But she'd glimpsed the shimmer of tears in her father's eyes, tears that seemed to vanish instantly.

Nothing was ever said of that moment. But on the long drive back to London, her father had held Julie tight beside him in the old carriage, hugging her with what seemed a sadness and a desperation.

"What in the world are you thinking, Father?" Julie had asked as he looked out over the passing fields.

"Nothing, my dear," Lawrence had said, "except how much all of us give up in this life, sooner or later, because we can never have all that we want. You'll find out soon enough. We're blessed, my dear. Quite blessed, but no life is without sacrifices."

Couple with that so many random impressions of Elliott over the years, bored and tired, on the periphery of parties and balls.

Well, now Elliott had the world. Elliott need never sacrifice again what he might have sacrificed years ago to marry an American heiress who had paid his debts and given him a handsome son to carry on the family name.

It did not surprise her in retrospect that Elliott had suspected Ramses of being a creature beyond normal comprehension from the moment they'd first met. It was Elliott who had followed him to the Cairo Museum on the night when Ramses awakened Cleopatra. And it was Elliott who had cared for the resurrected revenant queen Ramses had awakened after Ramses fled from her in terror.

Perhaps as penance for this, after their great journey had come to an end, Ramses had given Elliott a bottle of the elixir to do with as he pleased. And it had not surprised Julie that Elliott had drunk the elixir.

And perhaps Elliott might never come back to London, if he could avoid it, until his son and his wife were both gone from the earth. Surely he would never allow the secret of his immortality to bruise or hurt either of them. He would send home his rich winnings from the gambling tables, of course, and he would seek out that gold mine as Ramses had instructed him to do, and he would be the distant mysterious grandfather of loving children in the future who would never see the eternally youthful man face-to-face.

Now it was Julie's task to deceive both Edith and Alex as to her own transformation. And whatever her plans for the future, Julie would use the betrothal party to express her great affection for Edith and Alex, keeping inside the pain of the gulf that now forever divided them.

Out of all the people who had joined them on their Egyptian adventure, Alex remained the only one who still thought Mr. Reginald Ramsey a mysterious Egyptologist who had simply fallen into their group, who still thought the mysterious woman with whom he'd shared a night of passion in Cairo was just an old friend of Ramsey's gone mad.

And it was Julie's conviction that Alex must never learn the truth. The shock of the truth about her, about Ramses, about Cleopatra, about his own father—it would destroy Alex utterly.

No, her every thought must be for the recovery of Alex from what he had already endured.

After Cleopatra had gone to her supposed death, Alex had retreated into himself. On the ship home to London, he had confessed to loving this woman he did not truly know, but he had also vowed to forget her. He would return to the motions of living, he had insisted. They all would.

And she'd thought it a ghastly phrase then. *The motions of living.*

She thought it a ghastly phrase now. Surely Alex was recovering. Surely his wanting to give this betrothal party was evidence of his recovery. Surely the flow of money coming from the earl had underwritten a new confidence in Alex, a new willingness to look about him at the many eligible heiresses who would value his breeding, his title, his subtle charm.

Ramses took her hand. Somewhere a church bell chimed. It was late, and the walkway along the Seine was deserted.

"You think now of Alex or his father?" Ramses asked.

"Alex. I must confess something to you because the confession of it will free me from the need to do it."

"Of course."

"There is a part of me that wishes to tell Alex everything." Was that true? Her own words had shocked her. But yes, it was true. It was the deeper truth beyond pity, beyond sympathy.

"This is a confusion of guilt. Revealing this truth will not change the fact that you never loved him. And you should feel no guilt for this. This marriage was almost forced on you for financial reasons alone. None of its architects cared what might be in your heart."

"Of course. Of course. But . . ."

"I am telling you how you feel. Forgive me. I was a counselor far longer than I was a king. The role returns to me with too much speed."

"I wish to change him, Ramses. I never loved him. But I care for him deeply and I wish to see him changed so that . . ."

"So that what, Julie?"

"So that he would be able to drink of the world as we do. So that he would see its colors and its magic. So that he would be willing to risk injury, to his body and his heart, if it be in the pursuit of deepening his experience of being alive.

"This is my great worry, you see? In fact, it seems my only worry now. That I will wish to share the change that has overtaken me with everyone for whom I care deeply."

"Share the elixir, you mean?"

"Of course, it's not mine to share. But you know what I mean. You must have felt similar things throughout your existence."

"I have, but know this. The experience you are having is yours alone. The elixir did not really change you. Oh, it's made you stronger, more resolute. Of course. I enjoy this very much, these changes. But it has not changed your heart. It has unleashed what was already there. It has set your loving nature free. It will not do these things in everyone to whom it's given. But I know it's tempting, this belief."

"But if the fear of death is removed, does the person not . . ."

"Not what? Become good? I brought Cleopatra out of death itself and removed her fear of it. And did she not bring death to innocents in Cairo?"

"That's different, Ramses. She is a different creature. One for whom we do not even have a name."

"The elixir cannot cure a broken soul. Trust me in this. Your experience of it, it belongs solely to you."

"And you belong solely to me," she whispered. "And you are

part of this experience I don't wish to share with anyone. Not in that way."

A kiss, deep and fearless and without regard for passersby. Then he pulled back from her and took her hand. "Come," he said. "To the cathedral."

"No, darling," she said. "Not on this our last night. I want to seek the dark corners of Paris again, the dark narrow lanes, the taverns and cabarets where I would never have dared to set foot in the past." She laughed. "I want to see all the dangerous places. I want to see the thieves eye us as prey and then instinctively, inevitably, as they always do, turn away from us—as if we were angels."

He smiled. He understood, as much as any man could understand, she thought. Any man, who had never known what it means to be a woman.

And off they walked together, away from the river, and towards parts of Paris unknown to them, two adventurers of which the mortal world knew nothing.

7

Monte Carlo

The Englishman made love like a Frenchman, and for this Michel Malveaux was blissfully grateful.

The waiters and croupiers in the casino had referred to the man as the Earl of Rutherford, and that was how Michel preferred to think of him now. The title was an elegant reminder of how different he was from Michel's other clients.

He'd taken Michel to bed with the same vigor with which he had played the casino's tables for several days now. The vigor of a man half his age. The vigor of a man half Michel's age, for that matter. There was no sense of hurried shame in his movements. Neither was there hesitancy or nervousness. Indeed, the handsome, blue-eyed aristocrat stroked and probed and tasted Michel's body with the same abandon as the young men Michel had experimented with in the vineyards behind his family's farm when he was a boy.

No, nothing at all like his other clients, those men and women who invited him back to their hotel rooms with furtive, coded signals. Who bid him a hasty farewell once the deed was done, but not before giving him the requisite gift. Money, jewels, or the promise of a fine meal, all intended to buy both his discretion and perhaps his return the next night under similar circumstances.

Even the room was different.

Michel had been inside most at the Hotel de Paris, but not this particular suite, with its wallpaper the color of a cloudless sky, its soaring windows so easily opened onto the sea, and its small balcony. And how fearless of the earl to leave the windows open, to allow the ocean air to kiss their naked bodies as they engaged in a passion most would find unspeakable.

But it was this very fearlessness that had first drawn Michel to the man several days before. The earl was one of the best gamblers he had ever seen. Possessed of an almost otherworldly ability to read the deck, the wheel, and the croupier's expressions. And at the very moment each day when it seemed he might draw the suspicion of the house, he would graciously push back from the table. Then he would generously tip the waiters, who had kept him well fed with a steady supply of the small nibbles that seemed to sustain him.

What were his tricks? Michel was desperate to know. For this was why he'd come to Monte Carlo years before: to learn the secrets of the best gamblers, to master luck itself, so that he could support his ailing, widowed mother.

His poor mother.

She believed he had achieved this goal. It would have broken her heart to know the money he mailed home came from servicing the private, sensual needs of the wealthy. He'd recently sent her an emerald ring encrusted with diamonds, and she'd written just the other day to tell him she wore it proudly and with great joy whenever her sisters came to visit. If she knew it had been gifted to him by a German general and his wife after he'd brought them both to simultaneous moments of release, she would be shattered, he was sure.

But he'd been a younger and more foolish man when he'd left home. And after only a few months of living in a crowded apartment with several croupiers, he'd been forced into realization. He was already an excellent lover, but it would take him some time to become a better gambler. No choice but to put his first gift to use while he sought to acquire the second.

But now there was so much more he wanted to know about this man, beyond his tricks at the tables. So very much more.

And when the earl brought him to climax, the cries that escaped from Michel sounded both pleading and ecstatic, and the Earl of Rutherford seemed to delight in them, for he increased his thrusts until the two of them lay in a heap in the tangled sheets.

Drowsiness overtook him.

His companion, on the other hand, didn't seem remotely tired. He stroked Michel's sweat-matted hair from his forehead.

"The Earl of Rutherford has many secrets and skills," Michel finally whispered.

"Perhaps after another moment like that, I can convince you to call me Elliott."

"You are a man of great mystery and skill, Elliott."

"Do you speak of my skills at the blackjack table or . . . ?" With one finger, the man drew a slow circle across Michel's stomach.

"Both."

"I see. And so the whispered rumors of you are true, young Michel Malveaux."

"What rumors?"

"That you're skilled in the art of seduction. That it's made you a handsome living. Perhaps this is why I was so eager to show you the extent of my skills as well."

"Are we dueling courtesans then?"

Elliott laughed. "No, hardly."

"I'm sure. You have a title."

"And what exactly does this fact allow you to presume about me?"

"Nothing," Michel whispered. "I can presume nothing about you, for you have already defied my every expectation. You have none of the reserve of an English aristocrat and none of the pretense. At least when compared to the ones I've met."

"How many have you *met,* dear boy?" he asked with an impish smile.

"Be kind, Elliott. We have not all descended from great wealth. We do what we must to survive."

"To you I wish to be nothing but kind," he said, and gave him a gentle kiss, "repeatedly and with great enthusiasm."

"And so the rumors about me don't disturb you?"

"Not at all. My life is in a period of great transition. As a result, I have been freed from old restrictions and labels."

"Is your title one of these labels from which you are now free?"

"If it is my title that permits me to access beauty such as yours, young Michel, I wish to never be free of it."

"This fearlessness, Elliott. It defines you. Where does it come from? Do your skills at the tables give you this confidence?"

"You wish to learn my tricks, is that it? You think I've been counting cards?"

"I wish to learn many things about you, Elliott."

Ah, and there it was, a little crack in the man's façade, a suddenly distant look in his crystalline-blue eyes. Had he said too much? Was there too much longing in these words? Almost sympathetic now, the way Elliott grazed the side of his face with his bent fingers.

"You might say I am on a grand adventure. But I am also working to repay some debts. Now I'm privileged enough to combine the two endeavors."

"Repaying debts. With your winnings?"

"Yes."

"And soon you will move on?" he asked, hoping he had poured ice into his voice this time.

"Yes."

"To Baden-Baden, or the next casino, where you will employ your *skills* until you draw the suspicions of the house."

"You are a clever boy, Michel. It is clear you have seen much of the world."

"I have not. I have seen much of Monte Carlo. And much of the world now comes to Monte Carlo."

"Much of the world that has money comes to Monte Carlo. But there is much of the world that does not have money. And there is much of the world that remains shrouded in great mystery."

"How much of this mysterious world have you seen, Elliott?"

It appeared as if Elliott had suddenly been captured by memories so vivid they took his mind far from this beautiful hotel suite with its commanding view of the sea. Now Michel felt as if he were merely a screen Elliott was gazing through, and this wounded him more deeply than he wanted it to. It was a cruel reminder that they would soon part. That soon the Earl of Rutherford would become just another traveler whose generosity and attentions he had known for only a moment.

"My dear Michel," Elliott finally whispered. He had clearly forgotten himself and the words that came from him now were unbidden. "I have of late seen things in this world that defy all explanation. Things which have led me to question everything I once believed about life and death. All thanks to a king."

A king? But he said nothing. To do so would be to shatter the man's sudden, hypnotic candor. But Elliott remembered himself almost instantly. A fearful expression passed over his face. He sought to conceal it with a sudden, warm smile, but he was a second too late.

"Wash, and then we shall sit on the balcony and enjoy the view."

The temperature seemed to drop several degrees the second Elliott's weight left the mattress. It had felt like a dismissal, but at least the Earl of Rutherford had not asked him to leave. Michel was not being hurried from the room. Not yet, anyway. And so he washed, just as the man instructed.

When he emerged into the bedroom, Elliott was seated on the balcony outside. The smoke from his cigarette rose in a serpentine curl next to his head.

There was a letter on the dresser next to Michel's wallet, and even though he had no need of his wallet in this moment, for some reason, their proximity seemed like an excuse to steal a peek at the few pages of handwritten cursive.

Knowing that this blissful evening would soon be at an end, that these words were perhaps the only real glimpse he'd get inside the man responsible, Michel scanned the letter with what felt like desperate hunger.

The author was the man's son, an Alex Savarell.

He was grateful Elliott had finally cabled to give the date of his arrival in Monte Carlo. The sums of money Elliott had wired home for his family were much appreciated. As a result, their estate in Yorkshire had been reopened and they had added staff to it once again. It was there that they would host a betrothal party for a woman named Julie Stratford and her new fiancé, a Mr. Reginald Ramsey.

On additional pages, he spotted repeated pleas for Elliott to return home. But there were no mentions of what exactly connected this Julie Stratford and Reginald Ramsey to the Earl of Rutherford and his son. References to a "grand, calamitous adventure through Egypt" but no other details, aside from the implication that Elliott was traveling, in part, to escape the implications of this "adventure."

A scrape of metal outside startled him.

He dropped the letter, stepped back from the dresser.

Elliott had simply braced one foot against the balcony rail so he could tip his chair back onto its hind legs.

His spying had gone unnoticed. Or had it? The man seemed to have a supernatural ability to read the gambling tables. Could he now detect Michel's furtive actions a few feet away?

He made a noisy show of sliding into his trousers.

When he stepped out onto the balcony, Elliott greeted him with a smile and gestured to the empty chair next to his.

The harbor below sparkled.

There were so many questions he wanted to ask the earl, Elliott of the beautiful blue eyes, so much he wanted to know, but he feared the effort would be the same as reaching too quickly for a falling balloon; a simple touch would send it floating away with sudden speed.

Things which have led me to question everything I once believed about life and death. All thanks to a king.

What could these words possibly mean?

And why was Elliott smiling at him now?

He knows, Michel thought, *he knows I read the letter. He could sense it the same way he could sense what cards the croupier might deal next.*

"You are young," Elliott finally said.

"Why remind me of this?" Michel asked.

"Because you wish to go with me when I leave. And so it is my duty to tell you that this would be a wretched idea. Splendid for me, perhaps, but terrible for you."

"And why is that?"

"Because you are young, my dear boy."

"And you have the confidence of someone as young as I."

"Why do you say that?"

"Because you assume I would leave here with you at a moment's notice." He managed a wry smile which Elliott returned.

"Tell me I'm wrong," the earl whispered.

He could not. Indeed, he could barely manage to meet the man's curious gaze, and he could feel himself blushing and pouting despite himself. "Your tricks at the tables. Perhaps that is all I'm after."

Elliott laughed warmly, unoffended. "Luck, my dear boy. That's all. Simple luck. The same luck that brought me such a lovely evening with the likes of you."

"You flatter me."

"No. I speak with greater directness than you are used to."

Yes, Michel thought. *Because you are fearless, and it is the source of your fearlessness I wish to know. To savor.*

"A wife is meeting you at your next port of call," Michel said.

"Not at all," Elliott said.

"She is. A wife and a family of small mewling children and it would be impossible to explain me as your new valet because I am so handsome and *young*. And French!"

"Ah! I knew it! You do wish to join me," Elliott responded.

"Your luck makes my tongue loosen, I fear."

"My wife and I have an understanding and separate lives, each lived with an appropriate degree of expectation of the other, and our only child is grown. And neither one is the reason I will have to bid you goodbye at the end of this night. But enough about me. What about you, Michel? Is there a special woman in your life?"

"I have made many friends in Monte Carlo."

"I see. But you prefer the company of men, don't you? I could feel it."

"Was it a feeling you enjoyed?"

"Very much so. But I can dance by the light of either the sun or the moon. If that's not the case with you, dear boy, you should feel no shame over it. But neither should you become smitten with the first man who doesn't make love to you as if it's a quick and shameful thing that must be dispatched promptly so as to avoid discovery."

"You believe you are this man to me?" There was a tremor in Michel's voice, and the presence of it turned his question into a statement, a confession. *Yes. You have been this man to me, Earl of Rutherford.*

"Do not allow me to be, dear Michel. This is what I ask of you. Take your memories of me and of this night, and allow them to inspire you."

"Inspire me in what way?"

"Inspire you to shun all those who would treat you as if you were something shameful."

Mustn't cry at these words. Must remain calm, poised. Professional, if such a concept could even apply to this night. After all, Elliott had not yet offered a gift, and Michel could not bring himself to ask for one. Indeed, this unhurried exchange, here on this balcony with its beautiful view, was gift enough.

"You are a complete mystery, Elliott, a mystery who says strange things about life and death and kings."

Elliott laughed and rose to his feet. When he cupped Michel's face in his hands, Michel could not help but gaze up into the man's dazzlingly blue eyes.

"Think of me as a mystery, then," Elliott whispered.

"A mystery soon to depart."

"The night is not over yet, and in your presence, dear Michel, I feel miraculously restored."

Astonishing. Could he really go again?

When Elliott threw him on the bed, Michel had his answer.

He thought suddenly of the statues of bare-breasted women that were part of the hotel's façade. They were only a few stories below them now, those statues, their arms spread like wings. For the first time inside this grand hotel, Michel felt as if he were literally supported by those bare-breasted stone women and their brazen and sensual courage.

* * *

It was not the first time he had walked home with the sunrise, smelling of another's skin. But it was the first time he had done so with a heart this heavy.

So he wasn't surprised it took him so long to notice the footfalls behind him.

It was their speed that finally drew his attention.

By the time he looked up, the woman was walking directly beside him. She looked neither drunken nor disheveled. A jeweled clip held her golden hair in a precise bun atop her head, but her corset seemed loose beneath her blouse; her gored skirt made it appear as if she was ready to spend the morning dipping in and out of shops. But the shops wouldn't be open for hours. Indeed, only the faintest blush of dawn kissed the harbor's waters.

There was something off about her shoes. They were hard, durable, designed for something other than a leisurely stroll.

"I trust you had a pleasant evening with the Earl of Rutherford." She had a perfect British accent. It was the night for them, apparently.

"And who are you, mademoiselle?" he asked.

"Someone who notices things as well as you do, Michel Malveaux."

On another night, he would have sought to charm her, to seduce her. To channel her curiosity into a sensual experience she would then wish to keep secret. This would in turn keep anything she might have witnessed between him and the earl a secret as well. This was how secrets worked. But his departure from Elliott's room had left him shaken and raw. To say nothing of the fact that he was utterly exhausted by the man's insatiable desires.

"If you will excuse me, it is quite late, and I have no desire to discuss my evening at this time."

In an instant, she had seized one of his wrists. Her grip was powerful, astonishingly so. And the eyes he suddenly found himself staring into were as blue as the Earl of Rutherford's.

"Whether or not it's early or late is a matter of some debate, wouldn't you say?" she asked. "And depends largely on how one has spent the hours preceding this one."

It was not the first time he had been threatened. Customers had pulled knives on him, menaced him with empty liquor bottles. But always he had managed to find a way to charm them. This woman, on the other hand, possessed a focus and a malice that was neither drunken nor desperate nor lecherous. And so Michel saw only one choice: to lie.

"Regardless of the hour, my evening was my own. I do not know who this Earl of Rutherford is and I wish you to release my hand at once."

She did nothing of the kind. "And yet, when I first said his name, you expressed no confusion. You only asked me what mine was."

"And you have still not told me. Please let me go."

He yanked his wrist free from her grip. She released it with a smile and a pronounced withdrawal of her own hand. Both gestures suggested she could have easily maintained her grip no matter how much he struggled.

"I am merely passing through," she answered, and he saw it was no answer at all. "But you are local, and you have a reputation to protect." She practically sneered when she said the word *reputation.*

"There is a code here, mademoiselle, but apparently you are unaware of it."

"Is there, now?"

"Yes. Those who are passing through have no power to besmirch the reputations of those who remain. That simply isn't how it works in Monte Carlo."

It was utter nonsense, this claim. A shrill complaint from a wealthy visitor to one of the hotels could get him banned for life. The prince himself might escort him to the border should his behavior in any manner threaten the flow of tourists to this little paradise by the sea. But the woman before him seemed impressed by his confidence, if nothing else. Perhaps a bit of the earl's fearlessness had rubbed off on him.

"Get some rest, Michel," the woman said. "I'm sure we shall meet again."

"I hope so. Perhaps under more pleasant circumstances, which might allow the two of us to see each other in a different light."

He lifted her hand and gave it a gentle kiss.

He should have tried this ploy sooner. Now it was probably too late for seduction. Now he had earned her ire, whoever she was. Whatever her motives.

She smiled, nodded, and then retreated with footsteps as swift as the ones that had brought her to him.

Where had she come from? The hotel? One of the boats in the harbor? And what had she been after? Information about the Earl of Rutherford or information about him?

Should he send word to Elliott that a strange woman had seen them together, had suspected something?

This last thought tormented him by the time he reached his tiny apartment.

Sending word to Elliott, making any attempt to communicate with him again, would be to break a confidence he maintained with all his clients, for there was only one way to do it, and that was through the front desk of the hotel.

Had the woman been an angry wife of some previous client?

Could she be Elliott's wife?

They were insane, these thoughts. They set upon him like a flock of seagulls and he the only man for miles with bread in his hand.

It has nothing to do with the Earl of Rutherford, he finally told himself, and these words, along with the ones that followed, became a mantra that ushered in sleep. *The Earl of Rutherford is fearless. The Earl of Rutherford does not have a care in the world and never will.*

He woke only a few hours later, feeling mildly rested but still unbearably anxious.

Before he could think twice on the matter, he phoned the front desk at the Hotel de Paris and asked to be put through to Elliott's room. When they told him the man had checked out hours before, Michel felt both piercing longing and a terrible relief.

He was grateful Elliott had departed so soon after they'd said goodbye, for that meant he probably had been spared a run-in with the strange night-wandering madwoman with the powerful grip.

He would miss Elliott terribly.

He would hope secretly for his return.

He would cherish every memory he could of their time

together, would use those moments to satisfy himself. Too dangerous to write them down and risk discovery, but oh, how he wanted to. His memory would have to do.

But as he ended his call with the hotel, he figured that would be the end of the whole brief affair.

Three days later there was a knock on the door to his apartment. He was almost dressed for the evening, almost ready to strike out for the casino in search of clients new and old. He was still fastening one of his cuff links when he opened the door and saw an envelope resting on the front step.

His cuff link forgotten, he tore open the envelope, removed a sheet of paper featuring a hand-drawn map of the harbor. An arrow pointed to a single boat slip.

Attached to this piece of paper with a tiny pin was the diamond-encrusted emerald ring he'd shipped to his mother weeks before.

8

He raced out of his apartment in trousers, dress shirt, and bow tie. To the tourists he passed along the way, he must have looked like a waiter terribly late for his shift.

But he didn't care what anyone thought. His only thoughts were of his mother. His poor, frail mother, only a day's travel away by train. His mother who had cherished the ring he now held in his pocket so much she'd worn it whenever someone had come to visit.

Someone had taken this ring from her.

Or they had brought her here to Monte Carlo with it.

Both possibilities terrified him.

Night had fallen by the time he reached the harbor. The boat slip in question was filled by a vessel almost as grand as the royal yacht of Monaco itself. It looked like a miniature ocean liner with its own lone smokestack and a long white hull lined with portholes.

The woman with the powerful grip was waiting for him on the deck. She had traded her morning dress for a dark and frilly tea gown. And this terrified him for some reason, that she would consider the terrible gift that had been left on his front step to be an occasion worthy of fancy dress. Now he saw the reason for her hard-soled shoes, and an explanation for why she had seemed to appear out of the harbor itself.

This boat, it was her home.

"Where is she?" Michel cried before he could stop himself.

"Calm yourself and you may come aboard," the woman said. Maddening, her superiority. He would have snapped her neck and thrown her into the ocean if he could. "We don't want to alarm her any further."

So she was here. This woman had somehow managed to bring his mother here. As a captive, surely, which meant she wasn't working alone.

The woman extended her hand.

She wasn't simply offering to help him on board. She was reminding him of the strength she'd shown him when they'd first met. Of course, he had no choice but to accept the offer of help, even though the touch of her skin sickened him.

Inside, the yacht was decorated as elegantly as the rooms at the Hotel de Paris. Brass fittings, sparse antiques, and pastel upholsteries, all of it bolted down in ways visible and invisible to keep it from being tossed about at sea.

Behind the wheelhouse, a long central cabin led to a more sunken room, behind which Michel saw a narrow passage leading to private cabins along a short hallway lined in dark hardwood.

In the center of this sunken room a woman of exactly his mother's size was bound to a chair. There was a sack over her head. She was flanked by two well-dressed men. One of the men was enormous. And while his long red beard was trimmed and fairly under control, it still gave him the appearance of a great Viking stuffed into what the British called evening dress. The other man looked positively spry by comparison. But they both regarded Michel with the same flat stare as the woman who'd brought him to this place.

Ghastly that they wore tuxedos and bow ties while executing a kidnapping. Ghastly and terrifying, for it suggested they were capable of committing such crimes without so much as snagging a seam.

"Good evening, Monsieur Malveaux," the smaller of the two men said.

"Let me see her." It felt as if someone had said these words through him.

The man removed the sack.

They had gagged his mother with a great loop of fabric tied around her head. Her gaunt and deeply lined face bore the fatigued expression she wore whenever she'd been exhausted by a crying fit. But when she saw him, her eyes widened and she made a desperate sound against the gag. In response, the giant man rested one massive paw gently atop her head. He stroked her hair. Did he have his female companion's strength?

Michel rushed to her, fell to his knees before her. They allowed him this display. And this terrified him further. They seemed so unafraid of anything he might do.

He placed his hands over hers. She cocked her head to one side, trying to convey some message through her eyes alone. He muttered apologies and assurances, even though he didn't know what events had brought them to this terrible juncture.

"Now," the woman finally said, "do you find yourself somewhat more inclined to discuss the evening you shared with the Earl of Rutherford?"

"Yes." Michel shot to his feet. The woman stood right next to him now. When he turned in her direction, their noses almost touched. "Everything. I will tell you everything if you promise to let her go. Keep me here for whatever purpose you intend for as long as you like, but, please, let her go!"

"Excellent," the smaller man answered. "Let us hear your account, then."

Insane, the casual tone of this man's voice, as if they had brought Michel here only to give them tips on the best dining establishments in Monte Carlo.

"My mother need not hear this. She knows nothing of this man."

"Or your life here, I take it," the woman said.

The smaller man said to his compatriot, "Take her in the back. Get her some water. If our new friend proves forthcoming, get her some food. I imagine she's quite hungry after our trip."

The giant picked up the chair holding Michel's mother in both arms. He leisurely carried her and it down the hallway and into one of the private cabins.

How could he have made this request? Once his mother passed out of sight, fresh panic seized him. How could he have sent her away like that?

These people, they manipulated so much in him. His love, his shame, his need for secrecy. Who were these wretched monsters?

His mother was just a short distance away, but under present circumstances, it felt like miles of mountainous terrain. And so in a breathless rush, he told the story of his night with the Earl of Rutherford.

Never before had he discussed his life, his profession, in so much unguarded detail. But no judgments radiated from these people, just a cold calculation disguised as attentiveness.

Whoever they were, his sexual secrets did not seem to concern them. The details of the Earl of Rutherford, however: those held these monstrous people in thrall. And when he repeated the strange words Elliott had shared with him about life and death and kings, the man and woman before him both took a step forward, wide-eyed fascination in their expressions.

All thanks to a king. They made him repeat this phrase several times.

And, oh, how it pained him to include the details of the letter written by Elliott's son. The betrothal party at their estate in Yorkshire. The names Julie Stratford and Reginald Ramsey. But he was also a son, and his mother, his poor, sweet mother's life hung in the balance.

"Say this name again," the woman interrupted him.

"Which one?"

"Ramsey, you say? A Mr. Reginald Ramsey?"

Michel nodded fiercely, and for the first time, the man and woman who held him captive looked away from him and stared piercingly at each other.

"*All thanks to a king,*" the woman whispered.

*   *   *

His mother's legs gave out by the time they reached the hill that led to his apartment.

Michel was still stunned they had been freed so quickly. Impossible not to keep looking over his shoulder as he and his mother had hurried from the harbor.

When they'd first left the boat, he'd pleaded with his mother to contain herself and stay quiet. The worst thing they could do now was to alert others as to what those terrible people had done.

But she'd been desperate to rush into the whole terrifying tale, to tell him how they'd simply entered her tiny house and taken her as if she weighed nothing, was nothing. Mattered for nothing. Soon after he'd convinced her to stay silent, exhaustion overtook her.

Now he was forced to carry her up the hill in both arms, like a groom hoisting his bride over the threshold.

She was delirious by the time he got her inside his apartment. But she managed to say dazed things about what a beautiful apartment it was, even though it was no more than a single room. About how proud she was of him. How very, very proud. How she had always been so proud. And he could sense that she knew the story he'd had to tell her captors was one of which he thought she would be ashamed, and she was now trying to rid him of his fear and guilt, and this brought tears to his eyes.

He set her down on his bed, filled a glass with water, and encouraged her to drink. As she did so, he felt the hard lump of the emerald ring in his pants pocket. He withdrew it and gently took her right hand in his. At first she seemed confused by this, then she saw him sliding the ring onto her finger, and a smile broke across her face and tears filled her eyes.

"My boy," she whispered. "My darling boy, you have saved me. You saved me again as you always do."

He embraced her quickly so that she would not see his tears, so that she would think him as strong as she needed for him to be, now and always.

After a while, drowsiness overtook her, and by the time he settled her on the bed, she was breathing deeply and evenly.

He felt suddenly alone, and once more afraid. He was sure this terrible affair was not over. That soon there would be another knock on the door and another awful gift. But when he got to his feet, he saw his partial view of the harbor across the tumble of neighboring rooftops.

He saw the ship on which his mother had been held captive sailing out onto the vast, dark sea.

Elliott, dearest Earl of Rutherford. May you be a mystery strong enough to hold back the dark force I had no choice but to unleash upon you.

9

The Mediterranean Sea

They sailed through the night.

Their destination was a craggy pile of rocks, several hours from the coast of Greece.

Few would dare call it an island. Fewer still even knew of its existence.

But deep inside its central cavern, their maker slept, walled off from the sun.

Throughout their journey, they argued over the implications of what they had been told.

When their brothers and sisters in London had cabled them weeks before about a mysterious Egyptologist in London—a man who had appeared out of nowhere, it seemed, only to suddenly stand at the center of a great scandal surrounding a recently unearthed sarcophagus from Egypt—they had accused their dear siblings of nurturing desperate, childish fantasies.

A particular shade of blue eyes and an uncertain past were not enough to brand someone an immortal. The pure elixir could not be found in time. Inventing phantom immortals who might possibly lead them to it, this would be an intolerable way to spend their final days, they'd insisted.

Undeterred, their siblings had sent news clippings to their next port of call, clippings they had now spread across the dining table in the yacht's central cabin. MUMMY'S CURSE KILLS STRATFORD SHIPPING MAGNATE, "RAMSES THE DAMNED" STRIKES DOWN THOSE WHO DISTURB HIS REST, and then HEIRESS DEFIES MUMMY'S CURSE, "RAMSES THE DAMNED" TO VISIT LONDON.

But when they had first read these articles, they had remained unconvinced.

Their master had granted them two centuries of life. No more. And he had never hidden this fact from them. He had even nicknamed them accordingly, his fracti, the *final* fracti. For when they perished, there would be no one left who knew of his island tomb. No one left to expose his withered form to the sun. And so their death would ensure a kind of death for him.

This had been the plan for two centuries. And they should continue to honor the pact they had all made; they should resign themselves to their fate. Within months, their bodies would begin to crumble and disintegrate, a process that would take only a few days. If only their brothers and sisters hadn't remained in London, if only they had also taken to the seas to enjoy as much of the world as they could before they decayed, they would not have fallen prey to such hopeful fantasies.

With such assurance they had said these things, by letter, by cable, and even by telephone, when the cables about this Reginald Ramsey and his strange connection to Ramses the Damned did not stop.

And of course, they had balked, their brothers and sisters, insisted that they were going to place the house in Mayfair where this Egyptian allegedly resided under constant surveillance. So be it, they had said to them.

Spend your final days in vain hope if you wish.

And then, they too had spotted a man they believed to be an immortal, an immortal they didn't recognize. An aristocrat, a skilled gambler. The Earl of Rutherford. So skilled, he seemed to possess senses heightened by the elixir. The purest version of it, or the corrupted form that had granted them two centuries of additional life? This they did not know, and now, in the wake of the young prostitute's account, they were desperate to find out.

But had they too now fallen prey to the same trap? They spent the hours at sea debating this and had come no closer to an answer by the time they reached their destination.

As they approached the island where their maker slept, they moved out onto the deck so they could watch the pile of rocks appear out of the dawn.

A special bond knitted them together, and always had. They had often lived separately from the other fracti. They were not surprised when their siblings declined to join them on their journey around the world by sea. The three of them, Jeneva, Callum, and the giant Matthias, had all been made on the same night over two hundred years before, plucked from their deathbeds in the same London slum. Provided with wealth and a new life by their maker.

And so if he was to be awakened, it should be the three of them to do it. And yet . . .

"His command was clear," Jeneva said. "We were to wake him only if the pure elixir was found. Not for the mere hope of it."

"Perhaps after two centuries of sleep, he will thirst for life," Callum offered.

"You believe he wishes to be awakened just in time to watch us perish?" Matthias said. Even when quiet, his voice seemed like a rumble from the depths of his giant body. But he did not speak of his eventual death as a mortal would, for he had lived two centuries and more.

"We wake him because there is a chance we will not," Callum said. "Not now, not ever."

"A slim chance," Jeneva said. "A ghost of a chance, really."

"Nevertheless," Callum said, "it is enough."

Matthias was apparently convinced as well. He went to help as their skiff was lowered into the water.

The island had no beaches and nothing resembling a dock, so they would be forced to row to its rock-strewn coast.

They maintained the smallest crew they could, a captain and a single deckhand, both paid small fortunes to turn a blind eye to all of their peculiarities. These men had assisted with the kidnapping of Michel Malveaux's mother as if it were one of the transfers aboard of prepared foods they made in every port.

It was a short and quiet journey to the tomb.

The oars dipped gently into the still waters. Their boots made scraping sounds here and there as they walked with balance and precision over the giant rocks.

Matthias, their patient giant, climbed to the top of the island by himself, removed the three boulders that had sealed light from the cavern below. Then he returned to the closest thing the island had to a shore, and the three of them rolled back the great stones blocking the tomb's side passage.

By the time they entered the central cavern, sunlight was pouring down onto their father's remains.

The regeneration had begun.

Strands of their master's great, leonine mane sprouted from a head that had been withered flesh only moments before. There was a fullness now to the face that rendered it something between pure skeleton and animate man.

The tomb in which he'd slept, however, was as empty as when they'd left him here a century before. It was perched above the highest tide, so only the faintest dappling of seaweed was visible along the bottoms of the rock walls. He had granted all his earthly possessions to them, his children. His final fracti. But now, Jeneva saw this desolate tomb for what it was. A temple to his despair, and all that he had lost.

For millennia he had tried to discover the formula for the pure elixir. Each attempt had been met with failure. As a result, every two centuries, he was forced to grieve for another generation of his children. This ceaseless loss had broken his immortal spirit, he claimed. He had once described it as being tormented by the gods themselves. To be able to extend the lives of those he had made, but for what was only a mercilessly short period in the life of an immortal.

And his regrets had followed him throughout the centuries with the persistence of angry spirits.

Why had he given all the elixir to his soldiers within moments of having stolen it? Why had he not predicted that their allegiance to him would crumble once they were gifted with eternal life? Why had he been so confident he would find the formula in the quarters of the queen from whom he had so brutally stolen it?

His insurrection. His uprising. A grotesque mistake. He should have tried diplomacy. Or, at least, subterfuge.

Would those regrets still plague him now?

Or would the story they brought him give him a true life, and a true resurrection?

"Rise, Saqnos," Jeneva whispered over his body. "Your children bring you hope."

*   *   *

His robes had decayed, so they brought him clothes from the ship. But he had not yet dressed. In the nude he chewed great mouthfuls of the fruit and bread they'd brought him. It would have been easier to tend to him on the yacht, of course. But they dared not ask him to board. Not yet. That would be presumptuous.

He had not yet decided to leave this island and this tomb.

For all they knew, he would listen to their tale and ask to be sealed away again.

They had prepared themselves for his anger as well. So far he had shown none.

He listened to the tale of the immortal gambler in Monte Carlo attentively, his eyes bright.

Jeneva marveled at his restored skin, his lustrous tumble of curly ink-black hair. In this modern age, his coloring would be described as Middle Eastern, but in the kingdom to which he had been born, he had served a black-skinned queen.

This ancient, fallen empire, he had told them, existed in a time before the sun had suddenly and mercilessly scorched the northern end of Africa, creating a desert out of his ancestral lands, driving the survivors of the great plague that felled his kingdom south and east. Starved and in dread of disease, these survivors of Shaktanu had aligned themselves into fearful tribes, united by the most primitive of reasons: the shared color of their skin or scattered bits of history, most of it myth, suggesting a common ancestry. And all of this had resulted in ceaseless tribal warfare. All of it, this legacy of scarcity, fear, and misperception, had formed the ancestral basis of the tribes and kingdoms that would rise in later years on the borders of a new desert created by a cruel sun.

But before that terrible time, his had been a truly global civilization, and in it, the concerns of race that afflicted this modern age simply did not exist, and Shaktanu, in what was now the vast Sahara Desert, had been the center of its power.

Shaktanu. Jeneva could count on one hand the number of times her father had been able to say the name without weeping.

He did not weep now.

He listened and he ate, and he allowed them to marvel at the sight of his beautifully restored naked body, bathed in the shafts of sunlight still pouring down from above.

Jeneva had never witnessed the awakening of a pure immortal before.

His confusion was slight and passed quickly. His consciousness returned fully before his strength did. Throughout, his hunger and thirst were enormous.

By the time they had finished their tale, he had eaten all the food they'd brought him. And so, they all realized with a heavy silence, a moment of decision had arrived.

There was more food aboard the boat. Would he join them?

"I did not make these immortals, if that is truly what they are," Saqnos finally said. "Is this why you have awakened me? To learn this?"

"In part, yes," Jeneva answered. "We fear the queen, as you always taught us to. If this Earl of Rutherford is one of her associates, or a child of hers, then we were right not to—"

"Bektaten sleeps," Saqnos said, too gruffly, with too much authority. But they allowed him this certainty. What other choice did they have? They had never meet this queen, the one with the power to destroy them all. He rarely shared details of her beyond the most frightening one. "She seeks to guard the pure elixir, not spread it. She would not make immortals like this. And so what you rouse me for, my children, is the hope of a quest. A quest none of you may have the time to complete."

"You will have the time, Master," Jeneva said. "That is why we awaken you."

"And so there is a choice before us," Callum said, "one we cannot answer alone, given that our numbers are limited."

"What is this choice?" Saqnos asked.

"Do we follow this gambling aristocrat on his travels, or do we assemble in London and seek to learn everything we can of this Mr. Reginald Ramsey of Egypt?"

A long silence followed. For Jeneva, it was torturous.

Saqnos gazed past them; at what exactly, she did not know. They could hear the gentle lapping of the sea beyond the cavern's rock walls. The sunlight penetrating the cavern had begun to dim.

Dusk would soon fall upon this island, and with it, their father might choose to begin another sleep.

"We travel to London," Saqnos finally said. "We travel to London so that we can learn all we can from this Mr. Ramsey."

Part 2

10

SS *Orsova*

The ship was infinitely more powerful than the one that had carried her to Rome thousands of years before.

Outside of a sandstorm, she'd never felt winds this strong.

Before she was willing to venture out onto the decks, she'd forced Teddy to assure her that she would not be swept away.

"This is how fast things move now, and their movement creates this great, sustained wind," he had explained. "If there had been no roof on the train to Alexandria, we would have felt much the same thing, my beautiful queen."

That had been on the first day of their voyage, and now, a few days later, she'd found the courage to release the rail and drink in the pleasurable sensation of the wind lifting her hair from the back of her neck.

Absurd, these thoughts. Absurd to believe the strength provided her by the elixir would not be enough to keep her feet rooted in place.

And look at the other passengers! They weren't being whisked off into the sea air like grains of sand. But this is why she needed the handsome young doctor with her: to illuminate the sudden and unexpected mysteries of this modern world with its flying machines and roaring trains.

If only Teddy could also reveal to her the mysteries of the elixir.

But for that she needed Ramses. Again this fact aroused great bitterness in her, threatened to make this modern journey across the seas towards London into a kind of death march of the spirit.

How was it that her thirst for revenge had faded so quickly?

Weeks before, she would have delighted at the prospect of torturing answers out of her old lover, her old counselor, her immortal king. Now she dreaded it. And there was no putting his life in peril, of this she was sure. Of course, there were the lives of those he now loved, those with whom he had toured Egypt. And so if he refused to offer some explanation for the strange visions that had begun to plague her, she could threaten one of them with ease.

And this marriage to Julie Stratford—did it mean he'd given her the elixir as well? She doubted it. A pale-skinned little weakling, Julie had been. Far too cowardly to embrace the challenge of eternal life.

But she doubted Ramses would have offered Julie the elixir in the first place. He craved only the illusion of attachments to mortals. At the end of the day, he wished to be free so he might move on to the next long slumber, the next new age. Why else would he have denied her request for the elixir all those years ago and brought about Egypt's utter ruin in the process?

He didn't deny your request for the elixir. Maddening to have the voice of her rational mind sound so much like his voice, Ramses' voice. *He denied Marc Antony's request for an immortal army. To you, he offered it, and you refused because you believed you would reign as queen until your body gave out.*

Such confusion still.

She pulled the cable Teddy had brought her from the pocket of her dress, and tensed her fingers to keep it from flying off into the wind.

FATHER ARE YOU WELL STOP ENGAGEMENT PARTY
FOR JULIE AND RAMSEY EIGHTEEN APRIL OUR

ESTATE YORKSHIRE STOP MOTHER THRILLED
PLEASE COME OR WRITE YOUR SON ALEX

"We'll make it in time," he said now. "Don't worry."

He'd approached silently.

"With you, I have no fear, Doctor," she answered.

"Nor should you." He kissed her earlobe gently, lips nuzzling against the nape of her neck. "Bella Regina Cleopatra."

But his words only served to bring to mind the last man who had called her by this beautiful name.

Alex Savarell, youthful and handsome and eager. Even amidst the mad disorientation of her resurrection, his gentlemanly attempts to control himself in her presence had seemed like a kind of worship. In turn, his desire for her had made him seem as new to this modern world as she was. How she longed to see that eagerness again, to feel it, to taste it. To feel and taste *him*.

And her thoughts of Alex only reminded her of how much more collected she was now than in those first fumbling and terrifying days after her resurrection. Days in which her sense of awareness of the world around her had been a fractured, jagged thing, its sharp edges waiting for her whenever she reached out and tried to grasp for her name, her memories, her very being.

She felt a terrible revulsion when she thought of the lives she'd taken, almost as terrible as the visions that had started to plague her.

"Come," she said. "Let's return to our stateroom. I'll tell you more tales of my royal past and you will pleasure me as you always do."

"You are troubled by thoughts, my queen."

"Thoughts in and of themselves are never a trouble, Teddy. Only the actions they might inspire."

She took his arm.

There was a brief, contented moment of seeing the empty, windswept deck before them; the miracle of such a solid, massive structure moving effortlessly across the open seas beneath a night sky teeming with stars. Then the stars seemed to vanish, and suddenly the sky seemed to be bearing down on her like the lid of a sarcophagus.

Her knees buckled. She heard her frightened cry as if from a distance. The sound of it enraged her, but her rage was impotent before the power of this vision.

A train. She could hear it.

Barreling towards her?

A memory of the accident that had almost killed her a second time?

No. These sounds were different; they were coming not towards her, but from all around her.

The ship's deck had been transformed into a narrow, shaking passageway of some sort, lined with vague points of shifting light.

"My queen," she heard the doctor cry. But his voice also seemed far away, his hand in hers suddenly as soft as overripe fruit.

I am inside of this train, she realized suddenly.

From the darkness, another voice. Not the doctor's. Not her own.

Miss? Are you all right, miss?

The voice had a different, unfamiliar kind of accent, harsh and guttural compared to Teddy's. She'd heard this kind of accent several times since she'd come back to life; it was American.

Shafts of sunlight pierced the train's windows as it hurtled through unknown countryside. The part of her that was stumbling down the hallway of this speeding train car was as unsure of her footing as the part of her that struggled to stay upright on the steamship's deck.

She was a being divided somehow, trapped in two places at once, the only thing she could feel, the only thing of which she was absolutely sure, was an overwhelming nausea and the terrible noise of the train's screaming metal wheels.

She heard Teddy's distant voice call her name. *"Cleopatra!"*

And then suddenly she found herself staring into a reflection that was not her own in one of the train's rattling windows. Bare suggestions of the same woman in her earlier, far-less-powerful visions. Pale skinned and blonde, the details of her face lost to a whirl of strange countryside beyond the glass.

She could hear her scream quite clearly, as clearly as she could hear the young doctor begging her to calm herself, as clearly as she could feel him placing one hand over her mouth to stifle her anguished cries.

The *Twentieth Century Limited*

"Miss Parker!" the porter cried. "Are you all right?"

Sibyl gripped the handrail just before she fell knees first to the carpet. The porter rushed to her and curved an arm around her back.

A dream, Sibyl thought. *But I'm awake. Wide awake in broad daylight and yet it came over me with the same power as my nightmares.*

She'd just left the dining car on her way back to her compartment when the entire train car filled with wind. A door of some sort had been left open, she'd been sure. Her mouth had opened to call out to the porter when the smell of ocean wind suddenly filled her nostrils. And that's when she realized that her clothes weren't ruffled in the slightest, that the wind she felt was just that and only that, a feeling. As for the scent of the ocean, the *Twentieth Century Limited* was still miles from the coast. Then she had felt the presence of a man next to her, gripping her hand. Impossible. There wasn't space enough in the narrow passageway for anyone to be standing next to her.

And then she'd seen him. Not the handsome Egyptian from her dreams.

This man had pale skin and a jutting, defiant jaw. But he looked just as terrified as Mr. Ramsey had in her dream, the dream in which she'd reached for him with skeleton hands. And he'd shouted something, a name, but it hadn't quite made any sense, and his voice had sounded far away, as if the wind in her vision were carrying it away from her.

She and the man were standing on the deck of a steamship at sea. And in one of the large stateroom windows beside them, she glimpsed a reflection that was not her own. The same dark-skinned woman with perfectly proportioned features she'd glimpsed in her dreams. The woman's great mane of raven-colored hair had been coming lose from its braid.

And then the vision broke, and now, here she was, the porter guiding her back to her compartment by one arm as if she were an aged invalid.

"You're motion sick, Miss Parker. That's all. We'll get you some water and you'll be just fine. There's time for rest before we reach New York. Plenty of time for rest. Yes, ma'am."

Lucy had heard the commotion and came rushing down the hall, her face a mask of alarm. She took Sibyl from the man's grip and guided her back to their compartment.

Once they were alone, Sibyl's breathing returned to normal. Lucy crouched before her, reached up, and took Sibyl's face tenderly in her hand. Her lady's maid had never touched her like this before; it was a testament to how thoroughly undone she was.

"Just a spell," Sibyl whispered. "That's all. It was just a spell."

"I'll fetch a doctor," Lucy whispered.

She stood quickly. Sibyl grabbed her hand. "No. No, there is nothing a doctor can do for this."

"But, madam . . ."

"Please, Lucy. Coffee. Just coffee. If you can fetch me some coffee, I'll be quite all right."

With a piteous expression, Lucy nodded and quickly departed.

To not share the extent of her condition with her lady's maid pained Sibyl greatly. Perhaps it was reckless, dangerous. But Sibyl had become convinced the most reckless thing would be to not make this journey at all. To not seek some form of answer.

She was not going mad. She could not be. For the handsome, dark-skinned man in her dreams existed. He was real, and she had never seen him before. This was proof of something so extraordinary her lady's maid might drive herself mad trying to understand it. And she needed sanity at her side, at least.

The bright countryside flying past outside seemed a universe away from her frightening vision. And yet, the ship's windswept deck had felt as real as the seat underneath her now, a vision she could not blame on the mysteries of her sleeping mind. It had taken hold with the force of an epileptic seizure.

It's getting worse, she thought. *No longer just nightmares, but something more powerful. But so far, the fear is the most dangerous part of it. If I can endure the fear, I will survive this.*

And whenever fear had threatened to deprive Sibyl of all reason and self-regard, she could rely on one thing to protect her soul—her pen.

She grabbed her diary and began to write the details of her vision as fast as she could, as if each quick pen stroke had the power to steady her heart. She'd brought so many of these hardbound journals on her journey they made her suitcase almost impossible to carry. But there was no analyzing what had taken hold of her without once again studying the dreams of Egypt she'd had as a little girl. They were all connected; she was sure of it. All she had were her journals and the desperate hope that a mysterious man she'd only glimpsed in a news clipping might be able to unlock the secret of her new condition.

Once finished, she closed the diary, savoring its weighty feel in her hands.

Writing had sustained her, had carried her through every storm: the loss of her parents, her indigent brothers, and the critics who called her work fanciful nonsense. They were liars, these critics. Stories of romance and adventure and magic helped us to imagine a better world into being, however gradually. In the telling of every fairy tale, the listener and the teller took another step towards nobility. But would her stories protect her soul if this mysterious Egyptian man, this Mr. Ramsey, turned out to be just another bewildering piece of this great mystery and not its ultimate solution?

The thought filled her with a sense of dread that, while painful, was still preferable to the panic that had filled her when the vision took hold. With it came sudden drowsiness.

As her mind relaxed, she heard once again the name the man on the ship's deck had called her.

This time, she could decipher its unfamiliar syllables.

Her eyes shot open. She reached for the diary and wrote the name down as if she were in danger of forgetting it.

For a while, she just sat there, dumbfounded, watching the ink dry as the sunlit trees and rolling hills flew by outside.

Cleopatra, she had written.

But the other pieces of the vision had been distinctly modern. The deck of the steamship; the large stateroom window. These were props of her own time, and yet someone in the vision had clearly and distinctly called the woman Cleopatra.

Had she simply filled in one of the blanks in her visions with a name plucked from so many in her obsessions?

These were questions to which she did not have answers.

Mr. Reginald Ramsey would. She was sure of it. At the very least, something about the man would point her to the next clue in this mystery. That alone was cause for hope. That alone was reason to continue on this journey across the world.

When Lucy returned with her glass of water, Sibyl closed her journal quickly, as if this decisive gesture could somehow contain the swirl of mysteries in which she now seemed to dwell.

12

SS *Orsova*

She couldn't remember returning to the stateroom, but she was on the bed, Teddy beside her, applying and reapplying wet towels to her forehead, her cheeks, her throat, all while her chest rose and fell from an exertion so desperate it gave her a dull ache throughout her torso.

He had comforted her through other visions, but none this powerful. Pain and darkness; these things had become alien to her once she'd left behind those first few terrifying days following her resurrection. And yet, without warning, they had descended on her like a cloud of locusts capable of tearing her limb from limb.

She had only the vaguest memory of other passengers responding to her terrible scream, of Teddy shooing them away with empty explanations.

Vertigo, that's all, he'd growled at them. *She didn't realize how high up we were before she looked over the rail.*

The face. A woman's face. Who was this strange woman?

Ramses, she thought, and the name filled her with rage. But this rage focused her, drove the last traces of panic from her restored veins. *This is because of what you've done to me. You call me back from death only to leave me tormented by madness.*

"Cleopatra," Teddy said. But his voice was tentative and weak, and he'd refrained from using her favorite title—his queen. And was that a surprise? Hers was the behavior of a mad priestess, not a queen.

"Stop," she heard herself say.

"You must rest," he insisted.

The repeated touch of the damp towel and the occasional slip of his fingertips across her throat felt like acid on her skin. She reached out suddenly in an effort to seize his wrist. Only when she heard a great clatter did she realize she had sent him into the dresser against the opposite wall of the cabin. She had forgotten her strength.

The expression on his face sickened her; it was the same terrified expression of the shopgirl she'd killed in Cairo. Wide eyed, uncomprehending, tinged with revulsion.

"You fear me," she said.

He didn't answer. He tried to shake his head, but he couldn't. He froze, eyes wide.

"You look at me and see a monster."

"No!" he cried.

"*Liar!*" she roared.

He went to her, sank to the bed next to her, took her face in his hands. It meant the world to her suddenly that he had done this. That her violent eruption had not caused him to flee the stateroom in a panic, as Ramses had fled from the site of her tattered, resurrected form.

"The only thing I fear is that I have no cure for what ails you. I am a doctor, but I can't treat what I don't have a name for, and to see you like this, it's a torment, my queen."

"He will know," she whispered. "That is why we must find him."

"Of course."

"I need more," she said. "That must be it. He has not given me enough and so my mind . . . it is . . . it is . . ." *Not mine,* were the words that almost sprang from her lips, but they terrified her, so she turned her face to the pillow like a frightened little girl as this horrible feeling tore through her with paralyzing strength. *My mind, my body. They are not my own.*

And the mere thought that an episode as severe as this one might come on again, it terrified her. She had asked Teddy to teach her about the modern world, yes, but if her condition worsened she would become his slave.

But he was stroking her hair, nuzzling his lips against her neck, trying to lure her out of her dark reverie with gentle passion. "My queen," he whispered. "I am here, my queen."

"Prove it," she whispered to him.

"Prove what?" he asked.

"Prove to me that I am still your queen."

She used her strength now in a focused way to throw him across the bed. She straddled him, tore his shirt from him with enough force to pop the buttons. And when she felt his thickness under her, saw the fear in his eyes replaced by desire, felt his lust for her even as she unleashed the more beastly side of her resurrected being, the terror receded, the taste of his lips a balm as sweet as nectar.

And once they were naked and enmeshed, the thickness of him buried inside her, he spoke the words she craved and he spoke them without hesitation or fear.

"Always," he whispered. "Always my queen."

13

London

"And when I told her that I have the title of a lord and none of the money to go with it, she responded in the strangest way, Julie," Alex Savarell said. "'I shall acquire the wealth, my lord, that's nothing. Not when one is invulnerable.' What on earth do you think she meant by that?"

"Alex, you mustn't torture yourself like this," Julie answered.

"It isn't torture. Truly. She was just so odd, so strangely confident. I can't help but wonder if she *was* invulnerable in some way. But if that were so, she would have survived that terrible wreck and all those flames."

"They were ravings of a madwoman, darling," Julie said. "That's all. Any attempt to decipher them is sure to drive you mad as well."

The only son of the Earl of Rutherford, the man Julie Stratford had once been expected to marry, brought his teacup to his lips with a quick darting movement that did little to conceal his shaky grip.

Afternoon tea at Claridge's hotel wasn't the place for raised voices, but if she fought too valiantly to rid Alex of his obsession with the mysterious woman who had swept him off his feet in Cairo, raised voices would most certainly be the result. But afternoon tea at Claridge's wasn't the place for deception either, and what other word could she apply to her current endeavor?

It was one thing to have never truly loved Alex; it was one thing to have never desired his hand in marriage—these facts had been readily apparent to all who knew her, even the relatives who had plotted to marry them off to each other for purely financial reasons. Even, it pained her to admit, to Alex himself.

But her despairing former suitor remained the only member of their traveling party still wholly ignorant of all that had taken place during their trip to Egypt.

Seeing Alex tortured by this combination of ignorance and grief was almost more than Julie could bear. And his upset seemed terribly out of place amidst the white tablecloths that seemed to float like clouds above the red carpeting, beneath the gold-painted arches in the ceiling overhead. And all the other guests, speaking in a polite, low murmur while they occasionally glanced over at the pretty young shipping heiress who was dressed not in a traditional tea gown but a man's suit with a white silk vest and a loosely knotted scarf at her pale throat.

She had arranged to meet him the day after she and Ramses returned to London. And she had not expected the meeting to be entirely pleasant.

Brittle, at best. Cold, at worse.

But it was turning out to be neither of those things. Indeed, she was astonished by the degree to which Alex remained utterly obsessed with the woman who had romanced him in Cairo, and the extent to which that obsession had transformed him into a different man altogether. Vulnerable and anxiety ridden, but also more vibrant and alive than she had ever seen him.

Her only hope was to let him tire himself with talk of her. All the while, the truth was as close to her lips as it had ever been.

She was a monster, Alex, and you were but a pawn in her scheme to punish Ramses, her creator. A terrible pawn. That's all. The ticket to the opera she offered you was stolen from a corpse. And while you were waiting for her to return to her seat, she crept off to the powder room, where she intended to break my neck so

she could lay my broken body at Ramses' feet. It was all revenge,
you see. Revenge for the fact that Ramses had refused to give her
lover the elixir thousands of years before.

But the risk in sharing these things was far too great.

"Your glasses are drawing some notice," Alex said, startling
her back to the present.

"Are they?" she asked. "The doctor has recommended them,"
she said.

"The doctor or Mr. Ramsey? He's full of ancient remedies, that
one. Or at the least talk of them. In the last letter from my father,
he wrote of some old tonic Ramsey gave him that completely
healed the trouble in his leg."

It has healed far more than his bad leg, my darling.

Perhaps a small revelation would ease her guilty conscience.

When she removed the glasses, when Alex stared into her eyes
turned dazzlingly blue by the elixir's transformative power, wonder filled his expression. The grief-stricken man was replaced by
a young man who seemed to be witnessing the sunrise from a
mountaintop for the first time.

"My word," he whispered.

"It's quite startling, I know," she said.

"And the cause?"

"The doctors say it's either some sort of reaction to stress, or
the damage wrought by the sun. The loss of my father, perhaps."
Was she changing this story, embellishing it? She hoped not.

"Grief and injury, then," he said.

"Yes," she said, placing the glasses back on the bridge of her
nose. "I didn't want to startle you with it."

"What a wonder," Alex said quietly.

"Is it?" she asked.

"That grief and injury could combine to produce something so
beautiful," he said, his voice sounding distant and far away. "But
I guess that's no mystery, really. They say diamonds are made by
the violence beneath the surface of the earth."

"They are not diamonds, Alex. Just my eyes."

"But they are as beautiful as diamonds," he said. "And I fear that's why you didn't want to show them to me."

"How's that?"

"Fear of stirring some of my old romantic feelings for you, perhaps."

"I'm not quite that vain, I hope."

"No. You are not vain at all. I only wish to assure you that I have released all old expectations, as it were. There was a time, before our trip, when I was content to wait forever. I was confident that one day you would come to see my feelings for you as something other than a burden."

"I never saw them as a burden, Alex."

"You did. And it's perfectly understandable. It was my father who wanted us to marry. My father and your uncle. And so what defense did I have against any man who truly captured your heart? As soon as Mr. Ramsey entered your life, it was clear I'd lost the game. I'm resigned to it now. My only regret is that I didn't lose with a bit more grace early on."

He was speaking of that ugly evening on the ship bound for Egypt when Alex had quoted all sorts of judgment-laced half-truths about Egyptian history in a manner surely designed to taunt his new rival for Julie's affection. Worse, he'd refused to retreat from any of them once it was clear how much he'd upset their Egyptian traveling companion.

Still, he was, as had become his habit, being mercifully unfair to himself. Spurned suitors throughout history had done far worse than start a small quarrel at a dinner table.

"You are a perfect gentleman, Alex Savarell, and you always will be."

"You are being kind."

"Because you have earned nothing from me but kindness."

"I simply mean to say you should not hesitate to show me anything which makes you even finer of feature. You are free now,

Julie. Free of any old feelings of mine which were unreturned, however politely. Freed by my obsession with a madwoman, I'm afraid."

"Oh, Alex. I'm not sure that's an acceptable price."

"Well, fortunately, I'm the only one who'll have to pay it."

"Only so as long as you insist on taking responsibility for someone else's lunacy and delusions," Julie said.

"Then there isn't some great weakness in me?" he asked. "Something that repelled you? Something that repelled her as well, that caused her to drive off so recklessly even as I begged her not to?"

"Of course not!"

"So I'm without flaw? That's good to know."

"You have the same weaknesses as so many men of high breeding."

"And those are?" he asked with a cocked eyebrow.

"A bit of stubbornness, and a tendency to dismiss strong feeling."

"Ramsey has certainly encouraged you to be more free with your opinions. I'll say that much. And so you don't agree with my father?"

"With regards to what?" she asked, straightening. She was hoping for more information on Elliott aside from the gossip that he'd been spotted in various casinos throughout Europe, and the few mentions Alex had made of the substantial sums he'd sent home. She missed Elliott.

"It's something he said a while ago," Alex answered. "I overheard him say it, actually. He told a friend that my salvation was that I felt nothing too deeply. What would he think of me now, undone by a tumble with a seductive delusional hysteric?"

"It was unfair of Elliott to say such a thing," she answered. She meant it. There was something so undeniably good in Alex, so undeniably innocent.

"Was it?" Alex asked. "Perhaps not. Not when he was convinced the person about whom he was saying it had no real feelings."

"But you are a man of deep feelings, Alex. That much is very clear. And if anything, this painful experience you had in Cairo, it's left you with a new sensitivity that you should embrace. I dare say, many women might find it very attractive." Alex smiled and averted his eyes like a young boy. "You see, sometimes, Alex, we have to lose things to learn compassion. And sometimes we are overcome by change that arrives with some measure of violence, but leaves us transformed for the better."

"Like your new eyes, for instance," he said.

"Perhaps."

"Do you remember what you said to me on the ship that night? When I made such a fool of myself quarreling with Ramsey over Egyptian history?"

"I'm afraid I only remember the quarrel."

"*What is your passion?*" he said, quoting her. "That's what you said to me. You asked me what my joy was. My passion. And in the moment, I couldn't answer. You don't remember?"

"I do now. Yes."

"It's to be loved, Julie. It's to be loved as that woman loved me. Or *seemed* to love me. I'd never known that kind of passion, that kind of devotion, before. In some sense, it's why I was able to set you free so easily upon our return. Because it was clear you'd never felt for me the way that woman did, and after she died, all I wanted was to be loved that way again. And every time I hear you or Ramsey say that her love was born of madness, my heart breaks again."

Better to believe she was mad, Julie thought, *than to know you were her pawn.*

But was she? What did Julie truly know of Cleopatra's murderous clone? What did she know aside from that awful moment of believing her life would end at the woman's hands? Had the creature in question felt genuine desire for Alex? Had she felt a love for him that was as frenzied and irrational yet genuine as her desire to exact revenge on Ramses?

She didn't know the answers to any of the questions, and she doubted she would ever learn them. Better yet, she hoped she would never learn them. To do so would mean encountering that awful creature again.

For now, she had no choice but to let Alex believe the flames had claimed her.

To let him believe that someday he would rekindle just as ferocious a passion but with a woman of pure heart.

*   *   *

Alex seemed in better spirits when they emerged from the hotel onto the crowded sidewalk. He pulled his silver pocket watch from his jacket and checked the time.

"No word yet on whether my father will return for our party," Alex said. There was warmth in the way he said the words. *Our party.* And so he wasn't hosting the event out of some grim sense of obligation, a desire to save face. This cheered her. "I think my father misses your father terribly and wants some time alone."

"Of course," said Julie. "But I hope Elliott will return. At least, I hope he'll consider it, and I hope you're urging him to in your letters."

"Indeed, I will. It took some work finding him. He's always on the move, it seems. He didn't linger very long in Cairo after we all left. I'm afraid the cable I sent him just sat there. I finally caught up with him at one of his favorite hotels in Rome. He cabled back to say he'd be in Monte Carlo within the week. I sent him a rather long letter there. No response yet. Here's hoping it reached him. It makes me rather nervous, I must admit. To have him abroad with all this talk of war.

"Mother, on the other hand, is beside herself with excitement. She's back from Paris. I don't believe she's spent this much time at our country estate in years. By the time she's finished her preparations, all of Yorkshire will be excited to celebrate you and Mr. Reginald Ramsey as a happily engaged couple."

"It's so very dear of you both to do this," Julie said. "Truly, Alex."

"Consider it an outgrowth of my new sensitivity."

He graced her with a polite peck on the cheek.

"Where's the Rolls?" he asked. "Didn't Edward drive you?"

"Oh, I decided to walk."

"My. That's a great distance. You don't want me to see you home?"

"I quite enjoy the walk, actually."

Because I can walk and walk now without fear of ever tiring. Much as your father is probably walking now, clear across Europe.

"Very well, then," he said.

But all she said was "It was a pleasure to see you, Alex. And I mean no offense when I say it is also a pleasure to see you somewhat changed."

He reached up and slid the glasses off the bridge of her nose, exposing her blue eyes to passersby. Then he folded them and placed them gently in her hand.

"The feeling is mutual, Julie."

And then she was gone, and after a few minutes, she decided to keep the glasses exactly where Alex had placed them.

14

"Alex must leave London at once!" Julie cried.

She burst into the drawing room without regard for who might be in it. But she could sense Ramses very nearby.

The doors to the adjacent library opened, and he emerged, alarmed by her cry.

The conservatory beyond was a riot of blossoms he'd planted before they'd left for Egypt. Blossoms which had exploded to fullness in a matter of minutes after Ramses had sprinkled them with only a few drops of the elixir. They would never die, these flowers, and soon the maid, Rita, would grow suspicious of their vitality and life, and Julie would have no choice but to drop them into the Thames and hope they floated away forever. And it was through the conservatory's stained-glass windows that the sun's rays had awakened Ramses months before.

But now all of this seemed menacing, somehow, even the low, insistent gurgle of the conservatory's fountain. Overwhelming, laced with darkness. She'd known a return to London might be less than blissful. But it was grief for her father she had feared once she was surrounded by his belongings again; not this overwhelming concern for someone who still lived. Perhaps her immortality gave as much strength to her emotions, be they joyous or grim, as it did to her grip.

Even after Ramses curved an arm around her, she still felt if she were standing on the deck of a keeling ship.

"He is obsessed, Ramses. He is utterly obsessed. I never could have predicted it."

"With you?"

"No. With *Cleopatra*." A wolf's growl, the way she said the woman's name. The queen's name. The demon's name.

Quickly, Ramses guided her into her father's old library off the drawing room, the one they called the Egyptian Room. The handsome bookcases had heavy glass doors to protect the precious volumes within from dust, and small statues and relics lined the top of each. Ramses closed off the drawing room, a sure sign that Rita was still about, preparing platters of food, no doubt.

They were alone now with her father's old journals and books with his notes scrawled in the margins. None of these things was a comfort. Not in this moment.

"We will tell him to cancel the party," Julie said, her words coming out of her in a rush. "We'll say you're being called to meet with contacts in India. Then we'll arrange for Alex to take a trip around the world. I can fund it, of course. Perhaps he can go to Paris with his mother. And Elliott's sending home all sorts of money. From every casino in Europe, it sounds like. So it should be a—"

"But why, Julie? Why now?"

"You want to see India, don't you? You've said so many times."

"I want to see the world and I want to see it with you. But to cancel the party? To send Alex away this abruptly? I don't understand what drives this."

"Don't you see? He's been shaken to his core by what's happened. And if we aren't to tell him the truth about it, he's just going to pine away for that awful, hideous creature."

"You didn't speak of her with this anger when we learned she was still alive. What has changed?"

"I didn't think we had anything to fear from her."

"And now we do?"

"Yes. Don't you see? Alex . . . He hasn't done what he vowed to do. He hasn't returned to the business of living, or some tepid definition of it. He's unrecognizable, Ramses. He's a new man, but he's a new man who pines only for her."

"And you feel jealousy?"

"No! It's fear, Ramses. I fear for him. For if she has his heart, imagine the damage she can do to the rest of him."

"And that's why you wish to send him away? To protect him from Cleopatra?"

"In part. In part, yes. But I also wish for him to have some adventure, some new experience. Something that will fill the need he feels for her. It's as if he's discovered new truths about himself. And if he simply crawls back into the cave of his life and licks his gentlemanly wounds, his obsession with her will grow. And then he might try to look for her. Think of what a disaster that could be, Ramses. What an absolute disaster!"

"But you cannot send him around the world forever, Julie."

"I cannot. But I can hope that if he strikes out with this new sense of himself, this new desire to be loved, as he puts it, it will guide him to something else entirely new. Some new passion. Some new woman. Something that will make his thoughts of Cleopatra a distant memory."

"But Alex Savarell has no passions. This is what makes him Alex Savarell."

"The old version of him, yes. But you didn't see the man I saw today, Ramses. He's as changed as we are, only he hasn't consumed the elixir."

"So you wish to send him off in search of a new lover?"

"Or maybe not. Perhaps many lovers! Let him lose himself entirely in the realm of the senses. Let him move to a tropical isle and read nothing but this D. H. Lawrence fellow. It doesn't matter, Ramses. What matters is that he satisfy this hunger he now feels in some way that doesn't involve that creature. If he needs a harem to do it, I shall fund every last courtesan."

"Your twentieth century, it has foolish ideas when it comes

to harems. Their members were not dolls or statues. They had feelings, requests, demands. The management of a harem was not quite the escape a London aristocrat would like to believe."

"Ramses. Be serious."

"I am, Julie," he said, stroking her hair from her face. "I see that in this moment you are very serious, and very much afraid."

"But you do not share my feelings."

"If Cleopatra truly wishes to do Alex harm, why did she linger in Alexandria with her handsome new companion? You asked this yourself."

"And you have said she is unknowable. It's possible she is not truly Cleopatra at all, but some vicious clone. How else to explain her callous disregard for life?"

"In her family, success was measured in how quickly one killed one's siblings and ascended to the throne. That is one possible explanation for what you now call disregard."

"I don't speak of her actions in Alexandria. I speak of Cairo only months ago. She murdered at random, Ramses. Men she seduced in alleyways. We have the clippings. We know it was her. Why are you defending her?"

"I don't defend her," he said quietly. "And I don't defend my actions in the Cairo Museum. Perspective, Julie. That is what I seek to offer you in this moment."

"Perspective," Julie whispered, as if she had forgotten the meaning of the word.

"I say this. If she has the callous disregard for life you claim and she wished to do Alex harm, he would be dead already."

"But don't you see? That's not the type of harm I fear."

"What is it, darling? What is it that you fear?"

"I fear that she will turn him into a kind of companion. That he will give himself over to her too fully and become a companion in her darkness."

"And you fear this because his feelings for her have made him unrecognizable?"

"Yes," she whispered. "Yes. Ramses. Exactly."

"I see."

But he seemed to have no response to this, and the silence that followed allowed the extremity of her thoughts to hang heavily upon her.

"Oh, I know it's absurd. Sending him on a trip around the world. He would never agree to it. But if there was anything I could do to make him impervious to her charms should she enter his life again, I would do it. I would do it right this instant."

"This is your guilt, Julie. You believe your lack of love for Alex made him vulnerable to her."

"You're right. I know that you're right. But to see him so changed, Ramses. On the one hand it was exhilarating, but to know that *she* was the source of it."

"And to know she cannot be stopped."

"That's precisely it, Ramses. That's precisely it."

"So I offer you this, and I hope it comforts you. She has made no effort to see him. She has walked this earth for months now. During that time, she has allowed him to pine for her, to *grieve* for her. Take comfort in this, Julie. She may have the power to seduce him. But she has shown no desire to use it."

"I hope you're right, Ramses. I pray that you are right, even though I am no longer sure to whom I pray."

He took her in his arms and kissed her forehead. "If I'm wrong, I shall do everything in my power to correct it. I promise you this."

"What else can be done?" Julie whispered.

Samir's men continued to watch each ship that arrived from Port Said. They'd also learned the possible identity of the man she traveled with, a doctor by the name of Theodore Dreycliff. His family had left London some time ago.

"Julie?"

"Yes, Ramses," she whispered into his chest.

"Cleopatra. You called her the clone. You insist she can't have

Cleopatra's soul. And I try to understand you, but I don't really understand you. Help me grasp this, Julie."

"I've tried to explain before," she answered. "I often reflect upon it when the hour is late. My father, he was more obsessed with reincarnation than I realized. I learned this from reading his notes in the margins of the books he loved. When he began to study Egypt, he thought Egyptians believed in the transmigration of souls. Of course, he soon realized this was a misunderstanding. And he studied it extensively, this misunderstanding. How the Greeks misinterpreted whole sections of the Egyptian Book of the Dead."

"Yes. Once again, Herodotus is to blame, I fear. During my reign, the high priests taught that the soul went through a succession of journeys. It grew and evolved during these journeys. But they did not take place in the physical realm. They took place in the afterlife."

"Indeed. But still, this idea that we come back again and again to this plane. It captivated him more than I knew. More than he ever *let* me know. What do you believe, Ramses?"

"I believe the spirit and the body take separate journeys through this world. And the spirit's journey lasts far longer."

"That's not quite an answer, my love."

"Tell me this first. Do you want to believe your father was reborn? Is that what drives this obsession with your father's obsession?"

"No. It's what I think of when I think of Cleopatra. For if her spirit moved on at the moment of her actual death, two thousand years ago, if that spirit dwells in another living, breathing mortal on this earth, then how can the creature you raised in the museum truly be her? From where did that creature's soul come? If it has a soul at all."

Did he still harbor some great love for his last queen, the last queen of Egypt itself? If so, he didn't loosen his embrace. His breath remained steady and even beneath her cheek.

"Surely, it must wound you, to hear me say these things," she whispered.

"What wounds me is that I have committed an act for which the consequences seem endless."

"It mustn't. It mustn't wound you. I don't raise these things to make you feel pain."

"Of course you don't. But I swear to you, I shall let no harm come to Alex."

"And neither will I."

"Good, then in this effort we are joined, as we are in so many other things, my love."

15

Cornwall

The agent and the prim, soft-spoken members of the family told her the castle was a ruin.

She would be foolish to take it off their hands, they insisted, even for only a year.

Clearly they did not want to take advantage of this tall, wealthy black woman from Ethiopia.

Large holes had opened in the roof of both the tower and the great hall, and they couldn't afford to repair them. And so renting it was out of the question, they said. They were in talks to sell it to a conservancy, some organization that might one day turn it into an attraction for tourists who could scale the stair-stepped slopes of the windswept headland on which it stood. Provided, of course, this organization built a strong enough walkway to connect the island to the mainland. It was a short distance, but the drop to the crashing surf below was precipitous, and the current bridge would not hold for much longer.

But when she pressed them, the family revealed that these supposed talks had dragged on for years now. They could not agree on a sum, and there were so many descendants, each having been given an equal share of the old Norman castle that bore their once-proud last name, they quibbled over every detail. Their pain, their frustration, was evident in the first cables and in their subsequent letter. They lacked the funds needed to maintain a piece of property which had been in their family for centuries, and this filled them with shame.

Bektaten promised to remove this shame from them.

She was weary of her London hotel, the venerable St. James' Court, she said, lovely as it was. She wanted retirement.

She made no mention of the fact that she had with her as always her precious journals, the full account of all her wanderings. And it had been some time since she had copied these into fresh leather-bound parchment volumes. And that work was not to be undertaken in the bustle and noise of London, nor in some fragile city building that might be burned to the ground through human mishap. Bektaten needed a citadel.

She did not mention at all, of course, that she'd completed her exhaustive search of the recent newspaper accounts of the mysterious mummy of Ramses the Damned discovered in Egypt, and the equally mysterious Reginald Ramsey soon to be betrothed to the famous Stratford Shipping heiress.

It had been the international gossip of Ramses and Ramsey that had brought her from her remote palace in Spanish Morocco to this cold northern land which she'd avoided in her endless wanderings. The name Ramses the Damned had particularly excited her and disturbed her.

Centuries ago she had relinquished the fabled British Isles to her old immortal enemy Saqnos. And up until a few hundred years ago, her spies had seen him often, with his fracti, in London. But where was he now? Was he still in existence? If not, she could not help but wonder what had destroyed him. If he did exist, hidden from the prying eyes of the world somewhere, would her presence here draw him out? She dreaded this. She knew that she was conspicuous. She knew that she herself might soon be "an item" in the London papers if she remained here. And that is why she was quite ready to retire to the country, without an attempt to glimpse Ramsey and Stratford for herself.

If the family would rent Brogdon Castle to her for a year's time, she said quietly, she would leave the building miraculously restored, to become the foundation of a new family fortune.

But how? they asked. And why?

She had been blessed, she told them, using a word for good fortune that meant little to her, but which she was confident would mean everything to them.

All because these blessings had rained down on her for most of her life, she spread them wherever she could.

Finally, the Brogdon family was seduced, and a two-year lease with an option to purchase was signed.

Of course, they did not know that the men who served her could mend the castle's gaping holes with their bare hands. It was a job ten mortals would need months to complete; Enamon and Aktamu could finish it in a week. But Bektaten shared none of this.

Let the Brogdons think her a member of the Ethiopian royal family on a northern sojourn to escape the African sun. Let them think her eccentric and willing to live like a scurrying animal in a dank old castle, where the rooms were ravaged by fierce winds off the Celtic Sea that could rip through the broken windows without warning. No need to tell them these winds posed no threat to her health, that she was strong enough to maintain her poise amidst powerful blows, be them from the fists of several men or the sky itself.

At last, she was here.

The long exhausting drive from London was over.

And with Enamon and Aktamu beside her, she found herself in the presence of the stark beauty and grandeur described in the history books.

Fully restored, it would be a marvel. And perhaps if she loved it well enough, it would be hers—a new sanctuary for centuries to come. She did not know her mind on this as yet.

Often new mysteries brought her to new lands. But the mystery of Ramses the Damned was not like other mysteries.

The curtain walls of the castle were largely intact, as was much of its proud tower facing the roiling Atlantic. The stones missing from the courtyard's floor allowed space for her garden, and as she and her beloved servants roamed the tower, they found multiple rooms where she could house the new volumes of her journals as well as trunks of artifacts and old scrolls and parchments which always journeyed with her. People had lived here at least as recently as fifty years ago. It was quite possible, what she envisioned.

"Set to work," she told the devoted pair. "Do what you can, that is, after you take me to the village inn where we'll lodge until all this is at least livable. Hire the local workmen if there are any. Spend whatever is necessary."

A week later the great shipments of furniture arrived, including tapestries, and paintings, and within another week after that, she had softened the harder edges of the castle's vast interior, made it glittering, and even grand.

But there was still much to be done. And the newspapers, always available at the inn, told her that she had time to ponder the mystery of Ramsey and Julie Stratford, who were quite busy in London visiting old friends at receptions and teas, touring galleries, and even, it seemed, riding bicycles in fashionable attire or dashing about in Ramsey's new motorcar.

But it was the story of the betrothal party that assured Bektaten she would soon be able to see the couple firsthand—when she was ready.

Until then, she roamed the surrounding cliffs, explored the caves carved by the surf. The nearest tin mines were some distance away, and so the place enjoyed the isolation she sought.

Only the lightest items could be carried by hand across the short suspension bridge between the mainland and the headland on which the castle stood, so a crane was brought in to swing the furniture and crates over the gap, high above the crashing waves.

As they worked, some of the men caught glimpses of her, a

lone, black-skinned woman, swaddled in timeless robes, gazing out at an angry northern sea with which she was largely unfamiliar. When they inquired impertinently as to her history, Enamon and Aktamu repeated the tale that she was a member of the Ethiopian royal family seeking long respite from the heat of her ancestral lands.

It didn't matter.

She had lived in thousands of places all over the globe, too many to call any one of them home. A network of castles and estates maintained by mortals who had sworn a kind of loyalty to her based in love and adoration. Many of them she had met in the same way she had made the acquaintance of the Brogdons: through an offer of salvation. They were the last descendants of once-wealthy families, struggling to maintain once-grand pieces of property falling to ruin. And then, out of nowhere, it seemed, she appeared to them, offering them restoration. And hope.

Only a few of these mortals knew her secret.

Not a one knew her entire story. That was contained within her journals, and she had allowed no one ever to read them. Written in the ancient language of her lost kingdom, they contained not only the history of her reign but all that had followed. She called them the *Shaktanis,* and she turned to them now as she awaited the return of Enamon and Aktamu from London.

In the tower room she had transformed into her library, the window nearest to her had been repaired and glassed in. And a cozy fire warmed her.

Ramses the Damned. She turned the pages of her journals, so recently copied, and within minutes, she had found the account that had inspired her to cross oceans, to settle for the first time amidst the cool and the green of an island on which she had vowed never to set foot.

*   *   *

In the time when Ramses II had ruled Egypt, plague swept through the Hittite Empire to Egypt's north.

It was not a plague on the order of the one that had brought down the last remnants of her ancient kingdom. But its victims were many, and so she and her servants had traveled into the Hittite Empire in hopes of tending to the sick.

During her wanderings, she had discovered many miraculous plants blossoming atop mountain peaks or thriving deep within dark caverns. Some were miracles only within the blood of those who had consumed her elixir. And one of them, the strangle lily, was an outright poison, discovered when the bold and magnificent leopard she had made into an immortal companion nibbled from its leaves and turned to ash before her eyes.

But she had never resigned her vocation as a healer, a role she'd played long before she rose to become queen of Shaktanu, and so she had discovered and formulated medicines of surprising potency that could be used to treat sick mortals.

She longed to heal the world, of course, but this was a dangerous desire and always would be; a passel of reckless emotions without a clear, organizing purpose. To administer the elixir was to risk exposing it to those who might use it for domination and control. And whenever she considered this possibility, bitter, angry memories of Saqnos paralyzed her.

But plague, its horrors and its ultimate cost, always drew her like a Siren's call.

Plague stirred her tortured memories of Shaktanu's final hours.

And so it was to heal those afflicted by plague that she entered the kingdom of the Hittites in the year they now called 1274 B.C., bringing her many medicines and potions with her.

There, in the land of the Hittites, a strange tragedy had befallen Bektaten. She had fallen under the spell of a fearless maverick priestess, a worshipper of the goddess of healing, Kamrusepa. Her name had been Marupa.

Marupa had been possessed of remarkable strength and independence. Weary of cities and courts, she had created a remote mountain sanctuary for her goddess, to which many came for healing. In the eyes of Bektaten, Marupa possessed a wild vintage beauty. Gray streaked Marupa's hair, and there were times when she would cock her head, listening to the voice of the goddess, and then break forth in frenzied dancing and singing that terrified those who came for her curative magic. But her gnarled hands brought comfort, and her potions could banish pain, even heal bones, it seemed, and Marupa turned away no one from Kamrusepa's altar.

Marupa had known without being told that Bektaten was no ordinary human being. But she felt only sympathy and awe for the strange Ethiopian who sought to share her own curative potions so generously.

Though Bektaten herself prayed to no god or goddess, and had long ago turned against all pantheons as lies, she marveled at Marupa's faith, Marupa's insistence that Kamrusepa spoke to her.

Marupa had become Bektaten's treasured companion. And at last, succumbing to the loneliness which had so often driven her to confide her secrets, Bektaten told Marupa everything. They had spent many hours talking together, hours which came to be weeks and weeks that came to be months. All her doubts, her griefs, her great fears, Bektaten poured out to this new friend, inspired by Marupa's tenderness.

The very worst secret of her soul, Bektaten confided, was that she wished she had never discovered the elixir; and she feared she would never know how to use it to help anyone. It was not like her other potions or curatives, she confessed. And Marupa listened with tears in her eyes without censure or judgment.

At last Marupa put a request to Bektaten. "Let me give this elixir to the doves of my shrine, the birds sacred to the great Kamrusepa. And let me put before the goddess herself a goblet of this strange concoction, and let Kamrusepa tell us whether this is bad or good, to be destroyed or used, and how it might help all humankind."

Bektaten had no faith that Kamrusepa even existed. But to Marupa's gentle voice and smile, to Marupa's faith, she yielded.

And so it was that an altar was set up in the mountain shrine, with a goblet of the elixir and even the secret of the ingredients spelled out in writing on a stone tablet. And indeed the elixir was given to the birds of the shrine. And Marupa told Bektaten to be patient and let the goddess deliver her verdict.

It did not surprise Bektaten when the goddess, so often talkative and forthcoming, said nothing to her devoted Marupa. Marupa would never have deceived Bektaten. "Wait," said Marupa. "Give the great Kamrusepa time to speak," she said. And Bektaten agreed to it. The altar, the tablet, the goblet, the immortal birds now circling forever about the shrine—all this gave Bektaten a kind of hope. Never mind that that hope might die with Marupa.

Bektaten went about her wandering in the mountains, visiting the lonely shepherds who had need of her cures, and gathering new plants for which she might have a use, her devoted Enamon and Aktamu with her.

Then one morning early Bektaten had returned to the shrine to find a small crowd of crude mountain folk weeping at the entrance. All shrank from her in fear when she questioned them. Going in alone, Bektaten found Marupa dead at the foot of Kamrusepa's altar. The elixir in the goblet had been drunk or stolen, and the empty goblet itself lay in fragments on the floor, mingled with the broken pieces of the tablet that had contained the formula.

Bektaten had let out a scream so dreadful that the country folk had run for their lives. Her devoted companions had been unable to comfort her. And it fell to them to bury the brave, maverick priestess who had known the whole life of her beloved friend Bektaten.

That woman, who had never asked for the elixir herself, a woman to whom Bektaten might have given the potion one day with her blessing, had been buried in an unmarked grave on a windswept mountainside.

"Who has done this thing?" Bektaten demanded of the mountain folk far and wide. "Who has done this sacrilege?"

She was never to find out. Those she sought to question cowered or shrank from her. Had it been Saqnos? Had he somehow pursued Bektaten here, and stolen not only the elixir itself but the secret of how to make the pure and perfect version?

Bektaten was never to know.

At last, she withdrew from the Hittite kingdom, leaving the murder of Marupa unavenged. She abandoned the kingdom to its pestilence and to its wars, as the great Ramses II of Egypt battled the Hittite king, Muwatalli, at Kadesh.

In time, fate did bring Bektaten close to Saqnos again, only for Bektaten to ascertain that he had not been the thief and the murderer. In the fabled city of Babylon with its one hundred thousand citizens, Enamon and Aktamu spied on Saqnos easily from afar, and bribed his mortal servants for intelligence of him.

It was plain enough that he had gathered alchemists around him, paying them absurd sums, and constructing a secret laboratorium where he and they desperately sought the pure, uncorrupted form of the elixir he had begged from Bektaten in Jericho. It almost saddened her to see him still lost in the grip of this obsession.

But she had not confronted him. She had left Babylon without ever speaking to him. However, from then on, she had maintained a network of mortal spies to report to her on Saqnos's whereabouts and doings. At times, the network had failed, and Saqnos had vanished only to be rediscovered at some later date, engaged in the same desperate experiments. Mortals passed on the tales of the mad one who was ever enticing new healers or alchemists with rich bribes and wild promises, the mad one who paid absurd sums for any new plant or cure or potion or purgative on the market.

Who had stolen the elixir from the slain priestess? Who had murdered Marupa?

Bektaten looked at the news clippings, both old and new, spread out on the table before her.

MUMMY'S CURSE KILLS STRATFORD SHIPPING MAGNATE, "RAMSES THE DAMNED" STRIKES DOWN THOSE WHO DISTURB HIS REST

HEIRESS DEFIES MUMMY'S CURSE, "RAMSES THE DAMNED" TO VISIT LONDON

And the latest:

ENGAGEMENT PARTY FOR REGINALD RAMSEY AND JULIE STRATFORD ATTRACTS FAMOUS NOVELIST FROM AMERICA AND OTHER DISTINGUISHED GUESTS

Could it have been Ramses II himself who blundered into that cave long ago? Could he have been the one who dared to drink the elixir to the dregs and strike down the helpless Marupa with his sword?

Tales of ancient times told Bektaten nothing. But what of the talk now of "blue eyes," the handsome blue eyes of the enigmatic Egyptian, and then that talk of Julie Stratford's blue eyes—a remarkable result indeed of a fever she'd contracted in Cairo?

Bektaten rose to stir the fire in the grate, and then to walk about the small stone-walled library before gazing out on the sea-carved landscape before her.

Time had cooled her rage. It was true. And though the pain she felt for the loss of Marupa would never entirely go away, she had to admit to herself that she felt curiosity now more than a desire for vengeance.

She settled in her chair once more and scarcely noticed when her beloved cat, Bastet, came into the room, sidling up to the chair to rub her back against its legs and to stir the folds of Bektaten's long robe. Without looking at the animal, Bektaten scooped her up in her arms and kissed her, Bektaten's long fingers massaging her fur and the bones beneath it.

Bastet gazed up at her mistress with blue eyes—just as she had for the last three hundred years, ever since the day that Bektaten had given the cat the elixir. It was not a cruelty for such animals, Bektaten mused, not for those tender creatures who lived effortlessly in the moment, as all creatures should perhaps, enjoying each moment of being alive without memory or anticipation of anything more than a meal of fish or lamb, or a bowl of clean cool water.

"There are times when I wish I knew no more than you know, my pretty," said Bektaten, lifting the cat so that she might feel the silken fur against her cheek. "There are times when I wished I knew nothing."

Ramses the Damned. Mummy's curse. Legends.

Three thousand years had passed since Bektaten had knelt weeping in that cave, and the dread pharaoh of Egypt led his armies on their rampage on the banks of the Orontes River in the land of the Hittites. Surely he had learned much since then, just as Bektaten herself had learned. And maybe that was far more important than bringing the doomed king's life to a close with a touch of the strangle lily. But then again, maybe not. Bektaten had more to study, more to ponder, more to learn about the man called Reginald Ramsey.

16

They gathered in the castle keep as dawn's first light broke across the roaring sea outside.

They had dressed the part of British gentlemen, her loyal servants, in shirt and tie and raglan overcoats and derby hats. Both men were so tall their clothes had to be tailored specifically for them.

Her own height was the reason she preferred the swaddling of robes and linens to elegant garments. She maintained a trunk full of fashions suitable to every social occasion, a wardrobe befitting a member of a royal family on perpetual holiday. But when she enjoyed relative solitude, she had no patience for such ensembles, no patience for foundation garments her tall, slender figure did not need.

The hats her men wore were an amusing touch. Far too small, teetering atop their heads like molded, ill-fitting crowns. As they began to recount what they had witnessed, she passed between them, removed their hats, and set them on the grand console table against the nearest stone wall.

Now she would not be distracted from their words.

Of the two men, Enamon had always been the more forceful. Aktamu, on the other hand, had a quiet, introspective nature complemented by his round, boyish face. Perhaps Enamon's bent nose, a reminder of his mortal tilt towards physical confrontation, only made him seem more aggressive, or perhaps it was his age; he had been a few years older than Aktamu when they were made.

But any mortal years which had once separated the two men made for a meaningless division now, Bektaten thought. Both had lived centuries. They were now equals in experience and acquired wisdom. And yet, this difference in temperament flared up every now and then, particularly when she asked them to work together on a mission of great importance. It seemed to exist in the very fiber of their beings, preserved forever in the elixir's grip.

"He is immortal, this Mr. Ramsey," Enamon said. "I'm sure of it. His eyes are the very right shade of blue and he does not sleep. The windows of the house in Mayfair glowed at all hours and he made love to his fiancée throughout the night."

"And his fiancée?" she asked.

"She wears dark glasses much of the time. The newspapers say that she experienced a fever in Egypt that changed the color of her eyes. We are almost certain that she is indeed immortal."

"But there is something else," Aktamu said, his voice a soft whisper next to Enamon's confident baritone. "We were not alone."

"What do you mean by this?" she asked.

"There were others watching the house," Aktamu continued, "they did not see us, but we saw them. I followed them. Enamon remained behind so as to collect a full night's report on the house in Mayfair, as you instructed."

"The fracti of Saqnos? Here, now?"

"We don't know. Perhaps not."

"What did you see when you followed these others?"

"It was one man who led me to others. He drove with great speed. I followed him to a vast estate halfway between London and the area they now call Yorkshire."

Aktamu's facility with the map of this island was good and

helpful. When she had taken several long sleeps in the past, she had set her beloved assistants free to explore the world. So Enamon and Aktamu had spent some time here, while she had not. This would be valuable.

"And this man, he was immortal?" she asked.

"It was dark and the hour was late," Aktuma answered. "But this estate, it is known and it has a name. Havilland Park. A grand place. Sprawling, with high gates. And others were arriving."

"Arriving? How do you mean, Aktamu?"

"Beyond the gates, I glimpsed a driveway filled with cars. Various types. The lights in the estate's front rooms were ablaze even at the late hour. And another car arrived shortly after the man I followed. A man and a woman, elegantly dressed. I was too far away to see their faces. Had there not been so much activity, I would have scaled the walls and explored further. But this seemed a risk. I thought to consult you first. Perhaps you wanted to take a different approach."

Aktamu cast a glance at the slinky, gray cat rubbing itself against Bektaten's ankles.

"This is good, Aktamu," she answered. "This is wise."

Bektaten scooped the cat up into her arms, ran her fingernails along the length of its spine with a pressure that made it purr and lick the fingers of her other hand. How she loved this creature.

"These people of Havilland Park," Aktamu said. "We recognized them as people we had seen in the streets of London, spying on Ramsey and his paramour as well. They gather at a late hour. They are either immortals, or people so caught up in the planning of something, that they find sleep impossible."

"Or both, my queen," Enamon offered.

"Indeed."

For a long while, none of them spoke. The sound of the surf crashing against the rocks below made for a kind of meditative chant that allowed Bektaten to absorb what she had been told.

"He is the thief," she finally said. "Ramses the Great is the thief of the elixir. I know this now. The sword that killed my beloved Marupa was powerful, bronze. I should have seen it. I was too fearful of Saqnos. I should have seen that Ramses the Great's near century of life was only the beginning."

"You did see it, my queen," Aktamu encouraged. "That is why we are here now."

He was being generous. She had seen it only recently.

And so, apparently, had someone else.

"We will learn what we can of these people of Havilland Park," she said to them. "But first, my garden. It is time to plant my garden."

They nodded, and departed.

*   *   *

Bektaten watched them from the second floor of the keep, from the room she'd taken as her private quarters. One window faced the restless sea; the other, the courtyard below. There Enamon and Aktamu planted her seeds in the large patch of exposed soil that had been waiting for them when they arrived. Several days before, they had smoothed out the edges of the broken stones until they formed the shape of a rectangle. If it hadn't been for the hunched-over, laboring forms of both men, the soil would have looked like a dark hole in the earth itself, framed by the care of a human hand.

The seeds, which had once traveled in satchels on their shoulders, now resided inside an ornate, jeweled box. They had retrieved them from her new library in the adjacent tower.

Enamon was keeping notes of the location of each plant, even though they would all be able to recognize them once they blossomed.

And they would blossom in only a few moments' time.

In the crook of Bektaten's arm, Bastet purred. Ah, such sublime contentment.

Once they were finished planting, both men turned and looked up to the window.

With a nod, she gave them permission to continue. Aktamu picked up the cup of elixir she had blended for them, tipped it ever so slightly, and walked down the center of the soil patch, raining drops to his left as he went. Then he made a return trip, and did the same to his left again.

She had taught them long ago that they must never speed through this process. They must never let the ceaseless march of their lives numb their sense of the elixir's magic. And so, as if on cue, the two men stood to the side and watched quietly as the first green shoots emerged from the previously barren dirt. They held their ground as the first leaves unfurled, the first blossoms taking shape amidst these rustling beds of green.

Life, she thought. *Within this elixir, life itself. It does not kill us and make us anew. It unleashes us. It makes life itself limitless and unrepentant.*

A few minutes later, the men came to her quarters. In one hand, Aktamu held a single flower: five thick orange petals, the ends curling in on themselves, a tangle of yellow stamens. Bektaten settled into the nearest chair, her cat on her lap, as she accepted this gift. She pinched off the end of the stamens and ground them into a fine paste on her fingers.

For this test, she needed only a tiny amount.

At the scent that emerged from the flower, Bastet sat up suddenly, eyes alight, as riveted as she would have been by a freshly caught fish. What did the cat truly feel? Bektaten wished she could know.

Bektaten lifted two pollen-smeared fingers to her face, drew a quick line across her lips and down her chin.

The cat went to work immediately, licking the pollen away from Bektaten's chin and lips as Bektaten smoothed more along its coat.

After several seconds of this ritual, after the pollen had been absorbed by both of their skins, Bektaten was staring at herself through the cat's eyes. This never failed to humble her, and over-awe her. The two of them had made this connection many times before, and each time, the purring creature came away more docile and attentive to humans; more bonded with Bektaten's every mood and need. Something close to a loving familiar of pure heart. Indeed, through the miracle of the angel blossom, she had made many fearsome creatures her loving and attentive companions.

Bektaten ordered the cat off her lap with a silent, mental command. It obeyed and she found herself gazing at her feet, Enamon's feet, then Aktamu's feet as he backed slowly out of the dear creature's path. To the window she sent the cat, and up onto the ledge so she might have a view of the fully grown garden below.

What a sight the newly born plants made, even by way of the cat's vision—great stalks and blossoms rustling in the ocean breeze.

Silently, she commanded the cat back to her lap.

Once it returned, once she found herself gazing up at her own ageless face, she reached up and smoothed the pollen from her own lips and cheeks. Odd, a little dizzying, watching herself perform this task. And it would take a bit of time for her system to absorb the blossom's pollen entirely, at which point the connection between her and Bastet would be broken.

For now, she sat cradling the cat on her lap, waiting for the miracle to fade. She told the cat to reposition itself, so Bektaten would not be forced to stare at herself as if through a mirror. The cat obeyed.

"Is she still a clever creature?" Enamon finally asked.

"Yes, Enamon. Very much so. She will have much to tell us in time."

And who knew how much more Bastet could do in time? Who knew what great discoveries awaited Bektaten and Bastet in the future?

*   *   *

When they came to her, she had just finished reading her journals from the time when Ramses II ruled Egypt.

It had reawakened her vast store of memories from that period. Her search for Saqnos had taken her far and wide during that time, but rarely into Egypt, for she had heard nothing from Egypt to indicate Saqnos was there. Were there signs she had missed even as she recorded them? Ah, so much to ponder. But not now. Now was the time for the conjugal blessing of this new abode.

When her men appeared, silently, determinedly, she was ready for them.

Hungry for them.

She led them into her bedchamber, where there could be no doubt of her intentions, as her bed had been strewn with flower petals, and incense burned to perfume the air.

Years had passed since the three of them had last lain together, and it seemed a miraculous thing, how effortlessly they came together now.

She allowed them to remove her turban and smooth her dark hair. She allowed them to strip away her robes, and then to remove their own.

Three splendid immortal bodies, embracing one another in the shadowy candlelight, ready to sink down into the bower of flower petals and pillows.

Only moments before, she had been reading of her experiences of lovemaking from three thousand years ago. She found the experience unchanged. *When one is immortal,* she had written, *one does not claim the touch of another in a desperate way. One is not fearful of losing it and so one does not seek to contain or restrict or describe it in language that must fail.*

"Take me," she whispered, closing her eyes. "Take me and make me forget the tragic heat of mortal lovers, the taste of death that always comes with their kisses, the taste of loss that darkens their embrace."

They lifted her and laid her down on the soft scented bed.

Aktamu kissed her, his tongue passing between her lips, his fingers caressing her nipples, caressing the underside of her breasts. At once, she was heated through and through, loving the weight of his hips against hers, loving the pressure of his organ against her nether lips.

She abandoned herself to him utterly as he rode her until she was crying out in that divine agony that was always so like pain.

"My Enamon," she said, groping for the other man with her eyes closed.

And now came these familiar hands, so much rougher than those of Aktamu, and these harsh kisses, Enamon's hands beneath her, lifting her, as he penetrated her, his breath filled with broken whispers, *My mistress, my queen, my beloved and beautiful Bektaten.*

Roused again, unable to hold back, Aktamu took her face in his hands and drew her away from his companion, but that companion would not relinquish her and she felt Enamon's mouth on her belly, and then on her left breast. She felt his tongue on her nipple, and his fingers groping through her hair. Aktamu sought to pull her closer, Enamon to drive her passion to the peak.

She delighted in this tangle of their bodies, in being utterly lost to their contest with each other to possess her, lost to their frantic efforts to vanquish her with pleasure, to conquer her completely as they might never do in life. It thrilled her, this helplessness at the hands of those whom she commanded day in and day out, this surrender to those who worshipped her with an awe she had never fully understood.

Aktamu pulled her up to her knees, embraced her from behind, holding her breasts roughly for Enamon to suckle, and she collapsed against them, all sense of time and place lost to her, all burdens released.

And we are this, this only, this ecstasy that flesh can give to flesh.

With each shattering orgasm that followed, there came visions to her, visions of the garden rustling in the courtyard below, with its great shoots and blossoms brought to life by the same elixir that had turned what was once for her, long ago, a painful and perfunctory ritual—into an unbridled celebration of the body and soul.

These immortal lovers knew the map of her body, the map of her senses, better than any god who might have claimed credit for her creation. These immortal lovers understood her hunger, her endurance, as no mortal lover ever could.

Life, she thought again. *Life made ceaseless. Life made unrepentant.*

All this from the elixir.

All this a reminder of why the elixir must be protected forever, why this glorious magic must never ever be stolen from her again.

Finally, it was finished. They lay together, silent, spent, and divinely empty of all longing. In a little while they would bathe together, and dress one another. But for now, they nestled against one another in sublime exhaustion. And in the ancient language of Shaktanu, they confided endearments, pledges of everlasting loyalty, kisses of pure affection, and soft laughter and tears.

"Sealed in ecstasy," murmured Aktamu in his deep baritone voice.

"Bound to you forever," said Enamon.

Suddenly she was sobbing, shaking with sobs. She pushed her face into Enamon's neck. "Beloved, beloved, beloved," her hand all the while clutching the back of Aktamu's neck.

"My precious one," Aktamu said. "All that I am is yours."

Enamon kissed her closed eyes. "Your slave, always and forever. The true slave who has given you his very soul."

In the hours that followed, they became her servants once more.

After the long and leisurely bath, they braided her hair.

They gathered small handfuls of the springy mass of tightly curled strands and made them into long thin braids—carefully threaded with fragile glistening gold chains studded with the tiniest pearls. It was a laborious task, so many fine long braids to be woven, but these two males did it as patiently and lovingly as had her mortal female servants of old. And when they brought the mirror to her so that she could see the finished result—ah, the perfection and clarity of these modern mirrors—she felt she was gazing on an Egyptian queen of times long before Ramses, when so many noblewomen had worn their hair in this style. Around her head they put a final circlet of hammered gold, a weightless crown.

And then came those last adoring kisses before they withdrew at her tender command.

Once again came her sobs. She lay against the pillows and wept with all her heart. She wept for them and for her and for all the bodies and souls living locked in alienation and forever seeking union, union that could only end again and again in this sweet and terrible pain.

17

RMS *Mauretania*

Sibyl was too frightened of another episode to take her meals in the first-class dining room. But her fellow passengers still greeted her with warm smiles and respectful nods when they passed her on deck, as if she were their trusted companion simply by virtue of having embarked upon the same journey.

A few of them, mostly British aristocrats returning from a holiday in the United States, inquired as to her repeated absences during meals. To this Sibyl invented a story about the trip being so last minute she didn't have time to pack the formal wear appropriate for dinner. Perhaps if these fellow travelers had been American they would have insisted on some breach in decorum, but to the British, her desire not to appear out of place or beneath her station seemed perfectly understandable.

She did not, however, share with them her very real fear that after her terrible spell aboard the *Twentieth Century*, it would not be wise for her to travel more than a short walk, or a short jog, from her stateroom, where Lucy always waited with a glass of water and some tablets she rarely needed.

And so she had arranged to take most of her meals there. This gave her time to pore over her journals, to form a coherent chronology of the strange mental disturbances which had begun to alter the very course of her life.

It was a connection, this thing that plagued her now. There was no better word for it.

She felt a powerful and inexplicable connection to another woman, a beautiful, raven-haired woman who went by the rather grand name of Egypt's last queen. And she thought it very possible she had imagined this part of it; that her own lifelong obsession with Cleopatra had resulted in a kind of mental misfire as she'd tried to process her most recent vision. But this woman, whoever she was, appeared to be moving through contemporary life, just as Sibyl was. And even if the whole thing were simply a series of hallucinations—and that was doubtful given that one of the nightmares in question had contained a very real man, this Mr. Reginald Ramsey—the nature of each vision was that she was suddenly and violently seeing the world through another woman's eyes. And for some reason, this connection had gathered enough strength to escape the confines of her dreams.

All of this seemed to make utter and complete sense when she put these words to paper. When she whispered them aloud to herself, she felt like a complete madwoman.

And those were usually the moments when she'd risk a walk around the *Mauretania*'s decks.

Her favorite time of day for this ritual was the late afternoon when the setting sun silhouetted the great ship's four matching smokestacks, making them look like ancient monoliths gone suddenly aloft.

She would pass knots of well-dressed first-class passengers getting their last breath of fresh air before dinner.

Sometimes she would peer far enough over the rail that she could glimpse the children in third-class jumping rope and playing excited games of chase on the lower decks. But her delight in their abandon would soon turn to bitterness. She had no taste for class systems that divided people into groups deemed upper or lower. It angered her that all the children aboard were not free to run the entirety of the ship in great breathless circles, imagining themselves pirates or Vikings or whatever great seagoing figures filled their dreams. Worse, she was confident her brothers and her late mother, and perhaps even her late father, would have vociferously defended such a system, even though it left children with only a small patch of deck on which to run and play and dream.

When her anger threatened to get the best of her—and it was threatening to get the best of her more and more of late; another strange by-product of the disturbances, it seemed—she would stare out at the gray, choppy waters and say a prayer for those passengers on the *Titanic* who had lost their lives in these seas a few years prior.

And then, once this ritual was complete, and usually when she was on the northward-facing side of the ship, with the sun having descended fully behind the smokestacks and most of the passengers having filed inside for dinner, she would do something dangerous.

She would attempt to open the connection herself.

She would take the rail in a dual, white-knuckled grip and summon every fragment of each dream and nightmare, every last scrap of the vision that had taken hold of her on the *Twentieth Century*. The deck of another ship, not quite as grand as this one. Charging across the sea; possibly this sea, maybe not. She had no way of knowing, but she tried to remember it in the clearest detail.

Who are you, Cleopatra? Speak to me. Tell me where you are. And while you're at it, please tell me, how is it you can justify such a grandiose name?

After several days of vain attempts, there was no response.

She remained entirely powerless, and this disappointed her. But this disappointment did something far more significant.

It proved to her that she no longer feared it, this connection. That it had, in ways both small and large, awakened a part of her which had lain dormant for too long. This part of her had been able to stand down her foolish brothers; it had given her the courage to take to the North Atlantic, to *London,* on her own. In some ways, these were miraculous things, as miraculous as the idea that she might be receiving glimpses of another part of the world through a strange woman's eyes.

Whoever this other woman was, was Sibyl drawing strength from her?

Were they drawing strength from each other?

She had no way of knowing, only the vaguest sense that this Mr. Ramsey would have answers of some sort. And until then, she had her journals, and the splendid and luxurious isolation of her stateroom.

*   *   *

On the third day of her crossing, Sibyl had just begun her afternoon walk when she spotted a man reading a copy of a book she'd published five years before.

It was called *The Wrath of Anubis,* and like so many of her novels it had been inspired by a lifetime's worth of vivid dreams about ancient Egypt.

The man was seated by himself and reading her words with such intensity she had trouble suppressing a smile as she passed him.

In the book, a powerful queen awakens an ancient Egyptian king who has been rendered immortal by a curse from the gods. The king agrees to act as her counselor. Soon the two fall madly in love. But their love is shattered when the queen makes an impossible request: that the king unleash the same curse that rendered him immortal on her own private army, granting her, in turn, her own band of indestructible mercenaries.

The king refuses and abandons her. In despair, she throws herself into a crocodile-infested stretch of the Nile.

Her editor had insisted on the preposterous ending, even going so far as to demand Sibyl add extensive descriptions of the queen being torn limb from limb in the maws of bloodthirsty reptiles. But she had managed to have a bit of fun with the scenes, giving her imagination over to them with abandon even as her stomach lurched with each new line.

For general inspiration, she had used only the loosest bits of actual Egyptian history. For her mythical queen, Aktepshan, Sibyl had blended the more dramatic tales surrounding Cleopatra and Hatshepsut, even though thousands of years separated them.

She had long given up on trying to make her books histori- cally accurate. The fights with her editor that resulted were too grueling.

Readers want stories, Sibyl. Not history lessons!

She didn't believe this, not for a second. But she'd lost the energy to argue, and most of the history in her novels was a melting pot's brew of ancient and Ptolemaic history, with, as she sometimes wryly noted to herself, the names changed to protect the truly interesting. And in some sense, it was a bit of a blessing. Being freed from the burden of historical accuracy had allowed her to let her own childhood dreams of Egypt, with all their strange abstraction, reign as queen over her creative process.

She had written so many novels that sometimes the plots ran together in her head. But for some reason, *The Wrath of Anubis* stood out from the others. Perhaps this was a function of the sin- gle dream that inspired it.

She delayed the rest of her afternoon walk and returned to where the man sat reading her book.

His wife had joined him now.

Sibyl wasn't sure what she was hoping to gain by sitting so close to them. She wondered if her newfound strength might lead her to extend her hand and introduce herself as the author. There was no photograph or illustration of her in most of the editions. She hadn't told anyone aboard of her profession and had yet to be recognized. Instead, she pretended to be enamored with the sea, every now and then casting a sidelong glance in their direction.

"Huh," the man finally said and shut the book with a thud. "I dare say this Sibyl Parker is a bit of a socialist."

"How's that, darling?" his wife asked, sounding thoroughly indifferent.

"It's a cracking good tale for the most part. But then there's a lecture right here in the middle I could have certainly lived without."

"A lecture? Of what sort?"

"You've got an Egyptian queen who falls madly in love with an immortal man who, it turns out, once ruled Egypt himself. They have all sorts of adventures together, and then, one night, he meets her in her chambers dressed as a commoner and demands that she do the same, all so they can walk through her own city without being recognized. As ordinary folk, you see."

And there it was!

Even the arch disdain of the man recounting her fictional re-creation of it could do little to dilute her dream's potency and power. She'd had it ever since she was a little girl, the sense that she had been an Egyptian queen and that an immortal companion had led her in common garb through the alleyways and streets of some royal city she couldn't identify. Perhaps it had been Alexandria. Perhaps it had been Thebes. She could never be sure. The specifics were too vague.

The dream was not so much a visual experience, but more a kind of knowledge that would settle upon her in her sleep. In the midst of it, she would know things with that magical certainty one can only seem to achieve in dreams: she knew the man walking beside her, her hand in his, was immortal; she knew that she was queen of Egypt. She knew that his love for her had taken the form of this tour through her own kingdom, as seen through the eyes of her subjects. But these were bits of knowledge with scant images to accompany them. And so the dream felt vague and incomplete. She'd never seen the face of the man next to her, and when she'd had to describe it in the book, she'd stolen the features of one of Chicago's most handsome stage actors.

"Seems a bit of a walk from there to socialism, dear," the man's wife muttered.

"Can you imagine the king dressing up as a beggar and wandering through the streets of London?"

"Perhaps," the man's wife answered. "But I can't imagine him learning much from it."

"And why should he? Filth is filth. It's to be overcome and nothing more. He's to engage only in that which makes for an effective ruler. Playacting at being a beggar would do nothing of the sort!"

And here it came yet again, her newfound strength, and before she realized it, Sibyl was addressing the man, her tone confident and steady. "And perhaps it's not possible for a king who does not truly know his people, *all* of his people, to be an effective ruler of any kind."

The man stared at her blankly. He tossed the book aside and rose to his feet.

"Darling?" his wife asked, clearly amused. "Have you no response?"

His back to Sibyl, the man said, "Those to whom I have not spoken should expect no response when they speak to me."

And with that, he trotted off, but not before grumbling something under his breath about idealistic Americans.

His wife gave Sibyl a piteous smile and rose to follow him. "Do forgive my husband. He can barely stand to be questioned by other men. It'll be years before he's comfortable being questioned by a woman, if ever."

But Sibyl was unfazed by the man's rudeness; it was his choice of parting words that had startled her, and after the wife left, she rose and walked to the deck rail.

Those to whom I have not spoken should expect no response when they speak to me.

She had tried many times since the *Mauretania* left New York Harbor to open the connection between herself and this Cleopatra woman, and each time, she had screwed her eyes shut, reached for some deep, invisible place within herself. And every attempt had been like trying to find her way through a dark and silent room with no senses to guide her.

And yes, she had called out to the woman in her mind, silently, occasionally with a whisper. But to truly speak to this woman, it had to be done during one of their rare moments of connection. Until then, how could she possibly hope to expect a response?

Sibyl hurried back to her stateroom. She encouraged Lucy to take a walk about the decks and get some air. Lucy demurred at first, until she saw it wasn't a suggestion.

For a long while, Sibyl sat and agonized over the exact wording of the message, then, after tossing a few crumpled sheets into the wastebin, she settled on one she thought might work.

The wording had to be simple and clear. If the next episode would be anything like the one previous, she would only have a minute or two to display her message to the strange woman who suddenly found herself looking at the world through Sibyl's eyes.

Once she'd written the message, she stared at it for a while.

Should she carry it on her person and pull it from her pocket at the first threat of disorientation? Was the paper itself big enough? Should she use a tube of lipstick to write it on the bathroom mirror, even at the risk of having Lucy think her mad?

Perhaps if her first attempt failed, she would resort to these measures, but for now, she left the note on the dresser, within arm's reach.

MY NAME IS SIBYL PARKER. TELL ME HOW TO FIND YOU.

18

SS *Orsova*

Teddy was awakened by a great crash.

It had come from the stateroom's washroom. Cleopatra lay sprawled across the doorway, shuddering. She'd suffered from another episode, and Teddy had missed it. He'd drunk almost all the coffee on board, and still he had not been able to stay awake.

What a failure he was. What a miserable, abject failure. He had assured her he would sleep only as little as possible. That he would be there for her if another episode seized her in its terrible grip.

Tears stung his eyes as he leapt from the bed and took her into his arms.

She stared up at him, her eyes wide. Impossible to tell if she was alert, or if her mind had been drained by this seizure.

"I'm here," he whispered, "I'm here, my darling, my Bella Regina Cleopatra."

It would destroy him to watch this beautiful, impossible creature die before his eyes. Perhaps her body would endure. But what of her mind? Would these episodes worsen over time, leaving her a beautiful, blinking doll, as mad as a resident of Bedlam?

He could not let this happen, but how could he prevent it?

Our only hope is this Ramses. We must get to Ramses.

"Sibyl Parker," she whispered, with sudden, startling clarity.

"Who?"

"She has told me her name." Her eyes met his for the first time since he'd taken her into his arms. "I saw the words. When the vision came, I saw the words. She had written the words. In English. *My name is Sibyl Parker. Tell me how to find you . . .*"

Cleopatra sat up suddenly, possessed of a sudden burst of energy. Teddy was pleased by this, until he saw the fuel for it was not anger or the shock of sudden realization, but despair.

"She threatens me, don't you see? She threatens me as she steals my memories."

"Steals your memories? My queen, how can this be?"

"The barge . . . the barge that took me to Rome, to Caesar. I can see it no more, Teddy. When I woke again in your hospital, I remembered it. I could describe it. And now, when I reach for it, it's as if my fingers scrape along the wall of a tomb. It is gone, Teddy. Gone. It has been taken from me, this memory. And there are others. . . . The face of Caesar. It fades and is replaced. The faces of men I've glimpsed aboard this ship. Until I am not sure which one is really his."

He'd never seen despair of this magnitude before. He'd never seen the symptoms of insanity married to this kind of terrible awareness.

"And as these memories leave me, she is there. Again and again. This woman, this Sibyl Parker. She is *taking* them from me. She must be. And now she seeks to find me."

"Don't," he said, pulling her to him. "Don't give yourself over to this explanation. Not just yet. Not before we reach Ramses."

A shudder at the man's name. But she went quiet against him, gave herself to his embrace.

Her miserable wails were consumed by the ocean wind whistling around the stateroom's porthole, the ship's sway causing the brass fixtures in the room to knock inside of their sockets, a sound he'd found soothing at the outset of his voyage, but which now seemed to taunt them both.

"What am I, Teddy?" she whispered. "What is this thing that I am?"

He grabbed her by the shoulders. He almost shook her, but managed to stop himself in time. He poured his anger into his words instead. "You are Cleopatra VII, the last queen of Egypt. One of the greatest queens the world has ever known. You are descended from Alexander the Great. You ruled an empire that fed Rome, and your capital city was the center of all learning, the center of all art. The center of the very world. And you, its queen. And your son. Your son, Caesarion. He survived you and became—"

For a moment, it had seemed as if his lecture had taken hold in her. But at the mention of one of her children, her expression twisted into a grimace.

Too painful, this memory? Had it been a mistake to include it? He'd also read the history books he'd purchased for her. Caesarion had survived her for only a short time before being slain by Octavian's men. But Teddy thought it would save her from despair, to be reminded that her suicide in defeat had not been the true end of her family line.

"Caesarion." She said the name as if she had never heard it before. "Caesarion . . ." She was testing the feel of it on her tongue.

And then, whatever alarm she saw in his eyes, brought the look of torment back to her own.

"Who is Caesarion?" she asked in a trembling whisper, tears sprouting from her eyes. His lips parted, but he couldn't bring himself to answer. "My son? My son, you say?"

"Yes," he answered. "The child you bore with Caesar."

She shook her head, as if she was trying to jostle the memory of him back into place.

It didn't work.

He would have preferred to see her tear the stateroom apart in a rage. If she had needed to hurl him into the nearest wall in a moment of forgetting her own strength, he would have allowed her to. Anything would have been preferable to this convulsive despair.

She shook with sobs as he carried her to the bed. He forced her to drink.

Water, first, and then some of the remaining coffee, black, in hopes that it might center her, perhaps bring some clarity to her mind.

But what a vain, foolish hope. What could a substance as ordinary as coffee do for a creature such as her?

What could *he* do?

This question tormented him once again as she curled her body against him.

Her sobs quieted, and then it seemed she had left the room in her mind, even as she lay in his embrace. Her stare was so glassy-eyed and vacant he gave in to the nagging urge to jostle her every few minutes to make sure she had not slipped into some kind of coma.

Sibyl Parker. He played the name in his mind again and again. Something familiar about it.

British or American? He wasn't sure. And why the familiarity?

Finally, it struck him. A book he'd read while working in the Sudan. A spectacularly diverting tale of magic and ancient Egyptian kings and queens. He could barely remember the plot, only that he'd fallen into it with utter enjoyment. The author's name, Sibyl Parker.

"I must leave you for only a moment," he whispered suddenly. "I'll bring more food and drink when I return."

No pain or fear in her expression when he said these words. But she did reach for him. He took her hand. She seemed to study him with pity. "You claim to love me, Dr. Theodore Dreycliff. Is it still so?"

"It is not a claim," he said. "It is a statement of fact."

"How? How can you when you do not know what I am?"

"I know what you are," he said, taking her face in his hands.

Even though their lips were only inches apart, her eyes studied him, coldly now. "I know who you are, even if you do not. And I know who will save you from these troubling visions. We will see him soon enough, and we will stop at nothing until he gives us the answers we seek."

No kiss, even though his position made him ripe for it. Instead she caressed the side of his face with one hand. Gently, absently, as her focus wandered past him, and she once again stared into the void of her own despair.

"Minutes, my darling," he said. "I will be back in only minutes."

Disorienting to be rushing about the ship now, after days of having been so isolated from its hustle and bustle while he'd watched over her in the stateroom.

He found the ship's library in no time.

They had not one, but two titles from the author Sibyl Parker. Neither was the one he'd read a few years ago, but a quick skim of the opening chapters told him they were both set in Egypt—rollicking adventures just like the one he'd enjoyed.

But there were no photographs or illustrations of the author included.

But still, the name, the connection to ancient Egypt. They were clues, were they not?

And then a cold suspicion gripped him, coating the pit of his stomach in ice.

Was she a madwoman? A madwoman who had read fanciful tales such as these and lost herself to them?

That couldn't be it.

That couldn't be the sum of it, anyway.

For it didn't explain her strength. It didn't explain the nurses who had sworn on their lives that she had recovered from horrific burns in a matter of hours. It didn't explain the striking similarities between her own face and those of the statues and coins hiding in the tomb outside Cairo.

But the nature of this connection, it lay somehow in these books. Not so much in the book as in their author.

Should he show them to her?

No, not yet. She was too fragile. She believed Sibyl Parker was in her mind, stealing her memories. It wouldn't comfort her to know the woman might be profiting from the endeavor.

No, for now, he must keep this to himself. Tend to her. Protect her. Guide her to the end of this journey. But he could not help but wonder if they were on the wrong journey. If it was not Ramses the Great they should be traveling to see but Sibyl Parker herself.

19

Havilland Park

Bektaten had not yet traveled this far north, and the great expanses of open country startled her. This stretch of Britain seemed far more isolated than the rugged coastline she now called home. There one found the spidery constructions of mines and the villages needed to house those who worked them. Here, great stone walls seemed to run forever. They fenced in seas of rolling green hills. Occasionally a grand house rode these hills like an ocean liner cut adrift.

Havilland Park was one such house, Aktamu had explained.

For most of the drive, she'd cradled Bastet on her lap. When they rolled to a stop, the cat sat up suddenly, placed her paws against the window, and stared out into the shadows.

From this distance, the estate was but a halo pushing through a dense canopy of branches, like a star rising over a sea shrouded in fog.

The car in which they'd traveled was intended for taxi service, Enamon had told her: a Unic Landaulette. In back, it contained two facing bench seats, which offered plenty of room for her to recline while the men stood guard outside.

She'd ground several flowers of the angel blossom into a fine powder and placed all of it inside a vial she now wore around her neck. She emptied it onto her palms, rubbed them together.

Once her hands bore an orange tint visible even in the shadows, she rubbed them through the cat's slinky fur, swirling the pollen across the cat's nose.

Bastet purred, licked at her mistress's fingers. Then once the cat had consumed her fill, Bektaten rubbed some across her own nose and lips.

A few yards from the parked car, Enamon had taken up his post like a sentry.

Aktamu held the Landaulette's back door open as he watched Bektaten work.

She'd demanded that both men find hats correctly sized for their giant heads, and they had. They wore them now, and together with their dark overcoats, these accessories helped them to merge with the shadows.

And then, silently, and without fanfare, the connection was forged.

The last thing Bektaten heard before Bastet's point of view claimed hers completely was the soft click of Aktamu closing the car door behind the cat as she sent it racing off into the night.

A small war with the creature's instincts was to be expected.

When Bektaten felt the scurry of a rodent through the nearby brush, she was forced to pull back against Bastet's desire to pursue it. Wordlessness governed this connection; she could control the cat best through visualizing what she wanted it to do next, and occasionally, great swells of want and need could drive the creature to respond. Language, for the most part, was useless.

They traveled up and over the stone wall bordering the estate, down onto the lawn beyond, and then the great house came into view.

She saw the driveway Aktamu had described, still full of the cars he'd seen days before. Whoever had gathered recently at this house, they seemed to have taken up residence here. Above this driveway, a massive porte cochere, itself the size of a London townhouse. The wings of the house ended in rounded sandstone towers.

Everything about this place appeared to be medieval in design: its blunt volumes, its general austerity. But the sandstone was too clean and new to be from that period. The estate was one of the many Gothic revivals that had sprouted up throughout the country during the last century.

What that suggested about the inhabitants, aside from a desire to convey a bit of menace, Bektaten was not yet sure.

She commanded the cat to circle the house's perimeter, passing walls veined with manicured ivy. In the rolling grounds beyond, outlying buildings were shrouded in shadows and thickets of trees. But beyond those trees, she could just make out the shadow of a lonely, three-story stone building sitting atop a gentle slope. It looked like a smaller version of the Tower of London. She'd seen drawings of it in the Victorian guidebooks of England's great country estates. Those books referred to it as the Cage, and they described it as having been built in the Middle Ages, designed so noblewomen could peer out its upper windows and watch their men hunt stag on the slopes below.

Perhaps she would explore it later if she had the chance, but first she had to learn who lodged inside this vast house.

She looked for a perch or an open window, found only a healthy full-grown ash tree kissing one of the house's side walls.

She imagined the cat climbing, and the cat began to climb.

The first ledge offered a view down into a massive Gothic drawing room. A succession of severe, pointed arches made up the ceiling.

It was a cool night, but not so cool as to justify the inferno roaring in the marble fireplace, its mantel carved with some sort of battle scene she could not make out from this height. Tapestries covered the soaring walls; their images of stag hunts seemed to flicker in the candlelight thrown by the massive chandelier.

There was some sort of gathering in the room below. Whatever this group, it had the makings of a gay assembly but the expressions of those present were somber, serious. Focused. They were finely dressed, these people. The majority of them were pale skinned. And all of them were blue eyed. And it was that particular shade, that telltale shade. All of them, she could now safely assume, were immortals. But she did not recognize a one.

Were they fracti? Did they have any connection to Saqnos at all?

For a while, she watched them from this safe perch, and then a man she didn't recognize entered the room through one of its swinging doors, a great bundle of rolled-up papers tucked under one arm.

He called the group to attention with verbal commands alone.

He was not poised to present anything so formal as a toast. He did not even smile at those present. His deeply lined face did not seem capable of smiling, and his mane of bristly salt and pepper was parted into two wings that seemed to contain the same tense energy as the rest of him. Then he began to unroll the papers he had brought, spreading them out across a round card table in the center of the room.

The table's chairs had all been pushed back earlier. This allowed the group to close in around this new display.

And then the door swung open again. A white woman entered, blue eyed, and dressed in a flowing tea gown that matched the dark, muted colors of the room. She was trailed by a towering giant of a man in evening dress and then a more spry and significantly shorter gentleman, also in a black jacket with a white dress shirt and bow tie. Those already present stood more erect at the sudden entry of these three.

The door swung open again.

Saqnos.

Did she shake at the sight of him? Did her lips quiver?

Impossible to know these things, for she had given herself entirely over to the angel blossom's connection. And she did not want to know. She wanted only to see, to learn. To not be waylaid by the shock of her old lover, the man whose betrayal had set the course of both their destinies. Any profound emotional upset might disturb the connection between her and Bastet, and so she had no choice but to contain it. To focus. And to look for a way inside the house.

She compelled Bastet along ledge after ledge. At last, they found a half-open window, and she sent Bastet hurrying across the Oriental carpet in an opulent bedroom, across stone floors and down a grand staircase, until the voices of the people in the drawing room became gently audible.

It was not the best way for a cat trying to avoid detection while entering a room, blind and without a sense of where the people inside were standing.

But Bektaten had no choice. The door was about to swing shut behind a new arrival. She forced Bastet to race through the gap. Then she commanded her to seek out the nearest vein of shadow and slink slowly along its length while she got her bearings.

A large burgundy sofa concealed the cat, she realized, which was why the man speaking had not missed even a word.

A few careful steps later, the cat was peering around the sofa's edge.

The man who'd brought the papers was leading this presentation. He reminded her of an ancient Roman she had once taken as a lover. Killed in battle. And she had not cared much for him after a while because he had so often made clear that it was the darkness of her skin that aroused him and little else. But it was a rare thing for an immortal to find a lover who could match one's appetite, and so she had made use of him for as long as she could stand his cooing talk about her ebony beauty. Fate had done away with him in the end, as it had so many she had loved and lain with, sending her back to her cherished immortals.

To dwell on memories of him now was a distraction and nothing else; a distraction from another man, actually present in the room, whose countenance inspired in her a storm of feelings she feared she would not be able to control.

Saqnos.

He was the only one seated. The group had parted, giving him a line of sight to the round table and the man addressing them all in a tone best described as brittle.

"And here is the Roman temple, built in the nineteenth century by the father of the present Earl of Rutherford. It's a rather small structure. But it will suit our purposes perfectly as it sits atop an old underground tunnel dating back to some earlier civil war. Today there is a wooden trapdoor in the temple floor, providing access to the tunnel. It is covered with the thinnest of stone tiles, yet undetectable. A Roman statue stands beside it. This temple stands on the western lawn. And if the accounts we've managed to collect from their friends are accurate, the house and the western lawn are the only two places where the Savarells have chosen to entertain in the past. And so—"

"A tunnel?" Saqnos asked, with an authority that silenced the man. "Explain all this."

He wore the sheen of a recent resurrection: the brightness of the eyes, the lush pinkness to his lips. She had seen these qualities in herself after an awakening, and she recognized their source now. They did not age visibly, but long sleeps could be restorative nonetheless.

"It is perfect for us, Master. There was much debris in the tunnel. Apparently the present earl used it in his debauched youth to meet there with friends his father despised. All that has been removed by us."

Saqnos rose to his feet.

"Get to the point!" he said. "You weary me with all this. What is the actual plan here?"

The entire group took a step back. This, along with the manner in which the elderly, supercilious man leading this meeting had referred to him as Master, was proof that Saqnos was the creator of these beings.

A mistake, she realized now, with equal parts dread and fear. A mistake to give this island of Britain to Saqnos, to allow him to create legions of his broken children, his fracti. How many generations had there been? How much trouble had they wrought?

Why had she not struck him down in Jericho when she had the chance? Or in Babylon, when her spies had found his secret alchemical workshop? Why had she chosen to rule him by one decree and the fear of the strangle lily? There was only one answer, and she had wrestled with it for centuries. To destroy him would be to destroy her most powerful connection to Shaktanu.

There was a coldness to these people, these fracti slaves of Saqnos. A coldness and a quiet, restrained delight in the mechanics of this business they now discussed. Were these qualities intrinsic to his fracti, a product of the corrupted elixir?

So many questions. Too many to answer in this moment.

She must bear witness now, and nothing more.

And what she witnessed was that despite the vitality provided to him by his recent resurrection, Saqnos was vacant eyed. Exhausted. Broken. When he rested his hands against the edge of the table and gazed down at the schematics his child had been using to give this little presentation, nothing but weariness radiated from him. He was far from being the energized madman she had spied on in his various secret laboratories over the years.

Yet these slaves of his were frightened of him.

"And so, Burnham, you plan to lure her to this temple and abduct her through its very floor?" Saqnos asked. "Is that it? And this during some gala affair in which guests roam the grounds? How do you propose to achieve this?"

"Master," said the one called Burnham. "As I mentioned there is a statue in the temple, before the trapdoor. It is a statue of Julius Caesar which functions as a lever. Several of us will ask Julie Stratford to give us a tour of the grounds. We shall be most insistent. Once we've surrounded her in the temple, we'll open the floor and send her through. Others will not see this."

"And then what?" Saqnos asked, brow furrowed, staring down at the schematics as if they had offended him.

"More of us will wait in the tunnel below, where we will at once confine her in a coffin. We shall seal her inside of it with our collective strength, and transport her to the distant opening near the pond. Close to there lies an access road. We'll have taken her from the party before anyone notices."

Saqnos smiled. "Very well," he said. "Not such a bad plan. And a coffin, a coffin will terrify her, this newborn immortal."

"Yes, Master. And with all light shut out, she will begin to weaken."

Saqnos looked away, as if he could not make himself attend to these plans. "It will take time for darkness to weaken her," he said.

"Yes, but she will be afraid. And she will know that she has been deprived of all light. And she will know that if she does not cooperate with us in future, she can be buried alive easily."

Saqnos smiled wearily. "Yes. And you will be sure to tell her beloved Ramses the Damned that she is in a coffin."

"That is our plan, Master," said Burnham. "We will most certainly tell him that she has been sealed within a coffin. But we will not be keeping her in this coffin all that long. Only until we reach our final destination."

Burnham smiled with delight as if inviting his master to smile with him.

"It is the Cage that we have in mind for her," he said, and he could not stop himself from laughing. "Come, we will show you, Master."

20

It was too much of a risk to follow at the heels of this group, so Bektaten commanded the cat up the grand staircase and out the window through which she'd come.

From the ledge, Bastet watched the group round the side of the massive house and begin their short trek towards the lone three-story building in the distance, the one they called the Cage. Once they were a safe distance away, Bastet descended the ash tree and began to follow them from the shadows.

They walked in silence, this man Burnham and Saqnos in the lead. Their shoes crunched the grass underfoot. The swells in the surrounding landscape were too modest to be called hills.

What an odd thing, this building they now approached. It was like the remnant of some town center otherwise destroyed.

The closer they came to it, the more some primal, defensive instincts awakened inside of Bastet.

Something lived within this building, something which stirred at their approach. She could smell it now. A strange mingling of musky scents. Somehow familiar, but seemingly out of place and therefore hard to pinpoint.

"What of the queen?" Burnham asked timidly. "How goes it with the queen?" he pressed.

"The queen sleeps," Saqnos growled.

"But how do you know—"

"She sleeps," insisted Saqnos as though he did not want to be questioned. "Or she has done herself in with her own poison. She thought she could spend eternal life posing as a healer and a trader. Wandering without end, in search of what, she did not know. A torment, this lack of ambition. This lack of clarity, it destroyed her. It has driven her into a tomb of her own making, I am sure. If not, we would have heard from her long before now."

Ambition, clarity, *so these were the twentieth-century words he now used for his avarice and greed,* Bektaten thought. *And he assumes me dead by my own hand because I did not share in his desire to clutch the entire world in one fist?* And what sneering arrogance in his tone. Did he truly believe this, or did he simply desire to make his children believe it?

"But, Master, we can't be sure that—"

"Speak no more of the queen, Burnham. She is my concern and always has been, not yours."

They were only a few paces from the Cage. Its entrance was a single steel door; Bektaten was sure it was not original to the building.

The windows on all three floors were dark.

One after the other, the group filed inside. She waited until the last possible second.

Again the shock of a blind entry. But Bastet's senses were assaulted by more than just the smell of animals within—a terrible, deafening sound. Howls, barks, growls; all of them echoing madly off the bare stone walls. There were no furnishings here; just a crude staircase without a railing. It was up these stairs she darted, to the thicket of shadows at the top, so she could turn and survey the group below.

The most notable feature in the room was a large steel grate in one corner of the floor. Perhaps it had once been the entrance to some basement. Now it seemed this basement had become a pit, and from it came this chorus of ferocious barks and howls.

Was it the cat's presence that had driven these hounds to madness? Or did they react this way to all intruders?

One of the fracti stepped forward, a compact, elegantly dressed woman, her great mane of blonde hair fastened to the back of her head with a jeweled pin. She opened her handbag and dropped several raw steaks through the grate—four, five, six . . . Bektaten was startled to count eight in all. Not until the last one passed through the bars did the chorus of growls collapse into the moist sounds of a ravenous feast.

Eight steaks it took to quiet this horde. How many beasts were down there?

Stunned into silence, Saqnos watched the creatures eat.

"They are immortal," Saqnos finally said. "You have given the half elixir to these . . . dogs?"

"Yes, Master," Burnham answered. "And it has made them quite hungry. And quite strong. They were fighting beasts before, trained to hunt and kill. Now they can do both with incredible strength."

"I can see this. I can see this, Burnham." His words were almost a whisper. Was he pleased or revolted?

From her vantage point, she saw flashes of the dogs' great chocolate-colored flanks as they wrestled and fought each other for scraps of meat. Massive heads, floppy ears. Mastiffs, these dogs. Great, powerful mastiffs given even greater strength by the half elixir.

The barks resumed. The steaks were gone. Eight steaks, gone in the span of a few seconds.

Monsters. In the bowels of this building meant for the idle habits of nobility long deceased, the children of Saqnos had bred monsters.

"You wish to put Julie Stratford in here?" Saqnos asked.

"Indeed, Father," Burnham answered.

Impossible to tell if the others were as horrified as Bektaten was by this.

"Surely you do not expect her to die?" Saqnos asked.

"No. And that will be worse. She may fight them off for moments at a time. Perhaps she will recover from their wounds as we might, or as someone of your strength might. But the cycle of attack and defense and regeneration will be ceaseless. It will not end until we decide it should. It will not end until Mr. Ramsey tells us everything he knows." And then this Burnham smiled primly at his brothers and sisters, and his father. "I have named them the hounds of Sisyphus."

Monstrous, Bektaten thought. But she felt a strange flutter of anticipation in her own human chest as she watched this scene through Bastet's unfailing eyes. What was this feeling? Was it hope?

It was an abominable crime, what this man Burnham proposed, what these people had created here. A form of torture that rivaled those of the Spanish Inquisition, an event that had sent her into the earth on a long sleep.

Did Saqnos feel the same way? Could he feel the same away? Was he even capable of such compassion? Did this explain his silence and the time he took to study the ravenous animals? Was he imagining some poor woman, immortal or not, fracti or pure, being forced to fight off these terrible beasts again and again? And if so, would this fantasy of barbarism resurrect the thoughtful, patient man she had known thousands of years before, before his thirst for the elixir transformed him into a man of pure appetite?

Reject this, Saqnos. Reject this plan. Throw its architect into the pit with his creations if you must so he may know the horror of his own actions. There is a part of you that knows no immortals or fracti should marshal their power against any human in this way. You know this. You must.

"Burnham?"

"Yes, Master."

Saqnos turned to his child and clapped his hands on the man's shoulders. "This is a good plan, and you are a good servant."

Everyone below suddenly spun and looked in her direction. The dogs erupted again. Only then did she realize her own anguish and fury had caused Bastet to yowl; this feline cry had given her location away.

She launched herself from the stairs, hit the stone between their scrambling legs, and raced out the open door. The fracti didn't pursue. Neither did Saqnos.

To them, Bastet was just a feral cat whose secret lair had been disturbed. Perhaps they would later question why a cat would willingly draw so close to mad dogs, but for now, she had time to escape. She raced across the lawn, scaled the stone wall.

Then, just at the moment when Bastet saw the Landaulette in the shadows up ahead, Aktamu seemed to appear out of nowhere. He scooped her up in one arm.

Once Bektaten saw herself through Bastet's eyes, Bektaten reached for her handkerchief. It was like groping in the dark, but she had practiced this movement several times earlier that night. She wiped her face clean of pollen. Gradually, the connection began to weaken.

For another minute or two she experienced the car's movement as Bastet did, and then feeling returned to her own legs, and she felt once again the kiss of her dress shirt against her skin and the weight of her silk wrap against her shoulders and arms.

Once she found herself staring forward at the backs of the two men in the car's front seat, Bektaten said, "It seems we have a party to attend."

The Rutherford Estate

Alex Savarell followed his mother out onto the stone steps leading to the Rutherford Estate's broad western lawn.

Edith Savarell, the Countess of Rutherford, was almost as tall as her son, her silver hair as lovely to him as her blonde hair had been years ago. Elegantly dressed in a soft belted jacket and narrow skirt, and with her hair exquisitely coiffed, she seemed to Alex a timeless beauty reborn.

Julie and Ramsey's coming betrothal party was already the talk of London, twice mentioned in the society columns. A famous American author was scheduled to attend along with a string of other literary and artistic luminaries. In just a few days' time, some of the wealthiest families in Britain would dot this very expanse.

In preparation, the estate, which had formed a terrible burden on their family for so long now, had been beautifully restored— what with Elliott's steady stream of bank deposits from abroad, and Edith's renewed enthusiasm. It had been brought back to life, and so had Edith, who strode ahead of him now, making broad sweeping gestures at the lawn before them as she described where the tents, tables, and chairs would go.

Over the past few weeks, the gardeners had managed to trim the walls of box hedges that ran the lawn's length. They'd cleared

away the vines that had threaded themselves through the surrounding trees over the past few years. Inside, the wood floors
had been waxed and polished, the tapestries cleaned and the
expansive windows shined to spotlessness, crystallizing every
available view of the rolling green countryside. The dreary old
Victorian wallpaper in the drawing room had been replaced by a
new William Morris print, which made it appear as if the greenery
surrounding the house had wandered inside and been somehow
trimmed and tamed by all the elegant furnishings.

Edith was a handsome, strong-willed woman, an American
heiress who had always been the perfect match for Alex's father, a
man prone to long trips and "fits of reclusiveness," as she'd once
described them. She had never complained of the family's financial situation, which had consumed her own inheritance years
ago, managing the household as best she could, and making the
requisite excuses for Elliott's often eccentric behavior.

A woman of greater emotional needs would have been unable
to endure all this, Alex thought. And it delighted him to see his
mother so irrepressibly happy. Though Alex knew nothing of
women's clothing or ornament, he knew this new jacket and skirt
were expensive, fashionable—indeed her closets were bursting
with such new clothing—and that the pearls she wore had been
restored to her after years in a bank vault as security for debts
now paid. This was good for his mother. She deserved this. She
deserved to be proud and filled with social plans, of which the
engagement party would certainly be only the beginning.

Was his father suffering from his usual rebellion now—his
endless refusal to acknowledge the social demands placed on
him? Did that explain Elliott's travels all over Europe? It certainly didn't explain the great sums of money he'd been sending
home. He had mentioned casinos in his letter, yes. And there'd
been a bit of gossip from old family friends who had spotted him
in Baden-Baden.

There had been talk at the bank of an inadvisable land purchase in Africa. But with the money streaming in, no one had complained. Certainly Edith had not complained. She had continued to invest half of each surprising new deposit wisely for a time when perhaps her gambling husband would not have such luck. And she had managed all this, this magnificent restoration, on top of it.

"It's somewhat odd Julie wants to have the party outside," Edith said, turning to face her son. "It's not quite the season yet, and won't be for another few weeks."

Alex had a reasonable guess, but he didn't think it was his mother's business. Julie was still strangely shy about the remarkable thing that had happened to her eyes. Out of doors, she'd have every excuse to wear those eccentric little sunglasses.

"But the weather seems well suited for it for now," Alex said.

"For now, perhaps. But the temperature could plunge. And then what? Sweaters and blankets for all?"

"We'd simply move the party indoors, which looks just as impressive, thanks to all your hard work."

"You give me too much credit," said Edith. "With the right amount of funds, one can do anything. And besides, you've been quite a bit of help yourself, you know."

"What you've undertaken here, it's nothing short of a miracle, Mother. And a beautiful one at that."

He looked back towards the house. The stone frames around its bay windows had been cleaned. They stood out like bare bone against brick walls that were now as bright a shade of red as they'd been in his youth. The Rutherford Estate had been restored to its original subtle Jacobean elegance.

"Perhaps," his mother said. "But you know who all this work is really for, don't you?"

"For Father? To lure him home, perhaps?"

Edith waved at the air in front of her as if to swat at a fly. "Nothing of the kind. I'm long past trying to rein in your father. And please. Don't take that as a condemnation of the man. I love him, truly. But we are drawn by different tides, he and I. Who knows? Perhaps we live under different moons. At any rate, we seem to thrive as we are, so I've never questioned it and I won't start now."

Edith mounted the steps. He felt suddenly bashful and red-faced under the full force of his mother's undivided attention.

"Besides, he's doing his best to see to us. All this money he's sent home. He claims it's a sudden run of luck at the tables. But it must be a new business venture of some sort."

"I can't imagine."

"Neither can I. But for now, let us just be grateful. And let us trust the wind to carry him as it always does. But let us also be clear about one thing. When it comes to this party, there's only one person I'm doing it for, and that's you, dear boy. Because you asked me to."

"Indeed."

"And I assumed you asked me to because it was important to you. Because something about the whole affair will allow you to let Julie go once and for all."

"Maybe so, Mother. Maybe so."

"Oh, and if you stay the night, there's a gift for you. Enrico Caruso's last recording of 'Celeste Aida,' which I've been told is rather marvelous. It's inside for you, next to the gramophone."

Astonishing how these soft, loving words struck him like a blow to the gut. "Celeste Aida." The opera. Cairo. The feel of her hand in his, turning, seeing her sliding into the box next to him, a magnificent jeweled creature, radiant with an energy that seemed almost otherworldly. And then burned. Devoured by fire.

"Alex? It's the right one, isn't it? *Aida.* Isn't that the opera you all saw in Cairo? The one you're so fond of?"

Urgency in his mother's voice now. She clutched him by one shoulder, turned him to her. Tears in his eyes. How ghastly. He had never cried in front of his mother in this way, not since he was a small boy.

"Alex. What is it? It's Julie, isn't it? You haven't truly—"

"No, Mother. That's just it. I've already let Julie go entirely. That's part of what ails me now."

"So there is another?"

"In a manner of speaking."

"Alex, I'm your mother. Let the only *manner* of speaking with which we address each other be the one that's most truthful."

"There is someone. Was someone, I should say. But it appears she's slipped from my grasp as well."

"Oh, dear. Someone you met on this Egyptian adventure about which you've said so little?"

"Yes."

"I see."

"Do you?"

He was so startled by the catch in his voice, he pulled away from her.

His vision blurred. It had been so long since tears had come to his eyes he was astonished by the physical consequences.

He stepped away from her quickly. Her arm lifted into the air behind him as if she thought she could draw him back merely with a gesture. She was still reaching out to him when he shot a shameful glance in her direction.

"It truly is a fearsome thing, isn't it?" Alex asked. "To unguard one's heart. One can't know the terror of it until one fully does it, I imagine. They tell me she was a madwoman, you see. Some old friend of Mr. Ramsey's. But she was . . . Well, I'd never met anyone like her, and I doubt I ever will again."

"But what's become of her, Alex?" Edith laid a hand gently on his shoulder.

"She was in a terrible accident. We had all gone to the opera and it had been an enchanting evening until then. Just enchanting. I had told her everything about me. Everything. That I had a title but none of the money to go with it." Edith winced and bowed her head, as if the family's financial troubles were a terrible personal failing of her own. "But these things, they didn't matter to her, Mother. Not in the slightest. What she had for me, it was a kind of adoration. And it was instant. And powerful. So very powerful."

"And you had such feelings for her," Edith replied.

It was not a question, and there was pity in her voice.

"And then she simply drove off into the night, and I could do nothing to stop her," he continued. "The car, it became stuck on train tracks, and she wouldn't get out. I kept begging her to get out. Pulling on her, even. But it was as if she had undergone some terrible transformation. She seemed so confused. So confused, by so many things. But what she felt for me. She was sure of that, Mother. She seemed absolutely sure of that."

"Oh, Alex. Why didn't you tell me any of this before now?"

"Because to do so would be to do . . . this."

Surely he could maintain some gentlemanly pose while he wiped tears from his eyes.

His mother, ever the American, ran her hand up and down the back of his jacket until he relented and leaned into her half embrace again.

"I blame myself for this," Edith finally said.

"Oh, but that's absurd, Mother."

"It may seem so, yes. But it's not. What your father and I have, what we've *always* had, it's a fine friendship, but it isn't much else. To describe anything that's ever happened between us as passion or a great romance? It would be misleading at best, a fallacy at worst. It was an arrangement of convenience and finance, much as your marriage to Julie was to be. And when you consider those things, it's turned out rather well, I feel. But nothing we've ever had, nothing we've ever done, has prepared you, our son, for feelings of this magnitude. And so yes, even though it may sound absurd, I blame myself."

"Well, you mustn't," he replied. "Besides, what could you have done to prepare me for the passion of a madwoman?"

"If she truly was mad," Edith answered.

He was stricken by her tone, which sounded both distracted and calculating. She gazed off into the distance.

"You believe she was something else?" Alex asked.

"I wasn't there." She met his stare and then averted her eyes quickly. Did she regret her words? "But it seems that if she were truly mad, some signs would have presented themselves before the accident."

"But there were signs. Don't you see?"

"I'm afraid I don't, darling. I haven't met her."

"Her desire, the speed of it. The passion. It was all out of sorts."

"You consider those who experience an instant attraction to you insane? My dear Alex. Tell me we raised you to have a higher self-regard than that."

"Be serious, Mother."

"I'm being quite so."

"Well, it doesn't matter, really. None of it. Nothing will reverse the accident and all those terrible flames."

"This is true. What matters is that you get beyond this, Alex."

"I am trying. I promise you. I am trying with all I have."

"Listen to the recording," his mother said suddenly. "I encourage you to find your strength and listen to it. Don't let all your memories of that night be poisoned by its tragic end. Savor of it what you can. Cherish those things about it that were precious to you. Maybe not now, or right away. But soon, Alex." She embraced him now. "Soon, promise me."

"I promise you, Mother. I will try. Very soon."

22

Yorkshire

"You mustn't go," Teddy cried for the third time since she'd started to dress. "You're in no condition!"

Unbearable, the thought of spending another minute in this cramped, dusty room.

Quaint, that was the curious word Teddy had used to describe this place, this *inn,* as they called it. To her, it seemed a sharp, menacing word; and the forced smile with which he'd said the word over and over again had become a kind of taunt.

From the moment they'd reached England, his attentions had gone from nurturing to infuriating. The idea that he would try to stop her now, when they were so close to their destination, when this party for Ramses had started not a half hour ago—it was insane, these things he was saying!

He had already helped her into a corset, but now that she was pulling up the shoulders of the dress he'd bought for her in Cairo, he seemed to be coming apart. She studied herself in the full-length mirror as he paced behind her. "We have traveled all this way. You cannot expect me to—"

"*I* will go," said Teddy. "I will explain everything to Ramses. He seeks to live under an alias now. If I threaten to expose him, he will agree to meet with you at once. He will tell you everything you need to know, and he will most certainly give you more of this elixir. I'm sure of it!"

"And that is the problem, dear Teddy," she said. She removed her hat from its box, along with its long, sharp pin. "You are too sure of it. You are too sure of everything you say in this moment."

"Don't you see? This condition of yours, it's worsened since we arrived. You must stay put until we—"

If only he hadn't grabbed her by both shoulders. If only he hadn't shaken her. There was something about the feel of his hands gripping her in that way that triggered an anger she could not control.

She shoved him.

His back slammed into the wall behind him with such force the full-length mirror next to him tilted to one side, sending her reflection askew.

"Enough!" she said. But the fear in his eyes filled her with remorse. So much fear in him now; fear of her great strength, fear of her *condition,* as he called it.

And he was right.

It had worsened since they'd reached this vast, green island. The powerful visions had been replaced by strange bits of fugue. She now felt the urge to sleep, but could not. The result was a kind of daze in which her limbs went numb and she could barely form words and found herself staring off into space for minutes at a time.

More, she thought, *I just need more. And then I will never have to see this frightened look in Teddy's eyes again. In anyone's eyes again. Whoever this Sibyl Parker is, she is a witch, a priestess, and she has used sorcery to exploit my weakened condition. A long drink of Ramses' precious elixir will make me strong against her.*

But the look in Teddy's eyes. The misery and the fear. Not since Ramses had fled from her resurrected corpse in the Cairo Museum had anyone gazed upon her with this abject, wide-eyed terror. She could not bear this. She simply could not bear it.

"It is *you* who is coming apart," she said. "And it is you who will remain here while I attend this gathering. I have asked for your care alone. I will not become your slave."

"My queen," he whispered, the tears flowing now. "Please . . . my queen . . ."

Impossible not to pity him now. When she reached for his face, she expected him to flinch or turn away. And she saw the flicker of such an urge. But it died quickly, and when she caressed the side of his cheek, his eyes fluttered closed.

"Trust in me, Teddy. Trust in that which you cannot fully understand."

False, these words. At least the confidence with which she'd spoken them was false, even if the words themselves were true. For she understood the condition that gripped her about as well as he did.

He turned his lips to her fingers and kissed them gently.

Did he believe her to be dying? Or, worse, a creature whose mind would collapse even as her body endured?

How else to interpret his misery?

There was no time for this.

The hat they'd bought in Cairo had a broad black brim and a band of ostrich feathers that arced over it like plumes of spray from a fountain. She had already pinned up her hair so that the hat could fit almost snugly over the top. But she'd forgotten to insert the hatpin itself. Terrified that her resolve would crumble under the force of another terrible wail from Teddy, she left the room quickly, driving the hatpin into place as she strode down the narrow hall.

When the sharp tip met her scalp, she cried out.

A careless mistake, and a teasing reminder of how out of sorts she'd grown.

She had already called for a taxi. It was waiting for her when she stepped outside.

Once she'd settled into the backseat and informed the driver of her destination, she dabbed at the area of her head where she'd poked herself. A few droplets of blood came away on her fingers. She licked them up. God forbid she stain her dress.

*   *   *

The train had just pulled into the station when pain knifed through Sibyl Parker's scalp. Crippled, she hit the carpeted aisle knees first.

Passengers on all sides extended helping hands. In seconds, she was back on her feet, apologizing profusely for her carelessness. Trying her best to give no indication of the searing pain that continued to strobe across the roof of her skull.

Thank God she had convinced Lucy to remain in their suite at Claridge's.

If her lady's maid and companion had seen this display, she would have insisted they turn around that instant. Whatever Sibyl's affliction, it had worsened considerably over the past day. Impossible not to believe that the closer she drew to this Mr. Ramsey, the more severe her condition became.

But nothing would keep Sibyl from this party. Her publisher had arranged for her to attend in response to Sibyl's inquiries about the strange Mr. Ramsey. And when Sibyl had arrived at Claridge's, the invitation had been waiting for her along with more recent newspaper stories about the mysterious Egyptian— and the assurance that the countess was quite delighted to have a celebrated American author coming to the event.

Once the train came to a complete stop, the attentions of the other passengers left her.

She felt safe reaching up into her nest of hair.

Had this painful little episode left a mark?

Her fingers came away dry. She felt no welt or open wound.

It was a strange, new, and inexplicable aspect of this experience. As strange as her new bouts of sleeplessness. If that was the right word for it. A change had begun to overtake her in the late-night hours following her arrival in London. It had begun to feel as if her body longed to stay awake but couldn't quite manage it, and so the result was something close to a fugue.

And now this. A phantom pain that left no mark and spilled no blood.

It is lovely to meet you, Mr. Ramsey. I know I may seem quite mad, but I have traveled far to see you because you have quite literally haunted my dreams these past few months and . . .

She would think of something better than this by the time she reached the party, she was sure.

She hoped.

23

The Rutherford Estate

The party seemed to be unfolding exactly as Edith had planned, and this delighted Julie to no end. Indeed, Edith had seemed so pleased by the temperate weather and the initial steady flow of arriving guests, she'd made no comment on Julie's unique ensemble: a man's white suit tailored just for this occasion, complemented by a white silk vest, scarf, and top hat.

Julie and Ramses mingled on the grass, while their hosts, Edith and Alex, greeted new arrivals at the house's front door. They were the guests of honor, and therefore Edith had positioned them outside, where they could be enticements for attendees to move quickly through the house and onto the western lawn.

To Julie's eye, this plan seemed to be working quite well.

Over the shoulders of the couple who had cornered her, she watched the stream of guests proceeding through those first-floor rooms, which had been left open to facilitate a quick passage outside. The rest of the house was closed.

Just outside the terrace doors, liveried waiters offered each guest a glass of wine, then gestured for the new arrivals to descend the stone steps leading to a lawn dotted with Oriental rugs, tables, and chairs.

Because the day was only slightly overcast, Edith had raised only a fraction of the tents she'd ordered. As a result, each arrival was welcomed by a perfect view of Julie and Ramses standing amidst parasols and handsome suits and flowing white dresses designed or inspired by Madame Lucile, all of it hemmed in by the parallel walls of hedge that bordered both sides of the western lawn, and the breeze-rustled ash trees dotting the rolling hills beyond.

The board members of Stratford Shipping were all in attendance, along with wives and older children, and Julie had spent a fair amount of time chatting with them all.

As penance for turning a blind eye to his late son's thieving, Julie's uncle Randolph had worked diligently to place himself back in the good graces of his board members while he righted the company's course. Their presence here was a sure sign her uncle's efforts were succeeding.

Despite the cloudy sky, it was still bright enough out that only one or two guests had commented on her sunglasses. Indeed, many of the guests wore sunglasses of their own, making them difficult to recognize when they first approached. Julie was tempted to get rid of the sunglasses altogether, and let the story of the mysterious fever do its work. Someday soon she would do this.

Many guests here Julie simply didn't recognize at all. But this didn't surprise her.

Edith had invited not only her close friends, but many acquaintances as well. After all, whether they realized it or not, those present were more than guests. They were witnesses. Witnesses with a tendency to gossip, and countless social connections to whom they would soon spread the tale of the happy couple and their beautiful engagement party. Edith had also shown no desire to enforce a strict guest list. Let the fashionable painters and writers bring their friends. As Edith saw it, if some meddlesome member of the press decided to show up, so much the better. Let them write a story about the happily engaged couple enjoying a breezy afternoon in the Yorkshire countryside. It would make all those lurid tales of stolen mummies and mysterious deaths easier to forget.

This party wasn't about privacy or exclusivity. It was an announcement. Not just of their engagement, but of their new stability.

But, of course, Edith had another motive, Julie was sure. To show to the world her family possessed no hard feelings over Julie and Alex's aborted engagement. And no doubt a number of future brides for Alex were in circulation, with Edith spending more than a few moments with each.

For most of the party, the string quartet had transitioned from Mozart to Haydn and back again. But the handsome black musicians from America had finally arrived, and the delightful sound of ragtime piano and horns now filled the air. Julie wanted to dance. She knew perfectly well Ramses was dying to dance, before she caught his glance and wink. But there was no dance floor at the party, and it was just as well. Ramses was too easily given to dancing madly for hours without cease.

The music wasn't so loud that Julie couldn't carry on a conversation, and now, she could even hear Ramses a few paces away. He had finally mastered the art of presenting his tales of ancient Egypt as the result of academic work and not lived experience. Gone was his tendency to discuss long-dead historical figures with bracing familiarity, as if they were old friends. Which, in many cases, they were. For the next few hours, he would be Reginald Ramsey, the Egyptologist, Julie's strikingly handsome fiancé.

It was dreamlike, this party. Dreamlike and perfect and everything she'd hoped it would be.

"You will stay in England, of course," the woman she'd been chatting with said to her now. Perhaps she sensed Julie's mind wandering, which made Julie feel terribly rude. "No more of all these travels, I'm sure. Not with a wedding on the horizon."

What was the woman's name? Julie had already forgotten.

Genève or something of that sort. Her gown was frilly and white with sleeves of sky blue; her hat was compact, one of the smaller ones on display, and so clustered with white feathers they looked like balls of cotton. Her husband was a quiet man. He studied Julie with unnerving intensity. And earlier she'd seen the two of them showing familiarity to a giant bearded fellow, who must have spent a small fortune obtaining such a fine suit tailored to his great frame.

They both wore sunglasses, just as she did.

"I'm afraid we haven't set a date," Julie answered. "And I can't imagine a better way to spend an engagement than traveling the world. Seeing its wonders. Enjoying them on the arm of your true love."

"How delightfully eccentric," the woman said.

"Yes. I'm terribly sorry, but I've forgotten your names."

"Callum Worth," the man said, extending one hand quickly, as if the gesture might distract from his wife's rudeness. "And my wife, Jeneva."

"And you are friends of the Countess of Rutherford?" Julie asked.

"In a manner of speaking," Jeneva said. "But as I'm sure you know, this party's not only the talk of Yorkshire. It's the talk of London as well. So you must forgive us for requesting an invitation through mutual friends."

"*Mutual acquaintances* is more like it," Callum added.

"Such an intriguing courtship, you and Mr. Ramsey!" Jeneva continued as if her husband hadn't spoken. "And we're all quite sure the tale of how you two first met is equally intriguing. You can't blame us for wanting to learn more."

"You must forgive my wife, Miss Stratford. She does love a good story."

"It is people that I love, Callum." The woman had tried to put conviction behind these words, but she'd fallen short, and the resulting moment was a frigid one, as her husband gave her a look that seemed full of reproach. Perhaps her self-proclaimed love of people rarely extended to him.

"Indeed," he added quickly. "Now, Miss Stratford, I'm hoping we can enlist you in a little plot."

"A plot?" Julie said. "Sounds intriguing."

"You see, we do feel a bit sheepish about having invited ourselves to this little gathering, so we thought we'd purchase a gift for the countess."

"I'm sure Edith will be delighted," Julie said.

"Indeed, but we'd like it to be for her husband as well, although I'm told he's occupied currently with business on the Continent."

Mustn't discuss Elliott with these, or any, strangers. Not until she had some greater awareness of what he was up to.

"What sort of gift?" Julie asked.

"We were told there's a replica of a Roman temple on the property designed by the Earl of Rutherford himself. We thought we might give him a bit of statuary to go with it. If you can give us a tour of it, it will help us select something suitably regal."

"But we'd like to keep our intentions a secret for as long as we can, you see," Jeneva added.

"And if you ask Edith to give you a tour, you're afraid you'll tip your hand," Julie said.

"Exactly!" Jeneva exclaimed, with a bit too much enthusiasm.

"Well, I'd be delighted to—"

A hand gripped her elbow with surprising strength. She expected to find Ramses behind her. It was Samir. He looked dashing in his white suit, but his expression was a mask of concern.

"If I may have a moment, Julie," he said quietly.

"Yes, just one second while I—"

"If you please, Julie. It's a matter of some urgency."

"Yes, of course." To Mr. and Mrs. Worth, Julie said, "If you'll excuse me. And later, perhaps after the toast, I shall be happy to arrange what we just discussed."

"Oh, that's lovely. Just lovely. And thank you for . . ." But Samir was already guiding her away.

"What is it?" Julie whispered.

"I beg forgiveness ahead of what I'm about to tell you. The men in my employ, they are not professional spies, you understand. They are assistants at the museum, university students. They've done heroically well so far, but—"

"Samir, of course I will forgive you. But you must tell me at once what has you so frightened."

"A ship arrived yesterday from Port Said. But my men, they became confused. They went to Southampton instead of the Port of London. By the time they realized their mistake, it was too late. The passengers had already disembarked. And then, these *boys,* they spent the rest of the day squabbling over whether or not to tell me. If I hadn't telephoned them this morning for a report, I might never have—"

"I see. But they've watched every arrival since our return, have they not? And it's been weeks and we've seen no sign of them."

"These particular men were new to the game. University students, as I said. Perhaps I should have monitored them more closely but—"

"Don't be ridiculous, Samir. You all have done an excellent job for weeks now. It's foolish of us to assume you'll be able to guard us forever. Ramses is right. If Cleopatra had wished to—"

"No, Julie, no. Wait. Please. I wanted to be sure, you see, so I telephoned the inns in the area. And a man and a woman matching their descriptions checked into the Red Crown Inn last night. And this woman left the inn only moments ago."

Because so many fears had been removed for her, Julie was paralyzed by the feeling now.

"She is here, Julie. She is here in Yorkshire, and I believe she is on her way to this party."

Amazing how the terror returned to her. The feeling of being trapped as Egypt's last queen threatened to snap her neck. But this was a memory, nothing more. A memory of something that could never happen again. *Immortal.*

She would not give Cleopatra this party.

Or Ramses.

Or . . .

"Alex," she said before she could stop herself. "Come with me, Samir. We will send Alex and Edith to mingle and we will greet the guests."

"But, Julie. She is—"

Julie began to walk; Samir followed.

"I am no longer a mortal woman who quakes at the sight of Cleopatra. She will not lay claim to this event, Samir. She is a queen no more."

Clearly startled by her resolve, Samir nodded and followed her inside the house.

A few guests reached out to her as she passed. She did her best not to notice their attentions without seeming abominably rude. Let them follow her to the front door. Let them greet her there. For she realized now what had quickened her steps.

Alex. He could not see Cleopatra. He could not fall prey to Cleopatra. Not now, not at this party. Not at the very moment when he was making himself so vulnerable by humbly and publicly releasing Julie to her new husband-to-be.

Alex turned at the sound of her footsteps.

The stream of guests had thinned. He and his mother stood chatting next to the open front door. His eyes lit up when he saw her. This party had cheered him, it seemed. He wasn't simply going through the motions of it, as she'd feared he might. His new sensitivity, it allowed him to take more joy from the presence of others than he had previously. The smile he gave her now seemed utterly genuine.

She would not see this day ruined. Not for Alex. Not for any of them.

"Let us trade duties," Julie said, as jovially as she could. But her aggressiveness startled Edith into silence. "I insist. I shall greet the new arrivals here for a time. That way, you can both take time to enjoy this marvelous party you've put together."

"But Mr. Ramsey . . . ," Edith began.

"Mr. Ramsey is being quite charming on the lawn, and I don't wish to draw him away from his admirers. Samir and I shall relieve you of your duties. Please. I insist."

Had she given too much of her fear away with this request? Edith studied her for a bit, then looked to Alex. "Well, I am rather parched."

"It's settled then," Alex said, taking his mother's arm. "We'll be back shortly."

"Don't rush on our account," Julie said.

And then they were gone.

Breath returned to her lungs. Blood returned to her heart.

Next to her, Samir whispered, "She's got a bit of a point, Julie. Ramses. Should he be here when—"

"Where Ramses goes, the party follows. Let us draw no further attention to Cleopatra's arrival than is absolutely necessary. Besides, if she's come here today, it is in part to see him; I cannot grant this request until her full motives are clear."

"I see, Julie. I see."

Just then, the guests she'd hurried past on her way to the front door appeared with hands extended and polite smiles. She was lost suddenly in a sea of chatter as Samir stared past her out the front door.

It was agonizing, this little charade. Every cell in her body wanted to turn towards the front walk as if Cleopatra's imminent arrival might be magically foretold by a rustling of the hedges, a strange wind though the branches overhead.

"Julie . . ."

When Samir seized her elbow, she was in midconversation with a charming young Swedish couple with whom Edith often vacationed.

"Julie," he said again.

Julie turned and saw her.

She was halfway up the front walk. She was alone. She had

tilted her head only slightly so those wide, expressive blue eyes were visible under the great, feathered brim of her hat. Her dress was several shades too dark for the occasion, a deep blue with slashes of gold running through it. But she was striking in it, devastatingly beautiful, in fact.

When she saw Julie, she went so suddenly still it seemed as if she were preparing her body to take flight. Some of her old poise was there, the poise and fluid grace of a woman once schooled by the best tutors in Alexandria. But it was strained now.

"If you will excuse me," Julie heard herself mutter.

Samir distracted the young couple with a burst of conversation as Julie descended the front steps.

It seemed to last forever, this short walk towards the woman, the creature, who had almost taken her life. With each step she could see more clearly that Cleopatra stood with a slight bend in her upper back, and that her breathing seemed labored. Forced.

"Why have you come?" Julie asked.

"Take me to him. Take me to Ramses."

"First you must tell me why you've—"

"Take me to him or I shall snap your neck like a reed." Desperation in the way she'd said these words. The desperation of an injured animal, not a powerful one.

In response, Julie reached up and removed her sunglasses, revealing her blue eyes.

"Do your worst, last queen of Egypt," Julie whispered. "Do your worst."

Difficult to discern the emotions in Cleopatra's expression now. A strange, leering smile. Almost as if she were relieved to have been spared the possibility of a physical confrontation. And there was sadness there too, sadness so deep it was sorrow. But it was the labored breath and strange stance that captured Julie's attention again.

Sick, Julie realized. *My God, she is sick. Is this even possible? Can one who has absorbed the elixir actually fall ill?*

She was not prepared for this, this strange sense of both kinship and pity that welled within her at the sight of another immortal struggling to stay upright and focused.

"Come," Julie said. "We'll speak privately first. And then I shall bring Ramses to you. But whatever we must do, you and I, we cannot do it in front of all these people."

Without thinking, she extended her hand, as she would to anyone elderly or ailing. Only when Cleopatra stared down at it in astonishment did Julie also realize how strange the gesture was, given their tortured history. But there was that sadness in Cleopatra's eyes. Sadness and yearning, as if the comfort offered by this hand were a cool drink of water after a long desert journey.

But she did not take Julie's hand. Instead, she turned a suspicious glare upon the grand house behind her, upon the sight of Samir staring at her from the front porch.

Again Julie pitied her. For it seemed she was imagining the embarrassment of appearing amidst all those people in her hobbled, weakened state.

"We are equals now, whether we wish to be or not," Julie said. "Whatever has brought you here, we must discuss it as such."

"Equals . . . ," Cleopatra whispered, as if this word disgusted her. "What foolish notions this modern world draws from old Roman laws."

"Surely you did not come this far solely to disrupt this gathering. Am I mistaken in this, Cleopatra?"

"You are not. You are not mistaken."

"Very well, then," Julie said.

With one outstretched arm, she gestured to the eastern wing of the house, opposite from where the party was currently taking place. They'd round it and then proceed straight to Elliott's beloved Roman temple. It was a good distance from the western lawn and would offer them all the privacy they could ask for.

After what felt like an eternity, Cleopatra began to walk.

Julie followed. They walked silently in between an empty,

manicured garden and the side of the main house, before they emerged onto the great expanse of rolling green. As they walked, Cleopatra turned her head at the distant sounds of the party, at the brief glimpse of guests standing on the western lawn before the high wall of hedge concealed the party entirely.

Impossible for Julie to read her expression.

Suspicion? Longing?

With each step, Julie had to remind herself that it was safe to be alone with this creature now. That she could not be overpowered, and if she could not be overpowered, then there was no need for her to be afraid. And every second she kept her away from Alex felt like a victory.

The temple stood atop a grassy swell in the landscape, tucked against a dense wall of oak and ash trees. Its heavy steel door stood open.

Inside, shadows and statues awaited them.

24

He would save her.

He would show her his value once again.

He would rescue her from some terrible scene in front of all these aristocrats and then she would declare him her protector and guardian and she would use him for something more than sensual release and guidance in the modern world.

She would call him *dear Teddy* again and they would go back to traveling the world.

Teddy was sure of this.

He was sure of this because he was drunk.

But not so drunk he couldn't scale the service gate he'd found the night before.

Liquid courage. That was all. What he'd come to do would require a sip or two of brandy, and so he'd had several dozen before leaving the inn. Why he'd brought the small sharp knife he'd stolen from the inn's kitchen, he wasn't sure. Which immortal did he plan to use it on? The one he'd come to threaten or the one he'd come to save? It wouldn't work on either. But this hadn't mattered to him as he left the inn.

Because he was drunk.

Was he more drunk now than when he'd left?

Mustn't be distracted by these senseless calculations. Must

instead get the lay of the land so he could avoid a receiving area and the possibility of a guest list.

What mattered now was that he was on the property, and that he had finally stopped crying like a humiliated little boy.

The night before he had walked the perimeter of the estate. Learned its gates and access doors and the various points at which the height of its stone wall varied. He'd assumed she might want to enter in some secret fashion. With him, of course. And so he'd mapped out several ways in.

The service road on which he now stood traveled towards the back of the property. There were fresh tire tracks in the dirt, probably from one of the catering vehicles. Although why it had ventured so far from the house was beyond him. Where had it parked? Next to the pond he'd glimpsed the night before, the one behind the small replica of the Pantheon and its accompaniment of trees? That was a great distance from where it sounded like the party was taking place.

Directly ahead was a small manicured garden. Just beyond it, the main house. This area was positively gloomy with shade at this hour. No wonder they'd chosen to host the party on the western lawn. The stone terrace on this side was also smaller. And through its multi-paned windows, he saw no shadows or movement in the house.

If the doors were unlocked, this would be his way in, for sure. Victory!

He slipped through them, found himself inside a small sitting room–cum–library. Heard instantly the clop and clatter of servants rushing up from the basement with their silver trays of steaming hors d'oeuvres. This side of the house was almost entirely devoid of guests, and if he lingered here, he would draw attention.

He moved on.

He stepped into the hallway and was almost run down by a tall, tuxedoed man who offered a brusque smile and said, "Party's this way, sir."

Teddy nodded and gave him a dumb smile. The servant continued on, consumed with his business.

He was a footstep away from entering the house's front hallway when he heard a name that stopped him in his tracks.

"Sibyl Parker!" a woman's voice cried.

*　*　*

Sibyl froze.

The woman walking towards her now with her arms out in welcome was surely the hostess of this party, and she was greeting the sight of an uninvited guest as if it were a joyous occurrence.

How many scripts had Sibyl prepared and rehearsed for this moment? Now it seemed as if none of them would be necessary.

She managed her best smile.

"You are Sibyl Parker, are you not?" the woman said. She took Sibyl's hands gently in hers. Nothing less than delight in her smile. "There's been an illustration or two of you in the *Daily Herald.* Do tell me I'm not mistaken or I'll be horribly embarrassed. You are Sibyl Parker, the author?"

"I am, indeed, and you must be the Countess of Rutherford."

"Please. Call me Edith. I'm a great admirer of your books. I must confess I prefer them to actual travel. Oh, of course, you must meet our mysterious Mr. Ramsey!"

"Mr. Ramsey, yes." It left her breathless to say the man's name in such an ordinary exchange. For in her mind, it had taken on connotations almost mythic.

"Do come inside. A glass of wine is waiting for you in the drawing room and then you'll find Mr. Ramsey on the western lawn right outside. What a privilege," Edith said, drawing Sibyl up the front steps with a hand against the small of her back. "What an absolute privilege! If I had my copies of your books here, I would ask you to autograph them. But I'm afraid I'll have to settle for your signature on a napkin, if that's quite all right."

"It's absolutely all right," Sibyl whispered, so relieved by this turn of events she felt near tears. "Whatever you would like, Edith . . . I am sure it would be absolutely all right. I cannot thank you enough for your hospitality."

"Say nothing of it. Alex, my dear boy. This is Sibyl Parker, the Egyptian novelist. You have your memories of your recent trip to Egypt. I have her delightfully entertaining books. And so it shall remain, as I have no desire to travel to any Egypt that does not resemble the one depicted in her novels."

Her son was youthful and handsome. But there was a sadness to his eyes that seemed to intensify as he studied her.

"I must say, Miss Parker," he whispered, "you do look familiar to me."

"Well, of course she does. She's a world famous novelist."

"I'm not much for books, I must confess. Certainly not fiction. Most of what I tend to read is rather . . . dry." He spoke this as if it were a realization he'd only recently come to, and his embarrassment over it was fresh. "Is this your first time in Yorkshire?"

"It is my first time in England after many years."

"Ah, well . . . perhaps you simply remind me of someone, then."

She felt these words, and the intensity with which he'd said them, might be the first sort of clue to what had brought her here. But it was impossible to question him now, on the front steps of the house.

Edith glanced quickly over Sibyl's shoulder, a sign that more guests were arriving behind her.

"I cannot thank you enough for this reception," she said, with a bow of her head. "You have been most gracious. Both of you."

There were more thank-yous and smiles. Then she found herself stumbling down the front hallway, towards a sunlit drawing room. Just outside the open terrace doors, tuxedoed waiters stood at attention with trays full of wineglasses. Beyond, a small sea of guests mingled on the vast green lawn in between two high walls of hedge.

"Care for a glass of wine, miss?" one of the waiters asked.

But she had already seen him, and the sight of him rendered her silent.

Mr. Ramsey. Handsome, Egyptian. Nodding and listening attentively to the person who was speaking to him now. Every detail of his physical being, from his olive skin to his handsome jawline to the startling blueness of his eyes, flooded her with such overpowering memory she found herself speechless and breathless. This was not the vague ink drawing in the news clipping. This was the man from her dreams, in the flesh.

For now she could see the man a short distance from her had appeared not just in her more recent nightmares, but in another dream as well, a dream that had stayed with her throughout her life, a dream which had formed the basis of her novel *The Wrath of Anubis*.

This was the man with whom she'd walked the streets of some vague ancient city. She was absolutely sure of it! The man whose face and bearing she'd never been able to recall once she was awake; whose presence had always been an awareness and little else. This was the man who had provided her with common garb and requested she view her own kingdom and her people through the eyes of one of its ordinary citizens. And his living, breathing presence before her now was like a dab of watercolor bringing richness and color to something that had been but a pencil sketch seconds before.

It had not been just a dream. *He* had not been just a dream.

Again this question shook the earth on which she stood: How could she have dreamed about a living, breathing man she had never before met?

Unless she had met him, somehow, somewhere. Unless it was not a dream, but a memory. A memory of a man named . . .

"Ramses," Sibyl whispered.

His eyes met hers through the crowd.

At that very moment, an arm encircled her waist. Too close, too suddenly intimate. She almost cried out, but she was immediately startled by a blast of hot breath against her neck. With it came the stench of hard liquor.

"Do not move," the man whispered fiercely, giving each word terrible emphasis.

The man stood behind her now like an old lover who had come to surprise her. But he was causing a sharp pressure against the base of her spine. "That's a knife you feel," he said. "Sharp as a scalpel. Move one inch and I shall drive its sharp blade into your spine. You'll lose the use of your legs instantly. You might never walk again."

When she tried to speak, her breath came out in a series of weak gasps.

"Come with me," he whispered. "Don't make a scene. We are old friends. Act any differently and I'll cut you and flee this place before anyone can see you're bleeding to death. Walk."

He was deranged, this man, deranged and drunk. But the grip with which he held the knife against her seemed utterly, terribly confident. And so she obeyed. He walked behind her, with only an inch of space between his chest and her back, one arm looped around her shoulders to give the illusion of intimacy.

They couldn't walk a good distance like this. It was too strange, too conspicuous. But he guided her quickly in the opposite direction of the guests, into the deserted first-floor rooms behind them, past the procession of servants and waiters traveling up and down the basement stairs. With each step that took them farther away from people, from the comfort of the string music outside, her terror intensified, and he relaxed his pretentious pose.

Now he gripped the back of her neck. He steered her through an empty library, down a short hallway.

"Who are you?" she gasped. "What do you want?"

In what seemed like one motion, he'd thrown open the door to a small washroom and hurled her inside. By the time he'd drawn the door shut behind him, he'd brought the knife to her throat.

"Who are *you*, Sibyl Parker? Who are you really? And why do you seek to destroy my queen?"

*   *   *

Impossible.

He was seeing things, imagining things. Thoughts of Cleopatra had nagged him all day. The idea that she might make an appearance here, it was possible, of course. For what purpose, he had no idea.

But Samir and his men had been watching the ships, the ports. So far, no reports.

And that was all well and good.

But still, she was on his mind, as they now said, and always would be. And that's why he'd recognized her gaze in the face of the pale-skinned, golden-haired woman who had appeared just inside the terrace doors. Her eyes. The woman had Cleopatra's eyes. Her eyes before the resurrection. Before their color had changed. Brown and wide and expressive and full of intelligence and perception. And her poise. Perfect, upright, assured.

And then she was gone.

Lost behind a sudden shift in the sea of guests all around him. Nowhere to be seen on the terrace or the steps or the lawn on either side of him.

He had begun to rudely ignore the guests to whom he'd been speaking seconds before. He managed the most polite excuse he could and departed.

Where had she gone, this woman? Perhaps her resemblance to Cleopatra was a trick of the mind. But her sudden disappearance? This was cause for immediate suspicion.

A hand gripped his elbow.

Alex was standing next to him. "Don't go too far, old chum. We're toasting you both in just a few minutes. Fetch Julie if you can."

"Yes, of course, Alex. Thank you."

Yes, he would fetch Julie. But first, this strange vanishing woman with Cleopatra's eyes.

*   *   *

Fear moved through her in a wave.

What was there to fear in this small temple? A replica of the Pantheon, it seemed, with a gallery of Roman statues in alcoves lining its walls and a statue on a pedestal in the center. Was it Caesar? She could not tell. Her memories of his likeness were entirely lost to her now.

So where did this fear come from? Not dread. Not anxiety. But a sudden, violent paralysis throughout her entire body.

Sibyl Parker. From Sibyl Parker, this fear comes. Does she send it willfully? Or is that what she now feels? It was exhausting her to try to make sense of this.

"You are ill," Julie said.

No trace of malice in this statement, just a kind of gentle fascination.

Still gentle, this Julie. Why so gentle?

"How is it that you are so ill?" Julie asked her. "Haven't you healed completely from the fire?"

"I healed from the fire. The illness . . . it is in my mind."

"Whatever it is you want, I will give it to you, or I will have Ramses give it to you, on one condition."

"And so we negotiate now, you and I? The queen who fed Rome and the aristocrat who wept her way into the arms of a pharaoh?"

"Wear your cruelty however you like. It doesn't fit you anymore. You need help. You are here for help. And that is what I offer you now. *Help.*"

"But on one condition. So tell me, dear, sweet Julie Stratford, what is this condition?"

"You must stay away from Alex Savarell. Forever. You must leave him be entirely."

"Leave him be entirely," she whispered.

How unexpected, the anger she felt at this request. The rage she felt when she saw the fear in Julie's eyes, so similar to the fear in Teddy's when she'd left him a few hours ago.

"Leave him to forget me and our time together, you mean."

"Yes," Julie whispered, "that is exactly what I mean."

"And so he thinks of me often, does he? And this pains you? Do you love him still?"

"I never loved him. Not as a woman should love her husband."

"I see. So you think of me as poison, his thoughts of me as a corruption."

"He is tortured by memories of your madness."

"My madness?" she roared. "My *madness* born of your lover's guilt and arrogance! This is how you describe what was done to me? As a madness that comes from the fiber of my being and not his? Tell me, sweet, dear Julie, how did he offer you the elixir? Did he anoint you with oils? Did he uncap the bottle in some palatial bedchamber while musicians played? Did he explain to you its power and its defects? What you would gain, what you would lose? He did me no such kindness in the Cairo Museum. He rendered me a monster and abandoned me."

"He offered it to you two thousand years before. You—"

"And I refused it! I refused it and still he forced it upon me two thousand years later in death. In a death I chose!"

Why did Julie cry now? Was she simply afraid? Or was there such pain in Cleopatra's words, she too was overwhelmed by it. It seemed almost as if she felt guilty herself.

"He has said these very things, hasn't he?" Cleopatra asked. "He knows what he did. It tortures him, because he knows."

"He loved you," Julie whispered.

"Twice he abandoned me. Once as my empire fell, then again at the very moment when he brought me back to a life I did not want. May you, his new bride, be forever spared the kind of love he showed me."

"I am offering you what you want, but I cannot erase the centuries between you two. And neither can he."

"What I want ... ?" she muttered, circling past Julie. The answer to this question seemed to stare down at her on all sides, from the strange, stoic face of every statue in this shadowed tribute to the empire that had conquered her. "I want to know who these men are, these men of Rome. These men whom I should know. Even if these statues, these faces, are but caricatures, there should be some facet of them I recognize. Something of the cut of their chin or their hair or their armor. And yet my memories of them fade to nothing. More vanish with each journey of the sun across the sky. Caesar . . ." She turned towards the statue in the center of the floor. "Is this meant to be Caesar? I would not know. The man I lay with, the man with whom I bore a son, his face is lost to me. His smell. The sound of his voice. Lost to me. And my son. I am told I bore a son by him, a son who briefly became pharaoh after my death, and yet when I reach for any memory of him I swim in a great yawning blackness in my mind. His name, it is meaningless to me. And what next? What next will be consumed?"

"Caesarion," Julie whispered. "His name was Caesarion."

"Do you delight in this, Julie Stratford? Do you delight in my undoing?"

"Do you still wish to snap my neck solely because you know it will hurt Ramses?"

"That is not why I have traveled this far."

"Then I take no delight in your anguish, Cleopatra. And neither will he. But you have still not told me what you want."

"I want the elixir," she said bitterly. How she hated the sound of her own desperation. "He did not use enough when he brought me back. There were holes all over my body. I could see my own bones and it drove me mad. Now there are holes in my mind, my memory. They grow bigger each day. There is only one possible thing that can heal them. And it lies with him. And it is the only reason I would ever wish to lay eyes on him, or you, again."

Relief in Julie's eyes.

But just then Cleopatra felt a sharp pain in her throat.

Her hand flew to the spot where she'd felt it. Her fingers came away bloodless.

Julie advanced on her quickly.

Cleopatra recoiled, bracing herself against the statue's pedestal.

"Stand back," said Cleopatra. Impossible not to interpret this woman's advance as an attack. As Julie seizing upon a moment of weakness. But the woman's expression was one of absolute concern. Absolute pity. Somehow this only made the pain worse.

"Stand back," Cleopatra said again, but it was a tortured whisper. "Come no nearer to me."

"Pain," Julie said quietly. "You've told me of lost memories, but not pain. And it's pain you feel now. You have trouble walking. You have trouble standing upright. This is all a result of what's happening to your mind? It can't be."

Cleopatra couldn't answer, couldn't speak. To speculate on Julie's question was to return to those terrifying thoughts that had plagued her on the journey there: that her mind was no longer her own. That she had been invaded by one who was exploiting her current weakness. But that was too great a vulnerability to admit to in this moment. Not until she had the elixir in her hands.

She held to the pedestal, laboring for each breath.

Worse than the pain was this terror. This paralyzing fear that came once again in unstoppable waves. Where did it come from, this terror?

"Cleopatra," Julie whispered, her hand extended.

"Don't," she cried. "Please, don't . . . touch me. Stay back."

* * *

"Why do you torture her?" the man growled. "Why?"

Sibyl's urge was to shake her head, but if she moved an inch she might die in this tiny washroom, only steps from the pleasant chatter of aristocrats and servants. Nothing she had said so far calmed this man.

He gripped the back of her neck with one hand. With the other, he held the knife to her jugular vein.

Could she cry out for help before he managed to cut her throat? He was a doctor, he'd said, after he'd shoved her into this tiny space and there'd been no hope of an escape. A doctor who knew just where to cut and slash and cause instant death.

"Why do you do this to her? Why?"

"I don't know what you—"

"You torment her! You have entered her mind. How have you done it? Sorcery? Are you a witch?"

"I . . . Cleopatra. You speak of the woman who calls herself Cleopatra? You say *I* have entered *her* mind? But this is what I have been—"

"You sent her a message. You demanded to know where you could find her. Now you are here. You are stalking her. To what end?"

"For help. I thought we might help each other. But I had no idea she would be here. I came because . . . Oh, this is confused. This is so terribly confused. If you would just please calm yourself. If you would—"

"If I would just end you, then her visions would stop," he growled. "She would be healed of her pain. She would be healed of *you*."

A sharp knock on the door.

It surprised them both so badly she was terrified the mad doctor's hand might slip, allowing the knife to slice into her vein, where the blood pumped wildly thanks to a racing heart.

"Come back later, please," the doctor said, in a voice of maddening, terrifying calm.

Silence from outside.

Oh, how she wanted to cry out. She was desperate to cry out. Torture now to listen to whoever it was depart. To have been so close to rescue. But now the mad doctor's nose was inches from her own again, his grip on the knife steady.

"Now," he said, "give me one reason why I shouldn't—"

The door was ripped backwards. The knob fell off and landed on the floor at their feet with a loud thud. Sunlight flooded the tiny bathroom.

There stood Mr. Ramsey. Having torn the door off its hinges, he propped it against the wall behind him as if it were a small work of art. Then he grabbed the mad doctor by the back of his neck and dragged him into the hall with one hand.

Just as she felt relief, her legs went from under her. The mad doctor had been the only thing holding her upright.

The back of her head slammed to the dressing table. Pain thundered through her, followed by a great wave of darkness that seemed to swallow her whole.

*   *   *

"Cleopatra, please. Take my hand."

She stood there with her own hand out in warning. *Stay back.*

Julie was not surprised.

The queen's knees were bent, her eyes slits. She seemed to be fighting a terrible sense of disorientation.

But Julie could sense something else. A presence she could not identify. Many of them, in fact, and her heightened senses told her they were underfoot. Somehow underneath this very stone floor. This presence seemed to be coming to life at the sounds of commotion from above.

Suddenly, Cleopatra stood upright. But at just that moment, her body pitched forward as if she'd been struck from behind by a great and terrible force. She bucked forward, her arms flying out blindly in front of her. She seized the upraised arm of the statue.

At first, Julie thought it was Cleopatra's pure strength that had bent the statue's outstretched arm like a lever. But there was a great grinding sound from all around them suddenly. The floor beneath Julie began to move. Instinctively, she backed up and away. The stone that had been underfoot a split second before shifted dramatically to one side.

Impossible to make sense of it. It was all happening so fast. And Cleopatra was wholly unaware. Perhaps she couldn't distinguish between her spinning mind and the very real changes in her physical environment.

She rose upright suddenly.

"Stop!" Julie cried. "Cleopatra, *stop*!"

Did she even hear?

There was no telling, for just then, Cleopatra stepped forward and disappeared through the hole that had opened in the center of the floor.

*   *   *

She fell, expecting the plummet to end at each terrifying second. Clawing for the mud walls on either side of her. They were too far outside her reach.

Falling and falling, until she crashed into some sort of hard metal surface. No pain, but a kind of dazed bewilderment. Then just above her, scraping sounds and a metallic whine. The darkness became impenetrable as a lid was drawn shut over her.

She writhed and flailed, summoning all the strength she had. This was a coffin! She was trapped within a coffin! The lid was held down by a strength as formidable as her own.

Was she the only one who heard her screams? Was she the only one deafened by them? Trapped, confined, unable to move.

And then, motion.

This sarcophagus—what else could it be?—was being carried away, jostling from human movement. Her screams went with it, far beneath the earth, unheard, she feared, by all those except the ones who had just taken her captive.

*   *   *

Ramses had not expected this kind of fight out of the man. These wild punches, this desperate clawing.

Who was he? From where did his rage come? He was mad and stinking of alcohol. He made Ramses afraid of his own strength. If he wasn't careful, he would break bones or shatter the man's skull by mistake. And he didn't want that at all. But if the man didn't stop fighting!

His goal was to pin the rogue against the wall, thereby making his own strength known. Then the rageful drunk would have no choice but to answer his questions.

But it was not to be.

The man slipped free of his grip suddenly, his steps turning into a drunken dance as he ran away.

Someone was waiting for the man at the end of the hall.

She was tall and slender, and her skin was as black as a Nubian's. Her gold turban matched the color of her flowing dress, which was complemented by a shawl of yellow and gold brocade; its intermingling of color made it look like a form of armor. Her neckline was exposed, and despite the jagged gold plates that composed her necklace, this expanse of visible skin made her seem terribly vulnerable to the madman's careening approach. But she held her ground with utter confidence.

Would she move out of his way?

She did not.

Instead, just at the moment when the drunken fool seemed ready to plow her off her feet, she reached out and seized the back of his neck. He froze under her powerful grip.

For the first time, Ramses saw the woman's eyes. They were as blue as sapphires, as blue as his own.

The madman snarled, "Unhand me, you black—"

She slammed the side of his head into the wall.

The plaster dented.

He collapsed in a lifeless heap.

From behind her appeared two men, also black skinned, *and blue eyed*, both impeccably dressed.

"Remove him," she said. "Bind him if need be."

Silently, the men lifted the unconscious body. Together, they carried it away as if it were a rolled-up rug, offering Ramses polite nods as they passed. They headed in the opposite direction of the front hallway. Away from the party, away from the clamor of guests outside.

And then he was alone with her, this mysterious woman who had appeared out of nowhere, it seemed, who closed the distance between them with a warm and patient smile, as if the ugly business in this hallway were merely an inconvenience.

"Who are you?" he asked.

"Find your fiancée. They are preparing the champagne toast. You must not drink. Either of you. You understand me? You must not drink. I will take care of this one."

He'd forgotten about her, the golden-haired woman with Cleopatra's eyes, whose sudden disappearance had lured him into this little mess.

She was unconscious, slumped on the washroom floor.

"Go, Ramses the Great," said the black woman with the fiery blue eyes.

"Who are you and what have you done?" he asked.

"Only those who have come to do you harm will be harmed. Provided you and Miss Stratford do *not* drink the champagne. Do as I say. Find your fiancée. Now."

As if she had no doubt he would follow her command, she sank to her knees and turned her attention to the sleeping beauty on the bathroom floor. She drew her great shawl from around her back and wrapped the comatose woman's body on it. Then, without the slightest struggle, she picked up the golden-haired woman with both arms. An immortal, this powerful, black-skinned woman. There was no doubt in his mind. But . . .

The champagne. Do not drink the champagne . . .

He ran.

25

Julie ran.

She spotted Ramses on the stone terrace. Was he looking for her?

Yes!

When he saw her racing across the vast expanse of green on the other side of the hedge, he rushed down the steps, weaving between waiters passing out flutes of bubbling champagne to all the guests.

When he reached her, she fell against him, not just to seek comfort, but because it would allow her to whisper everything she'd seen. The wall of hedge concealed them from the party, but they were close enough that frightened talk might be overheard.

"She's here," Julie rasped. "Cleopatra. I took her to the temple to keep her away from Alex. She is sick. Something ails her. She thinks more of the elixir will cure it. She tried to explain, but there was some sort of trap. Ramses, the floor itself, it opened and swallowed her, and I could hear movement in the tunnel below. Someone took her, Ramses."

"We must end this gathering at once," Ramses said. "And we must do so without creating a panic."

"What is happening, Ramses?"

Memory struck. A memory only moments old. That strange,

brittle woman, Jeneva Worth, and her husband, Callum, asking for a tour, not just of the grounds, but of the very temple from which Cleopatra had just been abducted.

"Julie, come with me. I will explain everything as I—"

"*There you are!*" Alex Savarell shouted. He'd just appeared around the side of the hedge, and now he was bounding towards them with drunken glee.

"Do not drink," Ramses whispered fiercely. "Do not drink the champagne. Only pretend to drink. Don't let a drop of it touch your lips. Nod to indicate that you understand."

She nodded. And so there was more to this, she realized, more to this strange plot into which Cleopatra had stumbled, and Ramses was aware of it, and the only choice was to follow his instructions.

From behind, Alex steered them towards the lawn.

"We've been looking all over for you two," he said, sounding as if he had already imbibed a great deal. "I've been preparing this toast for weeks now. Force me to wait another moment and I'll suffer an attack of nerves all the wine in Yorkshire won't cure."

Seconds later, Alex had positioned them at the base of the terrace steps.

The crowd turned to face them. And there in front, Jeneva Worth and her husband, Callum. Impossible to believe they weren't connected to what she had just witnessed inside the temple. How else to explain their strange, overly detailed request for a tour of that very place? Now their expressions were unreadable, thanks to the sunglasses they wore. But they were certainly staring in her direction. Were they noting the little smudges of dirt from the temple on her dress?

As he spoke, Alex's gentle voice carried across the quiet lawn, occasionally drowned out by the breeze moving through the trees overhead.

It seemed a perfectly respectful toast, full of gracious, humble sentiments designed to tell the group before them that he and his entire family had truly moved on, that all those present should accept Mr. Reginald Ramsey and Julie as destined for each other. But Julie heard only every few words of it, and so it came as a surprise when Alex said, "And so I ask you now to lift your glasses in celebration of Mr. Reginald Ramsey and his bride-to-be, Miss Julie Stratford."

All of the guests complied.

She only pretended to take a sip, just as Ramses had instructed. But what could this mean?

She looked from glass to glass to glass to glass, searching for a mysterious cloud or flecks of some strange particle. But she saw only sparkling fluid in each.

There was a smattering of applause, some polite laughter, a few murmurs about what a lovely champagne it was.

Jeneva Worth dabbed the side of her mouth with a napkin. Then she went suddenly and conspicuously still. The sight of something on the terrace behind Julie had paralyzed the woman with fright.

She reached up and removed her glasses. Julie saw the woman's eyes were as blue as her own. Then she gripped her husband's wrist, whispered something to him that caused him to also stare past Julie.

He too removed his sunglasses. His eyes were also startlingly blue.

Finally, Julie looked over her shoulder at whatever had captured their attention.

She was one of the most beautiful women Julie had ever seen, and she was emerging slowly through the terrace doors. Her gold turban glinted in the sunlight, and she lifted her chin gradually as she crossed the empty stone terrace, until her features were visible to everyone on the western lawn who had noticed her arrival. Her skin was dark as ebony, her eyes as blue as an immortal's, and the gaze she leveled on the crowd before her seemed as steady and immutable as the Sphinx.

Many had noticed her arrival, but were trying not to openly stare. This was not the case with Jeneva and Callum Worth. Or with the giant bearded man she'd seen them mingling with earlier. Or with several other guests, who had noticed the arrival of this beautiful black woman with an evident horror that caused their jaws to gape and their hands to tremble. Each of these terrified guests wore sunglasses they now removed. Each revealed the crystalline-blue eyes of an immortal.

Ramses seemed less surprised by this woman's entrance than Julie was, but he stared up at her now, as well. He recognized the importance of her quiet arrival.

Most of the guests had gone back to chitchat.

But Julie felt as if every muscle in her body had coiled.

Do not drink, Ramses had told her. *Only pretend to drink.*

And now . . .

There was a soft thud against the grass a few paces away. Jeneva had dropped her champagne flute. She stared down at it as if it were a serpent preparing to strike.

"The queen," Callum Worth whispered.

And then Jeneva hit the grass knees first. The blue drained from her eyes, replaced by what at first appeared to be a fiery shade of red, then her eyes became empty, black sockets.

When Callum Worth reached for his wife's shoulder, he saw that his own hand was withering before his very eyes, as if every ounce of blood and every drop of water had been sucked from his flesh in one swift and silent instant.

Jeneva's hands appeared exactly the same. But this didn't stop her from reaching out for Ramses and Julie even as her jaw fell away from her face and turned to a drift of ash that danced gracefully on the cool breeze.

And then the screams began, piercing, terrible screams.

For it was happening to all of them. All of the terrified immortals who had removed their sunglasses at the sight of the magnificent woman now standing proudly on the empty terrace, staring down at all of them like a monarch preparing to address her subjects. Only her address was silent, Julie realized, and it unfolded with terrible and destructive speed.

All over the lawn, the immortals had begun to wither and decompose, creating little pockets of chaos among the guests. Here a withering arm reached out for nothing; there a desiccated torso collapsed onto a pair of suddenly hollow legs, both becoming clouds of swirling ash.

Chairs and tables were overturned as everyone raced to make an escape.

When a hand seized the back of her dress, Julie screamed.

It was the stately black woman, the architect of this, Julie was sure.

"Come with me," she said. "Both of you."

She held Ramses in a similar grip and pulled them both backwards up the steps as chaos reigned.

"Who are you?" Ramses demanded. He was masking dread with fury.

"I am your queen," the woman answered.

"I answer to no queen."

"Perhaps not," the woman answered. "But you still have one."

26

Inside the house, servants fled down the front hallway.

The woman led them through empty rooms, then out a side door and across a terrace much smaller than the western one. Then they were hurrying through a shady, manicured garden towards a wide gate that stood open across the entrance to the staff road.

Beyond, two gleaming motorcars sat parked. Standing next to each one, a tall black man in a beige suit and tie. Both cars were Unic Landaulettes, each with a pair of backseats that faced each other.

"We can't just leave!" Julie finally cried.

"Why not?" the woman answered. "Everyone else is."

"But Samir and Alex and—"

"No mortals have been harmed by what I've done."

"We cannot abandon our mortal friends to this panic," said Ramses.

"I sent a message!" the woman replied. She whirled on them. Her eyes blazed with anger. "I destroyed those who came to abduct your fiancée. In this way, I have sent a message to the one who sent these lackeys. And the message is this. I am awake, I walk, and I know of his evil designs. These actions of mine call for your gratitude, Ramses the Great, not your disapproval."

Whoever she was, this self-proclaimed queen, she seemed coolly satisfied by their reactions to her shocking words. And she spoke his former title with just enough disregard to indicate she would not be cowed by it.

"We have much to say to one another," she said, more quietly. "And we will do so once there is safe distance between us and this place."

She started for the car parked in front.

Her tall servant continued to hold open the back door to the one parked just behind it.

"That's not enough," Ramses said firmly.

"Enough for what?" she asked.

"Enough for us to feel like anything other than your captives. Captives to whatever poison you used on those guests."

"If I wished to poison you, I would have done so already."

An excellent point, Julie thought. And she now feared his pride might get in the way of whatever revelations this mysterious woman held in store.

They were staring at each other, Ramses and this woman, this queen. Each assessing the other's strength and resolve, it seemed. Two monarchs establishing ground. Would it fall to Julie to prevent an all-out war between them?

"You do not understand the forces that wish to do you harm," the woman said. "You were not even aware of them before now. Make no mistake. I am not one of them." She held his gaze. "I am Bektaten," she said, "queen of Shaktanu, a land that perished before your Egypt was born."

With that, her other servant opened the back door to the first car and she stepped inside. As she did so, Julie glimpsed a beautiful, golden-haired woman spread across one of the car's facing backseats, wrapped in some sort of blanket or shawl.

She couldn't just be sleeping. She must be unconscious.

Bektaten. Shaktanu. Julie could see that Ramses was mystified. He stood there staring forward, clearly in the grip of a storm of questions.

"Come, Ramses," Julie said, pulling him towards the other car. "Come. We have no choice."

Part 3

27

Cornwall

She had yet to wake, this golden-haired woman who walked with the same poise as Cleopatra, so Julie had volunteered to prepare her for bed.

How suspicious and apprehensive Ramses had been as he watched the man called Aktamu carry this strange woman in his arms across the swaying rope bridge! What if the poor mortal woman woke suddenly? What if she saw the perilous drop to the crashing surf and let out a scream that startled her caretaker so badly he dropped her by mistake?

When in all his long existence had he ever stood by silent, and helpless, watching the actions of another male immortal, whom he could not control?

Nothing of the kind took place, and now they were all safely inside this immense castle with its soaring walls and smooth floors of polished stone and its roaring fire and its lustrous draperies.

The furnishings in the great hall were new and suitably grand; there were great expanses of Oriental rugs, their colors muted so as not to compete with the purple and gold that defined the drapes and upholstery throughout. Each chair gathered around the massive card table resembled a kind of throne with a carved wood frame and thick, tufted cushions. The iron chandeliers overhead had been wired with electric replicas of candles, their glow steady and insistent. It was Norman, this castle. The arches in the windows and doorways were rounded and subtle. Ramses preferred it to the jagged severity of the Gothic, a style with which so much of this country remained utterly enthralled.

The man called Enamon lit some of the torches in the hallways. And so it seemed the castle had some corners electrical wires did not yet reach.

They were alone now, he and this queen, her turban like a crown. And in her bearing and in the fluid and patient way with which she moved about the great hall, her demeanor, that of a person who might have come into the world long before his own time, he sensed her age, sensed her deep reserve of control.

She studied him silently, and without any suspicion or disdain that he could see.

"You are my great folly, Ramses the Damned," she said finally. "Do you realize this?"

"How so?"

"That I did not see you. That I did not see the touch of an immortal in Egypt's long history."

"It was not every ruler who called me into service. And there was only one with whom I shared my story."

"Which one is this?" she asked, approaching him.

An astonishing feeling, the presence of one who could act as an authority over him—who outmatched him in experience, wisdom, and life. Indeed, she was the elixir's creator; she must be. For he could feel the quiet strength of her many years.

How would she react, this queen, when he told her what he'd done to Cleopatra? Would she consider it an unconscionable crime? Were they members of a special race of beings, he and this woman? Did she consider herself the arbiter of their laws?

"In time, Queen Bektaten of Shaktanu," he said. "I may tell you all you want to know, in time." *And she can destroy you with that potion of hers, the potion that infected those blue-eyed immortals you saw destroyed all around you.*

He took a deep breath, and tried to wipe the slightest expression of dread from his face.

She furrowed her brow a little. Mild disappointment in her expression, but not anger.

Just then, Julie returned. She took up a post next to him as if she meant to physically guard him. It was a loving gesture, this protectiveness, and under different circumstances he would have taken her in his arms to show his gratitude.

"The man," Ramses said. "The drunken one who attacked her. Where is he?"

Bektaten walked to the open window and stared out at the sea. "You know this man?"

"I believe so," he answered. "I believe he is a doctor named Theodore Dreycliff."

"A doctor," she whispered. Surely she did not find the word unfamiliar, but she exercised care in whispering it, as if she found it exotic. "And how did you come to know him?"

When neither Ramses nor Julie answered, she turned and gave them a long, steady look. "I see," she finally said. "And so we have yet to establish trust."

"Is that not what we have come here to do?" Ramses said. "Establish trust?"

"Let us begin to do it, then," Bektaten said. "I killed this man. The blow you saw me give him, he did not survive it. It was not my intention to end his life. I believe it was not your intention either, for the blows you threw at him were cautious and reserved. Am I correct in this?"

"You are," he answered. "I wanted only to prevent him from harming the woman—"

"Sibyl Parker," Julie whispered.

"How do you know her name?" Ramses asked.

"She's an American, a novelist," Julie said. "She writes popular romances." Julie eyed Bektaten warily. "My father thought her very clever and clipped an article written about her in the *Daily*

Herald. It's still in his study." Again, Julie looked uneasily at the queen.

Another long, uncomfortable silence passed, filled only by the pounding of the surf against the cliffs outside.

"This will not serve us," Bektaten finally said. "This suspicion, this concealment of our histories."

"I agree," said Ramses. "May you take the lead here just as you have taken the lead in so much of what has occurred today."

"Ramses, please," Julie whispered, caution in her tone.

"You fear me, Julie Stratford," Bektaten said.

"I fear your poison," Julie answered quietly.

"This was not my intention, to fill you with this fear," she answered. "The plot that I disrupted today, Julie Stratford, was to have seen you placed in a pit with trained fighting dogs who had been given a version of the elixir. They were to be starved, these dogs, so that they would set upon you again and again with ravenous hunger and terrible strength."

Ramses felt his heart beating silently in his head. *Who would do this to his beloved Julie?* He felt a tremor pass through his body, a mounting rage.

"To what end?" Julie asked innocently. "What have I done to make enemies such as these?"

"It was to force your beloved king to reveal the formula for the pure elixir, the one that has made us all what we are, and what we forever shall be."

"Of whose design was this plot?" Ramses could keep silent no more. "Who are these possessors of a corrupted elixir?"

"Come," Bektaten said quietly. "To the tower. To my library. Allow me to once again take the lead, as you so put it."

28

She was being chased and giving chase.

The labyrinth through which she ran was occasionally pierced by great shafts of sunlight that came from odd angles. She pursued the raven-haired woman from her dreams; she chased the woman as she rounded corners and slipped down alleyways.

Then she became the raven-haired woman.

She was no longer Sibyl.

She was being chased by Sibyl.

It repeated again and again, this pattern, with sinuous regularity, a continuous dance of pursuing and being pursued. And all of it was far more vivid than a dream, and much more substantial than the fleeting visions that had plagued her since she'd started her journey.

A child called out to her now.

She didn't recognize the voice, couldn't tell if it was a boy or a girl. *Mitera, Mitera, Mitera,* the child called. Distant, but urgent. Echoing through the strange and endless alleyways and tunnels through which she ran. There were glimpses of blue sky overhead.

She was not deep beneath the earth. She was in a city.

Alexandria, a woman's voice said.

Suddenly she stood at the edge of a slender canal that cut between great sandstone walls. Its banks were paved. Sunlight poured down through the break overhead, washing the rippling water in gold. And there she was, the raven-haired woman she had only caught glimpses of before now. Perfectly clear, practically an arm's length away on the other side of the canal. She wore a modern dress, deep blue, a lustrous shade, and she gazed back at Sibyl with as much astonishment as Sibyl felt.

Are you the one who took me? The woman's voice echoed. Her lips did not move, but the pain in these words swam in her expression, in her blazing blue eyes.

It was she. It had to be. The woman who called herself Cleopatra. And they were together now, for the first time, but in some place that was neither dream nor hallucination. But was it truly Alexandria, or some vague recollection of it, sanded free of detail, rendered immutable and stark?

No, I did not take you. I would never mistreat you.

Then leave me. Then leave my mind.

I cannot. You have entered my mind just as I have entered yours.

The voice. The voice again. The child's voice calling. The raven-haired woman turned and looked over her shoulder. But Sibyl felt as if the voice was coming from behind her as well. *Mitera, Mitera, Mitera.* It was Greek, this word. *Mother,* the child's voice called over and over again. *Mother.*

Where do you hide him? Where do you hide my memories of him?

I don't understand. I seek to find you. From you, I would hide nothing.

The woman spun to face her, as if astonished by these words.

Something in the rippling water caught her attention.

She let out a terrible scream.

When Sibyl looked down, she saw that her reflection was not her own but that of the woman at whom she'd been staring only seconds before.

29

When Sibyl jerked awake, a tall handsome man with black skin rose from the chair next to her bed. He had an elegance about him. He extended one graceful hand as if he thought she might leap from the covers.

She felt no such urge. The bed in which she found herself was a small sea of luxury. Soft sheets kissed her bare legs. Her head rested on a veritable field of soft pillows. All of it was so soothing she had no desire to sit upright. Not yet.

But when she realized that someone had undressed her down to her undergarments, she stiffened. Even the corset had been removed, all without waking her. Had this strange seductive man done this?

The thought embarrassed her into a deeper silence.

"It was a woman who prepared you for bed," the man said, his voice a low, comforting rumble. He was incredibly tall, black skinned, with a sweet, boyish face. "A woman, I assure you. Your modesty was protected."

She could only nod in response to this.

Gone was the dream. The strange vision of Alexandria. The sight of her reflection replaced with that of another.

Now there was just this bedroom, with its high stone walls and iron chandelier filled with flickering candles. No, they were electric, these candles. And for some reason this comforted her, to still be connected to the modern world even amidst these austere walls and the thundering surf outside and the roaring fireplace across from the foot of the bed.

It was a windswept coastline she'd been brought to.

How far was this place from Yorkshire?

She didn't know the map of England well enough to even guess. But it was a warm place and it had been cared for and the man near to her showed no malice or aggression. All of these things calmed her.

"A man," she said. "A man tried to kill me."

"You are safe. This man, you need not think of him now. He died due to his own rash behavior. He cannot harm you ever again."

From a crystal pitcher on the nightstand he poured her a glass of water, gestured for her to drink. Of course, it could be poison. Of course, this man could be an abductor far more fearsome than the mad drunk who had attacked her at the party. But she was not confined or restrained, and he was kind, this man. Very gentle and kind and possessed of a quiet strength for which she did not have a name.

"I am Aktamu," the man said.

Such a strange name. She had never come upon this name in all of her dreams or studies.

He held her gaze in the silence that followed, and she realized he was asking for her name without demanding it of her.

"My name is Sibyl Parker," she said. "And I would like very much to know where I am."

"I will tell them you are awake," he said. "I'm sure you will all have much to tell each other."

She nodded, even though it wasn't possible for her to know what this meant, who *they* were, or how she had come to be in this place.

At least it was beautiful, she thought.

At least she could hear the sea.

She felt movement on the blanket next to her and cried out. But then she found herself staring into the watchful gaze of a slinky gray cat. The gentle creature approached with careful steps and then sprawled out across her chest as if to comfort her.

This was no ordinary creature, she was sure. Sibyl began to stroke its fur anyway, and watched as it gently closed its blue eyes with a drowsiness that appeared almost human.

30

Havilland Park

Her scream was loud enough to awaken a pack of dogs nearby.

She could hear them howling, somewhere out there, somewhere beyond where she was now confined. Her reflection in the canal's water had vanished and been replaced by another. By Sibyl Parker. But were the woman's words true? Did she truly seek to hide nothing, to steal nothing? Was she as tortured by their connection as Cleopatra was?

A confusing jumble, these thoughts, none of them strong enough to distract her from the cold stone under her back, the pebbles and rocks digging into her flesh, and the damp, earthy smell of the cell in which she now found herself.

Her eyes needed no time to adjust to the darkness. For that she could thank Ramses and his elixir.

The grooves in the stone floor were clear, as was the outline of a formidable door made of some kind of metal. Also in this dark place, the lingering stink of some animal. Had the creatures howling somewhere nearby been housed inside this cell at some point?

A curse in this moment, these heightened senses. She would have savored a second or two of disorientation. Another few minutes of feeling as if her dream of Alexandria and the woman named Sibyl Parker were slowly falling from her like a shroud.

Gone was Alexandria. The sense of pursuing and being pursued through a vague impression of its backstreets and canals.

Gone was the terrifying sight of Sibyl Parker's reflection where her own should have been. Gone was the sound of a young boy's voice calling out to her again and again in Greek. *Mother, Mother, Mother.*

And now . . .

There was a terrible scraping sound. Similar to the sound her captors had made when they closed the lid over the coffin that brought her here.

Dim orange light fell in a small rectangle across the floor at her bare feet.

Through the sudden opening in the metal door, she saw three faces. She did not recognize a one. The man in the middle had cascades of black curls and exquisitely balanced features. To his left, a man who looked much older, with a pinched, sour expression and two wings of wiry gray and white hair with which one might scrub pots. To his right, a woman with a great mane of blonde hair who bore no resemblance to the other two. Immortals, all of them, and they studied her coldly, as a scientist might a failed experiment.

"It is not her," the man in the middle said, a quiver of rage in his voice.

"Master," the older one began. "I am so very sorry, but you—"

"Go," the man in the middle said.

"In the tunnel, they acted too soon and now with everything that's—"

"*Go!*" the handsome man roared.

The servant, or whoever he was, complied, and the woman went with him.

In the tunnel, they acted too soon. She repeated these words in her mind. And so the trap into which she'd fallen had not been meant for her. But still they had confined her. Unwanted yet imprisoned. *It is not her,* the man had said. So the trap had been set for a woman.

As she had fallen, she'd been sure it was Julie who had done it, who made the floor in the temple vanish from underfoot. That all of it had been a terrible ruse; Julie Stratford's sweetness, her repeated statements that she desired only to help. But she remembered now the startled look on Julie's face, the way she'd flung her arm out to stop Cleopatra from teetering and then falling through the hole.

It is not her . . .

Julie Stratford hadn't set the trap. These immortals had set the trap for Julie Stratford.

But why?

And more important, would she herself now be released?

Whoever these immortals were, better were her chances of escape if they didn't learn her identity.

The slat closed with a terrible grinding sound.

The darkness closed around her. She blessed it. It gave her time to think and breathe.

Her heightened senses couldn't detect departing footsteps. And so the door was incredibly thick, incredibly heavy. Designed to hold back the strength of one like herself.

But did they know she was immortal? Had they peeled back her eyelids while she'd been lost in her dream?

No telling . . .

The slat opened again. She jumped.

"Look at me," the man said.

She turned her face to the wall.

"Look at me!"

She refused.

"Did you hear those hounds? Do you hear the dogs, still barking at the sound of how you cried out? Obey me or I will set them loose upon you, right here in this cell."

"Then I will tear them limb from limb with my bare hands," she cried. It was the contempt in the man's voice that caused her to snap. And in doing so, she'd turned her face to the light and given him a perfect look at her blue eyes. A terrible mistake. For now he gazed at her with a wondrous expression. His smile looked triumphant.

Too late, she turned her face to the wall again.

"And so our trap may yield the wrong woman, but it has snared another immortal," the man said. "This is interesting. This is most interesting."

"Bring me your dogs and I shall do what I can to deepen their interest in me as well."

"They are as strong as you are. It should make for quite a spectacle. Do you fancy yourself a Roman gladiator? I watched many of them work in the Colosseum. You lack their build."

"They lacked my sharp eye."

He laughed.

But still, the thought of immortal, powerfully strong hounds descending upon her in this cell, it chilled her. But she couldn't display this feeling. Not to this strange being. This strange male who had sought to place Julie Stratford in this very cell, perhaps so he could menace her in just this way.

But he has the elixir! He must!

And how awful the choice seemed now. How impossible. To charm the cure to her ailment from this reluctant, vile captor, or to seek her escape so she might confront Ramses once more.

If she could get free, would Julie take pity on her as she had in that temple turned trap? Would this be enough to convince Ramses to give her another dose?

Mustn't show any evidence of this struggle to her captor. But once she'd done it, she realized turning her face back to the wall did that very thing.

"I must say," the man said, "even though your arrival here is most unexpected, you do look remarkably familiar. Yours is a face I've seen before, long before. . . ."

And then, as if to torture her with these words, he closed the slat with a great scrape she could feel in her bones. And outside, somewhere on the grounds of this place, his dogs continued to howl.

31

Cornwall

Shaktanu...

Ramses had heard the name before. In the time when he had ruled as king, a name that conjured legends and fantasy and a naïve belief in a more perfect, golden age. A time free of warfare and strife, brought down by the inexplicable fury of remote gods. Shaktanu, an African kingdom, a fantasy connected with remote jungles now covering innumerable rumors, jungles from which ivory and gold and jewels and slaves had once come.

Not so naïve, this belief, he now realized.

As Bektaten spoke of its lands, of its networks of ships that had sailed the world, of temples whose ruins had yet to be discovered and might never be, of a world lost to the plague and tribal warfare that succeeded its fall, it was clear she told only the truth. Indeed, she had settled into her role as historian, archivist, and storyteller with absolute ease, and Ramses now found himself entirely under her spell. If her wide-eyed gaze was any indication, Julie had fallen under the queen's spell as well.

Shaktanu.

When he had first awakened in this century, he hadn't noted the absence of this kingdom's name from any of the history books he'd devoured, even the popular mythologies of ancient lost kingdoms. But he was keenly aware of it now.

And this woman before him had been queen of Shaktanu; and the man who had sought to abduct Julie that afternoon, its prime minister.

He should have known.

This thought returned to him again and again as she spoke, as she showed them her leather-bound journals written entirely in ancient, unrecognizable script. Like no language he had ever seen, this script. Pre-scribal. Closer to the Roman alphabet than hieroglyphs, but with symbols interspersed that seemed almost like pictograms. She called these journals the *Shaktanis,* even though they also chronicled her life in the thousands of years since that kingdom's fall.

I should have known, he thought again.

He should have known that something as magical and momentous as the elixir could not have been dashed together by a madwoman living in a cave. Had this been naïve of him or just reckless? But by Bektaten's own admission, the elixir's discovery had, in fact, been an accident. She had not even been searching for the secret to eternal life, but for tonics and cures for everyday ailments. And so perhaps he should forgive himself his blindness, just as she sought to forgive herself for not seeing his immortal wisdom as it had guided so many rulers of Egypt.

But her discovery of him had been no accident.

And she had spared his life, even though she had the power to destroy him.

Before the expanse of her history, he felt a great humility. And with this humility came relief, for he was no longer the lone ancient among newly made immortals.

But had she brought him here to stand trial?

If so, why was she being so generous with her story?

Why was she taking great pains to care for this Sibyl Parker?

Perhaps, for now, she sought only to educate him and be educated in return.

But would all that change when she learned he had used her creation to awaken Cleopatra?

Footsteps startled all three of them. It was the one she called Aktamu, the one with the young face.

"She is awake," he said. "Sibyl Parker is awake."

"Then we will go to her," Bektaten said.

*   *   *

In a great four-poster bed, Sibyl Parker lay propped up on a mountain of pillows. As Ramses approached, her face seemed to dance in the flickering light from the fire. He was relieved to see her pale neck free of wounds. Curled next to the twin lumps of her feet was a slender gray cat who watched his approach with unnerving intensity.

Even though he had entered this bedchamber with Bektaten and Julie at his side, Sibyl seemed to see only him. And in her expression, he saw the same recognition he felt when he'd looked upon her across the crowded party.

Aktamu and Enamon stood silently in the far corner, closest to the window, and Bektaten next to the fireplace, as still as a statue, as if she thought a safe remove from all of them would allow her to absorb whatever strange story Sibyl Parker had brought to her castle.

"You saved me," Sibyl whispered. "You saved me from that terrible man."

"Are you well, Sibyl Parker?" Ramses asked. "Are you unharmed?"

"How do you know my name? Do you recognize me as well?"

Before he could answer, Julie stepped forward and said, "It was I who recognized you. I know your books quite well. My father, Lawrence Stratford, enjoyed them."

"And now I have thoroughly ruined your engagement party." Tears filled Sibyl's eyes. Tears and a piteous expression made worse by exhaustion, he was sure. "I hope you can forgive me."

"No, no." Julie rounded the foot of the bed, then sat down

on the opposite side of it so she could take Sibyl's hand in hers. "Nothing of the kind."

"She speaks the truth," Ramses said. "You were but one of several extraordinary and unexpected guests."

"Well, that is a most polite way of putting it. I thank you. But that man. That crazy, drunken man—"

"You have nothing more to fear from him." The note of finality in his voice brought about a long silence. "Now, please, Miss Parker. You must tell us what brought you all this way. You are American, are you not? Your accent."

Ramses said nothing of the woman's mysterious demeanor, nothing of her expression so suggestive of the long-lost Cleopatra, the Cleopatra who was as dead as ever now. He said nothing of the bizarre effect upon him of this woman's manner and voice.

Sibyl seemed to realize for the first time that Julie held one of her hands in between her own, and this made her smile. "Oh, Lord. Where do I begin?" Sibyl whispered.

"Wherever you would like," Julie said, "for we are in no great hurry."

"This is most kind. You are most kind. It is like a dream that you are all being so kind. You see, most of my life I've been a woman of distinct and powerful dreams. Dreams of Egypt, mostly . . . Oh, I'm afraid it makes so little sense, what I've been through."

Ramses smiled. "You have come to the right place, Miss Parker. We are experts in that which does not make very much sense."

"Good," she said, through her gentle laughter and her tears. "Good."

Julie filled Sibyl's water glass and pressed it into the woman's trembling hand.

After she drank, she began again.

"As I told you, all my life I've experienced vivid dreams of Egypt. But there was one in particular which recurred again and again. I could always remember only fragments of it when

I awoke, and those fragments felt more like an awareness, or a knowledge of what had taken place, rather than an actual recollection. But in this one dream in particular, I am aware that I am a queen. And you, Mr. Ramsey, or a man who looks exactly like you, you are my guardian. And I am also aware in this dream that you are immortal somehow.

"One night, you arrive at my chambers carrying the clothes of a common woman, and you ask me to dress in them so that we may walk through my kingdom. So that I may view my people through a different pair of eyes. A commoner's eyes. Compassionate, sympathetic eyes. And I obey. Because it is you, my immortal counselor, who has made the request, I obey. And together, we make this journey on foot.

"But when I would awake from this dream, I would remember almost nothing of the city we've walked through, and nothing of your face. Only the sense that I felt nothing for you but love and respect and awe. I have written and published an entire novel inspired by this dream, you understand? And then when I saw you at the party today, I realized this man, my immortal guide, was you.

"You see, I crossed an ocean because you've appeared in other dreams of mine. More recent dreams. *Terrible* dreams. And then someone sent me a news clipping with your picture in it, and there you were. But only when I laid eyes upon you in the flesh for the first time did I realize you were the missing piece from a dream that has been with me my entire life. So I ask you now, how can this be? And is it possible that it was more than a dream?"

Ramses reflected. If they continued on this path, if his suspicions about what had brought Sibyl Parker here were correct, he would soon have no choice but to reveal his great crime to Bektaten. But Julie's look implored him to answer Sibyl's question as honestly as he could.

"Yes, it is far more than a dream, Sibyl Parker. The city was Alexandria. I was, indeed, your immortal counselor. And you were Cleopatra."

Like a thunderbolt this news hit her. She tightened her grip on Julie's hand. It seemed she might lose her tenuous hold on the moment, on this place, and slip into dreams so deep she might never come back from them. But she struggled to concentrate, to ignore a vast undiscovered country of memories and sensations and voices.

"It is not a dream," he said. "It is a memory. A memory from a former life."

"And from your former life?" Sibyl whispered.

"No," he answered. "No, from my continuing life, for I am immortal, and I have lived for thousands of years. And so what you experienced today at the party, it was an experience without compare."

"How do you mean?" Sibyl asked.

"You, for the first time, looked upon someone you had known in a past life. And not a reincarnated version of the person, but the person himself. In the flesh. And this experience by itself was powerful enough to make your vague dream into a coherent memory."

"You. You are from a . . . past life?"

"Yes."

Sibyl shook her head gently and Julie pressed one palm to her forehead to comfort her. Again it seemed Sibyl might lose her hold on the moment, and that the long shadowy and undiscovered country would claim her. But against the pull of a dark wonderland, she clung to a purpose. *To live now, to live and think and know now.*

For a while, no one spoke, and there was only the rumbling of the sea.

A sense of resignation quieted Ramses. He did not look back over his shoulder at Bektaten, to see how the great queen responded to this new intelligence. No one in this room understood better than Ramses the prerogatives of ancient monarchs, the divine authority that had surrounded them, and the swiftness with which they might judge or act. *But I too am a monarch,* he thought, *born and bred a monarch, born and bred with authority, and I must protect not only myself but my beloved Julie. Whatever is to come, I will be Ramses as I have always been.*

"These other dreams," Julie finally said, "the more recent ones, the ones in which you also saw Ramses. Describe them to us."

"In the first one, it was as if I were coming out of darkness, out of death itself. I saw you standing over me, and when I reached for you, my hands, they were a skeleton's hands, and you were terrified."

"My God," Julie whispered. "The Cairo Museum. Almost exactly as it happened."

"In another, there were two great trains, bearing down on me out of darkness, and then fire. Terrible fire everywhere. And then, in another . . ." Tears spilled from her eyes now, but she still bravely tried to recall every detail. "I took life. My hands. I closed my hands around a woman's throat and I took her life. It was as if I did not know what I was doing. And the very fact that life could be taken by my bare hands, it was a source of great confusion. . . ." And then it became too much for her, and she shook her head as if to banish these thoughts.

"It's exactly as I suspected," Julie said.

She looked to Ramses, but he could not speak.

Guilt paralyzed him, filled his throat with something that felt like cloth, for here it was again, another consequence of the crime he'd committed in the Cairo Museum, the crime against life and death, against nature, against fate. They were ceaseless, the repercussions of this terrible event, and now this poor mortal woman had been laid low by it, and his terrible actions were being exposed to a queen whose existence had been entirely unknown to him before this day. He could think of nothing to say in this moment, nothing to do besides take Sibyl's other hand in an effort to comfort her. The face he revealed to Julie was strong, confident, a monarch's mask for the turmoil within.

Julie had slipped one arm around the woman's shoulders, and

brought Sibyl Parker's head to her breast. Tenderly Julie supported her even as she rested amidst these silken bed pillows and luxurious covers.

"Our Cleopatra of the Cairo Museum is ill," Julie explained. "In the temple today she could barely stand upright. She had difficulty walking. Her skin was shining and her eyes too vibrant. She bore all the marks of one who had consumed the elixir. The vitality, the physical health. But there was an illness within her. A deep illness in her mind, she said. And at the very moment when you, Sibyl, were assaulted by that awful man, it was as if she experienced the assault as well. Every blow. There is a connection between you two, a vital connection that was awakened when our Cleopatra opened her eyes in the Cairo Museum."

"When I awakened her," Ramses said, "which I never should have done." He gave a deep sigh, his eyes moving over the ceiling. "These dreams you had, Sibyl Parker," he said. "These nightmares, they were all connected to this newly arisen Cleopatra as she roamed Cairo only months ago. The two of you have been connected since she woke."

He shook his head, all Julie's talk of soulless clones returning to him, deepening his sense of horror for what he had done.

"Because you, Sibyl, are Cleopatra reborn," Julie said excitedly. "You're the vessel for her true spirit."

"We don't know this, Julie," Ramses said. "It may be true, but maybe it is not true. You speak of things no one can know for certain." Such anguish. What had possessed him as he had stood there in the museum with the vial of the elixir in his hand? He'd been a man then in the most tragic sense of the word, a fumbling and imperfect human being, struggling with a god's power and a lover's broken heart.

"We don't know this?" Julie questioned him. "Ramses, what other explanation could there be? This resurrected Cleopatra is an aberration. I've always known it. She was never meant to exist. The true soul of Cleopatra, queen of Egypt, had long ago moved on in its journey—living and dying in countless others, and finally being reborn in this all-too-human American woman, Sibyl Parker. The clone reaches out desperately for the soul in Sibyl Parker, because the clone has no soul. And Sibyl profits from this, while the clone sinks deeper into a decline."

"You see me as profiting from this?" Sibyl whispered.

Julie was startled into silence by this response. She appeared flustered, unable to find the right words for what she had meant to say.

"I have been besieged by visions," said Sibyl, "many of them terrifying. Paralyzing. They grip me in public places and quite literally bring me to my knees. What were once only nightmares, they have begun to spill into my days. This process you describe. In which one of us rises, while the other one falls, it is not what I have experienced, Julie. It is not what I experience now."

"Maybe not," Ramses said, "but would you say it became ever more real as the two of you drew closer to each other? Intensified? That is the modern word."

"Yes. Most definitely."

"And after today, when you were both on the grounds of the same estate, did the nature of this connection change in any way?"

"It changed the minute I arrived in London. It felt as if . . . Well, it felt as if we suddenly enjoyed the type of connection often described by twins. I felt pricks of pain that seemed to come from nowhere. I felt myself unable to sleep, despite great exhaustion. And emotion. Great swells of emotion that swept over me without warning, without any connection to what was unfolding in my immediate environment. As if I was suddenly privy to the feelings of another."

"She does not sleep," he explained. "No one who has consumed the elixir does. We can enjoy a kind of slumber for only a short while. It is never really sleep. Both of you are fundamentally different beings. Yet you are connected somehow and so your different natures struggle with each other."

"Well, we must find out if it's the same for her," Sibyl said, as if it were the most obvious of suggestions. "We must find her and bring her here. If this is a refuge for me, among sympathetic beings, then can't we provide the same refuge for her?"

Silence.

"In the dream," said Sibyl, "the one where we spoke, she asked, *Are you the one who took me?* She's being held captive somewhere, isn't she?" Sibyl studied their faces. What she saw in their expressions seemed to frighten her. "You will help me find her, won't you? Is that too much to ask of you? That you help me bring this to an end?"

Ramses smiled, but it was a small, secretive, and sad smile. After all this woman had endured, she wanted only to help the resurrected Cleopatra. Here, surrounded by immortals, privy to revelations that should have shaken her to the core, she thought only of the other, the horrid revenant that he'd brought into being, as if she had no choice. *That is it,* he thought. *They are so intimately connected this woman can't think of anything else.*

"An end," Julie said, as if she dreaded the thought. "What end do you imagine to this, Sibyl?"

"An end to this confusion will surely help us both," Sibyl said. "How can I tell you the urgency I feel to be with her, to look into her eyes, to hold her hands?" She paused. "Yes, Ramses," she said finally. "To answer your question, something has changed in the wake of the party. For the first time, we seemed to share a dream, she and I. We chased each other through the streets of some city. A child's voice called out to his mother. In Greek. The word *mother* again and again. And then we stared at each other across a canal of some sort. For the first time we gazed upon each other without vagueness or distraction. We spoke."

"What words did you exchange?" Ramses asked.

"She asked me where I was hiding him. Where I was hiding her memories of her son. And I told her . . ." Tears again. "And I told her I would never hide anything from her."

"She's losing her memories," Julie said. "She said so in the temple today. Specifically she mentioned her son, Caesarion. She can remember nothing of him at all. The knowledge that she even had a son torments her now. *A great yawning blackness.* Those were the words she used to describe the place where the memories of her son should be, but are not."

"Did she mention Sibyl specifically?" Ramses asked.

"No, but there was something she was holding back, something she would not say. I asked her why an illness in her mind would cripple her body so. She wouldn't answer me. But that was the moment in which it seemed she was being tossed about by invisible forces. The very moment when Sibyl was assaulted, I believe." Tears hovered in Julie's eyes. "I felt sorrow for her," Julie confessed. "Much as I loathe her—I can't help but loathe her—I felt such pity for her." Julie's voice softened, became little more than a murmur. "What must it be like to have no soul, to be groping for a soul that resides in another? What is it like to be conscious that one is an empty shell?"

"The man who attacked me," Sibyl said, "he knew my name. He accused me of invading her mind, of trying to destroy his queen."

"Ah," Ramses said, "and so it was that one, just as I thought. The doctor with whom she traveled. This Theodore Dreycliff. And so we know that Cleopatra is aware of you as well. That she detects your presence just as you detect hers. And that she was able to do so before the party today, before you two were within a stone's throw of each other."

"I sent her a message," Sibyl said, as if it were a shameful admission. "I sent her a message when I was aboard the *Mauretania.* I told her my name and asked her how I could find her."

"And did you receive a response?" Julie asked.

"Only the man who brought a knife to my throat," she answered, lips quivering from her tears. "I wanted to help her. I wanted to help us both. And now I feel as if I have done a terrible thing."

"You have done nothing terrible, Sibyl Parker," Julie said quickly. "Nothing terrible at all."

"But you believe that she has, don't you?" Sibyl asked. She was fighting sobs now, and it put a miserable tone to her voice that made Julie hug her closer. "You see her as a villain, as a monster. And so you will not help her, because you believe that I will be better off if she continues to decline, as you put it. And if what you say is true, she will experience a madness that is permanent because she cannot die. And I am supposed to be relieved by this, comforted by it, even. And if I tell you that I feel a connection to her more profound than the love I have felt for any person, for my departed parents even, you will not believe me, will you? You will think me blinded by emotion and the strange nature of this connection, as you call it. You will think me unable to see her accurately. Unable to properly judge her crimes."

"She has taken life wantonly, Sibyl," Ramses said as gently as he could, but even these soft words caused Sibyl to screw her eyes shut and shake her head. "She has struck down humans as if she were a lawless being, *soulless,* as Julie has said. She is capable of doing this again."

"I know," she said miserably. "I know this. It feels as if I was present for it. But I was also present for her pain and her confusion. I feel those things now. I feel her fear. I feel her terror in the darkness. And it overpowers me, and it will overpower anything you say to me of what she truly is. I crossed the world for you, Mr. Ramsey, thinking you might be the key to my dreams. But now I treasure you, implore you, because you are the key to her. She and I, who we are . . ." She broke off, her words failing her.

"We are glad you have come, Sibyl," Julie whispered. "You must know this. You must know that we are glad you have come."

"Then find her. Please. Find her and free her so that we may learn if her experience matches mine. Find her so that we can discover if another meeting between the two of us will change the nature of this connection in some way that will prevent it from destroying us both. At the very least, let her face your judgment.

Not the judgment of whoever holds her captive now. For I can feel her fear of these people as I would a second heartbeat in my breast."

She had silenced the room with this plea. She collapsed into Julie's half embrace and let her sobs claim her.

Ramses had done this to her. He and he alone. He had done this to this woman, and he had no choice but to fix it. Like Sibyl, he was not sure if he believed Julie's theory, or if he simply thought Julie's current version of it, which cast Cleopatra as a declining aberration, and Sibyl, the custodian of her true spirit reborn, was too neat. Too simple. But did this matter now? Did anything matter more than healing the despair he had brought to this poor, sobbing woman, who had traveled so far under such duress only to almost lose her life at the tip of a drunkard's knife? Yes, there was something that mattered more: providing rest to that horror that he had resurrected in Cairo. That mattered more.

Sibyl needed more than rest just now, he thought. She needed truth. She needed a truth that they did not yet possess, despite their powers and their knowledge.

These thoughts swam in Ramses' head.

Julie looked up suddenly. He felt a gentle pressure on one shoulder. A hand coming to rest there, a voice in his ear, Bektaten's voice. "It seems we have more to consider."

"Go," Julie whispered. "I will stay with her."

32

"Cleopatra," Bektaten finally said. "This is the only ruler of Egypt to whom you told your entire story?"

"Yes," Ramses answered.

They were alone. With an upturned palm, she had ordered her men to remain upstairs with Sibyl and Julie. Now she stood with one hand on the stone mantel of the fireplace in the great hall, gazing into the flames. Impossible to tell if she was quietly furious with him or if his revelation had plunged her deep into thought.

Did this give him hope? He wasn't sure.

"And you did not say her name earlier because you did not want to confess what you had done?" she asked.

"Yes."

"I see."

"What I have done," he began carefully. "Have you any knowledge of it?"

"Knowledge of it?" She turned from the fire. "With using the elixir to bring one back from death itself? No, Ramses. Of this I have no knowledge at all."

"How? In all your thousands of years, how could you not have once tested it?"

"It never entered my mind."

"But surely you must have faced death, a loss, a tragedy that tempted you—"

"Never," she said. "We are different beings, you and I. Once the soul has left the mortal body, one is indeed left only with an empty shell. This is the truth as I know it. I have never been tempted to rouse that empty shell, to grapple with a monstrous being whose nature I could not possibly know in advance."

"You had your poison, your strangle lily."

"And so, what? You suggest that to test a theory I might bring a body back from death, and then murder it if the experiment went wrong? I have never been an alchemist. That was the realm of the man who betrayed me and destroyed our kingdom."

"Surely, at some point, you must have become curious. You must have—"

Bektaten smiled and shook her head.

"We are different, you and I," she said again. "But don't seek to confuse me. In all your centuries in Egypt, did you ever once test the elixir in this way? No. Only when you gazed upon her again in the Cairo Museum, your beloved Cleopatra, this queen who humbled Caesar and seduced Mark Antony, this fabled seductress of a thousand talents, were you overcome by this urge. *It was not curiosity!*"

Her words wounded him, but he would not reveal it, and he saw only patience in her eyes.

"Be truthful, Ramses," she said. "It was not curiosity. It was nothing of the kind. I seek common ground with you, but do not seek to make me your partner in this particular endeavor so that you may avoid the consequences of what you've done."

"There is no avoiding the consequences of what I have done!" Ramses declared. Her words and her patience had infuriated him, as much as the quiet precision with which she'd delivered them. "Those consequences, as you put it, have pursued me across oceans. Does it mean nothing to you, my queen, that I was awakened without my consent? That I walled myself off so as to bring myself as close to death as I could. And yet, all that time, from the fall of Egypt to now, I . . ."

"You what?" she asked quietly.

"Had I known there was something on this earth that could have ended my life, if I had known of this strangle lily—. Had I at least known that I was not alone."

"I see," she whispered. "So I am your wayward mother. And I'm at fault for not having cared for you as if you were my creation, and not the thief of that which I sought to guard from the world."

"But why? Why did you seek to guard it from the world?"

"You can answer this question. Did you not do the same? Only when you were blinded by love did you reveal your truth. Until then, did you not find Egypt in the hands of ruler after ruler unworthy of knowing your secret? Incapable of being trusted with the elixir's power? Did you not see the seeds of the very things that destroyed my kingdom in the eyes of every king and queen you counseled?

"Consider it the fire of Prometheus if you must. But you knew. You were wise enough to see what I learned when Shaktanu fell. Should this fire touch the earth, it will ignite a conflagration that will incinerate everyone in its path, bringing more death than it could ever remove. In the smoking ruins of my kingdom, I saw this truth. In the warfare that webbed the land. In the bodies mauled by plague. This is history, as I have lived it, as I have known it. Sources of life fall into the hands of those who seek to profit from and abuse them, bringing great death as a result. I will not have the elixir meet such a fate. And if it's loneliness you fear, Ramses, you will join me in this purpose. And you will humbly admit it when passion has blinded you to its importance."

He felt foolish, like a young boy who had made desperate excuses for childish acts. Yes, he was a monarch who had been bred to believe that his every whim should be acknowledged, but he had been born and bred to duty as well, born and bred to uphold justice, reason, what was right. He had been born and bred to a mortal life of ritual and sacrifice that many a humble human would have found unendurable, and when he had slipped from the pages of living history into the legend of Ramses the Damned, he had remained bound by duty, bound to be the advisor of the rulers of Egypt. . . . And what was he now in this woman's presence? Why was he so vulnerable to her, so willing to suffer this?

He must have appeared chastened. She crossed the room and gently took his hands in her own.

"You must never do a thing like this again. Never, Ramses."

"I will not," he said. "The gods of Egypt must have cursed me in that moment if such gods exist."

"You condemned yourself, Ramses," she said. "You were your own god of old. And you must understand, before you say another word, I will not give you the strangle lily solely so you can dispatch into eternal darkness this revenant Cleopatra, the consequence of such an act."

"I would never ask for such a thing," he said. "To do so might endanger this fragile being, Sibyl." He paused, looking at Bektaten.

"Do you not understand how this affects me," he asked, "that the soul of the true Cleopatra may be inside of this tender mortal woman? In the very moment that I glimpsed Sibyl Parker I *saw* Cleopatra. My Cleopatra. I sensed her deeply." He put his hand over his heart. "And we do not know what the connection is between this new tabernacle of Cleopatra's soul and the risen body of Cleopatra that exists now."

"And so you don't believe Julie Stratford's explanation? You don't believe Sibyl Parker is claiming her rightful spirit back from the creature you raised, and that soon this creature will descend into madness?"

"I do not," Ramses answered. "If it were true, Sibyl would be flush with new memories, the very memories Cleopatra is losing. Yet she speaks only of dreams that have been with her all her life, long before I woke this miserable Cleopatra. This connection, whatever it may be, it is more complicated than Julie suggests. I love Julie, but Julie is blinded by animus. When Julie was still mortal, she almost lost her life at the revenant Cleopatra's hands."

"I see," said Bektaten with the same maddening patience. "I think you underestimate Julie Stratford, great king. But I do see what you mean."

Remarkable the unguarded way she studied him, almost as a lover might study one she was preparing to kiss. But there was no such need or hunger in her expression. Just a quiet fearlessness.

The glimpses he had seen of her anger suggested that she was slow to rage; that her anger, when it showed itself, gathered strength gradually like a storm far out at sea, moving inexorably towards a distant shore. Had her attack today, her slaughter of the children of Saqnos, been the terminus of such a journey? Or was it as she'd said: she had simply sought to send an efficient and indisputable message to the man who had betrayed her thousands of years ago?

Too soon to ask her these things, especially in the wake of his confession. But to converse with her like this, intimately and in relative solitude, was a sobering thing. He was as absorbed with studying and interpreting her every graceful gesture as he was with pleasing her with his insights. At the same time he was quietly on guard.

She released his hands and slowly returned to the fire.

"Would you really have ended it all those years ago?" she asked. "If I had become known to you. If I had showed you how to turn yourself to ash."

"It is a distinct possibility."

"A *distinct possibility*," she whispered. "You have mastered the language of this age. In particular the queer mannerisms the British use to put strong feelings at a safe remove. So many languages swim in my head. Sometimes it is as if I hear all of them at once, and I am unsure of which one will come from my lips. I envy you, Ramses."

"How so?"

"Your awakening, what it allowed you after such a long slumber. To drink in the twentieth century in great thirsty gulps after having known only desert kingdoms of the time before Christ. To experience it all without the distractions of the ages in between. The fall of Rome, the darkness that followed. The rage of the Mongols, and the Vikings. The slave ships bound for the Americas. The revolutions that rocked Europe. These things did not crowd your head as you discovered the motorcar and flying machines and powerful medicines that can now prevent plague. But to my existence, these things arrived slowly, as inevitabilities. Not magical constructions. I imagine when you first saw them, they seemed as if they had just arrived from the temple of the gods."

"Yes. This is true. But still, I would have liked to see Rome fall. For reasons which I'm sure are now clear."

She smiled. "Do you still think this age magical?"

"I have always dwelled in a kind of magic. It was magic that rendered me immortal."

"In a manner of speaking, perhaps," she said. "But I ask you this now because I wish to know if you have been freed from your anguish, freed from the same anguish that drove you to wall yourself away for all time."

"May I ask a question first?"

"You may."

"If you had met me then, as Egypt fell to Rome and my queen lay dead by her own hand, if you had met me then, and I told you I wished to end it all, would you have given me your strangle lily?"

She answered without hesitation: "No."

"Why not?"

"Because you needed then to be freed from your vocation, not from your eternal life."

"Counselor to kings and queens, you mean?"

"Yes. Yours was not a failure of spirit, Ramses. It was a failure of imagination. For that is the deepest and gravest challenge of immortal life. How to imagine it when we are bred and trained and shaped to see our existence as a brief, fleeting thing in which we skate helplessly across the surface of a violent earth."

"And from where do you summon your great imagination, Queen Bektaten?"

"Careful with your tone, Ramses. I don't seek to indict. Merely to address accurately and with experience behind me."

"And so you too have suffered these failures of imagination, as you call them?"

"Indeed," she said. "Many times over."

"And how did you survive them? Aside from long sleeps?"

"The risk comes when you find yourself looking upon the mortals around you as puppets. Tapestries. Tiresome children at best, shallow creatures of appetite and ignorance at worst. Once these thoughts take hold, the sense of isolation is soon to follow. There is only one thing that will stop it. You must go to where mortals are most wounded and seek to care for them, heal them. But your entire immortal life cannot consist of journeys like this. Ultimately they would produce an anguish all their own. To dwell only amidst the plague stricken, to walk only those nations brought low by war. But when you feel as if you are but a dry leaf carried by the endless winds of time, and you can bear the thought of what seems like a haphazard wandering no longer, you must go where there is pain and seek to alleviate it."

"To alleviate pain. Did I not do this as I counseled the rulers of Egypt? As I sought to guide them to wisdom and strength?"

"You sought to empower an empire. I do not dismiss this goal. But it is a different thing from what I describe. If you wish to be free of the despair that can grip an immortal, you must reach beyond the very concept of empire. You must go to the place where the pain among mortals is so great it has brought villages and even cities to their knees, and you must do what you can to end it."

"Without using the elixir," he said.

"Yes. Without using the elixir. Use your strength, your knowledge, your wisdom instead."

"And so this is what you would have told me, had we met in Alexandria. Had I told you of my desire to end my immortal life."

"Yes," she answered. "So I ask again. This despair, this anguish. Has it left you? Is your love for Julie Stratford enough?"

"She is a true partner. The first I've ever known."

"Because you made her an immortal."

"Because she is a wise and clever and independent woman, such as I've never known." He hesitated, but then he said it. "I saved her from the very despair I felt in Alexandria all those years ago, when I had lost all those for whom I'd cared most. Wise and clever as she was, she was poised to end her life."

There was more to say. "I drove her to this despair. It was I, the revelation of who and what I was, the assault on her rational mind made by my very being. I had driven her to the brink."

"I see," she whispered.

She retreated to the window and its view of the dark sea. Perhaps she didn't expect an answer right away.

"And so it seems we have an understanding," he said, hoping to steer them back to cooler matters of the business at hand, and away from these great philosophical questions, which she navigated with utter ease even as they filled him with confusion. "You will not give me the strangle lily to end Cleopatra's life."

"Not to end her life, no," Bektaten answered. "But there are other secrets in my garden. Other tools which might bring about an end to this trouble."

Just then, Sibyl's piercing screams echoed through the castle.

33

Havilland Park

Must not show them the extent of her humiliation. Then they might suspect they held a former queen in their rank cell.

She had just resolved to conceal the depth of her misery and her rage from her immortal captors when the door swung open. The handsome, curly-haired man who had menaced her earlier entered with a confident stride. Outside there were others. Just out of view, but she could detect their breathing and the occasional scuff of their boots against the stone floor.

"Tell me your name," her captor said.

His face was in shadow. She would not show him her own again unless forced.

"Hound catcher," she whispered.

He snapped his fingers. Shadows moved through the doorway behind him. Not just the two immortals she'd glimpsed earlier, but others. Five in all. As they gathered, they blocked out the light from the hallway even further. In their hands, they held chains. By themselves these implements would not have been enough to bind her, but when wielded by those who possessed her strength they would be more than enough to hold her prisoner.

"Tell me your name," he said again.

"Hound slayer," she whispered.

They seemed to work as a single mass, these people.

She was yanked to her feet. Her wrists were bound behind her. A heavy ring snapped closed around her neck. They pushed her out of the cell and into the stone hallway. With the chains, they dragged her up a set of stone steps.

When her bare feet touched the dirt outside, it at first seemed a cold, soft relief. Then she heard the dogs once more, so much louder than before.

A star-filled sky above, but when she tried to look back, the chain attached to the metal collar around her neck was pulled tight. She stumbled forward several steps before finding her balance. Ahead, a tall building rose out of the dark, rolling landscape. Isolated amidst the shadowed hills. The closer they came to it, the more fearsome the baying of these hounds became.

The steel door to the building's first floor was thrown open.

She was shoved through. Empty, this room. Empty with stone walls that made the riot of these fearsome animals all the more loud and overpowering. The sound came through steel bars in one corner of the floor. And when she saw the writhing shadows below, she realized there were many more furious hounds down there than she'd first suspected. So many, their shadows seemed to form an almost-solid mass occasionally pierced by a glint of teeth or a flash of pink gums.

No fear. Show these people no fear. Remember that you are a queen.

They shoved her towards the grate, these immortals. She fell to her knees. The stink of the hounds assaulted her in ceaseless waves. As ceaseless as their hunger, as ceaseless as their strength. She trembled not just from the humiliation but from the stark terror of what might await her should they shove her through.

There were too many of them to subdue. Too many to fight off. And if their hunger was anything like the hunger the elixir had left her with, they would tear into her with abandon. Would they work faster than her body's capacity to heal? Impossible to know this. She still knew so little about her condition, given that her attempt to confront Ramses had ended in this terror.

"Tell me your name." Her captor was forced to shout above the barking dogs.

Again she refused. He shoved her face against the bars. For the first time she saw how little space there was between the grate and the heads of these writhing hounds. A jaw snapped shut only inches from her nose.

"Cleopatra!" she screamed. "I am Cleopatra the Seventh. The last queen of Egypt."

But another string of words formed itself in her mind. *Help me, Sibyl Parker. Please. Help me.*

At last, he pulled her head away from the grate.

"And so it is true," her captor said. "It is as I suspected when you showed me your fine features."

To her astonishment, he pulled her to her feet, across the floor, and out the door. Before it shut behind her, she saw the other immortals dropping something down into the grate, which suddenly quieted the hounds below. Food.

Once they were outside, this man stood before her as if he were welcoming her to these vast grounds for the first time, and with pride. But she was still confined. Two immortals flanked her, holding the chains attached to the ring around her neck and the manacles that bound her wrists against the small of her back.

"I attended many of your triumphal parades in Alexandria," he said. "I was a great admirer of yours. Forgive me for not receiving you as I should. But it was not your acquaintance I expected to make this day. We shall dine together, you and I. I'm sure you are as famished as my dogs."

A pretense, this politeness. Perhaps a quieter form of torture.

But did it matter? He had broken her, and he knew it. He was reveling in it. A monster, this man.

"Clean her up and bring her something to wear. Her dress is in tatters. Hardly fit for a queen."

And then he was striding off into the darkness. For the first time, she saw the main house of this vast estate some distance away. The tall windows glowed against the scabbed and barren tree branches. It was a far-grander place than the one from which she'd been abducted. But in its size, she saw only room for even-greater horrors.

34

Cornwall

Sibyl had stopped screaming by the time Ramses and Bektaten burst into the room.

Now she was curled into a ball amidst tangled covers. Ramses was as distressed by her mewling as he'd been by her piercing cries. Apparently she had suffered some sort of seizure. Her water glass was smashed to the floor next to the bed, and there was a large stain on the front of Julie's dress shirt.

Julie took no time to dab at it; she was too busy trying to embrace Sibyl again.

The cat, who had seemed to be guarding Sibyl earlier, was now perched on the mantel over the fireplace, watching the entire scene with human focus.

Aktamu and Enamon stood on either side of the bed. Did they think Sibyl might fly from it and need to be restrained? How severe had this eruption been?

Once Julie managed to take the woman in her arms, Sibyl's words came in a breathless torrent. "They're torturing her. With beasts. Terrible beasts. I can smell them. I can feel the heat of their breath. She screams through me because she will not scream before them!"

Ramses turned to the queen. "These animals. Are they the dogs of which you spoke?"

"I assume so, yes."

Ramses studied Bektaten. "You know where Cleopatra is being held? You have been inside this place where they hold her now?"

"In a manner of speaking, I have been inside it, yes."

"And so you have met with this Saqnos in his own domicile?"

"No," she said. "Aktamu, to the garden. Bring us some étoile blossoms. That should soothe her."

At the mention of her garden, Julie gave Bektaten a fearful look. Ramses, before he could stop himself, did the same.

"They are well suited to her current condition," Bektaten answered. "My garden has yielded countless miracles and only a handful of poisons."

"Save her," Sibyl whispered, "you must save her, please. You must. She cries for my help."

They said nothing. Sibyl was in such a state she might not have heard them if they had. Her eyes were slits from which tears still flowed. She clung to Julie as if a great wind might tear her away the minute she let go.

When Aktamu returned, several blue blossoms in one hand, Julie slowly withdrew from the bed, but not before settling Sibyl down onto the pillows.

Bektaten's faithful servant tore apart the blue petals and the flowers' stamens and ground them all into a powder in his hand. Then he poured water into a fresh glass and began to release this fine blue powder from between his fingers, which he continued to rub together. Graceful and quiet, this process. When they brought the glass to Sibyl's lips, it seemed to work its effect almost immediately. The tremors throughout her body came to an abrupt end.

"Do we know if it will affect Cleopatra?" Julie asked.

"We do not," Bektaten answered, "but if it does, it will make her predicament more endurable as well. Come with me. Both of you."

They did as they were told. Enamon followed. Aktamu stayed behind.

To the first floor of the tower she led them and, from there, down a set of stone steps to a kind of basement chamber with two barred windows literally carved out of the side of the cliff.

Items of great and secret value were stored here, Ramses realized. Although what could be of more value than the enchanted garden in the center of the courtyard, Ramses was not sure. But the garden would be useless to someone who did not know its secrets. And he was sure that here, in this chamber, the garden's magic was distilled, seperated and rendered useful, sometimes fatally so.

The stone walls were covered with weapons from throughout history. Great gilded swords of silver, gold, ebony, and ivory. And on the long central table, a row of silver daggers, each in its scabbard. At the table's far end, several jars of brightly colored powder, labeled in the same script he'd seen in Bektaten's journals. Various pollens, he was sure. Various pollens which had, in some manner that wasn't clear, been applied to the weapons on the table before him. Alongside one end of the row of daggers lay several bronze rings, each containing a bright red stone. These rings were suspiciously larger than ordinary, modern jewelry, for there was a chamber under the stone in each that must have contained one of Bektaten's secrets.

It was an armory, this room. There was no better word for it.

"You seek to arm us with the fruits of your garden," Ramses said.

"I do not *seek* to arm you. I arm you. The daggers have been dipped in a substance that will stun an immortal for several hours on the clock. Each one is good for five effective strikes before the blade is exhausted. The rings contain the permanent solution you saw today." She uncapped the jewel from one, revealing a small bronze pin underneath. "Complete penetration of the strangle lily is required for it to do its work. On the surface of your skin it will not harm you. And it will harm no mortal at all."

"The sedative," Julie asked, "the one in which you've dipped the daggers, will it work on mortals?"

"No," she answered. "But the dagger will, of course, if your aim is good and your strike is strong. Are you confident in these things, Julie Stratford?"

"It's not entirely clear what you're sending us to do," Julie answered.

"I don't send you anywhere," Bektaten said. "I grant hope of success to a mission you're sure to undertake with or without my consent. That is all."

"And is this all?" Ramses asked. "These daggers and these rings?"

"No." Bektaten turned to the mahogany cabinet behind her. Its matching doors were inlaid with pearl designs. When she opened it, Ramses glimpsed shelves of glass bottles inside. Some large, some tiny vials, each filled with fluids of different colors and luminosities.

How he wanted to explore this cabinet! To hear her describe every magical potion within it. Surely they weren't all pure seeds from her garden, but various mixtures of plants still unknown to man. Given how long she had walked the earth, some of the plants she kept and harvested might now be long extinct. But there was no time for this now. For in this chamber with them was an almost spectral presence: their fear that Sibyl might soon suffer another episode and alarm the castle once again with her terrible screams.

From the cabinet, Bektaten removed a large vial, the length of her hand and the thickness of several fingers, full of some sort of orange powder, and passed it to Enamon.

"And what is that?" Ramses asked.

Enamon placed it inside his jacket pocket. When Ramses met his eyes, he responded with only a blank stare, a quiet, polite reminder that he was under no obligation to answer Ramses' questions.

"It's pollen from the angel blossom," Bektaten said.

"And it requires no ring or dagger to be effective?"

"It's a more complex tool," she answered. "It is how I was able to see inside the estate where he now holds Cleopatra."

"And how does it work?" Julie asked.

"You'll see," Enamon answered.

"You are not to use it yourself," Bektaten said. "Either of you. You don't have the experience."

"You're giving us your men as well," Ramses said.

"I am," she answered.

"And we're to leave you and Sibyl unguarded?" Julie asked.

"Dear Julie," Bektaten said, running one long-fingered hand down the doors of the mahogany cabinet, "I am not unguarded."

Julie nodded.

In the tense silence that followed, Ramses picked up one of the sheathed daggers by its handle, tested its weight in his hand. When Julie did the same, a protective urge flared inside him, and, as if sensing it, she met his eyes quickly. She was daring him to forbid her to join this mission. So he did nothing of the kind. But he could not help but smile at her show of defiance and strength, the way it tensed her lips, making them look succulent and kiss-able at the very moment when he knew a kiss might be seen as a crass dismissal of her resolve.

Bektaten studied them both. So did Enamon, as if they thought they might not have the strength for what lay ahead.

"I have armed your mission," the queen said, "and so now it is my right to apply conditions to it."

Ramses placed the dagger back on the table. "If these conditions are not agreed to, will your arms be withdrawn?"

She ignored this question. "You will bring Cleopatra here so that we may confine her and assess the true nature of her being, as well as the nature of what she is becoming and how it affects our new friend Sibyl Parker. You are not to destroy her with what I give you. You are to destroy only her captors and all else that stands in your way. As I have already said to you, Ramses, to kill Cleopatra in haste may place Sibyl in great peril. I will not allow this."

Ramses looked to Julie. Julie nodded her agreement.

"We agree. And your second condition?"

"Bring me Saqnos."

Difficult at first to pinpoint the source of anger in the room; the great heaving breath that sent currents of tension rippling through the silence that followed. The anger came from her servant Enamon. He was the one who had reacted to her order with a great inhalation. It was the first outward display of emotion Ramses had seen from this man, and it suggested he was more than just a servant. A constant companion. Had this Saqnos left wounds in him as deep as those he'd left in his queen?

Bektaten gazed back at Enamon silently, pain in her eyes, but a cold resolve to the rest of her expression.

"Do you feel that's wise?" Ramses asked.

"Wise?" she asked, turning her gaze from her companion to him.

"He seeks the pure elixir and always has. And you have it here."

"I have its ingredients here, scattered among many. It has not been mixed and it is never stored. Should he get free—"

"He will not get free." Enamon's voice was a deep, startling rumble. It startled even Bektaten. There was more than protectiveness in his tone. Also a note of reproach.

"Should he somehow find my garden," Bektaten began carefully, and it was clear her cool rephrasing was the only concession she would make to her servant's fear and anger over her choice, "he will once again be at a loss for how the ingredients are assembled."

Another tense silence.

She looked at each of them in turn.

Was she giving them the opportunity to challenge her?

They did not take it.

Instead, Enamon looked to the floor at his feet, a subtle gesture of surrender if Ramses had ever seen one, and Julie picked up one of the daggers by its handle once again.

"Do you agree to these conditions?" Bektaten finally asked.

Ramses was prepared to nod, when Julie broke the silence. "I must ask something first."

"Speak."

"Why have you not poisoned Saqnos before now?" she asked.

It was the first time Ramses had seen the queen flinch, as if Julie's words had literally struck her. She turned from the table and then to her mahogany cabinet, and for a moment, he thought she might remove a secret scroll or tablet which might somehow answer Julie's question with an ancient tale. But she did nothing of the kind. Rather, it was as if she could only collect herself by turning away from the expectant look in their eyes.

"He is all that connects me to my past," she answered. "He is all that connects me to what I was. If I am to destroy him for all time, the reason for doing so must confront me in the flesh once more."

"I connect you to what you were," Enamon said. "Aktamu connects you to what you were. We freed you so you could become what you are."

"Yes, I know this, and I'm eternally grateful for it," Bektaten said. "But Saqnos held the other half of my kingdom in his hands. If he is gone forever, so goes Shaktanu."

Ramses said nothing. It was not his place to say anything. But he felt she was blinded by love, not for a man as much as a lost kingdom. Or perhaps it was both, and she was unwilling to admit it. But to point these things out to her would be to risk their new and fragile alliance, Ramses was sure.

"There is a final chance," Bektaten said. "Bring him here so that he may have it."

"A final chance?" Ramses asked. "For Saqnos?"

"Yes, for him," Bektaten said quietly.

"You believe he can redeem himself?" Julie asked her.

"I believe I will give him a choice." She turned to face them again, enunciating each one of these words with a quiet emphasis that had the threat of anger at its edges. "There are many secrets in my garden. Far more than have been displayed for you on this table. This exchange . . . I am done with it. Do you agree to my terms? May we begin?"

Ramses answered by reaching out and taking one of the daggers in hand, just as Julie had moments before.

"Yes," he said. "Let us begin."

35

Havilland Park

It was impossible to tell how much time had passed. She felt as if they'd left her in this cell for hours.

Were they preparing the food? Or was this isolation another form of bloodless torture?

And how to explain this sudden calm that seemed to move through her? Was it resignation, surrender?

The door to her cell swung open.

The immortals who had placed her in chains earlier now brought her a dress, a porcelain basin full of warm water, and a cloth with which to wash herself. They presented these items to her as if they were royal tributes. It took all her effort not to sneer at the absurdity of this. Royal tributes in this dark cell that smelled of earth and rotting leaves? Who were these wretched people?

But there had been a shift in their manner. She was their prisoner still, but they now believed her to be a queen.

The dress was a thin and insubstantial thing, studded with pearls and glittering stones, that reminded her of froth on the Nile. Less of a garment than a silly form of adornment. Jewels in clothing form. It would diminish her to wear it, but not as much as it would to remain in this wretched little cell.

So she glared at her captors turned gift-bearers until they departed, then she disrobed.

If she had not just suffered the terror of almost being fed to their immortal hounds, she would have been unable to bear this indignity, washing herself with a single cloth she had to wet from a basin at her feet. But the rag was soft and the water just the right temperature, so she found herself grateful for them both.

And when she slid the dress over her skin, a wave of comfort washed over her. She knew instantly it was not solely the result of the material coming to rest on her skin. Perhaps the feel of this new garment had triggered this suddenly overpowering feeling, but its true source was far away. It was Sibyl Parker. Sheets of silk and a heavy comforter; that's what Cleopatra felt the kiss of in this moment. Someone was caring for and comforting this Sibyl Parker. Someone had placed her in a luxurious bed with fine linens. Just at the moment when this thought filled her with envy and anger, she heard Sibyl's voice, as clear as it had been in the dream.

We are coming, Cleopatra. Do not fear. We are coming for you, I promise.

She could hear the ocean, a great roar of surf, and when she allowed her eyes to drift shut, she saw the spectral outline of a blazing fireplace and the shadows of people passing before it. But then the vision was gone; Sibyl's voice, however, her memory of it, remained clear as the toll of a bell.

"Who?" she called out before she could stop herself.

The cell door opened. Her captors had never left, it seemed. And so, to cover this small outburst, she said quickly, "I am dressed. I'm ready to dine."

Who is coming, Sibyl? What real hope of rescue do they provide?

No answer.

Erratic the frequency of this connection, not as clear as it had been in the dream. And it seemed now to be based more in physical sensation than wild visions. Was it possible Sibyl chose not to answer, refused to tell her who was coming? Did Sibyl truly send a rescue party, or was Cleopatra about to fall prey to a second kidnapping?

No home on this day. No home, no refuge, no temple, no palace. Only those few memories she could still cling to and a resolve that felt like ice under her skin.

Scuffling sounds of boots on stone.

This time her gift-bearers brought chains once more.

She didn't fight them. What was the point? They were as strong as she was, and they outnumbered her.

They left her wrists free, but secured the ring around her neck and extended the attached lengths of chain on either side so that they might hold the other ends at a safe distance as they all walked together from the cell.

She wasn't just their prisoner anymore.

She was Sibyl Parker's as well.

36

Beneath sparkling electric chandeliers, the long dining table was set with a feast that could have served ten mortals. But the only person seated at the table was her host, who greeted her with a stare so immutable as to be statuesque.

Around the edges of the tablecloth, she caught glimpses of woven-pearl designs. The hardwood floors underfoot gleamed. The purple draperies on the wall of soaring windows off to her right were so long they puddled on the floor.

She was brought into this grand dining room in chains and delivered to the end of the table, opposite her handsome host at the head.

As she settled uneasily into the high-backed chair, she saw a small slip of paper resting on her empty plate.

It was a newspaper clipping. A story about a great cache of artifacts from Ptolemaic Egypt recently sold to private collectors. Archeologists and museum curators throughout the world were outraged. For these statues and coins may well have contained the actual likeness of Cleopatra VII, and they belonged in a museum.

What madness had beset the sands of Egypt? they cried. Was this just another fraud like the discovery of a tomb occupied by a madman pretending to be Ramses the Great? An illustration accompanied this article. A surprisingly accurate rendering of one of the statues she'd hidden inside the tomb to which she'd led Theodore Dreycliff. An illustration that bore a striking resemblance to her.

So this was how he had recognized her. Had he known her real name even as he tortured her with his hounds? How else to describe the speed with which he'd believed her?

But is it your real name? Will you still consider it your real name once your last memory of Alexandria is gone?

She blinked. Must not shed tears before this man. Must be strong. For soon, this strength might be all she had left.

If he had known her name as he tortured her, then he sought to break her spirit as well, and she could not allow him this. So she took the newspaper clipping and crumpled it in her fist as one might a dispatch from an enemy in war. Then, once she had crushed it into a ball, she dropped it to the floor.

She looked to her surroundings, willfully ignoring whatever reaction her host might have to this gesture of disrespect.

Through the windows, she saw only darkness. She could just make out the dim outline of the lone faraway building where they'd almost driven her into their pit full of hounds. On the walls above, tapestries depicting animal hunts and battles from times that had passed during her sleep of death. She felt here, as she had felt during her visit to Rome thousands of years before, as if all the adornments and lush fabrics were meant to hold back the ever-encroaching threat of wilderness and great forests and fields of green. Windows could not be left open without fear here. Fear of animals, fear of rain, fear of wildness.

And so there was that memory; that long-ago judgment of verdant, untamed landscapes; that longing for the clean simplicity of the desert coast. Could she hold on to it? Could she capture this memory, and others like it, in her fist?

Standing against the wall opposite the windows, three other immortals. All pale-skinned blue-eyed men who seemed to hail from this land called Britain. More of his children, no doubt. Was this the entire lot of them, the two who held her in chains and the three who watched her every move warily?

"Eat," her captor said.

Could she? There was silverware before her, and her arms and hands were free. Within easy reach, a platter piled with small cooked birds.

She tore the first bird apart with her bare hands, pulled the meat from its tiny bones with her teeth.

Her captor observed her display coolly. Was her refusal to use a clumsy modern knife and fork an insult? his gaze seemed to ask.

She had no desire to answer. She just ate. Her captor ate as well, but without once looking to his food. There was incredible patience in this man. A steadiness that frightened her as much as the callousness with which he'd almost tossed her to his dogs. But he ate with the ceaseless appetite of an immortal.

I know that I have charmed many men, she thought. *I know that I have charmed rulers of Rome. I cannot remember how, exactly, but the history books tell me I have done it and so I must be able to do it again.*

But this man was no ruler of Rome. Rather, there was an absence of emotion in him which made him seem not quite human.

"And so you faked your death," the man said suddenly. "The tale of the serpent. Your suicide. Another of Plutarch's lies?"

She said nothing. What would happen if she let this man know her death had, in fact, taken place, that she'd been brought back from it two thousand years later? Had he been made in this way? If he knew she had not been, would he see her as inferior, deserving of more torture?

"I wish to know your story," he said.

"And I wish to know yours."

"Let us begin with what we do know of each other, then. You are lucky to have survived the events of the day. Our abduction of you, it spared you from slaughter."

"What do you mean by this?"

"A poison was unleashed at the engagement party for Julie Stratford and Mr. Ramsey. A poison that works only on immortals. Which can reduce them to ash."

He gave her a moment to absorb this. She found herself chewing more slowly. Her hands shook. Poison that could kill immortals? Ramses had never alluded to the existence of such a substance in all the years they'd spent together.

"I take it you didn't know there was such a thing?" he asked.

"Did you know?"

He sipped wine from his silver goblet.

"How were you spared?" she asked.

"I didn't attend this party."

"I see."

"What is it you see, Cleopatra?"

"You unleashed this poison."

"Why would you say this?" He seemed intrigued.

"You have heard tales of Mr. Ramsey. Tales of the tomb that was discovered right before his sudden appearance in London. You recognized in these tales the presence of an immortal you didn't know. And you had no desire to share the world with him. So you sought to poison him. To restore that which you define as order."

These thoughts had tumbled from her, but once she'd said them, *once she'd thought of Ramses poisoned,* a wave of sadness rose in her. Sadness that rivaled the grief she felt, not for her son, but for her very memories of a son.

Could the cruelty of these people awaken her old love for Ramses? Would such a result be worse than a broken spirit or merely the product of one?

"If your story is true," he said, "and I merely sought to poison *Mr. Ramsey,* how do you explain the trap into which you stumbled by mistake?"

"The trap you set for Julie Stratford, you mean?"

Finally, a flicker of some emotion in his blue eyes that looked almost human. But impossible to read. Anger? Simple surprise? Was he impressed by her deduction?

"I didn't seek to poison Mr. Ramsey," he said with ice in his tone.

"But you sought to abduct Julie Stratford?"

"I did."

"And the poison?" she asked.

"The poison was not mine. Was it yours?"

And so he'd brought them to the threshold of her strange origin story, a story too dangerous for her to reveal.

"It was not," she answered. "I didn't know of its existence before today. Did you?"

It was the second time she'd asked this question. This time his answer was silence.

The tension in the captors on either side of her was so strong she could feel it.

He had, she realized. He had known of this poison, and still he had dispatched some of his people to carry out this abduction. How many had died as a result? The survivors stood on either side of her now, she was sure. Had they been saved by their mission in the tunnel beneath the temple?

She sensed in their tense silence a division in this group she might exploit. If she was careful. If she was patient.

"You should be grateful to me," the man said, an edge to his tone now.

"Share your name with me so my gratitude may take proper shape," she said quietly.

"Saqnos," he answered. "And you are Cleopatra, last queen of Egypt. Friend to Julie Stratford and her inamorato, the mysterious Egyptologist, Reginald Ramsey."

He was mocking the name Ramses had assumed in this modern era. Goading her to reveal what she knew of his real identity. But all she said in return was "Saqnos. From where does this name come?"

"From my history, of course. From my past."

"From which land?"

He considered his response. "From the land that existed when all the lands were one."

"You speak of the continents before they were divided?" she asked.

"You are a student of modern science?"

"I read many languages."

"And you speak many. Or you did when you were queen."

"I am no longer a queen."

"You will always be a queen." Almost parental the way he said this, as if there were concepts that mattered more to him than the stakes of their present exchange. Concepts such as the endurance of royal titles. "Just as I will always carry the title I held in my ancestral kingdom. The burdens we have shouldered, the visions and dreams, they will forever shape our immortal lives."

"And so you were a king three hundred million years ago, when the lands were all united?"

"You speak of unity in the literal sense. In terms of continents. I speak of a kingdom that united most of the world through treaties and trade and shared knowledge. It was not three hundred million years ago. And I was not its king, but its prime minister."

"How long ago?"

"In the time they now call eight or nine thousand B.C."

She could only gaze at him.

"Shaktanu," she finally whispered.

"You believe it to be a myth."

"It is a myth."

"You say this to me with a confidence that can only be described as arrogance."

"You demand gratitude for the degradations I have suffered here because you saved me from a poisoning by chance. Arrogance is a topic in which you are expert, Saqnos. Prime minister of Shaktanu."

"Degradations? You refused to tell us your name."

"You took me prisoner."

"You stumbled into our trap. I remain curious as to how and why. What ties you, Cleopatra, to Ramses the Great? Did the tales of this mysterious Egyptologist draw you as they drew me? How is it this Mr. Ramsey makes such a splash in modern life, and you somehow remain in the shadows until today? Did someone awaken you? Did someone bathe you in sunlight so that you might walk again? Did they tell you an old lover had risen?

"Or maybe Ramses is nothing of the kind. Maybe he is an old rival, an enemy in war. I've heard tell you made no friend of the great King Herod in your day. Of course, history today remembers Herod for crimes far worse than plotting your assassination."

"Ramses was much more to me than any of these things you describe," she said.

"Was," Saqnos said. "And is?"

This was worse than the dogs, she realized, worse than being forced to reveal her name. To admit the complexity of her feelings for Ramses before this awful man. But what other choice did she have? How else could she steer him away from the strangeness of her resurrection, the destructive consequences of it? Hard enough to admit those things to Julie Stratford, but to this man, this brutal, coldhearted immortal? Impossible.

"He was my counselor and my guide during the darkest hours of my reign," she said. "He brought with him centuries of wisdom. He used that wisdom to help me. Against my own siblings, against Rome. And with Rome, when it was possible."

And so she had stumbled into another trap. If Saqnos chose to question her, she would not be able to answer specific questions about her past without revealing the speed at which her ancient memories were leaving her.

"That was not all he brought with him, was it?" Saqnos asked.

She met his gaze.

"The pure elixir," he said. "Its power. Its exact ingredients. Its formula."

Strangely specific, this statement, and the way he brought his goblet to his mouth quickly, as if to distract her from the eagerness in his eyes.

Its formula . . .

She tried to chase all emotion from her face, to assemble the pieces of information he'd provided her. And so he had not poisoned anyone that day. But he had sought to abduct Julie.

Had his plan been to leave Ramses alive so that he might use Julie's abduction against him in some way?

Its formula . . .

So that he might torture Julie into giving him the formula for the elixir?

She made a show of returning to her food. Chewing, tearing apart tiny bones, and spearing little beef Wellingtons with her fork, all of which allowed her to disguise the evidence of her rapid thoughts.

Could it be that this Saqnos, clearly immortal, did not have the elixir? That he had been transformed by it, just as she had been transformed, without ever possessing it or the knowledge to make it?

Was the same true for the other immortals who did his bidding? The ones who called him *Master*? Strange for them to call him *Master* if he had not made them. But there was no ignoring the particular hunger that had come into his voice when he said those two simple words. *Its formula.*

Did he believe she knew the elixir's ingredients?

Should she allow him to believe this?

And then she recalled another word he'd just used. His final phrase had distracted her from it, but now it came to her, bright as one of her visions of Sibyl Parker.

Pure. He had called it the pure elixir. And so the version he had of it was impure, incomplete. Corrupted.

She had stayed quiet for too long.

"And so you have no idea who's to blame for the poisoning today?" she asked.

"This is not so."

"Who is it?" she asked. "Who has done this thing?"

"We are exchanging information, are we not?"

"We are. I have told you of my connection to Ramses. I confirmed for you the man who calls himself Mr. Reginald Ramsey is in fact Ramses the Great. I now request information in return."

She felt a surge of triumph. She had tricked him. She could see it. He believed she knew the formula for the pure elixir, as he called it. His eyes were too focused as his jaw worked.

"The librarians in Alexandria," she said, "my Alexandria, they called Shaktanu a myth. A fanciful tale. A tale of a golden age, free of warfare. A comforting fantasy for those with no taste for war. Who could not accept its inevitability."

"Nothing is inevitable. Not even death. We are proof of that."

"I'm sure your children who died today believed the same."

"Don't seek to goad me, Cleopatra. I'm immune to these tricks."

"But you are not immune to this poison, whatever it may be. And neither are you immune to those who wish to dispense it."

"I am immune to her tricks and her lies and her deceit, as I always have been," he sneered, and then realized, too late, what he had just revealed.

"Of whom do you speak now, Saqnos?"

"You have had your volley. It's my turn now. Ramses the Great. Lover or enemy?"

"They are so often the same. Why force me to choose?"

"You have already chosen. The choice lies within whatever reason you had for attending the party today."

"Why would it help you to know?"

"I will know this when I know."

An alliance. Was he truly suggesting an alliance after the way he had treated her?

"Two thousand years ago he was my lover," she said. "Today he is my rival."

"I see," he said, "and so you attended his party to do him harm. Or to use his fiancée against him, just as we had planned to do."

"It is my turn to request information now."

He toasted her with his goblet to indicate his consent.

"The poisoner. Who is she?"

He chewed a bite of food.

"Lover? Rival?"

Again, he did not answer.

"I see," she finally said.

"What? What do you *see*?"

"She was your queen," Cleopatra whispered. "She is still your queen, which is why you cower here at your estate even after she slaughtered so many of your children."

"Nonsense."

"It's the absolute truth. You occupy yourself torturing me because you are powerless before her. You are not immune. You are impotent!"

"She would not dare." His voice was a low rumble.

"Why not?" she asked.

"Because I am all that remains of our kingdom. She's nourished no grand design for her immortal life other than petty, dithering historian. She envies me, and she feels a bond with me that is tangled and confused, and so be it. For I'm nothing she believes me to be and I never have been."

A brittle silence.

"You told us she slept."

The voice next to her was timid and weak, but the newness of it caused Cleopatra to jump. One of the immortals had said this, the one standing to her left, holding one of the chains to the collar around Cleopatra's neck. A pale-faced woman with huge, expressive eyes and a glittering, fragile dress much like the one they'd given Cleopatra. She was countering Saqnos's glare with one of her own, but this took all her strength, for the hands in which she held Cleopatra's chain now shook. Her jaw quivered. There were tears standing in her eyes.

"You told us we had nothing to fear from her because she slept."

Saqnos leapt to his feet and slammed both his fists down upon the table with such force it looked as if a wave had coursed through the tablecloth itself, jostling every tray of food along the way. She relished the sight. Knew instantly it would deliver information of value, to see him so undone by two simple remarks from one of his children.

"Weeks," he growled. "All of you. You have only weeks, days. If that. And it was you who woke me, believing this Ramses, this king, would be your great hope. The plan was not my own. You assembled it before I arrived. Now you seek to lay this slaughter at my feet solely because I took her centuries of silence to mean she slept. This is an outrage! I have been shown more respect by our prisoner."

"She won't kill you because you are the other half of her kingdom," Cleopatra said quietly, "but clearly she does not feel the same way about your children."

"You know nothing of this!" he declared.

"I know more than you would like. Now. Perhaps you should send your ungrateful children away before they reveal even more. Of course, they would first have to release my chains."

"We have lost sight of our exchange," he said.

"No," she said. "We have simply welcomed a new member. A new member who has only weeks of life left, despite bearing the marks of one who has consumed the elixir. If there is only one pure elixir, that is."

"It is my turn to request information."

"Then why not ask me what you truly wish to know?" Must sustain this upset that had just taken place, must open the wound further, sending her captors further off balance. "Ask me the question that's burned in you since you first saw the blueness of my eyes."

"You believe I have only one question for you? You degrade my capacity for inquiry and complex thought."

"I believe you have a need, a want, that outweighs all others, for which you are willing to endanger your own children."

"And what is this need?"

"You need the elixir. You were given it, but you were not given the knowledge of its ingredients or how it is made. And you've concocted some bastard version that does not last. And it's all traceable back to your queen, isn't it? The queen of Shaktanu. The one you served as prime minister."

"I served her as many things. As prime minister. As lover. As friend. And when she made the greatest discovery of human kind, she kept it secret. From me. From her subjects. This was a betrayal of our kingdom and all who served her."

"And yet you somehow managed to consume this secret?"

"I stole it. It was my right. The hours she spent in her workshop were a luxury wrought by my loyal service."

"I see. So it was a golden age. Free of war. All thanks to one man. You."

"It was a time unlike any you have ever known."

"I know what it takes to rule. And I know that no king and no queen ever rules with one man at their back. Yet most of their time is spent fighting off challenges from those in their own houses who claim the true source of power and success. I knew this before my resurrection. I know it now. You were a traitor, is what you were, Saqnos. You speak as one who served only for the promise of personal reward."

A silence fell over the room. He turned his back to her. He was gathering strength. Gathering focus. Her outbursts had not pushed him further into anger as she had hoped. They had quieted him instead. Paralyzed him in some way. She didn't seek his paralysis. She sought his outrage. She sought a chaos she might seize as a chance to escape.

"Perhaps, then," he said quietly, turning to face her again, "you should lecture me more on your history as queen. Surely it will benefit me to know which aspects of your known story are truth, and which are fantasy created by an empire that despised you and cheered your fall."

He closed the distance between them. His children had backed up several feet, but they still held the chains in their hands.

"Your victories were many, were they not? You were banished from Alexandria by your father and yet you managed to make it back into the city as Caesar held it in his grip."

No, she thought. *Not this.* Not this interrogation. Not this descent into a past that was blackness. Hadn't she managed to avoid this? To skip past it?

"Tell me what is true of this tale, Queen Cleopatra VII. Last queen of Egypt. The tale in which you smuggled yourself into Caesar's quarters inside a basket full of serpents. Is this true? Or fantasy?"

"No," she whispered. "Lies. It's all lies. That is not how I outwitted my father's army."

A greater silence now, deeper, and, within it, a kind of tense energy gathering itself, a new energy that seemed to unite everyone in the room.

What had she done? Had she made some error? Revealed her true, tortured nature?

Slowly, Saqnos took one end of the chain from the hand of the woman who'd spoken against him. He began to wrap its length around his wrist, tightening it, pulling her forward in her chair until she was rising awkwardly to her feet.

"It was not your father's army," he whispered. "It was your *brother's* army. He was the one who banished you from Alexandria before Caesar's landing." He yanked her away from the chair. They stood within inches of each other. There was no avoiding his blazing stare. "And it was not a basket of serpents. It was a rolled-up rug. And you do not know these things because you cannot remember them. And you can't remember them because yours was not an awakening, it was a *resurrection*, as you just carelessly revealed.

"Because you, Queen Cleopatra VII, are not a queen at all. You are a foul thing raised from death, losing your memories to one who contains your true reborn spirit. You are *nochtin*. That is the name I made for the vile creature you are. I have raised many like you only to watch their visions of those who contain their true reincarnated souls drive them to madness, leaving me with only one choice. To wall them away in darkness for all time. And this is what I will do for you, pretender to a throne who calls me a traitor to mine. Cast you into darkness before eternal madness will claim you."

The scream that tore from her was a piercing, primal thing that sounded more animal than human. She slashed at him across his face with her fingernails, using such force he almost released her. But he kept his balance and withdrew by only a half step. The chains at her neck were pulled taut once more. But they couldn't restrain her cry.

"*I am Cleopatra!*" she roared.

There was a crack like the sound of a whip. A windowpane behind him was suddenly spiderwebbed with cracks. Had her own screams broken the glass?

A mercy, the fear that swept the room. It distracted her from her despair, from the terrifying implications of her captor's words. A rock. That was it. Someone had thrown a rock at the window small enough that it didn't crash through the glass, but with enough concentrated force to crack it from frame to frame. Only an immortal would have the strength to do this.

The three men who'd stood against the wall drew oily black handguns from their jackets and hurried to the terrace door.

The other two captors, the male and the female, remained at her side.

In one powerful hand, Saqnos gripped the front of the hard

cold collar around her neck. But he'd turned his head to one side to watch the hasty exit of his men.

There was a moment of silence, which was quickly filled by a strange, rhythmic clicking. A blink of an eye later, the three gun-wielding men were backing silently through the doorway, guns raised, heads bowed.

They were followed by the hounds, who stepped through the open door one after the other, perfectly silent, perfectly poised, their gazes directed at the men who pointed their pistols uselessly in their direction. For a moment, it was impossible to believe they were the same animals to which she'd almost been fed. For they were utterly silent now and moved in perfect unison. They were mastiffs, their heads the size of a man's. The round blue eyes seeming more thoughtful now that their mouths were not contorted into snarls. In the twinkling light from the chandelier, she could see their shining coats ranged in color from black to dark brown.

Dumbfounded, the men stumbled backwards. One of them stabbed the air with his gun as if he thought this might stop their advance. It did nothing of the kind. She could count them now. Ten, twelve. Fifteen in all. And on most of their dark faces, faint traces of bright orange powder.

Some powerful enchantment had caused a miraculous change in them. It seemed as if they were now governed by a single consciousness.

"Burnham," Saqnos said in a growl.

Torn between holding on to one of the chains attached to her neck and responding to his master's request, the man called Burnham cleared his throat and let out a piercing whistle.

The dogs ignored it.

Burnham went pale. He tried again. The dogs once more ignored him. It seemed as if the lot of them, all fifteen, were gazing directly at the three men holding guns, and now, Cleopatra realized, these men were essentially cornered. They'd been backed all the way to the wall.

"Burnham!" Saqnos bellowed.

"They are not responding, Master. It's as if they've been spellbound."

To this statement, Saqnos had no response.

And then the dogs began to growl.

Never before had she heard a sound like it. Never before had she heard fifteen different hounds growling in perfect unison. The sound was like a cross between a swarm of angry bees and a boulder being rolled steadily up a hill. One of the men simply ran from the room without apology. Another followed, and then the third did as well. But first he inanely placed his pistol on the console table behind him as if it were an offering, a gesture that might placate this gathering of beasts.

The dogs swung their heads in the direction of Saqnos.

The woman who'd spoken against him earlier fled, dropping her chain to the floor with a thud. Burnham followed. And then the dogs began to bark. Deafening, this sound, and it came again and again. In perfect unison. Each bark so loud, the sounds so perfectly aligned, it shook her bones.

Beneath this terrifying chorus, other sounds. Breaking glass. Footfalls. Scuffles. Fighting in the adjacent rooms. Were there more of these hounds? Or had someone stopped the escape of Saqnos's children?

Her captor either did not hear it or couldn't bring himself to care, for the dogs were advancing on them now, moving once again in perfect unison.

"You are doing this," Saqnos whispered.

A pleasure to see him so afraid, but was she not in the sights of these beasts as well?

"I'm doing nothing of the kind. Let me go. So that we may both seek safety before it's too late."

He turned to face her. His eyes blazed. His lips curled into a snarl.

"You are doing this. This was your plan. You work with the queen."

"I have never met your queen!" she snarled.

He bared his teeth. His mouth opened. And then he was torn from her.

The dogs drove him to the floor. It seemed as if they had all taken to the air at once, piling upon him in a mad tumble.

She fell over backwards, the chair toppling behind her. They paid her no attention at all, these beasts.

Freed from immortal hands, she now had the strength to unfasten the collar at her neck. She tossed it aside and ran into the hallway.

She could not resist a glance back. The dogs tore at Saqnos's prone body, concealing it from view as they attempted to feast. More anger than anguish in the man's wails.

She spun round, then froze at the sight that greeted her in the passage. Steps from her bare feet was a pile of ash, in the empty dress of the woman who'd just held one of her chains.

The poison had done this! There was no other explanation.

Movement behind her. Again, she pivoted.

Ramses. Advancing on her. He brought a finger to his lips even as he pulled a dagger from a sheath in his belt. A dagger? How could she reconcile these two gestures? One to give comfort, the other to strike?

How dare he!

She reached out, grabbed the edge of a massive cabinet, its shelves lined with vases of various styles. Then, when he was almost within reach, she brought it crashing down upon him, sending him to the floor in a cascade of shattering porcelain and glass and shelves that pinned him to the hardwood.

37

The shattering of glass and porcelain on all sides of him left Ramses stunned and struggling to shield his face with his hands. A slash across his eye would heal quickly, but even temporary blindness during this quick assault could be disastrous.

He was sure he'd lost her. He threw off the massive weight of the cabinet and rose to his feet. There stood Cleopatra, yards away from him, gazing at something she held in one hand.

His ring. The bronze ring Bektaten had given him for this mission, the one with the tiny chamber full of strangle lily powder. It had slipped from his finger during his scramble and fall, and now she held it in her hands.

What a terrible strategic error they had made! Their most harmless poison, the sedative, had been applied to their most fearsome weapon, their daggers. And their most fearsome to their least conspicuous, their rings, rings that did not fit them, rings too large or too small. If they'd been attempting subterfuge and assassination, this would have been an excellent plan. But with Cleopatra, that was not their plan.

And if Cleopatra were to release the strangle lily, Bektaten would never believe that Ramses had not worked this deliberately.

Cleopatra gazed at the ancient ring as if it were a flower she had picked. She could see what it was, see the threads beneath the jewel, a ring with a secret compartment. She unscrewed the red jewel, revealing the bronze pin underneath. She looked to him, saw the fear in his eyes, and unscrewed the casing that held the pin, revealing the yellow powder underneath.

"No!" he cried. "You must not! You must *not!*"

"And so this is the poison," Cleopatra said to him, her eyes blazing. "The *queen's* poison."

"I did not seek to use it on you. I sought to subdue you with another substance, a sedative on my dagger. I did not come to destroy you or even to harm you, Cleopatra. You must believe this!"

"You seek to keep me alive?" She seemed dazed by the possibility.

"Yes. Please. Put down the ring."

"Put the poison aside, you mean. This poison you received from a true queen. Unlike me, a shade of one risen from death by your hand."

"We will discover who and what you are together. All of us."

"Ah, you seek to comfort me now. Would it comfort you to know I never wished to see you again? That I did not cross an ocean for you out of love."

"You seek the elixir. You believe it will make you strong against your connection to Sibyl Parker."

"Sibyl Parker." Her jaw trembled and tears came to her eyes. "Sibyl Parker, the vessel for my true spirit."

"I heard his explanation, his slurs. You must not yet accept them as fact."

"Give me the elixir, and then leave me to my own interpretations of my *condition.*"

"I did not bring it."

"Of course you didn't. Because you never planned to give it to me. Only to abduct me again. For the purposes of what? More torture? Some kind of test to make sense of this madness?"

"You must not believe this. You cannot."

"You come for me with weapons that can end immortals."

"We didn't just come for you. We came for him. To end his destructiveness."

"And what do you seek to end in me, Ramses the Great?"

"Your pain."

She lifted the ring almost to her nose. "I could end it in this very moment, couldn't I?" Her breath was close enough to the open chamber to send small puffs of yellow powder drifting to the carpet when she spoke.

"No!" he cried.

"You wouldn't be pleased if I ended my life right here? You would not be relieved? To be free of the burden of me? From the monster you raised?"

"Come with me, Cleopatra. Let us free you from all of it without ending your life. Without ending Sibyl's life."

"Sibyl," she whispered, eyes wide.

A mistake, he realized too late, to use Sibyl in this way. He'd assumed she'd feel the same loving connection to Sibyl that Sibyl felt to her. But in her leering smile, he saw nothing but jealousy and anger.

"Oh, but of course. The silken sheets. The great roaring fire. She is with you, isn't she? The rescue of which she spoke. It was you, Ramses. I see now. I see why you have come. She is very pretty, isn't she, Sibyl Parker? With her golden hair and her pale skin. Perhaps in her every gesture you see the parts of me you do not despise. For she possesses my true soul, does she not?—the migrant soul that abandoned this flesh two thousand years ago. And so you come not to save me, but to save her."

"Your anguish blinds you . . . ," he said. "We are the victims, all, of powerful mysteries. What can we do but explore them together?"

"Enough, Ramses. Enough of your pity. Enough of your guilt. If these are to be my final days of sanity, I will live them as I see fit."

"Cleopatra!"

He lunged for her.

She hurled the ring at him, its contents rising in a yellow cloud.

He cried out and threw himself against the opposite wall. When he looked up, he glimpsed her through the veil of yellow powder drifting to the floor; she disappeared around the nearest doorway, bound for the entrance to the house.

He went after her.

In the great drawing room, he caught sight of her as she ran. Impossible to tell what it was she was running towards, for there was no doorway in her path.

"Cleopatra!" he cried.

And she turned in place, met his eyes.

"Set me free, Ramses!" she cried. "You raised me from death with no thought of what I would become. And now I am doomed. There is only one way you can repay me. *Set me free!*"

*   *   *

Seeing that her words had frozen him in place, she turned and ran. He watched, helpless, as she hurled herself through the nearest window. Behind her, the glass fell in great shards between billowing drapes.

If she continued in that direction, the others would not catch her. Julie and Aktamu were on the far side of the property, Julie guarding the spellbound Aktamu, who was guiding the hounds.

Footsteps behind him. Ramses turned. In both arms, Enamon carried the seemingly lifeless body of Saqnos. It was not the dogs who had finally subdued the prime minister, Ramses was sure, but the potion from Enamon's dagger, an injection that would only last for several hours before another had to be given. The great gashes and wounds the dogs had left on his face and hands had already begun to heal.

"I must bring him to the queen before he wakes," Enamon said.

"And so if I pursue her, I do so alone. Is this what you mean to say?"

Without a word, Enamon disappeared through the doorway behind him, his steps confident, as if Saqnos weighed nothing at all.

Ramses stood motionless, staring at the broken window.

How quickly the fight had left him at the first sight of her.

He had not been prepared for her perfect likeness to his lost love. He had not been prepared for her agony and her despair.

Her final plea rent his soul even now.

Who was he to deny this request to live out her days as she saw fit before madness claimed her? Could he find her then? Could he use Sibyl's connection to do it? Would he have the courage and the strength to subdue her amidst her madness, to wall her off in darkness for all time, just as Saqnos had threatened, but for her own good? Or could he release her to the world once and for all?

If there was no peace for her, would there ever be peace for him?

38

They came trotting across the lawn in a single pack. At first they appeared to Julie as a patch of deeper darkness that blotted out the lights of the house behind. Then their individual shapes became visible.

Julie stepped from the car where the silent Aktamu lay half comatose on the black leather seat.

The mission had been completed, certainly, for why else would Aktamu guide these dogs back here to their den?

Julie fell into step behind them from a safe distance, even though there was no chance they would turn on her. Aktamu still held these animals in thrall. Somehow, through the angel blossom, he controlled them, and he could see the world through their eyes. A remarkable thing, for there were fifteen of them in all.

On the long drive to Havilland Park, Julie had deluged Aktamu with questions as to this mystery, as to how he meant to turn Saqnos's hounds against Saqnos through a spell that would render Aktamu himself unable to hear or speak. But Aktamu had no words with which to explain it to her, the workings of the angel blossom, and how he meant to unite somehow with fifteen distinct creatures and guide them through a mystic link. He had assured her repeatedly that he would do it, that once he dropped the meat, heavily laced with the pollen of the angel blossom, through the grating of the pit that held these dogs, they would be his to command.

Julie found it fascinating, marvelous, yet another revelation in the realm of revelations which she now shared with these powerful immortals—a realm so vastly different from her old world that at times she could not gain any perspective on it, no matter how much she tried. She was no longer Julie Stratford, really, and she knew it, and her fragile ties to the London of 1914 were dying most surely with every day.

Here she was in the darkness, walking slowly across the grass behind these enchanted animals, fearless yet awestruck, not for a moment repelled by the mystery of the angel blossom, only eager to know more.

She was enthralled by the spectacle of the great hounds moving as one as they approached their home building, at the single minded manner in which they approached the door to their lair. It was as mesmerizing as the sight of them ascending from the pit had been not one half hour before.

Now each and every powerful canine sat silently before this door waiting for it to be opened.

Trembling, Julie stepped forward and opened the door for them. She stood to one side.

They passed through, one after the other, and began descending the steps into their wretched little pit.

Once they were all inside, she took hold of the rope and lowered the heavy grate gently into place. With a shiver, she saw that each dog had turned to look over its shoulder. This was Aktamu's work, no doubt. He was waiting for her to close and lock the grate before he wiped the pollen from his face, releasing these beasts to their own natures again.

She slid the bolt into place with a loud clang.

But she could not bring herself to leave. Not yet. She had to see this miracle all the way through to its end.

Gradually, a change began to overtake the dogs.

Some of them quivered. Others shook themselves wildly as if trying to free their coats of water. A few of them erupted into barks, but they were not as vicious or aggressive as the sounds they'd made before. They seemed like pained questions. Were they confused by what had just been done to them?

Their paws clicked against the stone floor. Their movements seemed dazed and confused, until she realized they were each trying to move into the best position from which they could peer up at her through the bars.

These creatures had been changed. Whatever this miracle from Bektaten's garden, it had allowed these ruthless canine killers to dance briefly with a human mind. And as a result they appeared submissive now, subdued, and, in their longing looks, eager to take this dance again.

She was almost sad to leave them, for they were monsters no more.

But then the door behind her opened, and there was Ramses, breathless. No triumph in his expression; restrained anguish, but a great relief at the sight of her. Once she found herself in his arms, she realized she had no idea which one of them had initiated this sudden, feverish embrace. But what did it matter now?

"Where is she?" Julie finally asked.

"She escaped."

"Oh, Ramses."

"There was a struggle. My ring, the poison. She took it from me. It was either my life or hers. And so I let her go."

"Does she have this poison now?"

"No. She tore the ring open and hurled it at me to keep me from pursuing her. It lies on the carpet inside the house."

The sound of a car engine outside. Whatever the vehicle, its engine was much larger than those of the cars that had brought them here.

"We've found the van they used to transport Cleopatra here, and the coffin. We will use it for Saqnos. But, Julie, I must go with them so I can help subdue him if he wakes. Can you follow us in the car?"

"Of course, Ramses. Of course."

He turned from her, but as soon as his hand touched the doorknob, he froze.

"I have failed, Julie."

"No. No, Ramses."

"I could have pursued her. There was a moment, before she leapt through a window, where I might have driven her to the floor. But she begged me not to. This Saqnos, he said dreadful things about her nature, Julie, her nature as a revenant, her state of being, which may be true. *Nochtin.* That's what he called her. We all overheard him. Nochtin. They were appalling things."

"But what, Ramses?"

"That he'd raised creatures himself with the elixir as I'd raised her. And that these nochtin, as he called them, went mad. That is what he told her." Ramses stared off as he spoke these words. "And there was such anguish in her, Julie." He shuttered. "I was prepared for her cruelty or rage, but not her anguish, and so when she asked me to set her free, to live out her last days before madness claimed her, I let her escape."

She took him in her arms again. He was shaking, her pharaoh, her king, her immortal. Shaking from the power of his emotions.

"Have I done a terrible thing again?" he asked. "As terrible as bringing her back to life?"

"No, Ramses."

"But Sibyl? What will happen to Sibyl?"

"Sibyl is now free from whatever horrors Cleopatra suffered in this place. And so is Cleopatra."

"But that was not the extent of what we promised."

"Find her and free her. Those were Sibyl's words. And we have done so. The rest? It will be accomplished in time. Cleopatra is no longer the monstrous, plotting thing we knew in Cairo. We can be sure of this now. She is weakened. She is ailing. And in this moment, it is not Sibyl's expectations with which we should be entirely concerned. She was not the one who demanded we bring Cleopatra to the castle. That was Bektaten. So we must now see if our new queen is satisfied with the hostage we do bring her."

He cupped her face in his hands and kissed her gently. "You marry your wisdom to love, Julie. This ensures I will be forever your captive."

She returned his kiss.

The door swung open behind him, and there stood Aktamu. He had wiped his face free of the pollen, and his look was expectant.

"Come," he said, "we must go."

39

Cornwall

What must he have thought when he awoke to the sight of a comforting fire beside him and the sound of the sea outside? Was he flooded with relief to be freed from the hounds?

Ramses could not know.

When he saw his queen, seated only a few feet away, in a high-backed chair that matched his own, Saqnos went as still as a statue, and so Ramses could not determine the thoughts that went through his mind, but he remained desperately curious.

Saqnos gazed silently at Bektaten. She gazed back.

Did he find her beautiful, this statuesque black woman with the long, thin jeweled braids flowing over her shoulders? For gone was the turban she had worn earlier, and more clinging and flattering was her long red gown.

Was Saqnos still rising from unconsciousness? Was the sedative to explain for his continued silence? They'd given him something else as well. Ramses was sure of it. Some other potion from their endless supply of potions. Would he ever be privy to how many medicines and poisons they possessed?

Upon their arrival, Aktamu and Enamon had taken the man's seemingly lifeless body off to the armory and kept him there for several minutes before carrying him to the great hall like a giant rag doll. Perhaps whatever they had given him was intended to hasten his awakening.

Saqnos shook his head. For the first time he seemed to sense the presence of others in the room aside from Bektaten. He looked at Ramses, and then Julie. They stood close to the window and its view of a star-filled sky.

Slowly, his eyes found the daggers they both held in hand.

What was such a short period of unconsciousness like for an immortal? Ramses wondered. Had he experienced dreaming for the first time in centuries?

So many questions he could not ask, for this was not his trial to conduct. He and Julie were now witnesses. Witnesses and guards.

Finally, Saqnos spoke. "Am I allowed once again to call you my queen?"

Bektaten was silent for a long time before responding.

Ramses noticed for the first time the jeweled rings she wore, and the jeweled belt that defined her narrow waist, flattering her shapely hips. Were these ornaments worn for Saqnos? Was it for him that she had put aside the robes that concealed her physical gifts?

They certainly affected Ramses, but he used all his power to conceal this, to conceal the quickening in his blood at the vision of this regal black face framed in the gold- and pearl-threaded braids of an ancient Egyptian queen—at the vision of Bektaten's exquisitely shaped breasts.

Finally Bektaten spoke.

"You remember Jericho?" she asked.

"Every moment I have spent in your presence lives in my memory."

"There were many moments when you were unaware of my presence," she said.

"Tell me of these moments, my queen."

"Your laboratorium in Babylon. Your many gatherings of alchemists. I found them all, your elaborate laboratoria."

"You were there. Watching me."

"Yes."

"And if I had succeeded, would you have unleashed your poison against me as you did today?"

"I did not unleash my poison against you. I unleashed it against your fracti—henchmen unworthy of immortality. I unleashed it against your plot to abduct and torture Julie Stratford."

Amazing the gentleness between these two as they discussed these things, Ramses thought. To see them converse as if no time had passed. Did their great age allow for this mix of familiarity and reserve?

Bektaten stood. He noticed a faint perfume rising from her as she moved back and forth before her prisoner, the light glinting on her long shining raven braids.

Around her head, high on her forehead, she wore a circlet of gold that put him in mind even more of his ancient kingdom, of the magnificent women who had been in the harem of the king. Looking down, he put these thoughts out of his mind, yet they had endowed Bektaten with even greater power in his heart. How could an immortal man not muse on what it would be like to have such an immortal woman in his arms? And how could a proud king not deny such thoughts?

"You murdered my children," Saqnos said quietly.

"You speak of them with affection now. When you traveled with fracti in Jericho, you spoke of them with disgust. They were mercenaries and nothing more. You drew me away from them so they would not hear you tell me the elixir they'd been given was impure. Did you keep these things secret from your children as well?"

"They knew of your poison."

"Yes, I saw the terror in their eyes when I appeared before them today. And yet you also told them I slept. That I was no longer to be feared."

"How do you know this?" he asked.

"There are many secrets in my garden. This is how I maintain my rule, even if I have only several subjects left."

Saqnos looked to Ramses and then to Julie again. "It appears your subjects grow in number even now."

"Friendships, to one as driven by appetite as you, may not appear as such."

"And queens with no sense of their true burdens will always assume those who serve them out of fear do so out of love."

"Did you fear me, Saqnos? Is that what defined your time as my prime minister, before your betrayal?"

"I feared you would betray your people. And I was right."

"There was a moment when you spoke for the people? When was this? Was it when you raided my palace, stole the elixir from my secret chamber, and gave it only to the royal guards? This was how you spoke for my subjects, by rushing to secure the greatest power ever known for only yourself and your guards?"

"Ah, Bektaten. Once again we arrive at your great weakness."

"And it is?" she asked.

"Your belief that pursuit of power is a weakness."

"And so it is the pursuit of power by which you wish to be defined. This is an ambitious wish, Saqnos. For I'm your only historian, and I don't see you in this light. Not now, not thousands of years ago. Not in the centuries between."

"What does it matter? I've nothing left. You've seen to that. My children, all taken from me. Even my hounds you have turned against me. And what of my estate? Have you burned it to the ground just to spite me?"

"Until you answer my question, I'll answer no more of yours."

"What is this question?"

"How did your fracti become children in your heart and on your lips? From where did this love for them come?"

"You seek to know my heart?"

"I seek to know your motives. Your heart in its entirety I would do best not to explore. I imagine the endeavor would be akin to chasing a moonbeam off a cliff."

"You seek to delay your murder of me with chatter. My motives have always been clear to you. I seek the pure elixir."

"So that your children may never die?" she asked.

"How many immortals have you made? You have the pure elixir. You can't understand my anguish. Two centuries, Bektaten. That was all I could give them. Two centuries of life. But a heartbeat amidst immortality. And yet, those were the only choices I was left with after our kingdom fell. The incessant, crushing grief of another generation lost to withering and dust after two hundred years. The absolute isolation as I walked the earth alone. Or the absolute darkness beneath it. And so I chose the first until only the third was bearable. And those children, the ones you slaughtered, had little time left. So I placed myself in a tomb, knowing that once they had crumbled, no one would know of my location, and my sleep would be as permanent as death."

"And yet, they woke you."

"Yes. They heard tell of this Ramses the Damned and in him they saw the hope of the pure elixir."

"You could have easily dismissed them and returned to sleep," she said.

"I've explained my motives. What else do you want of me?"

"You've lied about them. I watched you among your children, Saqnos. No great love drove you. You treated them as incompetents and slaves. You sought the pure elixir for your own benefit, not theirs."

"You ask me questions to which you believe you have the answers. Why? Why delay for another moment what you have always longed to do? Turn me to dust! Punish me once and for all for this thing you call a betrayal. So that we may put our history to sleep forever."

"What I have always longed to do? Nonsense. You were the one entirely possessed by a singular goal. You squandered the millennia you were given on bitterness and appetite, the pursuit of that which you were not meant to have. You don't command me here or anywhere."

"No. I give you explanations which you then twist to justify whatever you wish to do."

"How dare you?" she said. "How dare you treat me as one governed only by emotion? You staged a rebellion without a plan. Without the barest knowledge of what you stole. In your jealousy and your rage, you allowed reason to abandon you. You didn't once stop to question what an army needs to remain intact. You didn't once stop to ask what would render a soldier loyal to you if they had no need of food, arms, or shelter. You assumed they would hail you for all time as the deliverer of a great gift, and this alone would render you a god in their eyes, and not just a calculating thief.

"And yet, the Saqnos I knew, the Saqnos who served me, would have asked these questions. He would have encouraged me to ask such questions myself had I told him of such a plan. But the man who burst into my chambers, with the arms of my own soldiers raised against me, he was not that man. And so I will not allow you to stand before me and claim that grief for your fracti has made you what you are now. You were changed thousands of years before then, before a drop of elixir ever touched your lips, when just the idea of it drove you insane."

"I don't stand before you. I sit and I do so in fear of your daggers and your poisons."

"And I stand before you, in fear that you cannot tell the truth of yourself because you do not know the truth of yourself."

"Then give it to me, my queen. Give me my truth, even as you refuse to reveal your own."

"You have always known my truth."

"*That is a lie!*" he cried out. "Eight thousand years later it is still the greatest discovery of humankind and still you keep it secret. Still you guard it as if it were just an ancient scroll."

"And what would you do with it if I gave it to you?" she asked.

"What would you have done then if your plan had not ended in ruin?"

"I would have made gods on earth."

"Yes," she whispered. "Yes, you would have. And to do this you would have extinguished anyone who was not godlike in your eyes. You would have used it to fortify our palace against all others. You would have fractured our kingdom into a million pieces small enough to lie at our feet like blossoms. You would have taken the glorious miracle I had discovered and used it to shatter Shaktanu, and to make a kingdom only out of what was within your reach. And you knew I would permit none of these things so long as I ruled. And that is why you raised arms against me the moment you heard of the elixir's existence."

"And yet you've allowed me to live all of this time," he said.

"I have nourished hope. I have wished that a man given all the time in the world might someday come to know his true self and wish to improve upon it. But with each passing century, you have proved these hopes were in vain."

"Grieving for my soul," he sneered. "It holds you in thrall the way some are held by strong drink."

"It has, Saqnos. But I'm relieved of this obsession now. I set you free."

Ramses worked to keep silent. Next to him, Julie stiffened, tensing her hand around the dagger's handle.

"Free?" Saqnos asked, giving voice, it seemed, to Ramses' own thoughts.

"Yes. Free to make your final decision."

In the doorway behind Saqnos, Enamon and Aktamu appeared, daggers drawn. But they allowed enough space between them for Saqnos to leave the great hall if he so chose.

As if he could not believe this sudden turn of events, Saqnos rose slowly to his feet and looked to each of them in turn. He seemed stricken by the confusion on Ramses' face, on Julie's face, as if any suggestion the two of them were not in on this plan meant it could not possibly be a trap.

His final decision.

What could Bektaten mean by this?

"You set me free now that you have taken everything from me," he said. "My children, my hounds."

"Your house stands. Your hounds are still there. Although they won't be as submissive to your evil deeds as they once were. A decision awaits you on the other side of the bridge that brought you here. I give this decision entirely to you. Cross the bridge before I change my mind."

For a while no one spoke. The only sounds were the crackling of the fire and the roaring surf, and then those sounds were joined by a third: the low rumble of laughter coming from Saqnos, a sound so full of derision and contempt, Ramses tightened his grip on his dagger in response. Eventually this rumble turned into a frenzied cackling, and it was then that Ramses thought the man had gone mad.

There was fury in Bektaten's expression, but she did not order Saqnos to leave.

"You're a coward, Bektaten," Saqnos finally said, left breathless by his own laughter. "You're a coward who kills only at a safe remove. You cannot even bear to see me brought down by your own men. You are a coward, Bektaten, and you always were. A coward who could not face the evil in her kingdom."

"There was only one evil in my kingdom. And it was you. And I have faced you for thousands of years. And I watched your children die only a few feet from where I stood. Every last one. There was no remove. You were the one who sent them unaccompanied to do your bidding while you remained at your estate." She took a deep breath. "Leave this place. And know that from this day forward, my back will be turned to you."

Julie squeezed Ramses' hand, distressed by Bektaten's order almost to the point of crying out in protest. She had not seen what

Ramses had just glimpsed when Saqnos turned his back to the fire and stepped into the more even light cast by the chandelier overhead.

"Fare thee well, my queen," Saqnos whispered.

Bektaten said nothing.

Saqnos turned, passed between her guards, who turned and followed him. Bektaten followed as well. Ramses did the same. Julie tightened her grip and held him in place. "Ramses," she whispered fiercely, "she cannot let him go. She must not."

"His eyes, Julie," he whispered back. "Did you see his eyes?"

40

Outside, the winds were fierce, the sky over the sea still dark and pierced by stars. But in the east, dawn's first light brightened the sky. There was a pale glow all around them, which allowed their group to see without need for a flashlight or a torch.

Steps from the garden that had brought him so much ruin, Saqnos slowed and gazed into the rustling blossoms.

Behind him, they all came to a stop. Enamon and Aktamu, who had remained on the man's heels ever since they left the great room; Bektaten a few paces behind them; and then Ramses and Julie in the rear, their hands still clutching daggers that had been dipped in the strangle lily upon their return.

Ramses looked back at the castle.

Above, Sibyl opened her window. The wind whipped through her golden hair and she was forced to hold the collar of her night-gown closed against it with one hand. Had she overheard their conversation in the great room? If so, had she been able to make any sense of it? Regardless, she was silent. She seemed to understand she was bearing witness to a departure of great significance.

As Saqnos lingered, Ramses expected words of farewell. But there were none.

Silently, he started once again for the courtyard gate, which had been left open.

When he came to the bridge, he gripped both of its rope rails to steady himself and then proceeded to cross it. Slowly. Carefully. The boards underfoot were knotted tightly together, forming an almost solid floor. But the entire construction swayed steadily in the wind. And the spray from the crashing waves far below created a constant mist that turned the boards slick.

"Ramses," Julie whispered. "Ramses, she can't—"

"Patience, Julie," he whispered back. "Patience, my love."

Light glinted off some sort of shiny object that appeared to be resting against one of the rocks on the other side. Some sort of gift waiting for Saqnos just beyond the bridge. But Saqnos had not yet seen it.

Once he had crossed, he looked back to find Enamon and Aktamu standing on either side of the bridge's headland side. Each man had taken one of the rope rails in hand and stretched it taut across the upturned blade of his dagger. Their meaning was clear: should Saqnos suddenly try to return they would quite literally cut the bridge out from under him.

At first, Saqnos sneered, then a sort of realization seemed to dawn.

Why would they think this a threat worth making with this silent, deliberate tableau?

An immortal could easily survive the fall. An immortal might be strong enough to cling to the nearest rock and keep the waves from sweeping him away. Perhaps it was then that Saqnos noticed the gift that had been left for him on the rocks nearby. Or perhaps this strange gesture on the part of Bektaten's men caused him to survey his immediate surroundings, searching for evidence of this final choice she had referenced earlier.

The mirror rested against a jagged outcropping of rock behind him. Its details were hard for Ramses to make out at a distance, but it was the size of an elegant ladies' hand mirror, with an oval reflective surface and a bright silver frame.

Saqnos lifted it and stared into his own reflection. The sound that came from him then reminded Ramses of the bellowing of some great, stricken animal brought low by spears. For now Saqnos saw what Ramses had glimpsed briefly in the castle moments before as the man had turned from the fire and stepped into the chandelier's glow; his eyes, once blue, were now brown again.

For what felt like an eternity, he did not lower the mirror. His weary bellows eventually faded into labored breathing they could not hear from this distance. He looked again to Aktamu and Enamon. Neither man had lowered his dagger or changed his stance by an inch.

Now Saqnos realized why the prospect of having the bridge cut out from under him constituted a real threat.

Saqnos was mortal again.

This was why they'd taken him to the armory before bringing him to the fire.

This was the secret in Bektaten's garden she had referred to before blessing their raid upon Havilland Park.

Saqnos raised the mirror in one hand and hurled it to the rocks underfoot. The glass shattered instantly. Ramses at first thought this act was meant to only vent rage, then Saqnos crouched down and carefully picked up one of the largest shards. Studiously, he ran one sharp end down the inside of his forearm, and then the other. He watched the blood flow. He watched the wound remain open and red. And he knew then, from the fierceness of the wounds and the speed at which the blood flowed, that he was no longer immortal.

"A choice?" he roared across the stormy gulf between them. "This is the choice of which you spoke? Where is the choice in this? You have now taken everything from me. *Everything.*"

"You have your life!" There was such strength and power in Bektaten's voice that it seemed as if she were calmly speaking, and not shouting, even though her words were clear above the restless sea and whistling wind. "And you have your half elixir. You have the choice to make more *children.* You have the choice to live among them for two more centuries. And now, you have the choice to truly love them as companions and partners and equals. For you will be one of them, Saqnos. For when they die, so shall you."

"And the alternative?" he shouted back.

Bektaten uncurled the fingers on one hand and gestured to the great gap of wind and waves that now separated them.

I shall spend the rest of my existence trying to find the word to describe the change that is overtaking this man, Ramses thought. Was it peace that came to him? Was there a word in any known language that could describe the moment in which an immortal thousands of years old casts off his memories, sets down his burdens, relieves himself of the weight of a lived experience heavier than most creatures will ever know? Was it a moment for which a word need be invented, and would he, Ramses the Great, Ramses the Damned, be the one to someday invent it? Or did the word exist somewhere in Bektaten's ancient language? Was it written somewhere within the volumes of her journals?

Saqnos stared down at his bleeding arms, studied them quietly and calmly. Then he raised his gaze and looked once more across the violent gulf that separated them.

"Long may you reign!" he sneered, and then he stepped from the edge of the cliff.

41

Sibyl screamed.

Saqnos plunged silently into the stormy dark, arms thrown out in a gesture of surrender.

His body was caught, then flipped, by a jagged outcropping of rock.

He somersaulted into curtains of whitecaps and then was lost to the roaring sea.

When he drew near to her, Ramses saw no tears in Bektaten's eyes. No evidence of triumph in her expression either. But she had an answer to her final question, an answer that could not be disputed.

No great love or passion had driven the man who betrayed her. No great love or passion held him to this earth once his immortality was taken from him. And so his tale of being hardened by grief for his fracti was truly a lie, proved so by his own final leap.

Would it bring her peace to know this?

"Sibyl," Julie said quietly, then she squeezed Ramses' hand and hurried back inside the courtyard.

The four of them remained at the cliff's edge, staring down into the foaming sea. The wind was powerful enough to make great flapping sounds as it beat Bektaten's red gown against her body.

When he noticed that Aktamu and Enamon both rested a hand on Bektaten's shoulder, he thought, at first, they were trying to steady her in the wind. But nothing about her posture seemed unsteady or unsure. Their touch was solely meant to comfort.

The look on her face was something he could not describe even to himself. A deep sorrow pervaded her, yet he could point to no one change in her expression or her demeanor. She stared down at the rocks below.

"Go," she finally said. "See if his body can be found."

They nodded and departed.

Bektaten turned back to the castle. She bowed her head and walked slowly towards it.

Ramses had no choice but to follow.

He drew the gate closed behind him, as if this gesture would somehow wall off the implications of what had just taken place.

The winds were not as strong inside the courtyard. But the plants and blossoms in Bektaten's garden still danced and shifted and made a whispering music as they rustled together. Some of the stalks were taller than her by half, and while many of the flowers seemed ordinary at first glance, upon closer inspection he saw a certain characteristic in each that marked it as miraculous: strangely shaped leaves and petals that reminded him of human hands, blossoms of such an intense hue and size it was almost impossible to look away from them.

As she paused in the aisle between the two rows of plantings, of secrets, of miracles, Ramses expected her to collapse, or at least to fall to her knees. Perhaps in grief, or perhaps from relief. But she stood steady and strong, fingering one of the blossoms closest to her.

There was a creaking metal sound from above. He looked up. It was Julie, drawing the window to Sibyl's room shut.

"And so there is something that can make us what we were," Ramses finally said.

"Is there?" she asked. "Could you ever again be the man you

were before you became pharaoh? Before you became immortal? Or have you been so marked by your experiences since then, the return of your mortality would simply usher in a new existence, however limited in years?"

"Have you ever wished to know this yourself? After so much life, you must have some desire to meet the gods, should they exist. Some desire to see what realm lies beyond this one."

She considered his words for a while. She began walking again with Ramses beside her, but her focus seemed to be on each plant she passed.

"Many times I have walked the length of the land they now call Africa. I visited other kingdoms lost to history, smaller, humbler, than my own. But no less glorious in their own way. I counseled the rulers of kingdoms still largely unknown to this century, kingdoms whose great monuments have yet to be discovered. But many of my travels were solitary. And thousands of years ago, I walked endlessly, it seemed, towards a great cloud of black smoke on the horizon. Eventually I came to a roaring inferno that swept across a landscape free of humans, with nothing to stop its advance. So large was this fire, it could have consumed Thebes or Meroë. Alone, I marched towards it. Knowing with each step that I would give myself to it. That I would test the limits of my immortality, alone, with the flames.

"I tied myself to a tree. I could easily free myself if I wanted. But the time it would take to undo the rope would give me time to reconsider my decision. I tied myself to a tree so that I could watch the flames advance. So I could behold their fury and their mystery as no other human could. So that I could watch the trees fall before it and turn to ash. So that I could watch the helplessness of the soil and the life it had given birth to against a power of such force.

"And the animals that ran from this fire. The lions and the giraffes and the other great beasts, some of them paused and gazed at me as if I were a creature beyond their understanding. As if my absence of fear made me a god. And then the flames arrived. They consumed me. And I did what I could to give myself to them entirely. I released screams heard by no one. Sounds that did not seem human to my own ears. It was as if I was singing to the flames themselves." She was close to him now. She gave him her full attention. "And they sang back," she whispered.

"You heard the words of gods? Is this what you mean to say?"

"I tasted death, Ramses. There is no way to measure the time it took for the flames to pass over me. Hours, days. I cannot be sure. These measurements did not exist then. Only the passage of the sun was reliable for this. And these flames, they blotted out the sun and the night darkness entirely. The fire, it moved like a lumbering and contented beast, and I gave myself to it until it had passed."

"But what did you see, Bektaten? What did you see aside from the flames and the ruin they brought? What was this singing you heard?"

"There is no heaven. There is no hell. There is no above or below. If there is a realm beyond this one, it is no more beautiful, no more significant, no more full of truth, than ours here on earth."

"How can you say this? What did you see in the flames that would suggest this?"

"I saw a spirit world so intricate and vast, so thoroughly laced through our existence here on earth, that the rivers of departing souls have no choice but to turn back to it. They were not lost, these spirits. They did not wander. They did not wail. They did not cry out for guidance or the resolution of some petty mystery that had plagued them in mortal life. They *returned*. They returned with hunger. They returned with joy. They sought no greater realm. And what could that mean but there is no greater realm than this, Ramses. And so why would I wish to ever leave?"

"You don't believe it was just a vision produced by madness?" he asked.

"It was not a vision. It was sustained. For the time it took the flames to pass me, I lived between this world and a world that is here but not clearly seen."

"And you emerged from this place believing there are no fields of Aaru. No kingdom of heaven."

"No," she whispered, "I emerged from this place believing that if such a place exists, it offers no wonder greater than those here on earth. For the essence of what I saw was this: our soul, once set free, seeks only to return." He looked away from her. "You hate this thought? It angers you. You have loved and nourished visions of a world beyond this one."

"I have, in all my many years, loved and nourished many visions which I have been forced to set free. Your experience suggests a far greater challenge."

"What is the greater challenge, Ramses?"

"It suggests that all immortals must have an experience such as yours with the great fire, or we are doomed to become Saqnos. Consumed by a singular, blinding pursuit. Lost to a loneliness we create."

"Don't be so certain of this," she said, taking his hand gently and leading him back to the castle. "Don't be so certain of anything. There are many experiences within the *Shaktanis* that I wish to share with you. You may read and absorb them at your leisure. But do absorb them, Ramses. Don't leap to rash conclusions. Don't diminish them into a hasty code of morals and laws for beings such as us. Let them embrace you so they may guide you."

"You will teach me your ancient tongue so that I may read them?"

"Of course."

He stopped suddenly, and looked back to the garden.

"And if I ever wish . . ."

"What, Ramses?"

"If I ever wish to be mortal again?" he asked. "If Julie ever wishes it?"

A long silence. She released his hand.

"I will grant that wish," she finally said. "But I will not grant it to any immortal you make in the days that follow this one, as I wish you to make no immortals at all. Can this be our treaty?"

Treaty. A deep sense of relief coursed through Ramses. A treaty. Ah, so we are equal, are we? This powerful being now honors me by speaking of treaties, rather than of judgment. Ah, the marvel of queens. Even in ancient times he had heard talk of queens protecting their kingdoms, while kings go forth to conquer new ones, of queens protecting their power, while kings seek more. And in modern times, he had heard tell of a great queen, Elizabeth of England, who had followed this very path, protecting her great kingdom and its far-flung colonies, but never initiating a war to gain increased power or land.

Ramses smiled.

"A treaty?" he asked. "You speak to me now as if I'm still a king."

"Are you not?" she asked.

"Beloved queen," he said. "I haven't told you of another to whom I gave the elixir."

"And you need not tell me, for I know of it. Elliott, the Earl of Rutherford—a learned and sober man."

"Yes," he said. "Nor can I swear to you that I will never give the elixir to another. I know too much now of loneliness and isolation to make such a pledge to you. Elliott Savarell, the Earl of Rutherford, is my responsibility now, just as is Julie Stratford. And Cleopatra, my wounded Cleopatra, remains my responsibility. No. I cannot swear to you that I will not give the elixir again. We stand before a new and modern world of which I never dreamed. We may become lost from each other in this world, Bektaten. And who knows what tragedy or wisdom or need, for that matter, might guide me or drive me to do?"

Bektaten regarded him for a long moment in silence, and then she smiled. How bright and beautiful she appeared with this smile.

"Spoken like a king," she said. "But this elixir, in all its purity and power, you stole from the one to whom I'd entrusted it, and when you did this, you stole it from me."

"Yes, my queen, I know this now," said Ramses. "But I cannot go back and right that wrong. And I cannot erase the secrets of the elixir from my mind. Thousands of years have passed since that great theft. And right or wrong, I now possess the secret. Do not ask of me impossible things."

"You know what I am really asking of you," she said.

"I do. That I never act rashly again, that I never go against nature, that I never traffic again with the dead."

"Precisely," she replied.

"I give you my word on this. How could I not? I will never again do what I did in rousing this revenant Cleopatra from her slumber. I have made a nochtin, as Saqnos called it, and would I could undo it."

He broke off, unable to say another word.

"Nochtin?" Bektaten pondered. "Nochtin—a species described by a fool. Perhaps your broken Cleopatra is not a nochtin. Remember, it was with a corrupted elixir that Saqnos worked his resurrections, the same corrupted elixir that doomed his fracti."

"That's true," he said.

"It was the pure elixir that you brought to the corpse of your Cleopatra. Who is to say that she is a nochtin or that she will go mad?"

"If only . . . ," Ramses whispered. "But she is going mad, is she not?"

"She is suffering. She is in confusion. She has a dark path before her. But again, it was the pure elixir that brought her into being, and very possibly more of it will help her now."

This almost brought tears to Ramses' eyes. "Perhaps . . ."

"As you have said, Ramses, she is your responsibility. And I do not presume to question you as to what you do with this creature so long as you do not seek to destroy her. That I cannot abide."

"I understand."

"I shall be watching. I shall always be watching."

"And you'll see me a chastened and wiser man for all this," Ramses said. "I promise you."

"Well, then, Ramses the Great. We have a treaty, do we not?"

42

The Rutherford Estate

They were saying he should never set foot on the property again. That no one should. He had even heard nurses at the clinic suggest that the main house and tenant farms and even the old Roman temple be burned to the ground, and the land blessed by priests from every known religion.

They had infuriated him, these words. For this superstitious gossip had also taken hold among the other party guests being treated for shock and exhaustion at the same clinic where he'd taken his mother. And all of it upset him as nothing in his life had before. Not the loss of his beautiful companion in Cairo, Mr. Ramsey's mad friend. Not the loss of Julie, who had never truly been his to begin with. And not the long absence of his father, who even now had not sent word.

And where was his father? Another casino? Perhaps when the story broke across the Continent, he would be in touch. But for now there had been no telegram, no telephone call, no word of any kind—only another large deposit at the bank.

Throughout the night, Alex had managed to control his anger. He'd managed to turn his back on the gossiping doctors and nurses before lashing out at them. To worry a handkerchief between his fists whenever he felt the urge to tell those who had not been present for the horror to stop flapping their gums about it.

Instead, he'd been a perfect gentleman, a good sport. But both those roles were tattered costumes incapable of containing his confusion and grief.

When the police had questioned him, the supposedly logical explanation they were assembling became instantly clear.

While they weren't accusing everyone at the party of having suffered from a collective madness, they kept insisting that there were facts that needed to be addressed. Such as why had no one at the party recognized or known the people who had subsequently undergone such a horrific death? The police had managed to collect a few of their names from those who had chatted briefly with them on the lawn. And yet not one of these names was familiar to Alex, his mother, or any of the other guests to whom they'd spoken. The police had also managed to talk to the secretary who had assembled the guest list. She'd confirmed the names appeared nowhere on it. These mysterious people had come out of nowhere and vanished into nowhere. Perhaps, suggested the police, they had never actually existed at all?

And then there was the matter of the strange tunnel on the property. Alex had known nothing of this tunnel. Yet the police said there were tracks in the tunnel, and tracks cut in the lawn where the tunnel opened near the pond.

They were connected, these things, the police insisted. It was all some sort of misdirection, some sort of sleight of hand. A grand illusion intended to distract with chaos while some criminal activity took place. A theft, perhaps.

When Julie had finally reached him at the hospital by telephone early that morning, he had shared all these things with her, and his anger had boiled to the surface. How calm she had seemed. How soothing her words. She was terribly sorry they'd been separated in the chaos, but she and Ramsey were quite well, albeit as shocked by what they'd witnessed as everyone else. And it wasn't as if she had an explanation of her own. Care for your mother, she had said, that's what matters now. Care for your mother. They, on the other hand, would soon travel north to speak with the police.

And she was right, of course.

She was half right. His mother was very dear to him. But the house still mattered. The estate still mattered. And the crazy notion that some sort of theft had taken place had to be either proved or disproved. And so, after the nurses sedated his mother once more, he slipped away and returned to the house.

The fact that it was still standing startled him, which was absurd, of course.

A childish part of him had assumed the curses he'd heard visited upon the place by the party's traumatized guests had somehow managed to punch out the house's soaring windows, tear pieces from its roof, shred the hedges lining the long, curving drive to the front door.

Was the possibility really so absurd when you considered what they had all witnessed? People, living, breathing people, guests of the party, dissolving to ash before their very eyes.

And how would the police ultimately explain this?

A drug. They had all been drugged and subjected to some piece of visual trickery that was a cover for a great theft. But the police had searched the grounds throughout the night, had brought him and his mother detailed lists of the rooms' contents, right down to the jewels his mother had brought from London two days before.

Everything appeared to be in place. Perhaps when his mother got her wits more about her, she would notice something missing from the lists that should be there. But would it be so large as to require a secret tunnel to carry it away?

Alone now, Alex walked rooms that had just a day before been filled with laughter and delight, and then panic and screams. Could he fill them with his memories of childhood, of the toy train set his father had once helped him to build across the living room? Of the hours spent reading in the windows that looked out over the broad lawns?

Must go to the lawn, he told himself. *Must face seeing it again now, or never.*

What was the old saying about falling off a horse? Perhaps it wasn't quite fitting, considering he would have much preferred a broken bone to the shock of what he'd seen the day before.

Drugs. An illusion. A trick. A theft.

He was merely tasting these words, sampling them, seeing if they would prove digestible. And the answer would come only once he gazed upon the scene of the crime again.

The glass doors to the terrace had been shattered in the panic. Strange that the police hadn't put some sort of barricade or a piece of wood over the opening. But they weren't in the renovation business. He stepped through the framework carefully, so as not to loosen the remaining shards of glass. And then he followed the path the guests had followed the day before, out onto the patio and then down the stone steps leading to the grass.

He should have prepared himself for the sight of the overturned chairs, the toppled umbrellas, their canopies flapping in the gentle breeze. The debris of the great exodus had all been left behind. But the piles of ash, and the emptied clothing and shoes, were gone, thanks be to God.

Still, the sight of the wreckage before him was more upsetting than he'd anticipated. Perhaps the clear, beautiful morning only made it worse, for it called to mind better, happier days of sunsets like great orange bonfires lighting up the western horizon beyond the line of green, rustling trees. The clink of croquet balls on the lawn. Not this ghostly, haunted silence.

Already, I am not the same, he realized. *Already, I am changed by what I have seen.*

How long did he stand there in the breeze? How long did he stand there amidst the ghosts of yesterday's terror?

How long before the music began to play?

It started quietly at first. During the first few warbling notes, he thought it might be coming from the neighboring estate. But the neighboring estate was too far away. And this man's soaring operatic voice, the Italian words utterly familiar to him, was coming from the drawing room, and the gramophone within.

Upon his return to England, with a longing for the woman

he'd known in Cairo pulsing within him like a second heartbeat, he had, in secret, rushed to the library where he had read the entire libretto of *Aida* in a single, hungry sitting. It was lyrics from that opera that he heard now, lyrics sung by the voice of the great Enrico Caruso, so powerful and insistent despite the scratches on the recording. It carried through the shattered doors behind him.

Celeste Aida, forma divina,
Mistico serto di luce e fior.

Had his mother been released from the hospital? For the recording was her gift to him. She'd mentioned it to him before the party. But it couldn't be her. They'd sedated her only a half hour before.

Perhaps he truly was going mad.

But if that were the case, would he still be perfectly aware of his name, of the country in which he stood?

He placed his hand upon the doorknob and opened the door gently.

He prepared himself to discover that perhaps the nurses and the doctors were right; there truly was some inexplicable evil underneath the Rutherford Estate; that he had stepped through some doorway into an alternate and fantastical world.

Del mio pensiero
tu sei regina
tu di mia vita sei
lo splendor.

When he saw her standing next to the phonograph, in a soft fashionable dress that showed more of her flesh than the great silver gown she had worn to the opera, his back came to rest against the nearest wall.

When her eyes, those sparkling, impossibly blue eyes, met his, his breath left him.

He was frozen now as she moved across the room towards him, barefoot on the hardwood floor. No words for the look on her face. Expectant? Hungry? Adoring? He could not be sure.

He could not be sure of anything except that she was there. She had set the music to play. She was closing the distance between them now.

"What do you see, Lord Rutherford?" she asked. "What do you see when you gaze upon me?" Tears in her eyes; tears in his eyes as well.

Must answer. Must answer, for if I can't, then this may actually be a kind of madness.

"I see . . ."

"Yes."

Inches from him now, she raised her head hesitantly, as if she were afraid to touch him yet wanted nothing more than to feel his kiss.

"I see Cairo," he whispered. "I see the opera I have attended again and again in my mind. In my dreams. My dreams of the time we spent together. I search the aisles below for any sign of you. And then I see you in the car. . . ."

She sealed her eyes shut at this memory, forcing tears down her cheeks.

"I see you consumed by flames," he whispered.

"Consumed, yes," she whispered, "but not claimed."

"But you are . . ." *Healed* was the word that first came to his mind. But it seemed pathetically inadequate. This was a miracle, her appearance before him. Her *life*.

With all the courage he had, he closed his hand gently around hers. He brought the tips of her fingers close to his nose, then to his lips. A smile now accompanied her tears, a desperate, almost pleading smile. When she brought her hand to the side of his face and he allowed her to cradle his cheek, it was as if some great tension left her.

"Is there a name for what you are?" he whispered.

"If there was not, could you love me now? Here? As we both are?"

He wanted to kiss her fingertips, gently. But he knew this

would be the end of him. The end of any life he might have once described as level and sane. And so he did it.

And then his mouth was on hers, his hands traveling up and under her frilly, white gown. The feel of her silky flesh, the smell of her, the taste of her, the startling strength with which she pulled him to the floor, wrapped her legs around his waist as he tasted her, kneaded her, ravished her with kisses. Each touch, each taste, more than an expression of passion, a confirmation of her existence. Her miraculous resurrection.

Again and again, she said his name. And she did this after confessing to having no name of her own, and that made the love with which she said his all the more powerful.

Need there be a name for what they were to each other now? For what they had been for each other in Cairo? And if madness was required to enter this place of unbridled passion and dreams realized, then let there be madness now and forever.

43

She had not exhausted him. Instead, he carried her upstairs to one of the bedrooms, and there he began to make love to her again as the morning sunlight streamed through the lace curtains. The wallpaper seemed as vivid and bright as the day outside, more beautiful and welcoming than anything inside the dark estate where she'd been held prisoner.

He did not stop until he'd brought her to a climax that shook her to her bones.

In the breathless aftermath, as he gently smoothed her hair from her forehead, he began to tell her everything that happened the day before. The party and the great poisoning, the absurd explanation being offered by the investigators.

She said nothing in response. She didn't want to stop the flow of his words. They were so honest, so sincere, so carefully selected.

Her memories of their time together in Cairo were whole and untouched, and so she was reminded once again of why she had become so enamored of him in such a short time.

There was a nearness to him. Always. In every moment. A sense that he was utterly present. When he paused now and then to collect his thoughts, she did not feel as if his mind were slipping away to tend some calculations he wished to keep secret. He desired only to express himself as clearly as he could, and for her benefit. So that she could know him. So that she could know all he had been through since they'd parted.

Did this set him apart from all her past lovers, with their tilt towards perpetual distraction; a preoccupation with battles, with empires? She was losing her ability to remember.

But she could remember her brief time with him in Cairo, and in this moment, that was all that mattered. She could remember lying with him in that beautiful room at the Shepheard's Hotel. And how marvelous this was, to visit a memory vivid and pure, as so many others were being taken from her. Not just to visit it; but to live in it, to swim in it, to taste it. And now, as he had then, he treated her as if she were whole. As if she lacked for nothing, as if she was far from being the terrible, doomed creature Saqnos had described.

Nochtin. Could she imagine such a brutal word coming from Alex's lips? Perhaps, but she could not imagine him whispering it with the same hatred as her former captor.

He was explaining to her now that he had undergone a radical shift in his thinking, in his view of the world, all based on what he had witnessed on the lawn of this very estate. And on her miraculous return. And on the terrible, crushing grief he had felt after watching the flames claim her.

It was clear to her now that her reappearance, her resurrection, had somehow made it easier for him to accept what he'd witnessed the day before, outside this very house.

He spoke of it again now. This poisoning.

"Ashes, my darling. They turned to ash quite literally before our eyes." With a kind of dazed wonder, he said this. But again, she said nothing in response. She did not reveal to him that she had been on this very property before these events unfolded. That she had been perilously close to promising Julie Stratford she would never try to see him again, all in exchange for a dose of the elixir; a dose that might quiet her torment, stanch the outward flow of her own past. She told him none of this. Her silence seemed to cause him no strain, but for how much longer?

He had worked his way backwards in his story, it seemed. All the way to the explanations Ramses and Julie had given for her appearance in Cairo. Painful to hear herself described as a madwoman. But the rage she might once have felt over these words was not forthcoming. For it was possible she was becoming something far worse. Something that was neither immortal nor mortal. A foul thing raised from death.

Nochtin, she heard Saqnos growl. *Nochtin . . .*

Alex fell silent.

He caressed the side of her cheek. And only in the brief flare of his nostrils could she sense the tension in him, the expectation.

He had told her everything.

Now it was her turn.

"I am sick," she whispered. "I am sick, Lord Rutherford."

He propped himself up on his elbows. In so doing, he caused the sheet to slide down his broad chest. It was dusted with black hairs she'd been twining her fingers through only seconds before. At first, she thought he was recoiling. But this was not so. He was simply trying to get a better look at her. There was no revulsion in his expression.

"Sick?" he asked. "How can that be when you survived the flames?"

"The very thing which allowed me to survive the flames . . . there is . . ."

"A curse?" he asked. "Is that what it is? Some sort of curse?"

"Yes, perhaps we should call it a curse."

"What would you have me call it?" The anguish in his voice stabbed her. "I would so much rather think of you as an angel. It befits my experience of you entirely."

"I am not, Alex. I am not this thing you call an angel."

"Fine, then. I shall never call you anything but what you wish to be called."

Tears in her eyes at this. Tears that blurred her vision of this beautiful room and this fine, handsome man. He embraced her when he saw them, brought his lips to her neck, enfolded her in his warmth, his luscious mortal flesh.

"I shall seek no answers from you that you are not ready to give," he whispered. "Just, please. Don't leave me again. Please."

Oh, if only she could promise this. But when she parted her lips, her breath left her. She could do nothing but return his embrace. And then a silence fell, a silence filled by the suddenly slow and uneven sounds of his breath. Exhaustion claimed him.

When she realized he slept, she felt suddenly and utterly alone.

She withdrew from him only so far that she could see his face. It rested against the pillow now, next to her own bare shoulder. She reached for his cheek, intending to brush his hair from his forehead, much as he had done to her. And it was then that her fingers shook. And her despair turned to something darker. Something that chased away all sadness, replacing it with the comforting certainty of rage.

She cupped his chin in her hand. Ran her fingers along the delicate line of his jawbone. Felt the hot flush of mortal blood beneath his cheek. Ran her fingers gently along his throat; the veins pumping blood to his now-dreaming mind.

Was he dreaming of a future with her that could never be? A future sure to be destroyed by her coming madness?

What choices did she have in this moment?

To refuse him? Abandon him? Cast him back to the same grief he'd described to her moments before?

Or was it better to snap his neck? One quick movement. That was all it would take. And he would die believing he had attained her forever. He would die loving her. He would die having called her an angel only seconds before.

A mercy for him.

A mercy for her?

Inches from his throat, her hand shook. Her fingers trembled.

And at first she mistook the ragged sounds of her own tortured breath for some creature scratching inside the walls.

Was this the fate of all beings, to destroy that which they found beautiful once they realized they could not possess it forever?

It was a sob that threatened to take her now. All her effort was required to choke back the sound as she withdrew from the bed, gently, so as not to wake him, but quickly enough that she could feel as if she were recoiling from the terrible possibility of what she had almost done. Snapping his neck. Ending his life. Claiming to spare him pain by quickly ridding herself of the source of her own.

It was torture now. Torture to be here with him. With his tenderness and his beauty.

He did not wake. And she wanted him to. But she knew it would be harder to leave him if he did.

And then there were sounds outside. She moved quietly to the window and saw men in dark suits emerging from several cars parked along the driveway. They passed the house's front door. Instead they walked in the direction of the lawn where the poisoning had taken place. They were the investigators he had mentioned earlier; they had to be. They'd come back to begin another day's work now that the full day had dawned.

An agony to remain here another moment. An agony she could not endure.

She raced down the steps, found her dress in a puddle on the floor of the drawing room, close to where they'd made love. She had just managed to slip it over her head and smooth it down over her waist and legs when she heard him calling to her. Heard his footsteps hit the floor above.

And so she ran. She ran through the empty rooms away from the lawn where the investigators were gathering. Even as she heard him pursuing her, she continued to run, out a side door and into a manicured garden. She realized now she was close to the path Julie had asked her to walk the day before. Perhaps she could escape using the very same tunnel through which she'd been abducted.

And then she heard the door fly open behind her.

"Cleopatra!" he called.

This name. To hear him call her this name. This name that soon might no longer be hers. It caused her steps to falter enough that he caught up with her.

"No," he said, anguish in his voice. "You mustn't run. You must not! If you think you'll spare me further pain, you're wrong. For nothing could be worse than being returned to my grief for you. Whatever this curse that ails you, whatever you fear, I will be here for you throughout all of it."

"You cannot say these things," she managed through tears. "You don't know what they mean. You don't know what's to come!"

"Do you?" he asked. "Do you know what's to come? I don't sense certainty in you, Cleopatra. I sense confusion and the fear it breeds."

No words. She had no words with which to answer this.

"Every day since my return from Egypt has been a torment," he said. "I was a different man when I traveled there. And then I met you and it was as if all of my designs and ambitions were the hobbies of a boy. Childish things I had yet to put aside. I knew. I knew, Cleopatra. That there was something about you that could not be explained. Something that was possibly dark. Dangerous. Disruptive to everything I held dear.

"And still, I could not let you go. Even the darkest fantasies of what you were, of what you might be. They were not enough to make me let you go. This is what love is, isn't it? It's not a thing for which you clear a certain space in your life. It takes over your life, and all else must be made to fit to it, or the result is endless grief or a willful numbness that results in the death of your spirit before your body. I have seen this truth in the eyes of Julie and Ramsey. And I see it in your eyes when I look at you."

"You chain yourself to a sinking ship, Lord Rutherford," she whispered.

"No," he said, drawing so close to her his breath kissed her lips. "You are unsure of what you are. There is confusion in you. You fear this confusion will consume me. Destroy me. And what I say to you, what you must believe, is that you have already consumed me. And if you abandon me again, I will be destroyed."

She could not tell if she had fallen against him, or if he'd taken her in his arms. What did it matter? His embrace was sure. His embrace needed no other name. In his embrace, there was no confusion, no despair. No fear of the madness to come.

"I cannot remain here," she whispered. "I must withdraw from this world that I still don't fully understand."

"We shall go together, then," he said. "Anywhere you wish to go, I will go with you, my Bella Regina Cleopatra."

She took his face in her hands. Caressed him. Kissed him. Gave herself to him as he gave himself to her. It was gone, the desire to end his life that had been there only moments before. Gone and replaced by a need for him that was more than a simple hunger for escape.

"I'm so tired, Lord Rutherford," she whispered, "so very tired."

"Then rest in me," he whispered back. "Trust in me."

Part 4

44

Yorkshire

As soon as it began, Julie realized it wasn't going to be an interrogation so much as a polite questioning. Edith had insisted the detective conduct it right there in her room, with all of them gathered around her bed like nervous relatives eager to secure their piece of an inheritance from a dying elder. Perhaps this explained the detective's reserve; he was humbled by the presence of a countess.

Edith appeared collected and groomed for the moment, dressed in an ornate silk peignoir, her hair brushed back from her pale face to make a halo against the pillow. She looked positively angelic, and Julie was much relieved to see her so energized and restored after just two nights in this place.

It wasn't a bustling hospital so much as a quaint village clinic, ill equipped for treating grievous injuries. And that was fitting, Julie thought, for none of the aristocrats who currently filled its rooms complained of anything more serious than shock and stress.

Still, she thought their current arrangement inappropriate and intrusive. But Edith had insisted. Now she could see why. The countess listened closely to every word out of the detective's mouth, hoping his new questions would reveal new information.

How fortunate she'd been able to reach Alex by telephone the day before!

If he hadn't told her so much of the detective's theory, the two of them would not have come so prepared. But now, Ramses could play the man like an instrument. Agreeing wholeheartedly with his claim that, yes, some sort of elaborate illusion had taken place, some hallucinogen married to a physical sleight of hand, all of it designed to distract from some crime yet to be determined. How else to explain the strange tunnel underneath the temple?

"And the African woman several have mentioned?" the detective asked.

Edith furrowed her brow. No such reaction from Alex, Julie was surprised to see. He sat in a chair on the opposite side of the room, his hands clasped in front of him, his eyes fixed on some point just over Julie's shoulder. Resolutely calm, it seemed.

"Ah, yes," Ramses said, "this was my friend, Abeba Bektul. She is an Ethiopian of noble birth. She traveled here just for our party, I'm afraid."

"And what is your relationship to this Miss Bektul?"

"She's provided funding and general support for several of my excavations in Ethiopia."

"Ethiopia? Never heard much about mummies being unearthed in Ethiopia."

"Africa is a grand and mysterious place, good sir. A place whose full history has yet to be discovered."

"I see." The detective's brusque dismissal suggested he did not wish to see much of Africa at all. Perhaps he recalled the great defeat Ethiopia had delivered to the Italians years before and thought them an imminent threat to the British Empire. "And where is she now?"

"She's taken a room at Claridge's. You see, she'd planned to lodge with us at our home in Mayfair. But after all the stress, she desired privacy. She will be happy to answer your questions there, should you have any."

The truth was different, of course.

Bektaten had reserved the room shortly before Ramses and

Julie had departed Cornwall, and solely to give foundation to this cover story. And her alias, Abeba Bektul, was one of many, and different from the one she'd used to lease the castle. She did not wish to remain completely invisible if her participation was required, but she had no desire to host strangers so near to her garden. Thankfully, having lived many lives on different continents, she had no shortage of aliases she could use should this investigation turn its focus to her.

"Not sure there's any need as of yet," the detective answered, "so long as you can vouch for her good character."

"We most certainly can," Julie added.

"If we wish to question her, we'll be in touch with you then. Will she return to Ethiopia soon?"

"No," Ramses offered, "she'd planned a long stay to begin with. After what she's been through, after what we've *all* been through, she has no desire to take to the high seas anytime soon."

"Very well, then." The detective cleared his throat. "So it appears now, as it did before, we are in search of a theft. In the two days since we've begun our investigation, no further details as to these missing guests have been brought to our attention, I'm afraid. And while I can assure you it's almost impossible to investigate a murder without a body, when no loved ones or friends or even acquaintances of the missing step forward, well . . . it's impossible to investigate nothing at all. So if the constabulary is to continue in this matter, it will have to do so as if this is a theft."

"Or a poisoning," Edith said, "but of *us*. Clearly, we were given something that made us hallucinate. It must have been in the champagne!"

"Perhaps, miss," the detective said, "but I'm afraid that in the panic, the champagne was spilled and the glasses smashed underfoot. We couldn't recover a single intact glass anywhere on the property, and all the open bottles had been dispensed."

"Well, then it's the most perfect and befuddling plot that ever was." Edith tossed her hands in the air and let them thud to the blanket on either side of her. Julie couldn't help but smile. There was energy and vitality in this simple gesture, a sign that Edith would soon be free of this clinic and back to her old self. "Why we couldn't have all seen butterflies and rainbows is beyond me. Why did we all have to see something so truly wretched? But then again, I'm not a professional poisoner or thief, so perhaps it's just beyond me."

There was a ripple of laughter in the room.

Alex did not join in.

"It is rather odd, though, isn't it?" Alex's focus seemed to be entirely on Julie, even as he addressed the room. "That we would all hallucinate almost precisely the same thing."

"Odd doesn't even begin to describe it, I'm afraid," the detective said. "But just so you're aware, we continue to take this seriously. The constabulary will be consulting several illusionists over the next few days. Perhaps they'll tell us how a trick like this might have been accomplished through the marriage of some physical magic act and a drug, as the countess suggests. I do ask, however, that you keep that information from the press. For all of our sakes. It isn't the easiest thing. Police seeking help from . . . *magicians.*"

A polite exchange of goodbyes followed. But Julie found herself unable to take her eyes off Alex. Was he in some sort of shock? Had his condition gone undiagnosed as the medical professionals present rushed to give their full attention to his mother, the countess?

"It was so dear of you both to drive all this way," Edith said.

Julie clasped the woman's hand. "After what you've had to endure on our behalf, Edith. I can't . . ."

The words failed her, and she felt the touch of Ramses' hand on her shoulder. Did he fear she'd say too much?

"We'll return to London as soon as we can," Edith said. "I can't bring myself to visit the estate just yet. As for Elliott, well, he sent another enormous sum of money from somewhere. I've lost complete track of where he is."

"Surely he'll come home when he hears of all this," Alex said crossly. "As soon as I have a new address."

"Don't be annoyed with your father, Alex," said Edith. "He needs this time to himself. And every time I turn around, it seems, the bank is calling to let us know of another deposit. Fortune has certainly smiled on him, wherever he is, and he shares that good fortune with his family, perhaps more than he enjoys it himself."

"I'm sorry, Mother." He mirrored Julie now, standing on the opposite side of the bed, taking Edith's other hand. "It's been an exhausting few days."

But he didn't seem exhausted, Julie thought. He seemed dazed, perhaps a little drunk. Strangely relaxed. And when he caught Julie studying him intently, he gave her a knowing smile.

"It has," Edith whispered, returning Alex's grip and then Julie's in turn. "It most certainly has. And you've been a wonderful son throughout all of it."

Alex gazed at her as if these words pained him. Then, in a whisper, he said, "We have always been a family, Mother, you and I. And Father. And we always will be, regardless of where any of us are in the world. Regardless of where any of us hope to be."

"Yes, I suppose so," Edith whispered. "And be assured, I do miss your father from time to time. Even melancholy has its charms now and then."

"Alex," Julie said, "do you care to join me for a walk?"

He nodded, but he continued to stare at his mother.

Edith's mind seemed elsewhere. Perhaps that was why she didn't notice the glint of tears in her son's eyes. When he bent down quickly, almost furtively, to kiss her on the forehead, she reached up and patted him gently on the cheek. But her expression suggested she'd returned to some silent deliberation over the strange events of the past few days.

*   *   *

They walked together through the tree-lined square just outside. They were surrounded by a mix of stone walls and shop fronts, and neither one of them seemed able to speak. She expected Alex to burst forth with some great outpouring of emotion. That's what the Alex of several days before would have done. But now he had been changed once more, it seemed. And so she was at a loss for how to determine his mental state without revealing details she didn't want him to know.

"What do you believe, Alex?" she finally asked him.

"What do you wish me to believe, Julie?"

"I don't understand." But she did. She did understand. He had suspicions, suspicions of her.

"Most people don't change, do they?" He'd stopped suddenly, his hands in his pockets, staring at a motorcar as it chugged past. "No matter what happens to them. No matter what they go through. They do everything they can to preserve their prejudices. Or their ambitions, even if those ambitions were cast when they were quite young and foolish. This is the business of living, as I once described it, isn't it? To explain away new experiences with old beliefs."

"The business of living," she said, "as you described it, as I understood you to describe it, was ignoring the pain in your heart and seeking to distract yourself with routine."

"Yes. Indeed."

"You have been changed by what you have seen, Alex?"

"Perhaps. But that's not exactly what I mean to say."

"What is it you mean to say?"

"I mean to say it's a reasonable expectation of most people. That they won't change. That they will reject the implications of new experiences." He met her gaze. "New information—"

"Alex—"

"And so it's understandable, I guess. And perhaps the basis for forgiveness when you learn that so much has been kept from you, even by those to whom you've bared your heart."

When she reached for his hand, he withdrew it. When she reached for his face, he took a step back.

"But this is new, Julie. This forgiveness. So I ask you not to test it just yet."

"What else do you ask of me?"

"I ask that it be my turn. For the time being, at least."

"Your *turn*? I don't understand."

"My father is never coming home. I know this now. I know it because he will make no promise, no matter how he's pressed by me and my mother. And I know as well that my mother is greatly relieved. She's quite happy to return to her duties as the Countess of Rutherford now with the new wealth supplied by my father, and to have full charge of the estates she struggled to maintain so miserably for so long. She says to me confidentially that it is her turn to rule the little kingdom of Rutherford, and she does not care if she ever sees my father again."

"I see," said Julie.

"And that is all well and good," said Alex. "But I would like it to be my turn too in a different way."

"I still don't understand what you mean, Alex."

"My father is enjoying his endless travels. You and Ramses have enjoyed yours. And you will again. I would now like to enjoy my own."

Ramses, he'd said. Not *Mr. Ramsey*.

"Alex, you mustn't—"

"Mustn't what? Please, Julie. I understand. Truly. I do. You thought it would spare my heart to think her a madwoman. Perhaps you thought it was a privilege to be the only member of our traveling party with no real sense of the true nature of our journey. No sense of the momentousness of it. Surely, my father knows, and that in part explains his long absence."

"Alex, you must understand, I—"

"I do understand, Julie. This is not sarcasm with which I speak. But it isn't easy to say these things, so I ask for your respect."

"Alex, you don't understand what she is."

"Neither do you!"

She recoiled from his anger; she'd never heard anything quite like it in his voice.

"And neither does Ramses," he said, "and that's exactly the point, isn't it? The two of you sought to protect me from a being you yourselves did not truly understand. You still don't. She does not even understand herself. Only one thing is clear. She now desires only to return to the shadows in which you both would have wished her to remain. And that should satisfy you both, shouldn't it? Even if I go with her. For the time she has left. And I ask you . . . No. No, I don't ask it. I demand it, Julie. I demand that you not follow us."

Us.

"Where is she now?" Julie asked. "One of the tenant farms? Alex, you must tell me."

"Goodbye, Julie." His voice had softened, and he took a step towards her, closing the distance he'd opened when he'd pulled away from just the thought of her touch. "Goodbye. It's clear to me now you and Ramses stand on the edge of a magnificent and terrifying new world that has yet to be fully discovered. No doubt this new *Ethiopian* friend of yours hails from it. I hope it will bring you much joy and magic, this world. But I have no desire to be part of it. And neither does she."

*   *   *

How was it these words could overwhelm her more than anything she'd seen these past few months? What was the true source of these tears that gripped her now? Guilt? Remorse? It didn't seem so.

He gripped her shoulders, leaned in, and kissed her on the

forehead. A blessing, this gesture, after the way he'd pulled away from her only minutes before. Then he was trotting across the square in the direction of his car. For now he was afraid. Afraid that she would pursue. Afraid that she would alert Ramses, and they would begin searching for wherever he was hiding her, the being that was, but was not quite, Cleopatra.

She wanted to go after him. But she was paralyzed. Paralyzed by his revelations and his directness—his earnestness and his flashes of anger which, just like the vulnerability he'd shown in the weeks prior, were so utterly new to him.

He could change. He could accept impossible truths. This was what he had just said to her, was it not?

She watched his car putter through the square and disappear from view.

A moment later, she heard footsteps behind her.

Ramses embraced her.

She turned to him, gave herself to his arms, buried her face against his broad chest. No sense in trying to hide her tears, she realized. He could hear their effect on her breath. He could feel them through his shirt, no doubt.

Did it fall on her now to keep this secret from Ramses? Was that the only possible way to honor Alex's request? His *demand*, as he'd put it.

"She's with him, Ramses. She's with him. He knows everything she knows. And now he seeks to go away with her, and he demands that we do not follow."

"And he was angry with you?" he asked.

She looked up at him.

"Not quite," she whispered, "not enough to explain these miserable tears. And I don't simply feel remorseful or guilty. So I can't explain this sense of overwhelming sadness."

"I can, my darling."

"Well, of course you can."

"The secrets we kept from him. Your concern for him. The

party. All of it prolonged the business of your forced engagement. It was the one thing that still connected you to your mortal life. And now, in asking to be set free, Alex has set you free as well."

"Indeed. He said we stand on the edge of a magnificent and terrifying new world that has yet to be fully discovered, you and I. But he does not wish to be part of it. And neither does she."

"They already are," he said quietly.

"Can we honor his request?"

"We can, of course. But we now have a queen to whom we must answer as well. And then there is Sibyl, whose desire to find Cleopatra is stronger than ours."

"Must we tell them?"

"We must tell Bektaten. Telling Sibyl will be her decision. But whatever we disclose, we mention Alex's desire that they be set free. The two of them. Together. If it's your desire to honor this request, of course."

"If I desire to be set free myself, you mean. If I desire to be freed from my last tie to my mortal life so that I can give myself to your magnificent and terrifying world."

"*Our* world, my darling Julie." When she looked up at him, he graced her slight smile with a kiss. "Our world."

45

Cornwall

Sibyl was leaving them.

She had announced as much that morning after two days of continuous rest.

Two days during which she would burrow more deeply into her blankets whenever they tried to question her about her connection to Cleopatra.

Enamon had reported sounds of sexual release coming from her room. Muffled and restrained, of course, but still audible during his regular trips past her bedroom door. And so the connection between Sibyl and Cleopatra remained, and it was still strong, and it now provided her with the more pleasurable aspects of Alex and Cleopatra's reunion.

At least her torment seemed to be at an end, Ramses thought. The mad visions gone.

But were they? Or had Sibyl's attitude about them simply changed? Did they seize her still, only she now gave herself to them without confusion and resistance? There was no telling, for, suddenly, Sibyl wouldn't speak of any of it. And now, with a burst of energy that seemed to have come from nowhere, she was eager to return to her hotel room in London and a lady's maid whom she insisted was coming apart at the seams with worry.

They waited for her in the great hall. It had the air of a formal ceremony, the way they all stood with their hands clasped, not far from where they'd met with Saqnos three nights prior. Enamon was missing from their group, but only because he was on the other side of the bridge, waiting to drive Sibyl back to London. Aktamu was off on some other mission, the details of which Bektaten wouldn't disclose.

"Is this wise?" Ramses asked once the wait became unbearable.

"Wise?" Bektaten asked. She wore a heavy robe of rich brocade fabric, and her tightly kinked black hair, so lustrous, was gathered at the back of her head by a device of emeralds and gold.

Ramses was distracted for the moment by her regal beauty.

"To simply let Sibyl go like this," he said. "With so many questions unanswered. Is it wise?"

"She is not my prisoner," Bektaten answered, "nor is she yours."

"And what if she were to tell all she knows of us, you and I and Julie—"

"Who would believe her? She is a writer of fantasies."

Ramses nodded.

It was bracing the way she spoke to him now. But when he cast a glance in her direction, she didn't seem stern or angry.

Finally they heard the clop of footsteps on the stone stairs.

A moment later Sibyl appeared, dressed in new clothes Julie had purchased for her from a dress shop in the nearest village. A lacy blouse with a pearl-studded collar, contained by a trim jacket the same shade of white. Her dress wasn't nearly as long as gowns worn by so many ladies of this era. The hem was short enough that she could run, dance, and twirl if she so chose. And atop Sibyl's golden locks was a small top hat, black as night and much like the ones Julie had been fond of during their travels through Europe. It comforted him to see how Julie had left her stamp on the woman's new attire. A sign, perhaps, that Sibyl might soon return, even if she did insist on departing now with an aura of suddenness and mystery.

"Do I look well?" Sibyl asked. "Or healthy, at least."

"You look positively stunning," Julie said. "I'm biased, of course. Given I'm the one who dressed you."

Julie closed the distance between them, took Sibyl's hands in hers, and spread them slightly so she could get a better look at the clothes she wore.

"You're sure you must leave?" Ramses asked.

Sibyl flinched slightly, as if she were startled to have the tension in the room described so directly.

"Yes," she whispered. "I'm very sure."

"What guides you in this decision?" Bektaten asked.

If she'd flinched at the sound of Ramses' voice, Bektaten's voice caused Sibyl to go still. Fear? Awe? Did it matter, if one of those feelings led her to answer the question honestly?

Bektaten took several steps across the stone floor. Cautious and restrained, as if she could see the power she held over Sibyl and didn't want to overwhelm her with a fast approach.

"We know she travels now with Alex Savarell. That they seek to escape London and Yorkshire and perhaps Britain itself. Do you know this, Sibyl? Can you glimpse them through that which connects you now?"

They had not told Sibyl of what Alex had revealed to Julie the day before, but she didn't seem remotely surprised to hear of it now.

Had Bektaten held this information back on purpose? Was this a last-minute attempt to keep her from leaving?

Sibyl was silent for a while.

Then she leaned forward and kissed Julie gently on the cheek.

And then, to Ramses' surprise, Sibyl walked past Julie and began to approach the oldest immortal any of them might ever know. She held her head up and fixed a welcoming smile to her face, both signs that this movement required her utmost courage. For her experience of Bektaten had been limited and shrouded in fear; she'd seen the queen as nothing more than a mute witness to her tales and the architect of Saqnos's fatal leap. A source of mystery and death. And through the fog of these feelings, she seemed to be selecting her next words very carefully.

"There's no end to the gratitude I feel for you," Sibyl said, "that I will always feel for you. It would have been so easy to abandon me to my confusion. To dismiss my piteous wails that you free Cleopatra from her captors. And you could have quite easily kept all that you have here a secret from me. But you did nothing of the kind.

"Instead, you've done far more than illuminate the strange nature of my condition. Or this connection, or whatever we shall now call it. All of you . . ." She glanced about the room now, surveying each of them in kind. "All of you have done so much more than that. You see, there were times throughout my life when most thought me utterly mad. My vivid dreams, my love of stories. My intolerance for monotonous everyday rituals. The intensity with which I seemed to experience everything. In the eyes of my family, these were things to be tolerated at best, even when my writing brought them considerable profit.

"And so I've always been made to feel like a creature out of step with most of the world. But after meeting all of you, after being brought here and cared for and listened to, after each of you revealed your true nature to me, I feel that way no longer, and I never will again.

"I'm now privy to a great truth. Our souls, the souls we believe to be part and parcel of our bodies, are immortal, and those souls follow their own path. I possess a soul that once belonged to another, and after I die, that soul will travel on. Most human beings live and die without ever having such a great truth revealed to them. But it has been revealed to me."

Bektaten nodded, and again she smiled.

"And so I thank you," said Sibyl. "And I will always thank you."

With that, Sibyl extended her hand to Bektaten. For a moment,

Ramses thought the queen might reject this gesture. Consider it beneath her to shake hands with a mortal woman in this way. And in a manner of speaking, she did reject it. She ignored Sibyl's outstretched hand and gently took hold of the woman's shoulders instead.

"You will always be welcome here," said Bektaten. "As you will be in any place I call a home." Bektaten bent forward and kissed Sibyl on the forehead. "Fare thee well, Sibyl Parker. Fare thee well and remain as brave as you have been so far. For the mysteries that lie ahead for you are unknown even to me."

Sibyl nodded, blinked back tears, then turned her attention to Ramses.

He kissed her on the cheek, released her to Julie's warm embrace, and then suddenly they were watching her depart.

Before Sibyl could step out into the light, Julie said, "Sibyl, do you truly believe we'd harm her if we helped you find her? Is that why you want to find her alone?"

Ramses was relieved she'd said it so specifically. That they hadn't brought this farewell to a close without addressing Sibyl's true motives.

"No," Sibyl finally said, "I believe she's harmed all of you, and too recently for those wounds to entirely heal."

"And if she wishes to harm you?" Ramses asked.

Sibyl swallowed. And so this fear was with her. And that was a good thing, Ramses thought. That she had at least considered this possibility. That it informed whatever she might plan to do.

"I have but one hope. To convince her that I'm the key to her restoration. If I fail in that, nothing can save either one of us. Not in this life."

Before they could question her on this, Sibyl stepped through the door and drew it firmly shut behind her.

"Restoration," Julie whispered. "What could this mean?"

"I do not know," Bektaten answered. "Let us hope Sibyl Parker does."

With that, she turned.

"Come with me," she said, "both of you."

*   *   *

As soon as they set foot inside the armory, Julie gasped.

Lying on the table where Bektaten had spread out her weapons for them three nights before was Saqnos. Lifeless, nude, with a slight bloat to his features that suggested he had spent some time in the sea. But not very much. Ramses had seen what became of bodies pulled from the Nile or the Mediterranean after several days. The corpse before them now was in far better condition.

They had taken a plaster cast of his face, a perfect death mask, which now hung from the wall so it could dry. Spread out on the table behind her were detailed sketches of his head and torso, each from a different perspective on his corpse. No doubt these would be stored away with the pages of the *Shaktanis,* or in some great library she had yet to reveal to them, the only records that a man named Saqnos had ever lived and breathed.

"Those sketches," Ramses said, "are they by your hand?"

"This is Aktamu's gift," she said.

"Tell me there are drawings of your kingdom somewhere in your journals," Julie whispered. "Please. There must be."

"Of course. But there are glimpses of Shaktanu throughout the Africa of today. Words of the ancient tongue live on in the language of the Ashanti. The headdresses and facial markings of young Masai warriors mirror those of the soldiers who defended my palace. And the sharp, slender pyramids of Kush and Meroë, they are much like the ones that covered our lands. Lands that became the Sahara Desert. Shaktanu's collapse sent great rivers flowing south into Africa, and they carried pieces of our history and our culture. To see which ones settled and took root in other places, in other kingdoms, among various tribes fascinates me."

"And only you know their true origin," Ramses said.

"And Enamon knows. And Aktamu knows." Bektaten gazed down at Saqnos now, twined her fingers affectionately through a long strand of his black curls. "And Saqnos knew."

These last words she said in a whisper.

How to define the way she touched this fallen man now? Was it a mother's touch, or a lover's touch? Or did the touch and attention of an immortal queen combine both things, creating something far more powerful?

What had she seen, he now wondered, as she watched this man's final plummet? Had she been seized by memories of him? Had her sense of him grown suddenly tender as he fell to his death? Or had she mourned the kingdom they had once shared? Had she seen her palace, her chambers, her kingdom's tall, slender pyramids covering lands destined to become desolate and dry? Had she seen the great flock of birds that had circled the palace again and again without ever tiring, the very birds that had given away her secret to the man who would betray her?

It was possible. It was more than possible.

Ramses' own immortality had deepened his capacity for memory, widened the corridors in his mind through which memories could now emerge and be received. He realized this was why he could not help but view Cleopatra as a doomed creature, for his own memories seemed to deepen and take on more richness, even as she claimed to lose so many of her own.

Bektaten turned to the cabinet.

She removed a vial. The color of the fluid inside was different from any of the other substances she'd revealed to them. But Julie must have thought it was the elixir, because when Bektaten uncapped it, Julie cried out.

"No. No, you must not—"

Bektaten gave her a gentle, dismissive wave. Then she poured the blue-tinted fluid in a slender line along the length of Saqnos's torso. Within minutes, the flesh—the *mortal* flesh, Ramses reminded himself—began to dissolve. She repeated this process in slender lines that ran from his nose to the center of his forehead, the length of his neck, and then down both legs.

It only took several minutes for his body to disintegrate into a fine powder. And even this powder itself had seemed to dissolve. By the time the process was complete, there were only faint snakes of it along the table; nothing to suggest the silhouette or outline of the body that had lain there moments before.

And so it was a funeral she had invited them to. His last rites.

The death mask hanging on the wall behind them, the sketches of the corpse that had just disappeared before their eyes. Along with all references to him in the *Shaktanis,* these items would be the only evidence that there had ever been a man named Saqnos, a man who had served as prime minister of a lost kingdom.

"One must have witnesses." Bektaten's eyes were full of tears. She brought her fingers to her nose, the same fingers she'd twined through Saqnos's great locks, and inhaled gently. Her last moment of contact with the man she'd just turned to dust. A tolerable farewell kiss, perhaps. Whatever the gesture meant to her, it held her tears at bay, placing them behind some great reserve of strength. "One's own hand, one's own pen, one's own mind; these things are not enough if one is to live for all time. And so on this day in the year nineteen hundred and fourteen, in the twentieth century, I say goodbye to one witness. And I welcome two others."

Such warmth in the smile she gave them now.

"It is my hope," Ramses said, "that we will be far more to you than just that, my queen."

"This is my hope as well," Julie whispered, "my queen."

"Mine as well," she answered with a nod.

There was a sudden commotion from the castle's great hall. But as Julie jumped and grabbed Ramses' arm, Bektaten only smiled.

"It seems Aktamu has returned," she said.

They heard barking just before they reached the great hall.

Julie hesitated until she felt Ramses' arm encircle her waist, urging her forward.

Bektaten continued past them, unafraid. The sight that greeted them once they rounded the corner seemed menacing at first. But after a minute or two, Ramses realized the great hounds circling the room weren't stalking Aktamu. They orbited him as if he were the sun to their universe. And when he occasionally crouched down to show one of them affection, the others moved in, hoping he would scratch them behind their ears or under their jaws as well.

A remarkable sight! So many great and powerful hounds under the apparent thrall of a single man. But these animals weren't under the spell of the angel blossom; not in this moment. Rather, it was as Julie had suspected. Just like Bastet, the attentive cat who had sat guard over Sibyl for her entire stay, these great and powerful hounds had been forever changed by their exposure to the angel blossom. By their brief dance with a human mind.

And now Bektaten moved among them, her palms open on either side of her. Like loyal subjects, several of the dogs approached and offered her their great heads for scratching, and she complied. He wasn't sure if it was the first time he'd seen her laugh. Perhaps it was just the first time she had released laughter that sounded quite this contented and rich.

"These are good animals," the queen said. "I like these animals."

It occurred to him then, as he watched her moving among these now-docile creatures so radically changed by the secrets of her garden, what she had truly done for him by making herself known, by sharing her story. By connecting him to an intricate and undiscovered history, she had brought his years of wandering to an end. For even in his joyous travels with Julie, there had been an element of restlessness and searching, a sense that if he did not soon seek to connect himself to some modern institution or some semblance of an ordinary, modern life, his existence would once again be defined by immortal solitude. Such solitude would have soon claimed Julie as well, even as they traveled together, loved together, partook in life's great sensual pleasures together. But she was too new to immortality to know what a crushing weight this loneliness could become over time. He knew. He knew it all too well.

He had known it for centuries.

And so he now knew as well what Bektaten's arrival truly meant.

Her history, the elixir's history, was also his own. And in her garden, and the potions, tonics, and cures she drew from it, unending magic yet to be discovered. He was confident now that this would be his salvation from the great failure of imagination she'd warned him about.

She would save him from so many things.

She had gained witnesses, and they had gained a true queen.

*   *   *

Early evening brought a certain measure of quiet, and an excuse to light the torches in those areas of the castle where the wires couldn't reach.

The song of wind and sea was interrupted now and then by debates between Bektaten and Aktamu as to how their fifteen new residents should be cared for and housed.

Would they be dispersed to Bektaten's various estates and castles?

It was agreed that too little was known about their changed natures to begin planning trips for these dogs around the world. And so for now, they would remain here in Cornwall, as would Bektaten and her men.

Or at least this was how the matter would be briefly settled before one of the dogs knocked over some priceless piece of furniture and Bektaten voiced her concerns anew.

In the morning, Julie would return to London to calm the frayed nerves of the staff at the Mayfair house. To assure them that Julie and Mr. Ramsey were, in fact, quite all right, and no, they had not decided to abandon Mayfair altogether. But for now there was peace and quiet, and a respite from poisonings, suicides, and funerals for those who had once been immortal, and so Ramses took the opportunity to withdraw quietly from the great hall and walk to Bektaten's library in the tower.

There, waiting for him where he had left it, was a key to Bektaten's ancient tongue she had drawn for him on a scrap of paper, a paper he was to burn as soon as he mastered it. For she kept the language in which she'd written her journals as closely guarded a secret as the elixir itself.

She had already tutored him extensively. And his immortal mind had absorbed portions of her language quickly, as quickly as he'd memorized passages from the history books he'd devoured upon his awakening in this century. But before he took a single step on the path ahead he had to be confident of his footing. So he sat once more with the key and studied once more how the symbols of Bektaten's ancient tongue connected to the sounds of the English language he had so recently mastered.

Earlier that day, he'd translated a page of pedestrian English sentences into the ancient tongue, and his work had met with Bektaten's approval. What other sign could there be that he was ready to begin?

And so Ramses the Great, once Ramses the Damned, rose to his feet, walked to the shelves, and removed the first volume of the *Shaktanis*.

Once he had lit all the candles in the room and settled into the most comfortable chair, he opened the volume's leather-bound cover and embarked upon what was sure to be one of the greatest adventures he'd ever known.

46

Isle of Skye

For days now, Sibyl had seen glimpses of this place, even though she had only departed the ferry moments before. For days, her connection to Cleopatra had shown her the rocky peaks of the Cuillin Mountains; the sea inlets that divided these landscapes like fingers of ink. This narrow harbor of Portree with its row of stone buildings. But now she beheld these things with her own eyes.

She had a bookseller in London to thank for guiding her here. Her plan required several copies of her own books, and once she'd located a shop in London that carried most of her titles, she'd described to the bookseller within the places she'd been seeing in her mind for several days. The dramatic cliffs plunging to the sea, the lone lighthouse at the tip of a long green strip of land that stuck out into the sea like the overgrown finger of a decaying god. She'd told him these were images once seen in a book, drawings that hadn't been properly labeled, and she wished to visit these places before she returned to America.

Ah, it's the Isle of Skye you seek, miss.

She sought a great deal more than that, but there was no sense in sharing this with the shopkeeper. He was too delightfully puzzled that she'd paid him a visit, only to request several copies of her own books. He'd offered them to her for free provided she sign the entirety of his stock, and she'd happily agreed. And as she'd signed each book carefully, he'd attempted to engage her in talk about threat of war on the Continent, and Sibyl had no choice but to plead ignorance. The last time she had looked at a newspaper at all was when she'd rifled through clippings about the Ramsey-Stratford betrothal party.

War? Had her foolish brothers been correct?

What did the prospect of war mean for one who had experienced things such as she had these past few weeks? What did the prospect of death itself mean?

While she trusted Ramses and Julie completely, and this mysterious queen who seemed to control them now only a little bit less, she still thought it possible they might change their minds about allowing her to complete this last leg of her journey on her own, so she had lingered in London for two days to be sure she wasn't being followed. Then, with a satchel full of slender hardbound editions of her own books, she headed north.

North to the far reaches of Scotland, to the place where Cleopatra now walked dramatic windswept landscapes with such frequency that some landmarks, the same slopes, the same stormy coasts, were transmitted to Sibyl again and again and again.

The nature of their connection had most certainly changed after the party, after they'd come so close to each other without realizing it. The visions were more stable, more rooted in their passing, everyday moments. And the great swells of emotion and physical sensation they now shared were entirely new. And, of course, they could, when they wanted, speak to each other as if across a telephone line that remained open for only a few minutes at a time. But alongside these visions came a great sense of despair, a sense of hopelessness that radiated from Cleopatra with such force Sibyl was tempted to speak to her, to comfort her with words.

But she knew this wasn't wise. She might tip her hand, say something to alert Cleopatra to her approach.

But if Cleopatra could see the world through Sibyl's eyes as well, there was no keeping her journey entirely secret.

On the train ride north, she read through her past tales of Egypt and used a pen to mark those passages she thought might be relevant to her new mission.

On the ferry ride that brought her journey to an end, she felt a strange tingling in her neck. A burst of energy seemed to course through her. The only way she could release it was to clench and unclench her fists. They were entirely new, these sensations. And she took them to be a sign that she was close. That Cleopatra was close.

Perhaps she would have felt these things at the party had she not glimpsed Ramses immediately and been overcome by the memory of him; had she not then been so quickly assaulted by Theodore Dreycliff and knocked unconscious soon after. As she set foot on the dock, these feelings continued.

And so you are here, Cleopatra said. *Come to the pub above the harbor, Sibyl Parker. Come to me so we can end this.*

It was perhaps the most reckless and foolish decision she had ever made, coming here by herself. Lying to Lucy once more about her destination and her intentions and the length of time she would be gone. Perhaps it would end with her neck snapped and her body cast into the sea.

She didn't believe it.

She couldn't believe it.

And so it remained between them, a connection much like those enjoyed by twins, but far more powerful. Surely, her emotions flowed across this connection into Cleopatra as much as those of Cleopatra flowed into her.

The pub wasn't too crowded, but there were several customers. The walls and floor were of such a dark wood, the gray sunlight streaming through the windows seemed blinding at first. And then her eyes adjusted, and she saw her seated in the corner, wreathed in shadows that complemented the dark dress she wore

and the heavy black shawl that seemed intended for both concealment and warmth. Perhaps it was the wariness in her expression,
the wide-eyed fear that seemed to exist behind a glaze of defiant
anger, or perhaps it was the dark colors in which she'd draped
herself. Or perhaps it was being this close to her. But it was in that
moment that Sibyl realized Cleopatra had traveled this far north
out of pure despair, a despair that led to utter surrender.

For the first time since departing London, Sibyl no longer
feared for her own life.

It felt as if it were the longest walk she'd ever taken, this short
stroll from the pub's entrance to the table in the far corner, and by
the time she'd taken a seat across from Cleopatra, her hands were
shaking and covered in sweat.

"How will this unfold?" Cleopatra asked. "How will you
exert your final dominion over me? Do you expect the last ves-
tiges of my soul to leave my body? Did you expect to claim me
the moment I was within sight? Perhaps it happens now, as invisible as the connection between us. What would these men think
if they knew?"

"If they knew what?"

"If they knew you came to claim me."

"I'm not here to claim you. I'm here to restore you."

"Restore me? You are the vessel for my spirit reborn, are you
not?"

"I don't believe these words."

"Why not? They were spoken by an immortal thousands of
years old."

"An immortal who devoted his entire existence to re-creating
the elixir. And when he learned that those he'd brought back
from death could not help in this endeavor, he walled them away
in darkness. I don't believe for a moment this Saqnos ever studied the complexity of what you are. Of what *we* are. You and I,
together."

"Ask him."

"I can't. He is no more."

She brightened at this. Briefly she wore the promise of a smile, then it vanished. There was a glass of wine on the table before her; she brought it to her lips.

"This pleases me," she finally whispered.

"He hurt you," Sibyl said, "he tortured you. I felt it."

"What else have you felt? What else do you steal from me?"

"I steal nothing from you. I see glimpses of your life as you are living it. I feel moments of what you are feeling. There is a man with you. A handsome young man who loves you very dearly, who refuses to believe you are as doomed as you believe you are. And I agree with him."

"Do you?"

"What do you feel of me, Cleopatra? What do you see through my eyes?"

"It is the same," she answered quietly. "It is as you've described, only in reverse."

"You see, so it is balanced, this connection between us. And it became more stable the closer we drew to one another."

"How can you say this?" she hissed. "How can you call this thing *stable*? This word, it means 'calm,' does it not? 'Even'? 'Flat'? How can you use words like that to describe what is happening to me? I have lost my memories, do you understand? I was raised from the black waters of death itself only to be stripped of all that makes me who I am. The loss. Can you fathom the loss? I have not lost memories of being a shopkeeper or a dressmaker. I lost memories of being a queen."

"But I'm not gaining them," Sibyl whispered. "Don't you see? If I were the vessel for your true soul, and you an aberrant thing that should never have been raised, then all your memories would be flowing across this connection between us. I would assume all of them. They would become mine. Your mind, it would belong to me."

"Does it not?"

"No. The memories I have received from you have come to me my entire life in a gentle and, yes, a steady way. In fragments, passed down through centuries. It is your life *now* to which I am most strongly connected. And this connection has driven me closer to you, and the closer we have come, the more my fear has left me and been replaced by a love for you for which I barely have words.

"Can't you see? Your soul is not some small thing that can be stuffed into a bottle and passed off to another. Neither is mine. No soul is like this. It can't be. What connects us is far more complex. More intricate."

Sibyl reached into her satchel and removed a copy of *The Wrath of Anubis*. She placed it on the table so that Cleopatra could read her name on the spine.

"They came to me as dreams," she answered. "All my life I've had vivid dreams, dreams of Egypt. Sometimes only a jumble of sensations and images. Sometimes moments and episodes. I've captured most of them in my books, without knowing that they were yours."

"Mine," she whispered.

"When I arrived at the party, when I saw Ramses in the flesh for the first time, I realized he was the man from one of my dreams. That a moment you shared with him came to me as a dream, and I in turn wrote it in these pages."

"And why do you bring me this book now? To mock me?"

Sibyl reached into her satchel and removed a copy of *The Fire of Thoth* and then a copy of *The Storm of Amun* and then *Horus Rising*. She made a row of them across the table so Cleopatra could once again see the spines, and see her name, Sibyl Parker.

"I bring you these books because in the dream we shared when you were being held in that terrible place, you asked me a question. Do you remember the question you asked me?"

"My son," she whispered, "I asked you about . . . my son."

"You asked me where I was hiding your memories of him."

"Yes," she whispered.

"And the answer is this. I seek to hide nothing from you, and I never will. But the memories of yours that have come to me, throughout my life, throughout my dreams, they are all recorded here, even though I didn't know what I was recording at the time. And my hope is that if you turn these pages, if you read them, you might be able to restore what you have lost. My hope is that there is something in my words that will affect you just as the sight of Ramses at that party affected me. Perhaps it's in the smallest details. The colors, the smells, the textures. Maybe one of them will produce a moment of clarity and restoration like the one I experienced at the engagement party when I first saw Ramses in the flesh. I am not here to consume you. Or to destroy you. Or to cast you into darkness or madness. I'm here to restore you."

"You believe we are a queen divided? Is that it?"

"I believe that I am Sibyl Parker. American. Novelist. Cursed with two dreadful brothers currently who spend my money on nothing but drink and women. And I am blessed to have a spirit in part from one of history's greatest queens. The mystery of that connection is still unfolding. But this is who I am. And you are Cleopatra the Seventh, last queen of Egypt."

Cleopatra stared down at the books before her as if she thought they might open by themselves. Then, tentatively, she laid her hands across the cover of *The Wrath of Anubis* and drew it slowly towards her. But she could not bring herself to open it, it seemed. Defiance behind this, perhaps.

"I will not force this on you," Sibyl said, rising to her feet. "But I will linger here in this town for as long as it takes you to test my theory. If you wish me to leave, simply stay silent. And I will take that as my cue to return to America, and I will cherish what moments of our connection you allow me to share."

Sibyl stood.

There was wonder in the expression with which Cleopatra now regarded her. But she didn't ask Sibyl to stay. Knowing full well that it might be the last time they ever laid eyes upon one another, Sibyl collected her satchel and walked from the pub and into the daylight.

It was hope that had brought her this far; it was hope that would keep her for a while. She would take a room at the Royal Hotel, but not before she put in a call to Lucy at Claridge's to assure her she was well.

Then she would wait. For how long exactly, she wasn't yet sure.

For now, she would walk.

Her satchel was considerably lighter now, her books having been delivered, so each step along the harbor reminded her that she had accomplished what she'd come here to do. She'd presented Cleopatra with her theory and her writings.

She came to a gravel shore, dotted with beached rowboats. From here, she had a view across the water to the mountains in the distance, their flanks painted by the shadows of the dark storm clouds moving across the sky. They looked pregnant with rain, these clouds, but the air remained crisp and dry, and the wind drove them so fast it seemed entirely likely they might pass over here, and this town, without spilling a drop.

And then, suddenly, she was gripped by a vision unlike any she had experienced before since this adventure had begun.

The gravel, the water, and the mountains in the distance were replaced by a glimmering canal not unlike the one that had separated her from Cleopatra in their shared dream. But whereas the periphery of that dream had seemed hazy and abstract, now the details were clear.

She stood on the bank of the canal in a vast courtyard fringed by columns topped with the carvings of acanthus leaves. Great shafts of sunlight came down from above, and there were white clouds moving leisurely across the sky. And a young boy ran towards her along the black canal; a young boy with a cherub's face and black curls. And his voice was clear now as he called out to her again and again, *"Mitera!"*

The sunlight reflected off the rippling canal, sending bright rivulets of light across his laughing face, and then, without warning, he did a cartwheel right before her, and then she scooped him into her arms so as to keep him from falling into the water. And he was laughing. Gazing up and laughing at her as she held him.

She had seen this boy again and again in her dreams. But he had been one of so many faces that visited her in her sleep. Faces without names. She had assumed them all products of her fevered imagination and her love of the ancient world. She had been wrong then. But now, she was right. For this boy. This boy whose features and bearing and delighted laughter she had given to scores of children depicted in her novels had a name.

He was Caesarion.

He was Cleopatra's son.

And the vision Sibyl experienced now was a memory awakened. Awakened by Sibyl's dreams, awakened by Sibyl's words, awakened by Cleopatra's willingness to open one of Sibyl's novels and read a passage she had marked on the train ride here.

The vision receded, leaving her breathless. Sibyl found herself on her knees on the gravel beach, once again gazing out at the black water of the harbor and the mountains in the distance shadowed by fast-moving storm clouds. Only she wasn't alone. She heard a voice, clear and gentle, speaking to her across the connection that had changed the course of her life.

Come back, Cleopatra called. *Come back to me, Sibyl Parker.*

Epilogue

They'd returned late in the evening, finding the house empty as they'd anticipated, with no meddlesome servants to intrude on this, their last night in London. Henry and Rita and the rest of the staff had been sent on their yearly visits home. And a splendid meal of delicious cold meats, cheeses, and pastries had been purchased at a country inn as they made the drive back.

Now it was just midnight, and Ramses and Julie had made up the fires in the bedroom and in the drawing rooms, as not even in August was London truly what Ramses called warm. They had packed up all the belongings they would take with them on their trip back to Europe. And just where and how they would begin, well, all that might be determined in the morning. It did not really matter now. What mattered now was their being alone together, alone to discuss or reflect upon all they had experienced, all they had learned, and to make their plans at leisure now that order had been restored to their own private world.

Ramses had to admit he found the Mayfair townhouse cozy, what with its dark wood paneling and its many soft glass lamps, and its innumerable lace-curtained windows, and the great cold banquet set out on the oval table in the Egyptian Room, as Julie called it, which was a library of sorts, or a second drawing room, depending upon whom one consulted and when. On that very spot, the spot now occupied by the table, Ramses had awakened from his long slumber, in his painted coffin, to first gaze on these rooms. Well, the sarcophagus had been removed to the British Museum, where officials still railed about the "theft" of a priceless mummy, but were at the same time mollified by the gift of all the Egyptian treasure Lawrence had collected over his many years of amateur Egyptology and discovery, the great passion which had led to his death.

Ah, such a tragedy, Ramses thought, *that Lawrence Stratford had been poisoned before he could ever know that the mummy he'd discovered was indeed a slumbering immortal who would soon be restored to full life.*

But this was not the time for regrets over such things.

This was the time for them to sit comfortably at the table and begin a meal that only two hungry immortals could fully appreciate for its variety and size. Red wine and white wine. Divine cheeses from France and Italy. Cold roast fowl and lobster, slices of rare beef, and salads, as they called them, of boiled shrimp or savory vegetables. And then the sweets, the sweets that never ceased to amaze him with their flaky crusts and layers of sugar, and the delicious cherries or strawberries that spilled out at the touch of the fork. Ramses had finally become used to forks.

There was a virtue to using these modern tools to spear one's food and lift it securely to one's mouth. It kept the hands from being sticky. And yes, these napkins even delighted him now as he carefully wiped his mouth, as the English did it, before lifting the crystal glass of wine to his lips.

Clean hands, clean lips, clean glasses. It was all about such fastidiousness. Well, he'd become used to it, and used to the smell of the coal burning in the grate, and used to the faint scent of "London" penetrating the walls.

Julie was in her pink peignoir once more, that long lacy garment he adored with all of its tiny pearls that were not really pearls, and its full ruffled sleeves that made her hands all the more lovely, her hair flowing down her back in shimmering waves that he wanted to take in his own hands now and press to his face. Enough. There would be time later for their heated lovemaking, when he would peel off this luxurious satin dressing gown, as they called it, get rid of this stiff linen shirt with its merciless silk tie, and take his naked and trembling beloved in his arms.

Ramses was just about to reach for the cold fruit—slices of peach and pear lying on a bed of green lettuce—when a noise startled him. Someone at the front door. Someone turning a key in the lock.

He rose. He could see the door easily through the double doors of the first drawing room that opened onto the hall. Now, who would this be? One of the servants returned early? Had to be.

But it was not.

A figure in a dark cloak and hood entered the foyer.

It was Julie who recognized him at once.

"Elliott," she cried out, and she rushed to take him in her arms.

Elliott came quietly into the brighter lights of the front room and enfolded Julie tenderly, pressing her head to his chest.

"Forgive me, my darling," said Elliott. He removed the heavy hooded cloak and threw it aside on a chair. "I saw the lights, of course. I should have knocked. But I was in a hurry to be off the street."

"Elliott, you have that key for a reason," said Julie, "to enter this house whenever you like." She led him towards the table. "I'm so glad to see you," she confessed. "I have missed you so very much."

"Come, join us," said Ramses. "It's a cold meal but a savory one, and plenty for three immortals twice over."

Elliott stood there before the table as if he were trying to collect his thoughts. He was drawn and tired, *As we all become,* thought Ramses, *if we don't yield to the constant hunger.* His eyes moved over the heap of suitcases on the carpet. And then to Ramses, as if he had just heard Ramses' words.

"Just arrived or leaving?" Elliott asked.

"Off to Europe to continue our wanderings," said Julie. "Our visit home has exhausted us. I can't wait to tell you of all that's transpired."

"Off to Europe," asked Elliott, "to continue your wanderings? My dear, what are you thinking of? Where have you both been?"

"Oh, I know, there's talk of war everywhere—" said Ramses.

"Talk?" Elliott interrupted. "My dear man, England is at war with Germany. The declaration was made an hour and a half ago! Have you no wireless here? Don't you realize what's been going on?"

"War with Germany?" Ramses sank down in the chair.

"Yes, war with Germany. And all of Europe is in this war. God knows what will happen next."

Indeed, they had been in another world, hadn't they, a world of their pressing concerns. Ramses had seen a newspaper or two in the last few days but utterly ignored them, and only now did all the talk of war come back to him with the dizzying ultimatums and the names of the different countries involved.

"Come, tell us all about it as we eat and drink," Ramses pressed.

Elliott escorted Julie to her chair and then sat down between them, facing the front of the house. He was dressed in a rather prim linen shirt and tie and gray wool coat, the basic uniform of males today. And his hair had recently been trimmed quite short and very neatly groomed. He looked as always like a young man with an older man's character, his blue eyes quick and curious and generous as he looked at his companions. But a great sadness overshadowed him. And Ramses knew it was this war.

"Perhaps this war will be over very soon," said Elliott. "But I fear it won't be. I fear the future." He went on to explain the conflicts that had led to the declaration of war.

He spoke quietly for some minutes.

Ramses couldn't follow it. All he could think was: *How can this magnificent modern world enter into war? How can these modern people who know so much, who've come so far, suddenly be on the attack against one another?* It was unfathomable to him.

He contemplated the power of modern weaponry, guns large and small. He contemplated a world of flying machines and telephones and giant metal ships—at war. It was too grim, too dreadful.

At last Elliott fell silent.

"Eat," said Ramses. "I can see that you're famished. I know the telltale signs." He offered a plate of sliced meats to the earl, and a pot of sauce with it, and the silver tray of freshly sliced bread.

The earl obeyed, listlessly, as if the food were merely fuel. He drank deeply of the chilled white wine, and sat back in his chair, eyes moving from Julie to Ramses and then back again. Slowly, the natural color returned to his cheeks. And his eyes began to move over the banquet before him. He reached for the plate of glistening oysters. And Ramses filled his glass again.

They all enjoyed the feast. Their hunger was too great for them not to enjoy it. Ramses devoured the cold lobster, dipping the morsels of pure white meat into different sauces, and consumed whole slices of bread. The wine, yes, the wine, again and again and that flush of intoxication which was gone in an instant. He set upon the pastries with the same fervor, only glancing up now and then to see his companions dining with the same obvious pleasure. And they were just a small family, then, the three of them, united with their secret, united in their hunger, united in this pleasure which would soon leave them wanting more.

"I've seen my wife," Elliott said. "Don't worry. It was a very guarded meeting. I protected her as best I could from the robust health I enjoy now."

"I'm glad you saw her," said Julie.

"I gave her a hundred trivial reassurances and a hundred falsehoods as to my future travels," said Elliott. "To tell you the truth,

I think she was quite glad to see me going off again. I have always been a demanding man."

"You've provided for her splendidly," said Julie. "She has come into her own in a wholly new way."

"Yes," said Elliott. "A great burden has been lifted from her, the burden of a chronically melancholy and unloving husband who was at his best a wounded older brother always in need of comfort and allowances. . . ."

"Don't torture yourself," said Julie. "Don't look back. You were always good to Edith. But you're right, she's happy now."

Elliott nodded. He drank more of his wine, drank it freely as if it were water.

"No doubt she thinks I have a lover," said Elliott. "She said something to the effect that she admired my courage to leave London behind." He laughed. "And no doubt she'll take a lover of her own very soon. The revenues from my investments are increasing." He glanced at Ramses. "What will happen to my investments now with this war, I can't know. But I've deposited capital in a number of American banks as well as European ones."

"Wise," said Julie. She watched quietly as Ramses drew a folded sheet of paper from his coat and handed it to Elliott.

"Another place in Africa," said Ramses. "Where you should purchase land as soon as you can. Wait six months, perhaps longer. Then search for the old mines in the jungles. You'll find them."

"You're too kind to me," said Elliott. "But with this war, you should be doing these things yourself."

"Oh, don't worry," said Ramses. "When we first returned to London, I met with Julie's sage advisors. Of course they had many reservations. But many ventures have been arranged. Can any war affect the value of diamonds or gold?"

"What of Alex?" asked Julie. "Did you see him?"

"No," said Elliott. "Couldn't take the risk with those young eyes that would see what Edith's eyes can't see. But I've watched him from afar. And I know that he's gone off with the mysterious madwoman from Cairo. I understand now what Edith does not understand and must never understand. Alex's life is poisoned with knowledge of the elixir, and of us."

"Yes, this is all true," said Julie. Quickly she recounted all she knew of Alex's self-willed exile. "But you cannot know what Cleopatra has endured, what she's become."

Julie told him the story, the whole story, of Saqnos and Bektaten and the gruesome deaths of the fracti at the engagement party. She described the strangle lily and its power, and the temperament of the ancient queen who possessed this secret. She explained the corrupted elixir of Saqnos, and the fragments of information regarding the nochtin, those like Cleopatra raised from the dead. In a hushed voice, on the edge of tears, she explained the dreadful threat that now darkened the future for Cleopatra, that she might soon go mad.

Then she went on to recount the story of Sibyl Parker. She spoke of migrant souls, and mysteries of life after death. She spoke of Sibyl's dreams and Cleopatra's dreams, and the link between them. She spoke again of the placid and unfathomable nature of the great Bektaten.

And she explained that Sibyl Parker was now welcome in the house of Bektaten, Bektaten who might share the pure elixir with the wounded Cleopatra should Bektaten be asked.

All the while Elliott listened in amazement. Finally Julie fell silent and looked to Ramses to go on.

"This great queen and I have a treaty of sorts," said Ramses. "She wants no more rash acts on my part, no attempts ever again to wake the dead. She has the power of life and death over me, over all of us, yet she accepts my bold claim to determine when and how I might pass on the elixir again."

He studied the earl, as always impressed with the quick intelligence evident in the earl's eyes.

"But at any time," said Ramses, "this queen may decide to assert her authority over all of us who share this immortal journey with her. And we must, all of us, beware of this danger. We must never underestimate the power of Bektaten. We must never count on her indifference. She is now part of our world."

Elliott nodded. "I wish that I had shared the chance to meet this woman," he said. "But perhaps someday, whether I want it or not, I will find myself in her presence."

"Yes, that could be," said Ramses. "She travels with only two attendants, men as dark of complexion as she is, and in their own way as impressive, Aktamu and Enamon, but there is no telling how many mortals she may have at her command. She has not told us the full story of her life."

"I admire her," said Julie with her usual sweetness and enthusiasm. "I trust her, trust that she'll never harm us, never subject us to caprice or pure will." She glanced for approval to Ramses, and seeing his impassive face she went quiet.

"You have a great heart, Julie," said Ramses. "You have managed to love them all—Sibyl Parker, my broken Cleopatra, and even this powerful queen."

"It's true, Ramses, but how can I not be a creature of instinct, even more now than before? If she meant to hurt us, she would have done it, surely."

"Yes, perhaps," said Ramses. "But we must never forget what we've seen with our own eyes. The queen tends a garden of many mysterious blooms."

He reached for the wine to refill Elliott's crystal goblet. And the earl nodded gratefully. Their eyes met again, and then Elliott spoke.

"I don't ask you for the elixir for my son, Alex," he said. "I've pondered this for some time. It is my belief that Alex has a destiny, and that is to marry, to have children, to continue the Savarell line—all of which the elixir would bring to an end. Of course there may come a time when he may ask for the elixir. I wanted it from the very first moment I suspected its existence. So why shouldn't he? But I see my son's youth and I see his capacity for love, and I do see a marriage and children in his future. I can't deny it."

"I see this too," said Julie. "But to the point, Alex knows of the elixir, but he has not asked. And now it seems Cleopatra no longer asks for more of it to make her well."

"We have time to decide these many things," said Ramses. He rose from the table and moved across the carpet of the drawing room until he found himself close to the fire. He reached out to feel its direct heat. He thought again of this war in Europe, this dark tragedy that had fallen over the world he had only just discovered.

"Well, I must be going," said Elliott, rising to his feet. "I must get out of London. I must not be seen again by Edith, and I must not be seen by Alex, and I must not be seen by old friends. I have no choice but to go back to the Continent no matter what the war brings, but I don't advise either of you to come with me. I advise you to remain here, to travel in England, to go north, perhaps, to find some refuge for yourself until we see what this war reveals."

"But, Elliott," said Julie, "when will we meet again?"

"I don't know," said Elliott. "I can reach you at this address, can I not, and through Stratford Shipping, and through your solicitors."

"Always," said Julie. "Or at least until—. But that won't be for many years."

"And I shall give you this," said Elliott, removing a card from his jacket pocket. "The address and number of my new private solicitor, unknown to my family."

Ramses took the card from his hands. He memorized the names, the numbers.

"And of course there are the family representatives," said Elliott. "After I'm gone, officially, that is, you'll have to rely on the new man. I may go from the Continent to America. I haven't yet made up my mind. I have a great desire to see South America in particular, to see Brazil, and to travel through the more mysterious lands. . . ."

He stopped. He picked up his hooded overcoat, and then he stopped again and looked at Julie. The tears in his eyes. She rushed into his arms. They embraced in silence, and Ramses heard Elliott's whisper. "Beautiful child, beautiful immortal child."

"I've come to a decision," said Ramses. "Before you leave us, I want to give you the secret of the elixir. I want the ingredients engraved on your minds, both of you, as they are engraved on mine."

"No," said Elliott. "I thank you for your trust, Ramses, but I don't want it. I can't trust myself with it. Not now."

"But, Elliott, what if this war or some other circumstance separates us?" asked Ramses. "What if it's years before we meet again?"

"No, Ramses. I'm not ready for that burden. I know I'm not. My heart isn't experienced enough. And it won't be for many years."

Ramses nodded. "You have always surprised me, Elliott Savarell," he said. "You are indeed a truly unusual man."

"There will come a time, yes," said Elliott, "when I may beg you for the secret. But you mustn't give it to me now."

For a long moment they remained there in quiet together, stranded in the drawing room, gazing at one another, and then finally Elliott approached Ramses and embraced him. He whispered the words "Until we meet again."

Julie and Ramses stood behind the lace curtains of the window watching the figure of the earl as he moved out of sight.

Noises came from the dark surrounding city, unusual noises, noises near and distant and out of keeping with the small hours, noises perhaps that spoke of dread and excitement on the part of the restless populace in the grip of the news of the war. Ramses longed for newspapers to read, for the conversation in taverns and cafés, for the wireless and voices of government speaking of what was to come.

But there was time for all that.

"I shall miss him terribly," said Julie.

"And what about you, my beloved?" said Ramses. "Are you ready for the secret I have to give?"

"No, I don't think I am, my dearest," said Julie. "I think I know precisely what Elliott means when he says he's not ready. I fear my love for Sibyl Parker, for Alex. I fear my heart. I think I must trust in you for now and perhaps forever, Ramses. I think you must be the one to give this gift, not me."

"You don't know what you're saying," Ramses replied. But he nodded. This would do for now. He turned and embraced her and held her close to him.

"Very well, my darling," he said. "And so we go on as before. So we begin our journey again through the world."

"Not now, precious one," she said. "Perhaps in a few hours, yes. But for now, it's quite enough for me if we journey one more time up those stairs."

"Allow me," he said, and he gathered her up in his arms.

Up the long stairway he carried her and into the bedroom, and laying her down on the bed, he closed and locked the door. He wanted no more sudden visitors, no servants returning with talk of the war.

It was still dark outside. A shivering night-light in a porcelain shade illuminated the room.

Julie lay back against the pillows gazing up at him, her pale skin almost luminous in the shadows, her blue eyes filled with love.

He marveled at the sadness he felt, at the sadness that had gripped the three of them earlier, because he was happier now, he knew, than he had ever been in all his long life. He was happy and filled with quiet courage for what lay ahead of them all.

Ramses the Damned he was still, yes, in ways no one might ever understand. He would be that always. But he was happy and he knew it, and he cherished every moment.

Enough of thinking when the heart tripped and the blood grew hot and his body came alive with the single wordless obsession with her presence, her beauty, her patient gaze.

He pulled off his clothes roughly, stepped out of them, and fell silently into her arms, his lips pressed first to her eyelids and then to her naked breasts and finally to her sweet upturned mouth.

All thoughts of his broken Cleopatra left him. All fascination for the distant and all-powerful queen. All fascination for the world and this war that threatened it. And he gave in to the source of strength for him that was greater than any other. Her tender acceptance, her surrender, her quiet unending love.

PRINCE LESTAT AND THE REALMS OF ATLANTIS
The Vampire Chronicles

In this ambitious, rich novel of vision and power, the indomitable vampire hero Lestat de Lioncourt, prince of the vast tribe of the undead, returns. Lestat finds himself at war with a strange, ancient, otherwordly form that has taken possession of his immortal body and spirit, and it is through this perilous and profound struggle that we come to be told the hypnotic tale of a great sea power of ancient times: a mysterious heaven on earth situated on a boundless continent in the Atlantic Ocean. As we learn of the mighty, resonant powers and perfections of this lost kingdom of Atalantaya, the lost realms of Atlantis, we come to understand how and why the vampire Lestat, indeed all the vampires, must reckon so many millennia later with the terrifying force of this ageless, all-powerful Atalantaya spirit.

Fiction

PRINCE LESTAT
The Vampire Chronicles

Old vampires, roused from deep slumber in the earth, are doing the bidding of a Voice commanding that they indiscriminately burn their kin in cities across the globe, from Paris to Mumbai, Hong Kong to San Francisco. Left with little time to spare, a host of familiar characters, including Louis de Pointe du Lac, Armand, and even the vampire Lestat, must embark on a journey to discover who—or what—is driving this mysterious being.

Fiction

THE WOLVES OF MIDWINTER
The Wolf Gift Chronicles

It is winter at Nideck Point. Oak fires burn in the stately flickering hearths, and the community organizes its annual celebration of music and pageantry. But for Reuben Golding, now infused with the Wolf Gift, this promises to be a season like no other. He's preparing to honor an ancient Midwinter festival with his fellow Morphenkinder—a secret gathering that takes place deep within the verdant recesses of the surrounding forests. However, Reuben is soon distracted by a ghost. Tormented, imploring, and unable to speak, she haunts the halls of the great mansion, drawing Reuben toward a strange netherworld of new spirits, or "Ageless Ones." And as the swirl of Nideck's preparations reaches a fever pitch, they reveal their own dark magical powers.

Fiction

THE WOLF GIFT
The Wolf Gift Chronicles

When Reuben Golding, a young reporter on assignment, arrives at a secluded mansion on a bluff high above the Pacific, it's at the behest of the home's enigmatic female owner. She quickly seduces him, but their idyllic night is shattered by violence when Reuben is inexplicably attacked—bitten—by a beast he cannot see in the rural darkness. It will set in motion a terrifying yet seductive transformation that will propel Reuben into a mysterious new world and raise profound questions. Why has he been given the wolf gift? What is its true nature—good or evil? And are there others out there like him?

Fiction

ANCHOR BOOKS
Available wherever books are sold.
www.anchorbooks.com